Freebooter-Foundation
A 12th Realm Adventure

Cover design: Gail Rust.
IMAGE: SHUTTERSTOCK

ISBN: **978-0-909497-17-0** *(PAPERBACK)*
978-0-909497-16-3 *(EBOOK)*
FIRST EDITION 2021
FONT CALIBRI 11.5 PT

Acknowledgements

Many thanks to my advance team and editors, these are the people who point out my mistakes and give me insight from a reader's perspective. Their advice and ideas help polish my work.

As always, despite all their efforts, final decisions are mine and any errors in the novel are mine alone.

Thank you for purchasing this book, I hope you enjoy the continuing adventures in the 12th Realm.

Cast

Crew of ITS (Independent Trade Ship) Drake

Captain Joseph Jones	Owner and CEO of JJ Trading
Cmdr. Donald Hopmann	First Officer
Cmdr. Bruce McGill	Chief Engineer
Lt Cmdr. Allison Thompson	Navigator
Lieutenant Doug Harris	Logistics Officer/Pilot
Lieutenant Gabrielle Simona	Engineer
Lieutenant Danielle St Clare	Loadmaster
Lieutenant Cobal Latric	Astrophysicist/ Pilot
Lieutenant Boris Adler	2nd Loadmaster
Lieutenant Molly Renwick	Sensor Specialist
Petty Officer Rajiv Singh	Engineer
Simon Carpenter	Ship's Doctor
Jennifer Turbut	Medtech

Crew of ITS Kidman

Captain Udon Tellyz	Skipper
Cmdr. Phillip Barton	First Officer
Lt Cmdr. Mahmoud Rashida	Loadmaster

Earth based cast

Melissa Sykes	Mercantile Agent
HG Mossberg	Senior Partner Mossberg & Partners
Michael Anderson	Senior Counsel Mossberg & Partners
Gail Mossberg	JJ Trading Legal Counsel
Nyah Diallo	PA to Michael Anderson
Ivan Pankov	Director CID (Coalition Intelligence Directorate)

Brian Bosworth — Deputy Director CID
Solara Zander — Section Chief CID
Alistair Naismith — Captain Lady Philomena
Lt. Adelle Simpson — First Officer Lady Philomena
CPO Max Collingwood — Chief Engineer Lady Philomena

Ensign Sharon Holloway — Navigator Lady Philomena
Admiral William Cartwright — Commander Coalition Space Corps

Ferdor Zhirov — Commander Frigate Scaramouch

Jefferson Holt — Head of CID Section 5
Graham Naismith — Chairman Galactic Freight
Michael Husan — CEO Galactic Freight
Ernst Frederickson — Scientist
Luthor Abercrombie — Incumbent President Earth Coalition

Steven Chang — President Elect Earth Coalition

Alfred Hawes — Leader Coalition Council

Senior Free Traders/Jones Supporters

Duncan McLeod — Captain Galway Lady
Izzy Dolando — Captain Eldorado
Maris Legrand — Captain Mistral
Silvio Cordoba — CEO Cordoba Corporation
Martina Ruso — Dir Corporate Relations Cordoba

Jasmine Cordoba — Head of Cordoba Operations
Melissa Stokes — Chief Operating Officer Aegis Mining

Phillipe Alvaris — CEO Omnicron

Krell Empire

Gorth Todarij	Emperor
Captain Nadroc	Commander Krell Battleship Zotrik

I have not failed. I just found 10,000 ways that won't work.

Thomas A Edison

Chapter 1: Accident

Joseph Jones entered his cabin, the door slid silently closed behind him. They were now only six weeks from Earth and the end of his last journey on the old ship.

Joseph was the youngest of five children from an ancient aristocratic family. As with many old families, the huge fortunes that they had once commanded had been whittled away by generations of ineptitude. Three days after his father's funeral, the lawyers had summoned Joseph and his siblings to their offices to open the will.

The will was simple – the family estate was to be divided equally between them, except for the tapestries. These were to go to Joseph on the condition he never sold them. He agreed and the deal was done. In all it took a little over a year to finalise things and sell the properties. After the taxes that Earth imposed, each received a reasonable inheritance. If Joseph had been so inclined he had enough to emigrate to one of the more hospitable colonies and live his life in relative comfort.

He watched as his brothers started to have fun, squandering their new-found wealth. His sister was already engaged to a young man who had excellent prospects, as his father used to say. They decided to move to the colonies, started an agricultural business, and were quite successful.

Joseph's path was dissimilar again. Already operating as an independent trader, he was looking for a ship with more capacity, and one he could afford. He used part of his inheritance to buy this old ship, the Drake. Old was a generous term, but he got her cheap. He contracted Abracorp to carry out the work needed and, much to his brothers' mirth, six months later he took possession.

The Drake was older than Joseph. She had seen many years of service as an interstellar cruise liner and then, when the cruise business became over supplied, she had been mothballed. The company that owned her went into liquidation and the old Drake sat for years, before she came to Joseph's attention.

His rebuild brief was extensive, and expensive. He opted to keep the old proven Hyzene reactors and propulsion system instead of replacing it with the new Greenbach MAM (Matter/Anti Matter) reactor and Gravitron drive. The decision had proved to be a sound, but expensive option. While the older system had proven dependable, it did take substantially more maintenance. Still, the old ship had been reliable and formed the foundation for what Joseph had built to date.

He stood in front of the mirror in his bedroom. At one hundred and twenty Joseph Jones was in fine physical condition, more than could be said for the old Drake. His memory slipped back to the day he first boarded her. It was a wet Tuesday morning but the old ship looked resplendent after half a year of work.

Drake was roughly ovoid, with a raised Bridge and accommodation section forward while the stern housed the engineering section. The redesign included external hyzene and plasma storage nacelles, freeing up a lot of space for two new holds. The updated reactor and drive system enabled her to hold a Displacement factor of six, faster than most other freighters of the time - his thoughts were cut short by a computerised voice.

Captain Jones, please stand on the scanner.

The computer's voice dragged Joseph back to reality. Earth was six weeks away and four of those he would spend in suspended animation. This was standard procedure to ensure that everyone on board a freighter would arrive at their destination with the same amount of work time, even the Captain and owner. Now for the part Joseph hated the most.

To ensure the process was successful, one had to fast for at least twelve hours and then undergo the scan and a purge. The scan would detect how much matter was in the digestive tract and prescribe the correct dose of laxative; the purge was the result of taking the potion. An empty digestive tract was essential for the suspension process to work, and the subject to survive.

Joseph stood on the base plate, a white light emanated from the top of the unit while another thin green beam traversed the entire length of his body. The computer spoke again.

Well done Captain. The elixir will be dispensed momentarily. Remember to take it in the next half hour. Sleep well. The machine was always so polite. Joseph stood down, waiting for the much hated elixir.

He felt something, a rumbling in the floor. Suddenly the ship lurched. Joseph fell to his left, losing his balance and crashing into the wall.

The ship lurched again. This time he felt a massive rumble through the entire room. He braced himself against the wall and carefully regained his feet.

He reached for the comm unit. 'Bridge, this is the Captain. What's going on?'

A panicked voice replied. *Sir, the starboard hyzene tank has ruptured; we're dumping fuel.*

This was something they couldn't afford. Hyzene, while being easy to synthesise, was the primary energy source for the reactors and the drive system. The tanks held enough for the return to Earth, but with only a small margin for emergencies.

'How much are we losing?'

The same voice replied, this time more calmly. *Not sure, Sir. I don't have exact figures from engineering as yet.*

Joseph made a quick decision. 'Ok, I'm on my way back. Is the Chief awake?' Chief engineer Bruce McGill, the only person Joseph would trust with the safety of his ship.

I don't know; he's due to sleep today.

Joseph shook his head. 'Then I suggest you find out and wake him if he's asleep.' He didn't wait for an answer, but stumbled through the door as the ship lurched again. This was one time Joseph was glad his quarters were close to the Bridge.

The scene that greeted him was one of controlled pandemonium. Alarms screaming, lights flashing and people working frantically trying to rectify the problem – but no-one seemed to be in command.

'**Stop**!' Joseph yelled, everyone stopped and turned to him. He walked calmly to the engineering station and silenced the alarm. Now that there was a degree of quiet in the room he took stock.

The readout wasn't good. So far they had dumped over half the tank's available fuel. He approached the control panel and initiated the shutdown procedure for that particular tank. Nothing happened. He repeated the process, with the same result.

'That's the problem, Sir. We can't action the controls from the Bridge!'

Joseph stood away from the console, his eyes boring into every person he saw. The faces told him they had the same fears, as he now did.

Hyzene is normally stable, and while it can be highly volatile, it requires either the reactor or some intense heat source to set it off. The plasma trail from the engines was exactly what was needed. If the hyzene now being vented crossed the super-heated plasma trail, things would be far worse.

'Who's the watch officer?'

A short, thin man stepped forward. 'Me Sir, Lieutenant Harris.'

Joseph studied the young man; he had come aboard at the beginning of this trip and so far, had impressed with his efficiency. 'So what are you doing about this incident?'

'I've just shut the engines down, that should give us a good chance of avoiding any flash-over,' Harris answered. 'We're using the docking thrusters to keep us on course and stop any movement issues.'

Joseph was impressed, but any further response was drowned out by the voice of Bruce McGill over the intercom.

What fucking idiot turned the lateral deflectors off? Joe... are you on the Bridge?

'Yes Bruce, I'm here. What's the score?'

Some fuckwit turned off the lateral deflector arrays. Except for the forward array, we're a sitting duck. We've got a hole about three metres wide in the starboard tank housing, I think you better come down here.

Joseph turned back to Harris. 'Ok Bruce. But first get the hyzene flow stopped, the controls on the Bridge don't work.' He turned back to Harris, no need for words as the question was obvious.

Harris pulled himself together. 'I didn't; Gabby, can you explain?' He turned to another Lieutenant.

The second engineering officer, Lieutenant Gabrielle Simona gave both her Captain and Harris a withering stare. 'Sir, we had a massive power surge in the array, it went into shutdown mode. Before I had time to check what was happening, something hit the nacelle.'

Joseph held up his hand for silence. 'Ok, start your investigation, I'm going to engineering.' He turned and left for the pod. Five minutes later he was down in engineering with Bruce McGill giving him an update of the problem.

'Bruce, I don't need every detail. Can you fix it?'

'Sure Joe... with a dock facility. I can't fix this mess out here; either we find a space dock or a friendly planet to land on. There's no way I can do what is needed in space.' He pointed to the view screen that showed the damage to the tank nacelle. 'And, this'll make your day; we can't use the displacement drive, and our speed through space will be limited to point five light.'

'Is that all?' Joseph asked, sarcastically. To anyone else this would have been the start of an argument, but these two had been together for over twenty years, their banter was part of the deal. 'Navigator,' Joseph spoke into the comm unit. 'How close are we to any space dock or a friendly planet? Oh, I almost forgot, our max speed will be point five light, in normal space.'

On the Bridge the Navigator, Allison Thompson, shook her head. 'I'll get straight on to it Sir; did I hear correctly... no displacement drive?'

'You heard correctly, Allison, standard drive only. See what you can find and have all senior officers gathered in the wardroom in fifteen minutes.'

Joseph turned to the engineer, who nodded knowing the question before his Captain could say anything. 'I'll be there.'

***

The wardroom was substantial and comfortable. Joseph wanted this to be a relaxed and informal area so the furnishings had been chosen to facilitate that. He entered and took his place at the head of the oval table.

'First, Lieutenant Simona, what have you found?'

'Sir, there was an overload on one of the deflector array relays. When the backup system switched in; its relay also failed, shutting down the array completely. I don't know what caused the overload, only what happened after.' Simona's report was brief and to the point.

McGill backed her up. 'Skipper I've been concerned about these relays for a while, we've all noted inconsistencies in our engineering reports, but I never thought they were this bad; they're just old, way past their use by date.'

Joseph nodded. 'Yeah, the old girl is in sore need of a refit. Any info on why the Bridge lost control?' This situation was a grave concern to Joseph, if he couldn't control the ship, then things would get much worse, very quickly.

Again Simona answered. 'We haven't found the problem as yet, but we have isolated it to a section of conduits between transfer node 5 and 6. I think we'll find a faulty optical connection.'

'We have a team heading there now, should have it sorted within the hour.' McGill added.

Joseph smiled as he spoke, his team was working perfectly. 'But what, do we do now? Allison got any good news?'

The Navigator stood, walked to the front of the room and switched on the old view screen. 'Depends on your definition of good,' she said, drily.

'First the usual bad news; there's nothing within several light years we can access, no outpost, definitely no docks, nothing that even vaguely resembles civilisation.'

'And the good news?' Joseph asked.

The screen in front of them came alive; Allison called up a star chart and started to speak again. 'Here approximately twenty-six trillion kilometres away, we have an M class planet, AG four eight five.' She highlighted the target planet. 'Slightly larger than Earth; climate, according to the survey, is very similar; gravity is a little harsher, but this is the only viable alternative we have. At point five light it'll take us about fifty-four hours, allowing for acceleration and deceleration.'

'OK, who is in charge of it?' Joseph knew they would need permission to land, and probably have to pay a hefty fee.

Allison grinned. 'No-one, utterly non-aligned... there's no ownership lodged, no Coalition claim, nothing... in essence, a free planet.'

Joseph sat staring at the screen for a few moments before he spoke. 'Does anyone have any other options?'

no-one responded, so he continued, 'Bruce, how soon can we start, and is there anything else you need?'

'The nacelle's as safe as we can make it, we can start whenever you want but, accelerate gradually, Ok? As for requirements, I'll need everyone I can get on deck, so we better make sure everyone is awake before we arrive.'

'Reanimation is already under way, what do you need when we land?'

'Solid ground, remember we'll be heavier than we think if the gravity is stronger. We also need a reliable source of fresh water to replenish our Hyzene supply, and an area to set up the Hyzene processing plant.' McGill concluded.

'Thank you; we now know what we need. Allison, set the course and start accelerating,' Joseph took a breath and looked at the engineer. 'Is three hours enough?' McGill nodded, so he continued. 'Three hour acceleration time. When we're within shuttle range we'll send a few out to scout the planet, select a site and guide the Drake in; any questions?' With no questions, he continued, 'well we all have jobs to do so let's get at it; dismissed.'

Thirty minutes later Joseph was sitting at his desk in the ready room when he felt the ship change course and increase acceleration, he looked up as the door opened; Bruce McGill strode in.

'Finally underway... we had to replace every relay in the starboard array, total bloody mess.' He walked straight to the ancient coffee brewer and poured himself a mug. 'I take it you do realise where we are headed?' It wasn't really a question, but he wanted it on the record.

'Certainly do Bruce. AG48-5 is close to the border with Krell territory, that's why no one, including the Coalition, wants to claim it. The Krell have formally ceded it and the

Coalition Council has refused ratification; should make for an interesting land fall.' Both men sat back to enjoy their coffee.

The ready room was Joseph's domain, the place where he was most likely to be found, so he had designed it to suit his tastes. The ceiling was high and the walls were covered with the old tapestries he had inherited from his father, some dating back many hundreds of years. Imposing solid wood furniture gave the room an air of stability and power.

Directly behind Joseph's chair, a huge ancient bookshelf made of oak. On its shelves were hundreds of old, leather bound books, again from some of the ancient estates his family had once owned. When he was sitting at his desk, in this room, he gave the impression of an ancient Scottish Laird, as his ancestors were.

Finally he put down his mug, and gave McGill one of his more intense stares. 'Bruce, you know what I've been trying to start, with the other independent traders?' Everyone knew his passion for this, so Bruce just nodded.

'One of the major sticking points is that we are all operating at the mercy of the Coalition Council. Most of us are based on Earth, or close to it, so we're forced to accept their rules. If we form any kind of guild or association, the conglomerates will call on their tame councillors and have us penalised, but if we don't do something, we'll be squeezed out of business.'

'Joe, listen. At the moment we have a bloody huge problem. We're on a crippled ship, heading into no man's land to effect repairs. The politics will have to wait; we've got much more to worry about.' McGill had heard all this, time and time again and nothing had changed.

'You're right, sorry,' Joseph added. 'How long will you need to effect repairs?'

Now the conversation came back where Bruce believed it should be. 'Looking at the damage, I think we'll need the better part of two to three weeks for repairs and to process enough hyzene for the trip back to Earth... but we need to consider something else, the gravity. How much more is it than Earth Standard?'

Every human colony had assumed an Earth relative standard for all measurement, distance, time, weight, even gravity, all referenced to Earth.

'We think about twelve percent higher, why?' Joseph inquired.

'Simple, we're fully loaded but the final load was done on Satria. They use their own reference system; they are the only colony that doesn't use Earth standard. I'm having the Loadmaster redo the calculations. **But**... I need definitive data from the planet before I can even consider letting the ship land.'

'What! Bruce, we're already on our bloody way, what's the problem?'

'If the load from Satria is more than we expect, or the gravity is higher, the ship's structural integrity may be compromised when we land. If that's the case, we may never leave. I don't think we have a problem, but I'd be a pretty stupid engineer if I didn't make doubly sure. So when you send the shuttles, one of the first tasks must be to carry out a detailed gravity analysis, well before the ship gets there.'

'I know the Satrian mass figures can be a bit rubbery but I thought the Loadmaster allowed for that?' Joseph added.

'She does, but it's all relative to Earth standards. If gravity is higher than we expect it'll have a cumulative effect. The landing gear may not be able to support the increased mass or, worse still, the anti-grav may not be able to hold her, or slow her descent enough. Either way, not something I want to find out as we attempt to land.'

Joseph considered this new information before activating the intercom. 'Navigator, can you come to the ready room, please?' They sat back and waited for her to arrive. The door opened and Allison entered.

'You want to see me Sir?'

'Yes Allison. Bruce, fill the Navigator in on your concerns.' Joseph watched as Bruce relayed his concerns to her. When he finished she nodded and answered.

'How about, I work out the earliest point we can send shuttles, and we launch the gravity team then. When we arrive, I'll set up an orbit that will allow us to wait for any data without compromising either fuel or structural integrity. But, what do we do if we can't land?'

Bruce shook his head. 'I'd suggest we pray, if we're that way inclined. Even if we're not, it wouldn't hurt because if this fails... we're clean out of options.' The meeting lasted only a few minutes more and finally, Joseph was alone, a feeling of dread crept over him. He shook his head, trying to clear the doubts and went back to his console.

His first message was to Fotheringham, Craig and Sykes, his mercantile agents. Time to let them know the bad news, and to advise clients that their shipments would be delayed. He emphasised the word delay and didn't even hint that it may be permanent.

His next message was unusually cryptic, addressed to Gail Mossberg his lawyer, and detailed his requests about

AG48-5. He drafted and re drafted it a number of times until he was, finally, satisfied with the contents. He ran it through his encryption program before transmitting the message. It would be several days before he would have any answer, due to the communication dwell from this sector of space.

The rumbling in his stomach reminded Joseph it had been nearly eighteen hours since he had eaten. He shut his console down, notified the Bridge where he was going and left for the ward room. Hopefully the cooks could rustle up something for him.

Chapter 2: AG48-5

Twenty two hours later, the sound of the comm unit dragged Joseph back to consciousness. He glanced at the clock, thankful he'd been able to grab five hours sleep, 'Jones here.'

The voice of his First Officer, Donald Hopmann answered. *Morning Sir, we should be able to launch shuttles in an hour.*

'Thanks Don, I'll be there shortly.' Joseph swung his legs out of the bed. His first stop was the head, to relieve the pressure in his bladder and then a shower. Finally awake, he returned to the bedroom and opened the wardrobe. He withdrew a large suit container and opened it.

Inside was something that he hadn't worn for many years, an old design combat survival suit. The original concept had been designed in the twenty-first century, when Earth was racked by civil unrest and war. The unit became standard issue to operatives of an organisation known as Citadel and was unmatched in its efficiency in keeping the wearer alive and protected in battle.

Joseph had done his compulsory military service in the Coalition forces, he had even been attached to the remnants of Citadel, and this is where he found the benefits of the suit. As a part of his hygiene routine he had kept his body hair removed, a requirement for the suit's function.

Carefully, he pulled on the gossamer thin inner layer, the interface between his body and the suit. Next he donned the suit. When fully functional, this provided the wearer with processing for body waste, allowing more freedom in the battle field. Finally he added the last layer. The armour made from Acrilan impregnated fibres, flexible and virtually impenetrable. Now fully dressed, he stood assessing himself in the mirror.

'Not bad... damn thing still fits,' he said to himself as he left the room and headed for the shuttle bay.

Drake carried twenty shuttles as standard equipment. Five were designated protection units and were heavily armed and very fast. Five were personnel units and the others were general freight vessels. This time they were taking three of the protection units and three personnel ships. Two of the latter had been reconfigured as survey vessels and would be responsible for mapping the gravity of the planet, as well as locating a suitable landing site.

The third personnel unit would hold twenty heavily armed crew members, just in case. Although the added cost of danger pay was horrendous, safety dictated Joseph's decision. He would be in the lead shuttle, with Allison Thompson in the number two seat. The other two shuttles were piloted by their normal crew and everyone was now completing pre-flight checks.

As Joseph entered the shuttle bay control room, all conversation ceased. Everyone knew of his service record but seeing him in his battle suit always gave pause for reflection on their boss. Not only was Joseph Jones owner of JJ Interstellar Ltd and their Captain, he was also someone who had extensive battle experience both in open warfare and the covert realm that Citadel operated in.

Even though the organisation was no more than a shadow of its former glory, it still commanded respect and to have one of its officers as your boss, actually gave most a feeling of security. Secretly this was why Joseph still used the old suit; the effect in a sticky situation was profound.

'Number One, are we ready?' He called as he walked in.

'Sir, Commander Thompson has programmed all navigation systems and is waiting to give the final briefing... when you're ready.'

'Thanks, Don.' Joseph motioned his second in command aside, 'You know what to do if we fail.'

'Yes Sir, but it won't come to that.'

'Let's hope not. Now I better not keep the Navigator waiting.' Joseph walked into the shuttle bay briefing room. Everyone in the expedition group was already assembled, and he acknowledged their salutes as he entered.

'OK, no time for long speeches, we all know what we have to do, and what's riding on us doing the job, so let's get it done; Commander?'

Allison Thompson took the stage and began. 'We will exit Drake in approximately fifteen minutes.' She brought up a star chart on the view screen. 'We will accelerate to this point where we will enter our worm holes, then a displacement transit time of twenty minutes followed by a deceleration and approach time of one and a half hours. At the end of this time we will be in orbit round AG48-5.

'This is where we will make the decision to land, or not. We will complete at least three orbits, mapping the gravity and other parameters; this data will be the deciding factor. All navigational parameters are programmed into each shuttle's computer so basically it will be an automatic flight once we enter the worm hole. Any questions?' The plan was simple and no questions were asked.

'Captain, do you want to say more?'

'Yes. Your safety is paramount so no heroics; do your job, and we'll all come through this,' Joseph scanned the faces before him; confidence was all he saw, no fear or trepidation. 'Good, let's get moving.'

Everyone filed out of the room and went to their designated shuttles; Joseph and Allison the last to board the lead ship.

'Ok, Commander, this is your show now.' Joseph said as he took the second seat, giving his Navigator command of the formation. Deftly she activated the drive system and brought the ship alive, sending the go command to the other shuttles as she lifted off the deck.

The deflector flared white as it matched frequency with the Drake's system, and they were in space. She turned the ship to port and watched as the rest left the shuttle bay. When they were all formed on her, she activated the navigation program and the six shuttles responded, accelerating and changing their heading for the insertion point. Minutes later all displacement drives initialised, and they each entered their own worm hole.

The view from a shuttle cockpit was unbelievable. Being such a small vessel, the worm hole was also narrow; Joseph felt he could reach out and touch the swirling kaleidoscope that made up the extremities of it. As with most space travellers, Joseph loved this sight, and he saw from the look on the Navigator's face she did too.

'First hop in a shuttle?'

'No Sir, but the first time I've been in the command seat... so beautiful.' She was awestruck by the swirling colours that made up the boundary of their tiny cocoon. Still, she had a job to do and, as she made to leave her seat, Joseph stopped her.

'Commander, you can sit and enjoy it for a few minutes, can't you?'

'Yes Sir, thank you.' Allison sat still for the next ten minutes, trying not to even blink in case she missed something. Finally, she tore herself away from the show. 'I have to get things started, Sir.' She moved back to the temporary console that had been set up in the rear of the cockpit as Joseph changed seats and took command of the shuttle.

Nineteen minutes and forty-seven seconds after leaving Drake, the six shuttles re-inserted into normal space. Allison began to interrogate the systems on the other shuttles, and link them all. Her navigation program was still running all the ships, leaving Joseph with little to do, so he began a detailed sensor scan of the region. Being so close to the Krell border made him feel uneasy. The scan showed nothing. But slowly decaying ion trails indicated that ships had passed this area, recently. Joseph noted this and logged his results.

Simultaneously the six shuttles were decelerating, heading for the fifth planet in the system. As they got closer it began to shine with a blue hue, indicating the possibility of vast bodies of liquid water, the rarest commodity in the known universe. The readings began flowing. Atmospheric conditions were similar to Earth, a slightly lower concentration of oxygen, but ample for human habitation.

As they closed, the indications of water were confirmed, at least three huge oceans and several land locked seas, or giant lakes were evident. The latter were of most interest as clean fresh water was essential for the hyzene distillation process. But the gravity readings were the most important. Not only the difference between AG48-5 and the Earth standard, but the size and rotation of the planet plus the proximity of its three moons and the other planets in the system would be part of the decision whether the old Drake could actually survive landing.

Ninety minutes after the reinsertion, the six shuttles settled into their individual orbits; this was where the Navigator's guesswork would prove accurate, or not. Each ship had been assigned an individual orbit, different altitudes and speeds as well as completely different trajectories.

Allison believed this should give a more complete picture of the planet and its gravity well. At the same time, comprehensive scans of the surface were being carried out, to locate the best landing site. Four hours of orbiting the planet allowed each ship to complete at least three cycles and gave Allison a basic picture of what Drake would encounter.

'Captain, I have the data. Drake should be able to land, if the Loadmaster has done her job correctly.' She brought up the calculations on the shuttle's viewer; then changed it to graphic representation. It showed that the planet had a twelve point seven percent higher gravity than Earth. If the ship was loaded to its full mass capacity, it should have an eleven percent safety margin landing here.

'Eleven percent safety margin, not much; let's hope the Satrian officials were more accurate than usual.' Joseph mused.

'Or that Dannie was more circumspect than usual.' Allison was referring to Lieutenant Danielle St Clare, the Loadmaster for Drake. Joseph was confident everything would work out – Lieutenant St Clare was, in his view, one of the most efficient Loadmasters in the game. In the five years since she had joined the crew he had never had an issue with load masses, especially where Satria was concerned. St Clare had proved many times that she was more than capable of correcting the mistakes they made.

'I don't understand Sir. Why are load outs on Satria such an issue?'

'Satria has a strange system. All their dock workers are paid by mass moved, but they don't have a check system in place. They take freight off the surface and weigh it; at that point the payment is calculated. From then on the less movement they make, the better for the dock owners, so they tend to cram as much into each container as they can. They don't weigh the containers as they leave, only the goods as they arrive.

'Fewer containers handled, more profit to the owners and eventually, more bonuses for the workers, but the Guild is trying to change it. Remember there have been three ships lost because of overloading in the last two years. But changing that sort of corruption isn't easy, especially when most of the politicians on Satria are tied to dock owners in some way.' Joseph explained as he looked at the data. 'Ok send this back to Drake and break the formation, time to go down and have a good look around.'

Allison transmitted the data along with her suggestions for approach vectors and orbit parameters; then signalled the others with her Captain's orders. The two shuttles equipped for the survey work and two protection vessels would leave orbit and begin to survey the planet. Joseph had chosen the southern hemisphere and designated the northern half of the planet to Lieutenant Latric and the second survey ship.

The four ships broke formation and began to descend towards the planet. The atmospheric layering was also similar to Earth, and they used a standard Earth approach, compensating for the higher atmospheric pressure and density. It seemed to work well. Lower and lower the four small ships dropped, now falling through heavy cloud cover above the equator.

At five thousand metres they broke through the clouds into a grey and violent storm, similar to a hurricane on Earth. The shuttles were equipped to handle these conditions but the additional gravity made it hard work for them. They separated and headed for their respective survey co-ordinates.

One thousand kilometres later, Jones finally saw clear sky. He increased height to seven thousand metres and got his first glimpse of land. An island appeared off their port bow, lush and green; it was small but looked habitable.

Boris Adler's voice broke the silence, *Shuttle Betty B, commencing survey run.* Joseph waited as the other vessel dropped down towards the island. The survey took longer than expected, mainly due to re-calibrating the ground sensors, but the results were encouraging. While the island wasn't suitable as a repair site, it did yield some clues as to the geological structure of the planet. With the new information, sensors were again calibrated and the two set off towards a sizable land mass they had seen while in orbit.

The plan called for six hours of survey, then the four ships would meet and a decision as to where the best landing site was, would be made. Four hours into the action, Betty B located a possible site.

Boris relayed the information to Joseph, and they met at the site. It seemed ideal, a substantial flat area that was geologically stable and possibly able to support the weight of the Drake. Located next to a huge clear lake, this site had it all so Joseph decided to land. He set his shuttle, Orion, down at the edge of the lake.

Gradually he decreased the anti grav power, placing increasingly more of Orion's mass directly on the landing pads; the ground seemed solid and held up well. Next he tested the atmosphere. As their initial information had indicated he found no bad surprises, just an acceptable, breathable mix of gasses. Oxygen was a couple of percent lower than Earth but nothing that would cause any respiratory issues.

He called Betty B and authorised her to land, Boris brought the shuttle in and repeated Joseph's cautious landing. This time it was different, the site he had chosen was further inland from the lake, where he would park the much larger Drake. Here the ground was covered with a tall grass like vegetation, so tall that Betty B disappeared from view.

As they touched down Betty B's sensor operator, Molly Renwick called out. 'Sir, I'm picking up biologicals, mammalian and quite large.'

'How far?' Boris called back.

'Two hundred metres abeam port.' Boris powered the port blaster bank and cut a swathe in the grass out to one hundred metres, as Ensign Renwick sent the details to Orion.

'Hold position, Betty B.' Joseph released one of the small drones each shuttle carried. This small unit flew to the second shuttle and the clearing that Boris had made.

As it arrived, the first beast emerged from the long grass. It was **huge**; Joseph estimated it weighed over one thousand kilograms. It had a big solid head with four long and dangerous looking horns, two facing forward and two, slightly longer ones, at right angles to the head. The body was covered in long, shaggy fur, or something resembling fur.

It moved confidently on four sturdy legs that terminated in huge, almost paw like feet. As it moved toward the shuttle, more emerged from the undergrowth. These were mostly smaller and many had young walking beside them.

'Bovine... they're bovine, or something like it.' Thompson quietly added from the rear of the shuttle.

'Cattle, you think they are some indigenous cattle?'

'Not only me, Sir. The computer has come to the same conclusion. The sub family Bovine has many animals in it, not just cattle. These appear more like some sort of marsh land creature. Look at the feet; they're designed to spread the weight to allow the creature to move easily through soft ground.' She stopped, mesmerised by the steady and graceful progress the herd was making.

They showed no fear, or even curiosity about the strange thing in their path, they simply walked around the shuttle and continued towards the lake.

'Betty B, start your ground integrity tests, Drake will be entering the system in another five hours.'

Joseph saw the herd emerge from the vegetation and head to the lake. There appeared to be a definite hierarchy with, what he assumed were bulls, standing guard while the smaller calves and females drank. Then, in rotation, the males all took their turn to slake their thirst with the largest and, Joseph assumed, alpha male the last to take a drink. When he finished they started to walk north, toward a distant valley that Joseph had noticed as they flew over, keeping a reasonable distance from both the water and the undergrowth. The younger males took both point and flanking positions and the alpha brought up the rear.

'Well that tells us something.' Thompson noted.

'Yes, they have a social structure and there are predators that they are wary of, something we need to consider.'

'And Sir, they seem to give the same respect both to the lake and the bush. I'd say there are threats from both!' Thompson spoke quietly, as she programmed the drone to follow the herd and record its movements.

Orion from Betty B, Boris Adler's voice again broke into the cabin.

'Go ahead, Betty B.' Joseph replied.

This site won't do. Ground integrity tests show structural weakness, it won't hold the weight. Sorry Sir.

'Better we know now, than try to sit the old girl down and lose her; Orion out.'

'Orion calling Caber.'

The reply was immediate and enthusiastic; *Caber here, Sir and I think we may have had better luck.* Lieutenant Cobal Latric sounded excited. *I'm transmitting coordinates for the site we have found; I think you should check it out Sir.*

'Roger that, Boris, what are your thoughts?'

Honestly Sir, this is the best site we've found in this hemisphere, so far. If Latric thinks he's found something that will work, we need to consider it, seriously. Betty B could stay down here and keep looking if you like.

'No, Boris. We'll head for Caber's location, now.' Joseph said. Although they had landed, he hadn't shut the shuttle's systems down, just in case, so getting airborne was quick. Boris had taken the same precautions, and within minutes they had formed up and were accelerating toward the northern half of the planet.

Three hours later they again made landfall, not their destination, but another continent. Here the land was different, apart from a verdant coastal fringe and areas of fertility around scattered water holes, the land was barren, a vast desert.

At the speed they were flying, the desert soon began to dissipate and suddenly they were over another area of lush vegetation, but only for a few seconds as the ocean again rushed to greet them. This didn't last long as they began to decelerate and descend to the coordinates Caber had sent.

This site looked much better, little vegetation, mostly rock with easy access to a lake almost as large as the southern counterpart. There was something about this site that twigged Joseph's interest. It looked like it had been carved out of living rock for the exact purpose they intended to use it. A call from Drake interrupted his thoughts.

'Go ahead Number One.'

Sir we have entered the system, we will be in orbit in another hour, but we need to land soon; we lost more fuel than we estimated. The upshot is we don't have enough to hang around for more than a couple of orbits. Don Hopmann wasn't one to be melodramatic; if this was his assessment, it was accurate.

'I hear you, Don. We're just landing on what we believe will be a suitable site. I'll call you as soon as we have confirmation, Orion out.' Joseph gently grounded the ship and completed the shutdown procedure. He waited for ten minutes, allowing the others to confer before he briskly walked down the boarding ramp.

He joined the group and discussion stopped. Gabrielle Simona, Boris Adler and Molly Renwick had been in the middle of a very animated conversation when their Captain walked up. 'Don't let me stop you, what's the verdict?' Knowing full well they were now out of options, Joseph let the team decide on what to do.

Simona was the first to speak. 'Sir, I think this is ideal. The ground is solid, the water is fresh and pure, plus we have plenty of room for the processing plant; and we are out of time, you know that Sir.'

Joseph nodded. 'Yes, you're right but if the others have any issues, please speak up.'

Boris joined the conversation. 'My only issue is how close we are to the lake. We don't know what the weather is like and,' he pointed to marks on the rock, 'there's evidence that this area floods, regularly. If the weather gods smile we'll be Ok but, once we have the old girl pulled apart, she's stuck. If the weather turns bad, though, we could have some issues.'

Joseph walked round the site where Boris had indicated. There was evidence of fairly major flooding, in fact that seemed the reason the area had been carved out as it was. He made his decision.

'We don't have much choice, unless anyone has an alternative, we have to bring the Drake down here. I know this is less than perfect, and we've surveyed what, five percent of the planet, so yes there are definitely going to be much better sites, but Drake doesn't have the time.' He turned to the Navigator.

'Navigator, plot the best re-entry for the ship.' Thompson turned and walked back into Orion to carry out her Captain's orders. 'Now, let's bring the other shuttles down, we need everyone on deck when Drake arrives.

The next four hours stretched everyone to the limit. All shuttles had to be moved off the proposed landing site, but luckily the surrounding terrain was able to accommodate them. The landing site was thoroughly scanned and then visually inspected before it was surveyed and the ground beacons installed. Finally, preparations were as complete as possible, just as the lower oxygen atmosphere, coupled with the higher gravity was taking its toll.

Joseph stood beside Orion, now perched on a small bluff away from the landing site. 'Well if we're not ready now, we never will be.' He said to himself.

He turned to Thompson. 'Navigator, give Drake final landing approval.' Thompson ducked back into the shuttle and issued the necessary instructions. Now there was nothing they could do, except wait.

Time seemed to stretch, minutes seemed like hours. It was only ten minutes after Allison had issued the final landing instructions, when she detected the first tell-tale of Drakes imminent arrival. The first atmospheric sensor reading to show that there was a massive disruption in the upper atmosphere.

'Drake has started its descent, Sir.'

Joseph didn't move; knowing the trajectory Drake would be taking, he had his eyes trained where he knew she would first appear. He was counting down, silently, and when his mind reached zero, he lifted the binoculars to his eyes. Seconds later he was rewarded with the sight of Drake breaking through the clouds. She was moving faster than he thought she would, but there was nothing he could do, the future of the crew and his ship was up to his First Officer.

***

On the Bridge of Drake, Commander Don Hopmann and chief engineer Commander Bruce McGill stood perfectly still, watching the slowly climbing speed indicator. McGill's main concern had been the antigrav system, could it sustain the increased mass it would need to if they were to survive? His simulations had indicated they only had one chance, and even that was slim.

The altimeter showed five thousand metres as Hopmann called for an adjustment in the drive parameters and their rate of descent slowed; now back in the range McGill had asked for. Four thousand metres passed and speed again leapt; another adjustment to the drive, and the speed responded as they wanted.

***

On the ground, Joseph's eyes were glued to his binoculars. He was almost not breathing as the huge ship seemed to drift down. He knew that wasn't the case. He could visualise what was happening on the Bridge. Don Hopmann and Bruce McGill were two of the best officers he had ever worked with, and he knew that if anyone could bring the ship down safely, they could.

***

Two thousand metres passed – McGill glanced over to Hopmann. 'Your call from now on Number One,' he was referring to powering setting for the antigrav system.

Hopmann waited for a few extra seconds – fifteen hundred metres passed.

'Antigrav to fifty percent,' McGill applied the required power to the system, gradually. Drake began to respond, sluggishly; it was as if she didn't want to slow down.

'Minimal effect,' McGill called, Drake was still plummeting toward the ground much too fast.

'Seventy five percent,' Hopmann called and McGill increased the power. Drake shuddered, ever so slightly, now she was starting to fight the gravity.

Eight hundred metres flashed by.

'One hundred percent!' the call slashed through the Bridge and McGill applied the power to the antigrav system. This time Drake voiced her opposition, groaning like a wounded animal and creaking like an old building lashed by a hurricane. But she was slowing, the entire crew now starting to breathe again.

Four hundred metres, – they were still way too fast.

'Engineer, one hundred and twenty percent,' Hopmann called. This time Drake screamed in protest! The massive load now being taken by the old antigrav coils far in excess of anything they were designed for. But they were still falling too fast – one hundred metres.

Hopmann called his final command. 'Helm, on my mark full reverse on the drive... engineer on the same mark one hundred and fifty percent!' No one argued – there was no alternative. Hopmann silently counted down till he reached three, then aloud 'three, two, one, mark!'

On Don's command, the massive ion drive system applied full reverse power and the antigrav howled in protest at the huge increase in power being fed to its coils.

Someone in the rear of the Bridge started calling the altitude.

'Twenty metres, ten metres,' all braced for impact as the count slowed 'five... four... three' At three metres, the twelve massive landing struts contacted the ground, not all at once, but in quick succession. 'Contact' the same voice called, enthusiastically.

'Drive, shut down. Antigrav, reduce power to ninety percent.' At this command the drive system was quickly returned to neutral operating parameter and the antigrav allowed more of the ship's mass to be taken by the struts.

'Antigrav to fifty!' Hopmann called. The ship complained bitterly at the increase in mass being supported by both the struts and anti-grav. But ultimately, it was the skeleton of the old ship that had to bear the load. It took a few moments for the sound to abate and then McGill called.

'We have four coils now at critical temperature, I need to shut the system down, or we'll never get off the planet again.'

Hopmann turned and looked at the engineer – he was never one to exaggerate. 'Ok shut down antigrav system.'

The ship's twelve huge magneto-hydraulic support struts groaned loudly at the sudden increase in weight, but they held.

'Well, we're finally down... call the Skipper and give him the news.' Hopmann instructed the comms officer as he proceeded to unseal and open the ship.

Chapter 3: Argos is born

Gail Mossberg stepped out of the elevator at 08:35 exactly on Monday, 17, October 2495.

She was in great spirits, having spent the weekend sailing with friends in Hawaii, but now she was back at work. The door in front announced she was entering *Mossberg and Partners, Attorneys at Law;* she smiled inwardly remembering her father's words when she started her law degree *"work hard but play harder".* Even today she still lived by those rules.

The receptionist, already at her desk greeted her.

'Good morning Ms Mossberg; here's your morning comm log.' She handed a small data pad over. Gail scanned the messages till she noticed one from Joseph Jones.

'When did this one come in?'

The receptionist called the log and replied 'eight am, Saturday morning.'

Gail nodded and walked through the next set of doors into the general office. She kept walking through the rows of clear cubicles that would house the general staff in less than half an hour. Already some had turned opaque indicating that there was either a confidential meeting or call taking place, or it could disguise another operation. She smiled, knowingly. It could also mean the occupant was desperately trying to cure a hangover from a wild weekend's activities. *Oh to be young and stupid again ...* her thoughts made her smile even wider.

She reached her office at the far end of the general area; it was a good size, but no larger than any of the other partners. HG Mossberg wanted it known that if his daughter was going to succeed him one day, she'd have to do it by merit, and not simply because she was his daughter.

HG had had introduced her to Jones and given her the account to manage; so far, she had been grateful. While Joseph Jones had a reputation for being eccentric, he had also proved to be a very astute and worthwhile client. Both Gail and the company had been well rewarded for serving the Jones account.

Gail had made several personal investments into Jones' enterprises, and they had all paid off handsomely. In fact, the last venture had financed her purchase of the thirty-metre yacht she had spent the weekend on, so when a message came from Jones, it always got her attention.

She downloaded the message and, as usual, it was encrypted; one of Joseph's little eccentricities. She opened the decoder and fed the message into it. Her mind raced as she read the contents – and then re-read them. *What are you up to this time, Joe*? The message, when decrypted read:

Drake damaged in meteor strike. Have to land on AG48-5 to effect repairs. Records indicate AG48-5 is FREE planet. Please discover all about title and if possible purchase same, use ARGOS Ltd as holding company.

It was simply signed Jones, as were all his messages. It was the three letters after the name that caught her attention; UDE. These were the first letters of "*Utmost Discretion Essential*", meaning Jones wanted this done without raising any suspicion.

'What **are** you up to Joseph?' This time she spoke out loud, as she started to interrogate the Coalition database for reference to AG48-5. UDE also meant that apart from her father and one other, no one else could assist in the matter; all part of the agreement they had with Joseph, an agreement that now spanned more than twenty years.

Two hours later, she had as much information as she could obtain. She activated her secure internal comm link and called her father. No answer. She knew he was in his office, so she sent him a text message.

We received UDE message from Jones. Need to see you urgently. Seconds after she sent it, she received a response.

Need five minutes.

Exactly five minutes later she left her office and walked the forty-five steps to the door of her father's office. The nameplate on the door simply read **HGM, Senior Partner.** Gail knocked and opened the door.

As Senior Partner her father commanded a massive space, his office was the size of a small apartment. There was a full bathroom, functional kitchen, formal sitting area, an informal lounge and two bedrooms. Gail remembered times, as a small child, spending days here with her father as he worked incessantly building his practice. The outer office had three comfortable lounge chairs, a small sofa - and Anderson.

Besides being an accomplished lawyer, Michael Anderson had been her father's PA and right hand for as long as Gail could remember and, although he had long ago passed the age when any sensible person would retire, he steadfastly arrived before her father each morning and left only when they had completed business for the day. Michael Anderson was also the third person who Jones would allow to work on one of his UDE projects. He stood as Gail entered.

'Morning Miss Mossberg, your father is free.' He left his desk after turning on the DND sign over the office door; nobody would try to enter now.

'Gail, has Jonesy finally asked you to marry him? I hope so. I'm not getting any younger and I don't have any grandchildren. Hell, bloody Anderson has five, so what's the answer?' HGM, Horatio Gordon Mossberg stood and stepped from behind his desk.

He was a large man, standing nearly one hundred and ninety centimetres, with the start of a sizable paunch around the middle. Too much office work and not enough time to play was his excuse. Gail believed differently - too much good food and wine was her usual comeback.

She gave her father a long look. His hair was almost white now and long. Today he had it tied back in a tail, as he did most days. He wore faded jeans and a plaid shirt, with leather, elastic sided boots. HG hated wearing business suits, believing they were something only useless arseholes wore to cover up their stupidity; her father was a man of strong opinions and convictions.

Be that as it may, she also believed him to be one of the most honest and honourable people she had ever met. His *shoot from the hip* attitude hadn't won many friends, but it had won many court cases, much to the chagrin of his opponents.

'No, he has not.' Gail wasn't in the mood for this, so she handed him the data pad. 'Here's the message.'

Horatio read it, let out a quiet whistle and flicked it to Anderson. 'Hey Mike, what do you make of this?'

Anderson read the message, and moved to the console on the desk and brought up the information on AG48-5. 'HG,' he started with the usual abbreviation of his boss's name, 'I believe our friend is onto something. Let me make a few discreet calls, I'll only be about five minutes.' Anderson stood and left the room. While he was gone, Gail went to the kitchen to make some coffee, her father followed.

'You pissed with me?'

She turned and faced him. 'Yes I am. Will you please stop with all this marriage crap, I'll marry who I want, and when I want; or nobody... got it?'

HG smiled, his whole countenance changed. 'Just like your mother, she knew when to snap the reins as well. I'm sorry, but I believe you and Jonesy are a perfect match, I also know you're very happy whenever he's back on Earth; hell, you hardly come into the office when he's around. I only want you to be happy, as happy as your mother and I were.'

Gail studied the man before her, this usually larger than life, bear of a man could also be so gentle and vulnerable. She remembered the day when they both suffered the loss. Andria, her mother, had taken Gail's younger brother, Steven, on a school excursion to the ruins on Zander 4. These ruins were some of the best examples of ancient life in the galaxy. A civilisation that existed many thousands of years before humans entered the stone-age.

Something happened, on their second day on the planet – something natural and horrific. An earthquake struck the ancient site, an earthquake of unprecedented magnitude. So great it actually split the land mass into three pieces. It was centred on the ancient ruins. A massive rift opened and the entire site simply fell in. Gail's mother and brother, along with over four hundred tourists and archaeologists, vanished. There was nothing ever found; this memory softened her attitude.

'OK, yes I am attracted to him, I love it when we're together, **but** that is so bloody rare. What's it been this time, eighteen months? And before that... over two years! When he's here, things are wonderful, but I don't want a part-time relationship, I want it all; career, husband, kids, home, the whole bloody thing! And Jonesy loves space above everything else. We'll never work.'

HG gently took his daughter's chin in his hand and lifted it, so he could look in her eyes. 'Have you told him this?' He waited a few seconds. The almost imperceptible shake of her head the cue for continuing. 'I thought not. Try telling him how you feel; it's the only way you'll ever know what to do.' Before Gail could answer, the sound of Anderson returning interrupted their conversation.

'I'll say one thing Mr Jones is one smart customer. AG48-5 is a free planet in every sense of the word; here's how it plays. Years ago, before the war started, the Krell Empire ceded that system to the Coalition; the idea was to have it as a sort of buffer zone between us. The only proviso on the document was that the system remained neutral, in perpetuity. The Council refused to ratify the agreement and ever since then, AG48-5 has been left, by both sides.

'If Mr Jones wants it, all we have to do is register the claim, but the claim will be for the whole system, not one planet. As the Coalition refused to ratify the ceding of the system, the claim will be registered and, for a modest fee, title granted. Believe me, from the calls I made, the bureaucracy would be more than happy to be rid of it, seems that it is a constant source of irritation. All we need is for a Director or Company Secretary to authorise the transfer.' Both men looked at Gail.

'Yes, I'm Co-Director **and** Company Secretary of Argos Ltd. Where do I sign?' Anderson had the documents already prepared on his data pad; Gail took it and entered her signature. The system scanned her right eye and took her left thumb print as verification of her identity. She handed the pad back to Anderson who transmitted the form back to the Ministry of Planetary Property.

The three took their coffee back to HG's office, they hadn't even had time to finish when Anderson's pad chimed. He opened the message.

'Well I'll be...' his voice trailed off as he read the message. 'I told you they were desperate to dump the planet! Ms Mossberg, as you are the Co-Director of Argos Ltd, it is my duty, and pleasure to inform you that Argos Ltd is now the sole owner and entity responsible for the planet Argos, formerly known as AG48-5.

'Not only that the office of Planetary Land Title has ceded the entire system, one star, twelve planets, and accompanying satellites, into the title documents. Argos now actually owns a whole solar system.' He read further, 'they've even gazetted it and the leader of the Council has signed off, even the President...' again his voice trailed off as he read further. 'Even the President has already agreed to the transfer, my contact wasn't joking when she said the Council wanted to be shot of this problem; I've never seen the bureaucracy work this fast... **ever**. It makes me wonder if Mr Jones has spies in the Administration.'

***

Joseph completed his external inspection of Drake; satisfied all looked in place, he walked up the personnel access ramp. First Officer Don Hopmann was waiting at the top.

'Well she's down, Don, and in one piece,' Joseph opened. 'Actually a bloody good job; must've been hard?'

'Thank you Sir. To be honest, I didn't think we'd pull it off, she did hit pretty hard. I've asked the Chief to carry out a full structural analysis of the ship to make sure.' Hopmann spoke as he fell into step with his Captain.

'Excellent, give me a few moments, I want to change. Meet you in the ready room in twenty,' Joseph said as they headed for the pod.

Joseph entered his quarters and began the process of removing the survival suit. He placed it back into its sanitising and storage compartment and headed for the shower. With all the fresh water here, the crew could now have water showers whenever they wanted.

Although he was weary, having had no sleep for over twenty-four hours, the shower reinvigorated him, at least temporarily. Back in normal fatigues he left his quarters and walked the short distance to the Bridge. Here, all was relatively quiet with only a skeleton crew on station. He nodded greetings to them and opened the door to his ready room. Don was already seated with a steaming mug of coffee in his hand.

'Just what I need,' Joseph said as he ordered one from the dispenser. 'Now Number One, I get the feeling you have some concerns about the ship's condition?'

Don Hopmann was younger than Joseph at eighty-five years old. He was tall and well-built with shortcut hair. His face was long with a square jaw, a thin nose, and flashing blue eyes. He and Joseph had been together for the past twelve years, and were a very strong team. He paused and took a sip of coffee before he answered.

'Yes I do have some concerns. We hit bloody hard, even with the antigrav at one fifty percent and the drive at full reverse. She's an old ship, Joe, extremely old, and she complained bitterly all the way down; but the final grounding was different... there were noises that aren't right. I'm concerned that she won't be able to take off again, so I've ordered the analysis.'

Joseph slowly digested the information. Don was a one of a kind – he felt the ship. That was the only way Joseph could ever explain how he knew problems before they happened and Don explained it the same way. He believed he could discern problems by the sounds the ship made. Joseph thought back to an old book he had once read that described space travel as being deathly quiet; this description always brought a smile to his face.

He nodded to Don. 'Remember I once told you about that old book I read?'

'You mean the one that describes the silence of space travel?'

'Yeah that one; written by someone who had never been in a space ship. We travel in a sealed tin can, for want of a better description. There is always noise, air being pumped throughout the ship, fluids moving about, heaps of mechanical noise and somehow, you can read all that. If you're concerned, then so am I. So what's the plan?'

Don stood and activated the console. 'I've got the chief working on the repairs and setting up the hyzene plant. Lieutenant Simona is coordinating the structural analysis and, as we only have two analysers, she has four people with her. The rest are working on the repairs.'

He turned the console toward Joseph, and they spent the next half hour fine-tuning the duty roster. 'Joe, you look beat. I've just come off four weeks hibernation, so I can handle things for a while. Why don't you go and get some sleep, I'll call you if anything happens.'

Joseph knew Don was right, he was tired and the planetary conditions weren't helping. Before he left he turned back to the duty roster. Don had already factored in the effect of acclimatisation, so he had nothing to worry about. He smiled 'Good job, thanks,' Joseph said as he left the room.

***

Twelve hours later, Joseph woke.

He was hungry — ravenous in fact — by his own calculations, he hadn't eaten for thirty-six hours or more. He climbed out of his bed and went to the head.

Returning a few minutes later, the ache in his bladder now gone, he went to the food dispenser, ordered his breakfast and took the plate of food to the table. Settling down to bacon, scrambled eggs, sausage and toast, Joseph ate with gusto and finished before he took the first sip of his coffee then opened his console.

There was an urgent message from Melissa Sykes, his mercantile agent. It seemed that some of his clients were less than understanding about the situation and were demanding to know when their goods would arrive on Earth. Joseph noted that Danielle St Clare was cc'd on the message and that it was ten hours old, so he made a mental note to check with her before answering.

The other messages were routine, so he quickly dealt with them before returning his utensils to the dispenser.

He returned to his bedroom, dressed in clean fatigues and left, his first stop was the Loadmaster's office.

The door was open and Danielle was sitting at her desk, so engrossed in something that she didn't notice her Captain enter. Joseph stood quietly in the entry, till she looked up, 'Sorry, Sir. I didn't hear you come in.'

'Dannie, don't worry. You were fully engrossed in something.'

The usual perception of a Loadmaster was a big, burly, ham-fisted male – someone who could move a container with his bare hands. Dannie, as she preferred to be called, was the exact opposite.

She was fairly tall, slender and incredibly feminine in appearance but, as many soon found out, appearances could be deceiving. She was a brilliant Loadmaster, using her brain and her crew instead of trying to do things herself. Her blonde hair was long, but she wore it tied up when on duty. Her hands were slender, more like those of a musician or artist, than a Loadmaster. Her physique was well-formed and, under her clothes, well-muscled and fit. In off duty excursions, she was a real head turner and one of the nicest people in the crew.

'Yes, I have a solution to the issue with our disgruntled customers. The Kidman is without a cargo, evidently there's a problem on New Britain, some labour dispute; the whole place is in lock down. So they're sitting there waiting on a resolution.'

'How far is New Britain?'

'Normally ten days but Udon Tellyz is her Captain, and he's Altarian.' She was beaming now. 'He knows the Rift Passage... he can be here in four days.'

Although her enthusiasm was infectious, Joseph called a halt. 'Hang on, I'm not risking another of my fleet landing here, at least until we're confident in the ship's ability to withstand the conditions.'

'No need, Sir. We can prioritise the cargo, use the tugs to haul the containers into space... they can handle anything. We arrange them in orbit so when Kidman arrives all they need to do is depressurise the hold, and we simply push the containers in.' Dannie sounded like a kid with a new toy, such was her excitement.

'Ok, how many containers are we talking, how much mass and how long to set it all up?'

Dannie smiled, sheepishly. 'I have a confession, I've already spoken to Udon; he's preparing to leave as we speak.' She looked up to her Captain, who simply smiled his approval. 'We have isolated the containers and prioritised them; in total we need to move twelve hundred, approximately one point two million tonnes. It'll be tight; **but** we can do it. We'll move the most problematic clients' freight first, that way if we have problems, the worst whingers will be placated first.' As she finished speaking she turned the console towards Joseph, with the plan she had outlined detailed on the screen, down to the last item.

Joseph shook his head. 'Impressive, you've thought of everything. I only have one suggestion.' The look on her face told the story, quickly she scanned the screen. Joseph laughed. 'No, you missed nothing I was going to suggest you should head down to the hold and start things moving.'

'No need, Boris is already cracking the whip. The first load should be about ready to leave; all I needed was your approval.'

'Officially, you have it. Damn good job, Dannie, damn good!' He turned and left the office *she is worth much more, I need to fix that.* Joseph thought as he headed to his next destination, engineering.

The atmosphere was completely different here. As he entered the primary power control room, Joseph sensed massive tension. Something was wrong, the room was deserted but for two figures in the OOD (Officer of the Day) office - and they were having a very heated discussion. Cautiously, Joseph moved to a better vantage point, he was absolutely unprepared for the sight that greeted him. The two arguing were his Chief Engineer, Bruce McGill and his deputy, Gabrielle Simona.

This can't be good Joseph thought as he made up his mind to interfere. He purposefully walked across the control room trying to give both antagonists warning that he was coming; neither paid any attention to his progress. He reached the door and, as noisily as possible hit the door actuator. It slid open as McGill spoke.

'I don't give a flying fuck what you think... this old girl can handle anything!'

'Chief' you're wrong. If you don't listen, you're going to kill everyone on board.' Simona wasn't backing down. 'Look at the data, **please**.'

'I don't need to, I know this ship.' McGill fired back.

'What data?' Joseph spoke loud and forcefully. Both engineers stopped, neither had noticed their Captain enter the room.

'Sorry, Sir, didn't see you come in.' McGill blurted out.

'I can believe that, if I hadn't arrived, what was next, Pistols at twenty paces? Now exactly what is so problematic that you two almost come to blows?

McGill spoke first. 'It's nothing... just our **junior** engineer's mistaken data.' His sarcastic emphasis on the word junior was totally out of character.

'Bullshit... Sir there is a significant problem with the structural integrity of the ship.'

'**Shut up**! I've told you, the old girl is a lot tougher than your stupid simulation makes out.' McGill shouted.

'No, Bruce, time you shut up!' Joseph interrupted forcefully. 'If there's even a tiny chance that the ship is unfit for space, I need to know. After all, I'm the **only** one who can make any decision about her space worthiness. Now, both of you, calm down, leave here and meet me in my ready room in ten minutes; then you can **both** tell your stories. Do I make myself clear?' Both McGill and Simona, nodded.

'I didn't hear that.'

'Yes Sir, you made yourself very clear,' Simona replied.

'Yes Sir,' McGill grumbled.

'Ok, now both of you leave, Gabrielle, you first.' Simona turned, gathered her gear and left. 'As for you, what the fuck is wrong with you, Bruce? In all the years I've known you, I've never seen you attack a junior officer like that; what gives?'

'You'll see when she shows you her data and simulation, but I **know** she's wrong!' McGill fired back.

'Alright, but I need you to piss off and calm down, and you better be a hell of a lot cooler in ten minutes, got that?' McGill turned and stormed out of the room, leaving Joseph absolutely bewildered over his actions, *something is seriously wrong* Joseph thought as he left the room, *something extremely serious.*

Chapter 4: Rift Run

Captain Udon Tellyz surveyed the Bridge of his ship, Kidman.

The newest in the Jones fleet, only five years old and currently state of the art for trade ships. Much smaller than something like the old Drake, she was being built primarily for trade; freight was a secondary duty.

Joseph had recruited Udon specifically for the new ship, something strange in freight or trade circles; usually the owner got all new ships, but Udon had a number of advantages over Joseph. The key attribute that had brought him to the attention of the Jones organisation was his heritage and knowledge of the Rift.

The Togarth Rift is a horrible expanse of space, almost as bad as the fabled Stygian Black. Gravity anomalies, huge shifts in orbits of asteroids and planetoids, coupled with massive cosmic storms made it almost impossible to traverse. Being located in the Illium System made the Rift a huge problem.

Over the past few decades, this system had become a gold mine; the Daldaro asteroid belt was one of the best sources of rare minerals. These minerals were essential for construction of the new ultra-efficient MAM reactors, and this in turn was essential for the continuing push into space. The Rift caused some huge trade and freight issues – the way round it could take as long as twenty days – but for those who could traverse it, the journey was no more than four.

Udon was Altarian, and only Altarians had found a way of navigating through the Rift. He was one of a select few of his race who had the knowledge and ability to pilot a ship safely through. Many others had tried to find the route – some owners had even hired Altarians and placed secret data recorders on board – all to no avail. The route was never the same, twice.

One brilliant example had been by one of the major corporate freight lines, Galactic Freight Inc. They had hired an Altarian and recorded his flight through the Rift. Once through, they disseminated the navigational data to their ships in the region, and sent four ships hauling time sensitive freight, through the Rift.

The corporate executives refused to listen to pleas from Altar not to do it – they were warned that their plan wouldn't work. But, as has been the case with many Corporations over the centuries, a new, young executive was placed in charge, and he was on a mission to impress. Impress he did, all four ships were lost, along with all hands and all freight. What happened to the executive, nobody knows, but from that day on no Altarian would work for any Corporation. Udon only agreed to work for Joseph after a comprehensive confidentiality agreement was signed.

'Pilot, disconnect umbilical.' Udon's voice, smooth and deep, reverberated round the Bridge. 'Comms thank the dock Commander for his assistance and give him my regards.'

The Pilot confirmed that the various umbilical lines that attached the ship to the dock were clear – they were ready for space. 'Back us out, Pilot.' Udon sat in his command chair at the centre of the Bridge.

He was a tall man, over two metres with a slightly green hue to his skin. As with all from his race, he was bald –

Altarians having no hair on their heads, unlike most other Humanoids. His face was long and his features soft but his eyes were striking; deep black pupil inside a brilliant orange iris. The sclera, the white part of human eyes, was light green and the effect of his gaze was hypnotic.

He watched as the ship cleared the dock and turned for their departure coordinates. As they reached the outer marker, Udon turned to his Navigator.

'Set course one eight five mark zero six seven, ahead full.'

The Navigator entered the course and the Pilot corrected the ship's trajectory, increased power to the Gravitron drive and reported to the Captain. 'Course one eight five mark zero six seven, drive now at full power.'

'Thank you.' Udon acknowledged the reply. 'Navigator, how long to our insertion point?'

'Twenty seven minutes, Sir.'

'Thank you, Mister Barton,' Udon addressed the Pilot. 'You have the Bridge. I'll be in my ready room, please call me fifteen minutes after we enter the worm hole.'

'Aye Sir, I have the Bridge.' Phillip Barton, Pilot and First Officer, acknowledged his Captain's orders. He left the pilot station and took the command chair as Udon left.

Altarians have many things in common with humans, and indeed most Humanoid races share much commonality in physiology. All Humanoids are bipedal, warm blooded mammalian creatures; some features, skin colour and other physical attributes, while similar, can set races apart.

But it is the unseen that is the real difference and for Altarians, this comes in an almost mystical ability to read spatial anomalies. It all stems from a small organ in the centre of their forehead, a third eye some call it. Udon had no clue as to how the organ worked, or why it didn't work the same with all Altarians. He only knew it allowed him to feel what was happening in space – but it had a downside. For him to utilise his skill completely, he needed to block out all other stimuli.

The door closed behind him, and he walked to the cupboard to the left of the entry. Here he removed a black storage case, and opened it with trepidation. It contained a full body suit and a dark helmet. The design of these was such that the wearer was completely isolated from any sensory input from their surroundings. Once he was in the suit and connected to the ship's systems, he would not hear, see, feel or smell anything outside. The normal background buzz of shipboard life would disappear. He would not be able to sense anyone near him, only the organ – the Dratarium Bud as it was officially called, would feed information to his brain. He would, truly become part of the ship. Udon shivered, remembering how Jones had once lent him an old human book that dealt with the writer's idea of space travel.

He chuckled to himself as he began to remove his uniform, he remembered thinking that it must have actually been written by an Altarian as only in one of these suits could anyone actually *feel* the total isolation that the book described. The idea made him feel better, he didn't know why, it just did.

Udon secured the suit collar round his neck; all that remained was the helmet. He took this out of the inner case, unrolled the cable that would be connected to the ship's sensors and inspected it for any damage. Everything was in working order.

Fifteen minutes, Sir. Phil Barton's voice broke through his thoughts.

'Thank you, Mister Barton. I'll be right there.' Udon picked up the helmet and walked back to the Bridge.

The sight of their Captain dressed in this garb caused most of the Bridge crew some unease. Although some had been through this many times, it was still against human nature to trust something they viewed as a form of magic. Udon smiled, knowing the feelings his crew were now experiencing.

'We are about to run the Rift once again. I know some of you are new to this, but it is something I have done many times. All I ask is that you do your jobs and allow me to do mine. If at any time, you feel you cannot continue, please let the First Officer know and return to your quarters; there will be no repercussions.' Udon nodded to Barton.

'As the Captain said, some of us have done this with him many times, but if you feel too uneasy to stay, please leave. But understand this, once we transfer control to the Captain, we cannot, and will not resume it until Captain Tellyz requests us to do so.' Barton waited, giving all a few moments to decide; no one moved. 'Very well, we reinsert in three minutes, Captain please take your seat.'

Udon moved to the Pilot's station, sat down and connected the helmet input to the console. Next he placed the helmet on his head, instantly images flooded into his mind. He was floating in a huge ocean of coloured bubbles, constantly changing, moving; rushing past him but never touching him.

His body was now the ship; what it felt through the sensors, he felt as well. He felt the power of the drive system, hurtling him through space. He felt the periphery of the worm hole; the beauty of space flashing past. Then he felt something different, something changed. The worm hole started to decay, like it was dying and normal space was being born to replace it.

Then he felt it, the massive, mad dissonance that was the Rift. He felt the ship, huge, heavy and ponderous. In his mind he also saw the controls at his fingertips. Gently he started to caress them, like he was making love to his ship. Then he took command.

He felt Kidman respond to his caress, obeying his desires. The entry to the Rift was easy, nothing much to sense, but further inside he could already feel the power building, like a raging beast, waiting for the chance to smash this puny tin can.

Phil Barton had done this with Udon many times over the last five years, but he still remembered his first time. He looked round at the crew; three were Rift virgins and the expressions on their faces told the story.

'Computer... initiate protocol Rift Run Alpha.' His voice was confident as he began the process.

Rift Run Alpha protocol initiated, please authorise. The digitised voice responded.

'Authorisation... Barton-six-delta-niner-x-ray-one-four.'

Authorisation accepted.

Barton turned to the crew. 'I would suggest that everyone take their seats and strap in; these runs can be a bit violent.' He initiated the ship wide broadcast. 'This is the First Officer. We have commenced our Rift Run, this may necessitate some fast and violent course changes all personnel please assume necessary safety protocols. That is all.' While the inertial dampeners should stop any internal damage, Barton always made the same announcement every time, just in case.

Udon felt the Rift – he was now part of it – and he moved with as much grace as he could, given that his body was now the trade ship he commanded. Ahead he felt a gravity well form; he altered his trajectory to skirt it. Another suddenly materialised below the ship, he fed more power to the drive and the ship responded, barely avoiding the trap.

In Udon's mind these looked like huge whirlpools in space. He felt the gravity fluctuations, felt their deadly pull. Now, something he had never experienced, a huge black mass lay ahead. But it wasn't a mass, more truthfully it was a huge black nothing, as if something had torn a huge piece out of space, blackness and emptiness had replaced it. This was the only way he could rationalise what he was now seeing, and it was rushing toward him.

Madly he flung himself to his left and dived below his horizon, slamming all available power to the drive.

'Inertial dampeners are overloading.' A panicked cry came from one of the new engineering officers.

Barton replied. 'The Captain is aware of that, keep calm.' But his thoughts were less than confident; he had never seen the ship thrown around so much this early in the run, and they still had several hours to go.

For Udon this was personal, the huge black emptiness was trying to swallow him. He ducked, dived, zigged and zagged; but still it came - relentless. He could feel the strain on his body, the ship was protesting. She was a trade ship, not built for these manoeuvres.

He could feel the stress, the loads on the drive and reactors, but he couldn't stop. The survival of the ship demanded even more. The tear was deepening, but he spotted a chance. Desperately Udon flung himself into the new course, the ship obeyed, reluctantly. He could feel the strain on her systems in his gut. She was close to the absolute limit.

The ship responded and together, they made the final dive to safely pass under the anomaly. Udon made a mental note to replay this from the sensor log. Something was dreadfully wrong with what they had just experienced.

Now in the clear for a while, Udon slowed the mad forward rush, allowing the ship's systems to normalise again. It also gave him a chance to rest, the last hour had been excruciatingly demanding.

Barton saw the Captain remove his hold on the control system, lift his arms and remove the helmet. Udon was now disconnected from the ship. He unbuckled his harness and moved to Udon's side.

'Are we through?' The question came from one of the new crewmen.

'Not quite half-way,' replied one of the older hands.

'That was some ride, Captain!' Barton said as he checked Udon's vital signs. Apart from extreme stress response, he was ok.

'Yes, Mister Barton, something I've never encountered before; we'll need to review the sensor logs thoroughly after this. Now I could use some coffee, we should be in null for the next hour or so.' Udon was referring to the part of the Rift that they were now traversing, very slowly so the ship, and Captain, could recoup and prepare for the next onslaught. He stood and headed for the ready room door. 'I'll be here.'

'Fine, Sir I'll start working on a ship status update.' As the door closed Barton turned to the crew. 'Ok, I want a full ship system status report in twenty minutes.' After an hour of total inactivity the Bridge crew leapt to the task, glad they had something to do to take their minds off what had just happened.

Udon entered the ready room, ordered a coffee from the dispenser and removed the suit. He placed it into the case where it would be cleaned and prepared for the next use. He ached, all over, his body felt like he'd been thrown down a long, steep rocky precipice.

What very few knew was now being evidenced on his body. Interfacing with the ship was physical, as physical as if he had actually done every move in person. To pilot ships in this fashion was hugely taxing, and sometimes deadly, for Altarians. Udon inspected his body in the mirror. Although he was tired and sore, he bore no permanent damage from the first run.

He commanded a bath to be prepared. A few minutes later, and with a fresh coffee, he entered the bath. The deep blue liquid was a unique Altarian preparation that could rejuvenate and reinvigorate him in minutes. He climbed in and immediately started to feel the benefit. He lay there for fifteen minutes before he felt completely normal and climbed out, the liquid had changed colour, now a very pale blue.

I was in a worse state than I appeared, Udon thought to himself almost in disbelief. He stood under the dryer and a wave of air blew over him removing the last vestiges of the liquid. Finally, Udon walked back into the main room and put the suit back on. As he finished, Barton announced he was at the door.

Barton started his report. 'The ship is in fine shape, Sir. We had a few minor incidents, but they've all been rectified. Here's our current position and course. We're slightly out of place compared to where we had projected, but nothing too problematic.'

Udon studied the data. He knew his mad piloting to avoid the tear had pushed them further away from their theoretical optimum trajectory than either wanted, but it was unavoidable. 'Thank you, Number One... time to go back to work.'

They left the room together. Barton took the command chair and Udon went back to the Pilot's station. He looked round the Bridge before replacing the helmet on his head. Slowly Udon reintegrated with the ship's systems. She had indeed been through a lot, he could sense what had been repaired or replaced. He felt a pang of guilt; it felt as though he had deliberately hurt a firm friend, but this soon passed, and he got back down to business.

As he assumed control of the ship, Udon sensed a huge ion storm approaching. Rather than trying to run through it, he turned away and skirted it perfectly. This added another two hours to their traverse time, but it was well worth it.

The rest of the transit was fairly quiet; the normal gravity wells, a couple of hugely charged ion storms but nothing too taxing. Four and a half hours later, Kidman broke free of the Rift and control was passed back to the crew. In all, the run had taken almost seven hours, much longer than usual, thanks to the strange black void they had encountered.

Udon removed his helmet. 'You have the con, Number One,' he said as he stood.

'Aye Sir, I have the con.' Barton's response was accompanied by a barely audibly sigh of relief from the new crew members. They had survived their first Rift Run and were all grateful they had.

Udon was exhausted; his usually light green skin was now more of a dull grey. He needed rest and lots of it. He returned to his ready room, commanded the bath to be prepared again and removed the suit, placing it back into the storage case. He coiled the helmet harness and stored it back in its container. With this finished he took a small breathing mask and attached it to an air feed beside his tub. He climbed in, placed the mask over his face and lay down, completely submerging this time.

Two hours later Udon surfaced. He removed the mask and went through the drying routine before he moved back to the other room, selected a clean uniform and began dressing. That's when he realised he was incredibly hungry and tired, mentally tired. He ordered a meal of steak and salad from the dispenser and called the Bridge as he waited.

'Number One, please come to the ready room.'

Moments later the door opened and Phil Barton entered. 'Thought you would like to know, we just entered our first displacement. We have another four to go, but we should arrive at AG48-5, in about seventy-five hours. I've changed the duty roster; third shift will take over in half an hour Sir.' Barton knew all too well how much the Rift Run took out of his Captain. 'You don't need to be back on the Bridge, the crew is handling things well.'

Udon smiled, he and Barton had developed a very strong partnership, and he was grateful for it. 'Thank you,

Number One. Truth be known, I'll probably sleep for most of the transit, but I'll be here in the ready room.'

'Aye Sir, I'd better get back for shift change. Sleep well.'

Chapter 5: Argos Defined

Joseph entered Drake's ready room.

In a few minutes he would need to somehow pacify his Chief Engineer and mend the rift that seemed to be forming in the engineering crew. He knew that having to land on this remote planet was having an effect. Lower oxygen level and higher than normal gravity was sapping everyone's energy. But he couldn't allow that to affect the efficient running of the ship, or the repairs.

Joseph sat at his desk, noticing a message icon at the lower left edge of his screen. He accessed it and saw it was encoded and from Gail Mossberg; just the thought of her gave him a warm feeling. Quickly he opened the message and dumped the contents into the decoder program. The message was simple –

AG48-5, and entire Zedak System, now owned by Argos Ltd. Coalition has changed AG48-5 name to Argos. What do you want to do with it?

Joseph sat back, a huge smile splitting his face. 'Well I'll be... they did it.' He started to construct a reply, as he finished, the annunciator announced that McGill was at the door. He finished transmitting the message as the Chief Engineer entered. Joseph looked up. 'First, have you cooled down?'

'Yeah,' McGill grumbled. 'I just don't like hearing what she has to say.'

'Does that mean you think she may have a point?' Joseph snapped, concern starting to grow in his stomach.

'Let's wait till we see the simulation.' As McGill finished, the door opened and Lieutenant Simona entered carrying a small data core.

'Right, before we go any further, this is the kiss and make up time. Both of you need to understand I can't have my senior staff at war, and you two are the most senior engineering staff we have.' Joseph's voice had a commanding tone to it. Both officers nodded and offered each other apologies.

'Excellent. Now Lieutenant what is your concern?'

Simona gestured toward the console. Joseph acquiesced, and she connected the data core she was carrying. 'Sir, I have been doing a full structural analysis of the ship, as per our standing instructions for any forced landing. I was particularly concerned because of the overloading and the gravity. When the First Officer noted that he felt the landing was particularly hard, I knew I needed to get the analysis done ASAP.'

She worked the console and brought the display up on the screen behind the desk. 'The old Drake is designed with a backbone structure; actually a double backbone... one top and one bottom. I initially sent in a remote to carry out fluoroscopic analysis.' The image changed and now showed the upper backbone of the ship under fluoroscopic conditions.

The evidence was troubling. 'All these lines,' she used her laser pointer to indicate her concerns. 'Are structural cracks in the backbone. So I decided to carry out a detailed x-ray examination.' Again the screen changed. 'This speaks for itself.'

The image was damning. Where the fluoroscope showed a myriad of surface cracks, the x-ray showed how deep they went, some almost clean through the central structural supports of the ship.

Joseph let out a tuneless whistle. 'Bruce, what's your take?'

McGill shook his head. 'I don't want to believe this,' he turned to Simona. 'Lieutenant, are you absolutely certain of the equipment? There are no calibration issues?'

'Absolutely, Sir, we have rechecked and done the analysis three times now,' she brought up the simulation. 'This is what I predict if we try to leave the planet.'

The simulation showed the ship lifting off and gradually gaining height. It concentrated on the damaged areas of the structure and clearly demonstrated a worsening of the damage, but the ship was able to leave the surface and achieve orbit.

'And this is what happens if we try to use the displacement drive.' This simulation was much worse. As the ship approached the event horizon to enter the worm hole, the stresses caused the backbone to fail; the ship literally tore apart.

'But what if we took off empty, leave the cargo behind?' Joseph suggested.

'That was empty. Am I right Lieutenant?' McGill's voice sounded defeated.

'Correct. I'm afraid the Drake is stuck here, at best we may be able to move her, with assistance, but she will never go back into space. Sorry Sir.' Simona was slightly bemused; the Captain seemed to be taking the news better than she anticipated. In fact, he was smiling.

'Ok, so the old Drake is finished as a space ship. What did you mean we could move her with assistance?' Joseph seemed to be thinking out loud.

Both Simona and McGill were at a loss to explain Joseph's attitude. His ship and crew were theoretically marooned on this planet, at least until they could arrange other ships to pick them up, and they were uncomfortably close to the Krell border. But Simona answered the question.

'We would need to use the tugs and some of the freight anti grav units to better support the weight. Then we could, I think, lift her off and drag her to a different location. But I don't see what good that will do, the old girl still won't be able to get home!' Simona felt the emotion as the facts were now sinking in.

'Yes, but what if she was home? How far could we move her?'

McGill couldn't hold back. 'For God's sake Joe... didn't you hear what she said? The Drake's days are finished. That's what I was so bloody angry about... for the moment we're stuck here.'

'Calm down, both of you,' Joseph turned to the comm system and called the First Officer to the ready room. They waited, and a few minutes later Don Hopmann walked in.

'Don, take a seat, and you two sit down, we have a lot to discuss.' Joseph waited as the others took their seats. 'Now, this is the situation, Don. The Drake is finished, she'll never go back into space and home, but, something else has happened.' He continued to bring the three up to date on the status of AG48-5.

'So AG48-5 is now Argos and you own it?' Hopmann inquired.

'That about sums it up. In fact, Argos Limited owns the whole system. The freight situation is taken care of. Kidman will arrive in less than three days now, and we are already placing critical freight into orbit. When she arrives, Kidman will take the freight, and a selection of the crew, back to Earth. We have a new ship complete and ready for delivery. The crew bring it back here; we transfer the rest of the freight and send it back to Earth.' Joseph was even more excited now.

'And, what else do you have in mind?' Don knew Joseph well, possibly better than anyone else. He could see the signs of a plan.

'Don, the Independent Traders Guild... we have a problem... we're all so splintered. What if the Guild had a permanent base, somewhere where we could meet, even have permanent bases for our ships? We could work together and beat the conglomerates at their own game and, as Argos is an independent, neutral colony as of now, we can all avoid much of the cost impost the conglomerates are having dumped on us.

'We could level the playing field... think about it,' Joseph was becoming animated now. This was his passion, his driving force; to create a truly free, Independent Traders Guild that could benefit **all** the small operators in the Galaxy. Don had heard this before, many times and, while he was a full supporter of the concept, he felt they had more pressing issues.

'Skipper, you know I support all that but, we have some issues that are far more urgent. We have a dead ship, a crew that is expecting to be able to leave here and return to Earth in the next few weeks. I think we need to focus on solving these problems... the rest can happen in time.'

Joseph stopped, looked at his First Officer and nodded. 'As usual you're the voice of reason. Here's the plan: Kidman will arrive soon, take on the critical freight and a partial crew. I want you to select a crew for the return journey. We have a new ship sitting in Abracorp's dock, waiting to be picked up.

'You Don, and the crew you choose, will collect the new ship and return. Between both you and Kidman we should be able to ship all the freight, and everyone who wants to return to Earth.' Joseph held his hand to stifle the protest he knew would come. 'Yes I know, at least three months before we can leave, but that will give me time to survey the planet and try to decide what to do.'

'And you're going to sell that to the crew?' Don asked the question everybody was thinking.

'I don't have a choice, do I? Neither do the crew. Kidman can only take a maximum of ten extra for the return journey, she's nowhere near the size of Drake. Even the new ship is smaller but by bringing both back, we can deliver the freight and give everyone the freedom to choose to stay, or return to Earth. Besides, what other option is there?' A smile crossed Joseph's face. 'Freedom, I'll name the new ship Freedom... remember that Don, when they officially launch her.'

Don shook his head. 'And the crew Sir? What do we tell the crew?'

'We tell them the truth, Number One, just the truth! I believe hold three is now clear, so we'll have a crew briefing there this afternoon... acceptable?' Joseph waited until the others agreed. 'Now we need a plan about what we do with the ship. We will still need shelter and power for the next few months. Bruce where are we up to?'

For the next hour they discussed the logistics needed for an extended stay; food, water, power all needed critical evaluation. Finally, everyone had their duties and the three dispersed. Joseph left the ship, took one of the small hover sleds and went to the hyzene plant site.

Hyzene was now in desperately short supply and if the plant wasn't up and running by the next day, they'd have to start to shut auxiliary reactors down. The chief engineer had assured his Captain that wouldn't be necessary, but from where Joseph stood, it was a brave commitment. Joseph climbed back on the hover sled, powered it up and headed away from the site.

He wanted a better idea of the land around the ship's current location. Joseph had a hunch that they would need to move the Drake to a better location sooner rather than later.

The ground began to gently rise away from the hyzene plant. He followed what seemed to be a natural pathway but as he got further away, he suspected that this wasn't natural. As he passed through a five metre ravine his thoughts were amplified. Here he saw indisputable evidence of drill marks, as though some machine had bored holes deep in the rock. He recognised these as blast charge drill holes; clearly they weren't the first mechanically capable creatures to be on Argos.

He followed the ravine until it flattened out to reveal a huge expanse of level ground. Joseph stopped; the sight before him stunning in its beauty.

The ground was well covered with native grasses and vegetation. Tall trees, low scrub and wild flowers everywhere, *well if I had to crash somewhere, this seems like a pleasant location.* The thought brought a chuckle to his lips. Wandering some distance from him was a herd of the four horned creatures he had seen on the southern continent, hundreds of them. Another idea began to coalesce in his mind.

The sky was clear, and he was watching bird like creatures circling, almost like eagles of old Earth. In the distance was a raised plateau, not more than fifty metres higher than the land in front of him, but enough that he could see what he thought was a waterfall cascading down the side. Joseph followed the waterfall with his eyes, it fed directly into a river that disappeared into the undergrowth. He assumed, it must be what fed the lake he could see about five kilometres away.

Something triggered his fight or flight senses, and he tapped the shield icon on the control panel. The quiet was split with a loud roar and a large creature slammed into the active shield. The shield did its job; the creature was flung several metres away. It regained its feet, all six of them, shook its head and started to cautiously circle back toward the sled.

The creature resembled a cat, at least the body did; it moved with typical feline grace and purpose. But the head was something else, almost canine like with two wide set red eyes. The creature bared its teeth and again let out the roar he had heard before.

Again the animal leapt at the sled, again the shield repelled it. Again it sounded, this time more of a howl, a howl of frustration. Seconds later it was answered by another howl, not too far away.

Now Joseph was worried; the shield system was not designed to repel attacks from large animals, it had done so twice already. It wouldn't take long for the battery to be depleted, if this attack was kept up.

As much as he hated it, he had no choice but to arm the sled's single disruptor. If one animal could attack with such force, then two would spell the end for him, in short order.

A third howl, from a different direction sent a cold shiver of dread through his spine – three animals. The sled's shield couldn't protect him for more than a few seconds – one concerted attack, and he was history. Joseph activated the targeting system, locked on the animal in front of him and waited.

The animal sat down, lifted its head skyward and let out another, different pitched howl.

It sat and waited. Seconds passed slowly.

Joseph placed his thumb on the disruptor trigger.

Another howl answered, this time from a different direction - then another from far ahead of him. The animal in front of him stood – Joseph deactivated the safety on the weapon. The red eyes bored into him then, as quickly as it had attacked, it turned and galloped away. Joseph followed it as far as his eyes could, noting that it left virtually no track. Within seconds of it passing there was no evidence it had been there.

Finally, able to breathe again, Joseph deactivated the disruptor but kept the shield energised. He looked at his watch, 14:30; time he was heading back. He turned the sled and started to retrace his course to the Hyzene site.

Captain Jones, this is First Officer, come in please. Don Hopmann's voice echoed round Joseph's helmet.

'I hear you, Don, what's up?'

'Sir, we have completed the tasks assigned to us. We would like to meet with you to discuss the results before you address the crew.'

'Ok, I'll be back in about fifteen minutes, assemble in the ready room Jones out.' Joseph reached the hyzene plant and approached one of the workers. 'Where's the site super?' The worker pointed to a shuttle on the far side of the site and Joseph turned his sled toward it. He stopped and powered it down as the supervisor came out of the shuttle.

'Captain, can I help you?' she asked.

'No, but I think I can help you. Has anyone seen any indigenous life?'

'One of the security guys said he thought he saw something... like a cross between a cat and a dog. We all thought he was hallucinating.'

'Well he's not. I've just had an altercation with one... a damn **big** one.' Joseph's face showed he was serious.

'How big?'

'Have you ever seen a Lion?'

The supervisor nodded. 'Yes in the zoo museum in Sydney, and in vids of course.'

'The creature that had a go at me was about fifty percent larger, with six legs. I would suggest you strengthen your security and even set up a perimeter shield.'

The supervisor saw he wasn't joking. 'Yes, Sir, I'll get a crew on it immediately.'

Joseph climbed back on the sled, powered it up and accelerated away from the site. Something in Don's message told him he had other problems and he needed to find out what. Five minutes later he was back at the ship, all four access ramps were down and none were guarded.

He guided the sled up the port ramp and back into its parking bay; downloaded the data from his encounter with the cat like creature and called the First Officer to meet him at the head of the ramp immediately.

The docking bay was huge, running almost the entire width of the ship. Each side was garaging for the land vehicles - sleds, ground tugs and personnel transports; the central section was marked and reserved for shuttles and space tugs. It was accessed both from the side, via the ramp, or from top via an airlock. Joseph moved back to the ramp and waited.

It was only a few minutes later when the First Officer was at his side, 'You wanted to see me, Sir?'

Joseph handed the data pad to him. 'Yes Don... have a look at this.' The data pad played the recording from the sensors on the sled. Don let out a soft whistle.

'Doesn't seem too friendly... what is it?'

'I'd say top of the food chain, round here at least, and we are a lot of tasty morsels for it. We need to tighten security; at the least a sensor grid and armed patrols. A shield wall would be better, if we have the power,' Joseph suggested.

'Not a chance, we're running on empty now. If the hyzene plant isn't up and running tomorrow, as engineering said it would, we'll have to start limiting shuttle flights and scaling energy demand back.'

Joseph thought for a moment. 'Ok, as of now all shuttle activity is for essential purposes only, everything else is cancelled. I want all available personnel working on the Hyzene problem; we can't afford to lose that. Also, every access point to the ship that isn't essential is to be closed and sealed, immediately, and armed teams to be placed at those that are still active.'

He turned and began walking toward the pod; glancing at his watch he saw the time was 14:55. 'We have our pre-briefing in five minutes.' He didn't need to remind Don. He was already on his comm link arranging for his Captain's plan to be put into action. Getting out of this area made sense as it would soon be flooded with shuttles and other vehicles.

***

The readout on the console read 15:03 as the door annunciator buzzed.

'Enter,' Joseph called. The door opened and the senior officers came in. Thankfully, Joseph had increased the seating in the room and all eight were now occupied. Don was the first to speak.

'Captain, the measures you asked for are being implemented. From now on only one of us can authorise a shuttle flight and all access points to the ship are now under guard, so one problem taken care of. Unfortunately it's not the last. I'll summarise then the others can elaborate.

'First the site isn't as solid as we first thought. It appears that there is an underground cavern, or cave system. Currently it appears to be supporting the mass of the ship, but we still have some anti-gravs powered, so it is actually only supporting round half of the ship's bulk.' Don's next words were tinged with sadness. 'The structural analysis has been confirmed... this ship will never get back into space.

'Crew acclimatisation is an issue, work shifts must be kept short and work on all repairs is slow... and food will become an issue in six or seven weeks.' He turned back to the other officers, seeking their confirmation. 'Bruce, do you want to add anything?'

The Chief Engineer stood. 'Thanks Don. Skipper, we will have the hyzene plant operating tomorrow and full production will be available by the next day, our energy problem will be solved. As for the ship... if we want to save her she has to be moved, and soon. To do that, we need to be able to scout and comprehensively survey a new site.'

'How long do we have?'

Molly Renwick, the senior sensor operator and the ship's ranking science officer answered. 'Not easy to say, Sir. We have very limited data on the structure of the planet I don't think this area is a natural formation, I think it has been deliberately constructed.' The room was hushed, everyone expecting some protest from the Captain.

'I agree Molly. Today I did a bit of exploring. I found evidence of construction as I passed through an obviously artificial ravine. I think sometime in the distant past, there was some intelligent habitation of the planet. Let's sort the survival issues, and then we'll work on a program for you to investigate, agreed?' Joseph's answer stunned all in the room, the realisation that they may not be alone on this planet wasn't something they wanted to hear.

Joseph continued. 'Food, Number One; you mentioned some shortage?'

Doug Harris, Drake's logistics officer answered. 'Yes Sir. We have enough to last the six weeks of the journey, plus another three in reserve **but**... that figure is based on our normal crew level. More importantly, our normal hibernation level is taken into the calculations. Now with all crew awake and working hard in adverse conditions, those calculations are meaningless. Food demand is up by thirty percent and climbing. At our present rate of consumption, we will be out within five weeks and that includes what's available from the hydroponic gardens.' Doug handed the room back to his Captain.

'We've seen some cattle like creatures, and there are sure to be many plants we could eat. Simon, can you sort out a program to figure out what's available and what we can eat, without killing ourselves?' Joseph handed the room to the Ship's Doctor, Simon Carpenter.

'Actually, Allison and I have been discussing this; she's an amateur botanist you know. I'm sure we can sample some of the local flora to check if it's edible. And I believe we have a couple of experienced hunters on the crew. Boris, the assistant Loadmaster, has quite a reputation as an adventurer... spends all his free time hunting. He would be the best to work the animal side of things... but I must have samples to test **before** we try to eat them.' Simon emphasised this requirement.

'Well, we have some problems, but also some possible solutions.' Joseph was happy with his crew's analysis and solutions. 'The most pressing is energy... then we need to move the ship. Bruce you are certain we will have hyzene production up and running tomorrow?'

The Chief Engineer nodded. 'Yes Sir, I guarantee we will be producing tomorrow. Another thought, while we were setting up the intake system for the plant, we noticed a number of aquatic animals... fish I suppose. Maybe we should try to catch some, test if they're edible?'

'Sounds like we have plenty to do... once we have power and the ship is safe. Bruce, how is the repair to the tank and conduits coming. We need that fixed before we can transfer any hyzene.' Joseph brought the discussion back on track.

Gabrielle spoke up. 'I'll answer that, if I may?' McGill gave his permission by simply nodding. 'We are almost ready to receive hyzene; the tank is repaired, and we are testing it now. The conduits should be ready by tomorrow night and about the same time we will have sufficient hyzene supply to use.'

Joseph looked round the room, proud of his crew. Here they were basically stranded, their ship dead, and still everyone was working as true professionals. 'Thank you, each of you has done a great job.' He glanced at the console, 15:45 was displayed. 'In fifteen minutes the whole crew is gathering in hold three, we need to make this situation as positive as possible and I need each of you there to help.'

Chapter 6: New Possibilities

Joseph stood on the small elevated platform that had been placed at the end of the hold.

There, before him stood his crew, all 165 of them; most had worked for him for a number of years. But others, like so many in the industry were itinerant; workers who signed on for the duration of a trip, or just from one planet to another.

His comm was active, so he moved forward and greeted them.

'Thank you for joining me. I'll give you an update on our situation and then details of an interesting opportunity we have before us... first the situation. As you all know, Drake suffered substantial damage when the deflector shield failed and we elected to land here to effect repairs. We have set up a hyzene production facility that our Chief Engineer assures me will be producing early tomorrow, so energy will not be a problem. We have also conducted a complete structural survey of the ship, and this is where we have a more worrying issue.

'To put it bluntly, the Drake's days in space are over, the old girl will never leave this planet.' As he said those words, a murmur of discontent rumbled through the crew. A couple of people started to shout questions, but Joseph was ready for that. 'Please, let me finish and then I'll answer your questions if I can.

'We are **not** stranded, and I emphasise **not**. The Kidman will be here in a few hours, and she will do a couple of things for us. First, she will take the time critical freight to Earth; this is the freight that will generate the largest portion of bonus for the ship, so everyone will still make a handsome income from the trip.

'Second, she will take our First Officer and a skeleton crew with her to take delivery of our newest ship. The Freedom, as we have named this new vessel, will return with Kidman to collect the remainder of our freight and the rest of us, if we want to go.' He paused as a rumble of disbelief started to run through the crew.

One of the crew, a Petty Officer called out. 'What do you mean if we want to? We've got no other option.'

Joseph smiled. This question couldn't have come at a better time. 'But there is another option, for those of us who like a bit of adventure. Let me explain,' he held his hands up to call for calm, again. 'Up until we arrived here this planet was designated AG four eight five, and was a free planet. What that means is that nobody had claimed it. It was ceded to the Coalition by the Krell years ago in a bid to separate the races and prevent the war from escalating further.

'The Coalition didn't even acknowledge the action, so I made some inquiries and have been able to secure title, in perpetuity, to the planet, and the entire system. It has been named Argos and is now mine. So we can stay here and build a new society, a new planet free from all the intrusions of the Coalition and Earth governments.' Again a rumble of voices was heard. 'Wait, anyone who wants to return to Earth can do so, no question of that, just a question of when.'

The Petty Officer again spoke. Joseph thought for a moment then remembered who he was; Petty Officer Rajiv Singh. He was a tall man with dark brown skin. His head was covered with a turban but his dark eyes sparkled, almost excitedly.

'And what if we decide to stay, what happens then? Some of us have families; we have homes and possessions... what happens to them?' His words were accompanied by a chorus from the rest of the crew.

Joseph again held up his hands for silence. When there was again quiet he continued. 'I don't have all the answers now, but we will work these issues out. More importantly, we now have to accept the fact that for the next fourteen weeks, we will be staying here.'

Before anyone could protest he continued. 'It will take the Freedom and Kidman that long to return, and before any of you ask, no, the Kidman can't take more than the ten we will be sending in the skeleton crew... she doesn't have either the cryogenics or the life support to do it. So, whether we like it or not, we are **all** stuck here for the next fourteen weeks, so we need to suck it up and get on with the job.' There were a few grumbles, but in all, most took the news in their stride. 'I'll hand over to our Chief Engineer so he can fill you in on the engineering details, Commander McGill.'

Bruce moved past Joseph and took the stand. He outlined the issues with the Drake and what was planned to alleviate the situation. Then Lieutenant Harris took over and brought them up to date with the logistical situation. This didn't go down well, the food issue brought howls of complaint and Joseph had to intervene.

'**Silence**,' he yelled, '**silence**!' Joseph waited until the noise subsided. 'This entire situation isn't what any of us wanted **but**, we have identified some sources of indigenous food that our medical and scientific staff will be analysing.

When they have cleared the food sources, and I am sure they will, we will have plenty to last. In any case, we don't have an alternative.'

'Bullshit,' a voice came from the back of the crowd. 'This's all bullshit! Why don't we just take our chance with this ship and head back to Earth?'

Bruce McGill moved past Joseph. 'I don't know who said that but **listen up**! If you want to commit suicide, then step forward and I'll personally arrange for you to be accommodated! But, if we take this ship back into space, then not only will you be committing suicide, you'll be murdering all your crew mates who want to live.

'Now, who's the first who wants to die?' Silence was the response. 'I thought as much... now here's some information for you. This was the Drake's last trip... Freedom is her replacement. What's happened is she is now part of Argos and not being broken up for scrap. So are you all with the program now?'

There was a murmur of agreement that came from the group.

'There is one other thing. Along with, what I believe will be some great steaks, there is an indigenous predator. The Captain had a run in with one earlier today. To keep it at bay we have set up a shield wall at the construction site and closed all unnecessary access points to the ship. From now on there will be armed patrols round the ship and at the hyzene plant. But hear this, these creatures live here, we are the invaders. We will only kill them if we have to. There will be no trophy hunting, is that understood?

'So here are the rules... pretty simple in fact. Nobody leaves the ship unaccompanied and there will always be at least one person in any group who is armed, and no one leaves without authorisation. As Number One is returning to Earth, I have assumed his duties and part of that is security. If anyone wishes to leave the ship, I must give authorisation. This will remain in force until we know exactly what we are dealing with. Is that clear?'

There was a chorus of grudging agreement; now everyone knew the score. For the next half hour, the command team answered as many questions as they could. Finally Joseph agreed to hold daily briefings to keep everyone in the loop and the meeting was disbanded. While McGill started to set up the security protocols, Joseph the other officers left the hold and went to the forward observation lounge.

Initially Drake was designed as a cruise liner but, as often happened, there wasn't the demand for the service and, after many years of Drake being mothballed, the company went into liquidation. It was about the same time that Joseph was looking for his second ship and the huge liner was offered for a fraction of its value, so he quickly snapped it up.

It took over six months to convert her to a freighter, selling off most of the luxury fittings to various ship builders. The transactions were beneficial for both parties. The builders got luxury fittings at a bargain price, and Joseph managed to make enough to pay for part of the purchase and the entire refit, in all, he considered it one of his better business decisions. He was so pleased with the deal that he kept an eye out for more cruise bargains. Over the following forty years, he had converted nine other liners the same way.

When Drake entered service with Joseph's company, she proved ideal as a bulk freighter and, as her fit out was still considered extreme luxury; attracting good crew had never been an issue. All senior officers had their own suite, junior officers their own private room, and all other ranks shared accommodation, no more than two to a room; and these rooms were larger than most Captains' quarters on other vessels.

Some of the cruise liner facilities hadn't been removed. There were three observation decks, four gymnasiums and three restaurants, now delegated as senior officers' ward room, junior officers' mess and crew mess. The forward observation lounge had been converted into the Captain's Lounge and private quarters as it was only a short distance from the Bridge.

The group of five officers followed Joseph into the lounge – he suggested they all grab a drink – and he operated the controls for the view port. Shields slid back into the hull revealing the magnificent vista of Argos outside the ship. Everyone was now sitting and Joseph poured himself a large, single malt before he returned to the windows.

'Beautiful isn't it?' He spoke to no one in particular. From this position in the ship, they had an uninterrupted view for 240 degrees. They could clearly see the hyzene plant, and the plateau Joseph had seen on his brief exploration.

Directly in front of the ship was the lake, or sea; the actual determination hadn't been made as there had been no time for a detailed survey. It was deep blue and seemed to go on forever.

To port was the gently sloping land that eventually merged with the distant mountain range and to the aft, plains as far as they could see. The air was clear, almost sparkling with a few clouds starting to form to port.

Allison Thompson, Drake's navigator, moved to his side. 'It certainly is beautiful and unspoiled. Sir, what's your plan? I know you've long held the view that the Independent Traders Guild (ITG) should have its own base. Is that what you're thinking?'

Joseph gave his navigator a long look. 'Between you and Gabby, I really don't have any secrets... seems that you two can almost read my mind.' Both officers had been with Joseph for years, and he desperately wanted to keep them. He returned to the bar, refilled his glass and sat with the others.

'You're correct, as usual. The ITG needs to throw off the shackles of the Coalition and the corruption that is evident with the trade conglomerates. What most don't know is that the Coalition has a new tax. We call it the Boot Tax.

'In essence, it is a tax on everyone who lands on a planet for the purpose of commerce. The rationale is that this tax will raise funds for the colonies to improve their space ports and make our life easier. But it fails any fairness test for a number of reasons. First it is levied every time someone lands on the planet, based on people, not shuttles. You all know how many times we need to send people to the surface on many colonies to ferry goods to the ship.

'Every time a person steps foot on the planet, the tax is levied but the interpretation has been clouded and some more enterprising bureaucrats have raised the stakes. On some colonies, every time they leave a planet, the tax is also levied. Last week it was extended to orbiting transfer stations and docks.

'The corporates have worked a scam where they are registering their ships on the planets that they trade with, thereby limiting the tax impost. Add to this the generous tax rebates for this registration and you understand that the Boot Tax is designed to purely target any non-aligned independents.' He took a swig of his drink.

'But how will owning this planet help?' Simon Carpenter posed the question.

'Simple. If the Guild registers Argos as its base of operations we can officially secede from the Coalition, thereby limiting their ability to impose the tax. Sure we will still have to pay local taxes, but I don't mind that. Local taxes stay local but this Boot Tax is being charged by the Coalition administration. Most of it will go in bureaucracy; almost nothing will get back to the colonies. So if we are separate to the Coalition, we should be able to negotiate around it.'

Simon spoke again. 'Well, I can only wish you luck. The Coalition has a pretty long reach when it wants something. If you can pull it off it'll be the coup of the century.'

Just then the door annunciator buzzed. 'Enter' Joseph called.

Gabrielle Simona and Bruce McGill entered, both smiling like Cheshire cats. 'Great news, Sir... the conduits have passed their pressure tests and the hyzene tanks are fully operational.' Gabby announced enthusiastically.

'And,' Bruce chimed in, 'we have started transferring hyzene. The process is easier than on Earth; the water is so pure, fewer contaminants, so the purification process is much easier.' Bruce reached the bar and poured a drink for himself and one for Gabby. 'We are also transferring water to top up the ship's supply; tell the crew they can have water showers from now on.' The news was met with a sigh of relief – ion showers were good and efficient, but couldn't beat an old-fashioned water wash down.

'Great work, you two... well ahead of schedule. Now, Allison, I have a new job for you, but first, can someone find Ensign Renwick.' A few minutes later Molly Renwick, senior Sensor Operator entered the room. 'Ensign, will you please fill the staff in on the situation under the ship?'

Molly began to describe what she had found in the rock strata below the ship. A labyrinth of caves and tunnels so uniform and geometric she didn't believe they could be natural. While this caused most in the room to pause, her next revelation was more urgent. The subterranean structure, coupled with the load the ship was exerting, could cause the rock to fail. So far, she had recorded only small changes but, the longer Drake was sitting here, the more probable a new disaster was.

Joseph thanked the Ensign and offered her a drink. 'Thanks, Molly. For those who don't know, Molly is a geophysicist, and a damn good one. So here is the task; Allison and Molly will head up a team to survey the planet and find a more suitable location for Drake's **final** resting place. A location close to here would be best, due to the need for us to refuel with hyzene, but it must be stable for the long term. The site we choose will be the start of our colonisation of Argos.'

He turned back to Simon. 'Doc, I want you to fast track the analysis of potential food sources and Bruce, I need you to come up with a list of equipment we will need to begin building a new colony... remember, we have two ships returning here in the next fourteen weeks. I would rather they returned with stuff we need and can use, than come back empty.'

Everyone noted how animated Joseph was; his dream, his obsession, was now closer to reality than ever before, and he showed it. Don decided to intervene, believing that if he didn't they would be here for at least another hour listening to the Captain postulating about his dream of a truly solid, Independent Trading Guild.

'Allison, as Navigator you are the best to fill us in on Argos and where it fits in this system.' All eyes turned to her, Don had been successful in diverting the conversation.

'We really don't know much. Argos is the fifth planet in this system. It is substantially larger than Earth but, because of the output of its sun, has a similar atmosphere and possibly, ecosystem. Interestingly, it has an almost perpendicular orientation... only one point seven degrees of axial inclination... so the seasons should be fairly even.'

'The orbit is elliptical... like Earth's... and this should deliver true differentiation between the summer and winter seasons... if I can use those terms?' She looked round the group for any dissension. 'I decided to keep Earth terms as we are all familiar with them. Each day is longer than Earth, approximately twenty-eight hours, and so far my calculations show a three hundred and eighty-five day orbit time so each year will be a bit longer. But apart from these findings, very little is known about the place.' Allison finished and handed the floor back to the First Officer.

'Then one of the first tasks must be to change the ship's chronometer... if we're staying, we need to start working to Argos time. Gabby, can you arrange that?'

Gabrielle agreed and Joseph took control of the meeting.

'Well, I would say we all have our work cut out for the next few days. Bruce, when we have enough hyzene, start fuelling the shuttles and the survey work can begin. Now, if you have nothing more, I think we should get started.' He waited for any further business. 'Ok, thank you all for your input; we'll meet again in three days for any updates. Don, can I have a few moments with you?'

Don waited as the others filed out of the lounge. Once the room was clear Joseph spoke, 'Don, we need to know what the crew's mood is. Personally I'd like everyone to stay and help with the colonisation but, the reality is that won't happen. I know this is asking a lot but can you try to find out what their feelings are, what the crew wants?'

'That shouldn't be too hard. Already I know that some of the engineering staff have started discussing what this all means and Danielle says that some of the load crew have formed a committee... I think they'll come to you fairly soon. What you need to do is work out what incentives you can offer, what benefits there will be for them to stay. But I'll keep an ear open for anything I hear.' Joseph nodded and thanked his First Officer. Don left and finally Joseph was alone in his favourite part of the ship.

Night was falling and the sky was giving a magnificent display, Joseph moved to the centre of the room, activated the antigrav disc and began to float up toward the ceiling. As he reached the top of the dome, part of it slid open and the disc he was standing on filled the gap it left. Now he was standing on the top of the ship watching the canvas of the sky change as the sun dropped lower in the west.

He stood still, mesmerised by the beauty of what he was seeing. Colours swirled; red to pink, orange to purple – colours he had never seen in any sky before. It was then he realised it had been many years since he had taken the time to do this; to stand still and gaze at the majesty of nature. Joseph suddenly felt very small, like an ant at the foot of a mountain.

The sky darkened as the colours started to dissipate. He stood perfectly still, his eyes transfixed on the sky. Suddenly he heard a screech to his left. Joseph turned and his eyes locked onto a large bird, or at least a bird-like creature. This was the source of the sound. He watched as it soared high, circling something.

Then he saw the object of its fascination, a smaller bird desperately trying to avoid the obvious predator. The smaller creature darted all over the sky, left, right, up, down trying to avoid what was now the obvious feeding habit of the larger bird. It was a dance that could have only one eventuality, and Joseph was the first human to witness this primordial and deadly ballet.

Suddenly, the predator let out another screech, but this time a flash of fire accompanied the sound. The smaller bird was engulfed in the fireball. Instantly, the predator folded its wings and dropped like a stone.

The prey was now fluttering slowly toward the ground, but only for a few seconds. The large predator flared out of its mad dive, unfolded its wings and grabbed the hapless creature in its talons.

It let out another screech. This time, Joseph was certain he could sense triumph in the sound.

He chuckled to himself. *Argos is going to be full of surprises.*

Chapter 7: Discovery

He was floating in a sea of tiny pinpoints of light. Weightless and free he gazed in awe at the beauty surrounding him. He was a tiny microbe in the vastness of the universe.

Suddenly it all changed! A deep black mass appeared; it was moving slowly, but definitely moving.

Voices, unintelligible, barely audible whispered in the darkness. As the blackness progressed, stars began to disappear. The voices became more strident.

This must be stopped... you must warn them... stop this madness.

Cries of anguish, of pain assaulted his mind; as though millions were crying out in terror - the whispering voices became louder.

Warn them, stop the madness. You are the only one. Warn them, stop the madness. You are the only one. The voices repeated over and over.

'Who are you? What must I do, how can I help?' He screamed at the cosmos.

He was sweating, the black mass was advancing; he observed planets in its path being drawn into its huge maw. Cities crumbling, people desperately trying to flee; but the end was unavoidable, the cries of despair flooding his consciousness. Then he recognised the city.

'Impossible, the vision is false. Organa is standing; I was there a few days ago.' He screamed.

The vision is of the future. Watch, learn; stop the madness. Only you can stop it.

The scene changed, more stars had vanished, the howls from the dead continued unabated - then the voices.

Watch, learn; see what will happen.

'Who are you?' he screamed.

Search your mind, you know who we are.

The scene changed again, this time a ship, sleek and new. It launched something from its belly; the object sped ahead and then vanished into a worm hole. Moments later, he felt something, what, he didn't know; it felt like flesh being torn from bone. He felt pain, more pain than he ever imagined could be endured; as if the whole Galaxy shuddered, but much more.

The pain felt deeper, much deeper, but he couldn't see anything. Then the blackness appeared, it looked like a piece of the fabric of space had been torn away, revealing something else, something sinister and ancient, then he remembered. He had seen this before.

The ship, the sleek silver ship was in the path of the advancing blackness; it tried to turn and flee. He felt the ship shudder as the engines were forced to emergency power, to no avail. He stared, helpless as the blackness engulfed the ship; he tried to cover his ears to hide from the cries of those on board. But their howls only lasted for a moment, then silence.

The voices returned. *Now you see, now you know. Warn them; stop them, before it is too late.*

Captain Udon Tellyz woke, his body covered in sweat but his mind focused on one word – Frederickson. He reached over to his communicator and called his First Officer.

Barton here, Sir.

'Number One, can you come to my quarters in half an hour?' Udon requested.

Aye Sir, half an hour it is. The First Officer's response was crisp and correct.

Slowly Udon rose, his muscles ached and his mind reeled. He was covered with a patina of sweat so his first call was the bathroom. He stood briefly under a cold shower, trying to wash away the exertion of his sleep. It didn't work, so he progressed to his morning exercise routine.

Like most Altarians, Udon was a devotee of L'trisk, and every morning he went through a complex routine designed to stretch both mind and body. Many humans had become exponents of the discipline, some describing it as a complex form of yoga, others Tai Chi; others considered it the most advanced form of martial art rivalling even the fabled Kung Fu of Earth.

In truth, L'trisk is similar to these and much more. Many Altarian L'trisk masters were sought after as body guards. Only the fabled Warrior Queens of Varga were thought to be superior in hand-to-hand combat, or so the mythology suggested.

Udon started concentrating on a single point in the room. He began the routine, stretching his muscles, focusing his mind. Fifteen minutes later he was finished, both his mind and body now in tune and relaxed. His morning ritual complete, he selected his uniform for the day. He had just finished dressing when the door annunciator chimed, Commander Barton had arrived.

'Enter,' Udon ordered as he turned for the door. Phillip Barton, second in command of Kidman, entered the room; he was a tall and wiry man, with a shock of flaming red hair and light blue/green eyes. He was not an overtly handsome man, but he had an aura that commanded respect from his crew and admiration from others. If he had to be summed up succinctly, confident would be one of the words used.

'Morning Sir, I trust you are rested?' he inquired as he walked through the door.

'There is a duality to the answer to that question. How long was I asleep?'

'Twenty three hours.'

Udon changed his stance and gave his second in command a long, hard stare. 'I was that bad?'

'Worst I've seen... you could hardly walk, so I thought it best to leave you to recover. There was something different, wasn't there?'

'Yes, Number One, vastly different. Powerful and troubling; something that should not be there, something I am at a loss to explain. Maybe our scan logs will assist.' Udon's voice sounded lost, almost fearful. Whatever he had seen in the Rift had almost destroyed the ship. Barton decided he really didn't want to run across it again.

'I thought you might need them. I have reviewed the whole run, a couple of times and there is one section that I can't explain... is that where you want to start?'

Udon nodded. 'Thank you, Number One, most efficient, as usual.' Together they sat and reviewed the sensor logs, the normal Rift denizens were there. Gravity wells, ion storms and the rest of the challenges, but the section they were analysing had something else, something that neither man could grasp.

Even the ship's computer had drawn a blank in trying to assign a description to what was there. For an hour they ran and re ran the logs. Udon tried to recall his vision of the action, but it seemed to be clouded and just beyond his reach. Frustration built, and finally Udon stopped. He looked at Barton and spoke.

'Phillip, I must ask something of you. Something you are not compelled to agree to, but something that may help us understand what we have encountered.'

'Captain, you know I trust your instincts. If you need me to do something, I'll do it.'

'I need to join our minds, link us at a subconscious level. That way we may be able to view what I am having difficulty with. Together, we may be able to define what we have just been through.' Udon's voice carried a level of concern Phil Barton hadn't heard before.

'Sir, you have brought us safely through the Rift... in there we encountered something that almost killed you, but you stayed the course. If you need my mind, you have it. What do we do now?'

'Thank you. If you were Altarian it would be much easier, but as you're human, there are differences, but we can still make the process work.' Udon retrieved a container from his sleeping quarters. He opened it and withdrew two apparatus. Each looked like some sort of skull cap, with five sensor pads – one for the front of the head, one for each temple and one for each side on the base of the skull. Udon quickly fitted the unit to Barton's head, before donning his own.

'Now this can be quite unnerving. You may feel my presence, in your mind. That is normal but this process will let me see through your eyes and may give us better understanding. There will be some transference between us. In other words we will end up knowing more about each other than we could ever do consciously, but that is unavoidable with this system. Now if you are ready?' Barton nodded and Udon tapped an icon on the side of the container.

What happened next is something that Phillip Barton would never be able to explain. He was floating outside his body. At first, panic began to well up in him; was he dead, where was he? There were no reference points, he was no longer in the ship; he was floating in space, but that was impossible.

Then he heard Udon's voice, not spoken, but he heard it somewhere in his mind. Udon was calling him, calling him to follow. Gradually Barton gathered his mind, concentrated on his Captain's voice and began to follow.

There he was, just ahead, in the Rift. A wave of panic flowed over him, but Barton quickly countered it.

'This is where I first felt the Blackness,' Udon said. 'Can you feel it?'

Barton concentrated, allowing his mind to reach out to the cosmos. 'Yes, I can sense something. Something not right, like an injury?' But his mind told him that space couldn't be injured.

'There! Just ahead... can you see it?'

Barton turned his gaze and followed the extended arm of his Captain. There in front of them he felt it, what he saw was nothing. It was huge, at least ten times the size of the ship and it was black; not the usual space blackness, but a total absence of anything blackness.

'I... see... something,' He stuttered. 'But it is really nothing. What is it?'

'Yes, I see it now. Barton follow me, we must go back. Follow me.'

At his Captain's words Barton turned and followed. Moments later he was back in the ship. 'What just happened?'

'You experienced what I did in the Rift, except from a different perspective. I perceived a threat to the ship and was engaged in preventing our destruction. You, on the other hand were able to look directly at it, I saw through your eyes.' Udon was excited – excited and concerned.

'This may sound strange, but what we just experienced was a tear in space. Like something had ruptured the very fabric of space and opened a wound to... to somewhere else. All I know for sure is that thing is real and destructive. You saw the way it consumed everything in its path?'

Udon busied himself packing the caps away. 'Anyway I recorded it. We need to have the data analysed so we know what we are dealing with.' He stopped, he had suddenly remembered something. 'Frederickson, we need to find out any information about a ship called the Frederickson. I'm certain it has something to do with what we saw.'

'Aye Sir, I'll start on that now.' Barton stood to leave.

'And Number One, say nothing of this to the crew. Until we know what we are dealing with, the less they know, the better,' Udon cautioned.

'Aye Sir,' Barton confirmed as he left the room.

***

Joseph rose early – before dawn – made coffee and took the AG platform to the top of the ship. This was his first chance to view an Argos sunrise, and he wasn't going to miss it. He took a small collapsible chair with him, unfolded it and sat, facing east. The first tell-tale signs of a new day delicately tinting the sky.

First a pale pink crept sluggishly towards the ship, then the sky adopted a more purple hue. Joseph sipped his coffee, enjoying the solitude of the moment, and the ever-changing sky show. Finally, Zedak, to give the star its Krell name, emerged from below the horizon, filling the sky with a pure white light. Joseph smiled to himself. Although this heavenly body had a name, he was sure it would eventually simply be called the Sun, as were most of the stars that human colonies orbited.

He donned sunglasses to counteract the glare from Zedak; the day would be hot and clear. Checking his watch, surprised to see he had been here for nearly an hour, the longest time he had to himself in quite a while. He sighed, stood and collapsed the chair and activated the platform.

Don Hopmann was waiting below. 'Looked like a beautiful sunrise, Captain.'

'Yes Don, worth the time.'

Don handed him the communicator that Joseph had deliberately left sitting on the table. 'We had a communication from Kidman. Captain Udon has requested a meeting as soon as he arrives. He sounded... concerned.' This word stopped Joseph; he turned back to his second in command.

'Concerned? Really, Udon sounded concerned?'

'That's the best word I could think of, but yes, concerned is an accurate description.'

Joseph looked directly at Hopmann. 'Did he give any indication of why?' As soon as he said it, he knew it was a waste of time. 'Of course he didn't. How soon will he be here?' Udon rarely gave away any clue of his feelings. To most, he appeared cold and aloof. For Don to pick up concern from his voice, then something was definitely wrong.

Don checked the time. 'Kidman should arrive at fourteen hundred hours and Captain Udon indicated he would be transferring to the planet immediately.'

'Well, that gives us plenty of time,' Joseph was relieved. 'Have you had breakfast yet?' Don hadn't, so they headed to the officers' mess.

After breakfast, they went to the shuttle bay. Two shuttles had been reconfigured for survey work and refuelling was almost complete. Joseph was keen to get the project underway and had given it priority, but Don had some reservations. While the crew of Drake were highly skilled in many areas, he didn't feel confident they could take the place of a full survey team, something Joseph had asked him to return from Earth with.

'Skipper, I know we have discussed this, but wouldn't it be better to wait until I return with a survey team?'

'I really don't know. I have a gut feeling that we may need to move the old girl as soon as we can; don't ask for reasons, I don't have any... only my gut.'

Don nodded. His years with Joseph had taught him not to argue with the Skipper's gut; it usually turned out correct; still, he would be happier when he returned with an expert team.

Next they met with the shuttle teams, led in this case, by Ensign Renwick. Although she was only an Ensign, Molly Renwick held a master's degree in geophysics and that gave her the expertise to lead the survey. She would be on Drake with the shuttles manned by flight crews she had chosen. To cover more ground, each shuttle would be controlling four drones; these would be coupled in swarm mode and slaved back to their shuttle. This configuration meant only one operator was needed for the swarm. Again, the lack of personnel numbers had led to another innovative solution.

All readings would be sent back to Molly on Drake, where she would evaluate each site they found. If one stood out, she had a shuttle on standby and a small crew to accompany her to do an on-ground examination, if required. Molly hadn't been too happy when she was told she must have at least two security people with her, armed security at that; but the threat of unknown locals won her over. Reluctantly she had accepted the condition.

'So, when will the shuttles be ready to leave?' Joseph inquired.

'As soon as they're fuelled, in about half an hour I think; everything else is ready.' Molly knew her Captain was asking more. 'Our first run will be a high altitude survey, so we can get the lay of the land. This should take about four hours. Once this is complete we will regroup, analyse what we have and start specific area surveys. Simultaneously, we will send a couple of pre-programmed drones on a detailed mapping mission. Hopefully in a week or so, we will have a new site as well as a complete map of this continent.' Joseph wanted to ask more questions, but he knew that Renwick had the situation under control.

'Only one other thing, how are the others coping, reporting to an Ensign?'

Molly grinned. 'Well, let's call it a work in progress.'

'Ok, I'll accept that, for now... but remember you have my full support... any issues, just call.'

'Yes Sir, I don't think we'll have any problems, but thank you.'

Joseph and Don left the control room and went to one of the observation portals. From here they watched until the shuttles were launched.

'Well Number One, you probably should have your team assembled, and I need to send some messages to Earth, to start things moving in advance. I take it, everyone has accepted the situation?'

'Most have, but we do have some associations forming and I'm sure they'll want to talk to you soon.' Joseph knew exactly what Don was referring to and knew he needed to form a plan urgently.

'Well it's only natural, given the situation. Let all section heads know that I will be available to discuss any issues from tomorrow, but normal protocols are to be followed.' Which meant appointments would need to be made; Joseph wasn't about to let disgruntled crew rule his days. 'In the meantime, I need our Engineers' list of requirements so I can arrange for some purchases to be made back on Earth... and all before Kidman arrives.'

'Aye Sir, I'll start arranging things for tomorrow. I think you'll have a very busy day.' Don chuckled as he left the room.

Joseph noticed he was being hailed. He answered the call and the face of the chief engineer filled his screen. 'Bruce, I was about to call you. Do you have the equipment list I asked for?'

'Sure do, just sent it to you. We also came up with a list of skills and expertise we are short on, the type of things we need to build a new colony. Damned if I know how you're going to arrange it all.'

Joseph was already reading the list; it included earth moving equipment, construction equipment, in fact virtually everything they would need to build a new colony. The list of skills and expertise was similarly thorough.

'Now, do me a favour; prioritise all this. You know Kidman's capacity and Freedom's details are on file. Consider what we will need for the next six to twelve months and re-configure the requirements. Also, leave out the earth moving gear for the moment. I have another idea for that.'

'Ok, I'll do it. Give me about an hour,' McGill said as he signed off.

Joseph thought for a while, and then began composing messages. The first was to Phillipe Alvaris, CEO of a mining and Terra-forming operation, Omnicron. They had met many years ago and formed an instant rapport. When Phillipe had decided to start his own company Joseph had invested quite a hefty sum in the venture.

So far it had proved to be a reasonable, but not exciting investment. In fact, it was one of the few things he and Gail Mossberg disagreed on, Gail believing he should divest himself of the holding. But Joseph disagreed and held on to the investment. The current situation could make Omnicron one of his best investment decisions ever.

Joseph paused, just thinking of Gail made him smile, but he shook off these thoughts; he had far more pressing issues to deal with. He continued with his messages for the next hour, until Don called – Kidman had arrived.

***

Captain Udon Tellyz studied his reflection in the mirror. Gone was the ever present gravity compensator; now Udon was dressed only in his uniform. Altar, Udon's home planet, had a gravity signature fifteen percent higher than Earth, hence the need for the compensator. While it did keep his muscles and bones conditioned to Altarian normal, he disliked how it felt and looked. Satisfied, he left his quarters and headed towards the shuttle bay. Phillip Barton was waiting at the entry to the bay, the data pad under his arm.

'Captain, I downloaded my impressions as you asked. Also, we can find no reference to any ship called Frederickson, not in any of the registry data bases.' Barton said.

'What, no reference anywhere?'

'Sir, we checked everything, general shipping, military, private, research. In fact, Commander Thompson ran some sort of generic algorithm using derivations of the name… nothing. There has never been a ship named Frederickson.'

Udon shook his head, the frustration showing on his face. 'Perhaps Captain Jones will be able to shed some light on it. Thank you, Number One.' Udon walked to the shuttle's airlock. 'Please expedite loading, I expect to be back in a couple of hours and want to depart soon thereafter.' He boarded the shuttle and sealed the airlock.

The shuttle was configured for crew transport, with a total of twenty seats. Udon took the Pilot's seat and began his pre-flight checks. Satisfied the shuttle was space worthy, he initiated the drive system and called the control room for clearance; this was granted, so he fed power to the drive, turned the shuttle and swiftly exited the bay.

Ten minutes later, Udon had the shuttle locked into an expeditionary orbit. Landing on Argos was a thrill for him. He had none of the usual data for the nav system, no topography, no atmospherics, no positioning systems; he felt like early space explorers must have felt. Landing on an alien world, with no idea of what to expect and his excitement grew.

Drake's beacon sounded over the comm system, now he had a location. He recorded it in the nav data and began his descent under manual control. It felt good, he was in command, actually flying the shuttle; something he got very little chance to do now.

Udon's next dilemma was solved even before he knew he had one. Being Altarian, he was a stickler for correct protocol, and he hadn't asked what the comm protocol was now, his comm system solved it for him.

Argos control to unidentified shuttle; please identify yourself.

Udon smiled. 'Argos control, this is shuttle Columbia from Coalition Trade Ship (CTS) Kidman, en route to CTS Drake, Captain Udon Tellyz at the helm. I request landing coordinates.'

A few moments passed, then, *Shuttle Columbia, landing coordinates being transmitted now. Please alter course to approach from the north.*

Udon checked the data sent, altered his heading and replied. 'Argos control, Columbia has altered course and will approach you from north.' Ten minutes later Udon was on the ground. He opened the airlock and stepped out. It felt good to feel the ground under his feet, and to feel real gravity.

He took stock of his location. The landing pad was on an elevated area to the south of Drake, the lake to the east. *If one had to crash, this is an ideal place to do so* he thought. The sound of an approaching land vehicle caused him to turn. It stopped beside him and the canopy opened. Inside was Joseph Jones.

'Captain Tellyz, welcome to Argos.'

'My thanks, Captain. I must congratulate you... you certainly picked a beautiful place to crash.' Udon's attempt at humour brought a chuckle from Jones.

'Haven't thought about it like that, but yes, I agree. Now climb in, I believe you have something you want to discuss?' Udon climbed into the small vehicle and the canopy slid back into place. Joseph took a long path back to Drake, giving him time to fill Udon in on where things stood. As they finally arrived in Drake's primary hangar, Udon spoke.

'So you actually own the planet, Captain?'

'Yes, not just the planet but the entire system. The Council was only too glad to be rid of it.' They climbed out of the transport and took the pod to the ward room. As per Udon's request, the senior officers were waiting for them. After the customary greetings, Udon began to explain what had happened on the Rift Run. To assist he replayed the sensor data and his own recollections as well as Phil Barton's recordings; the heavy silence in the room confirming everyone's concern.

'Any idea what it was?' Joseph asked.

Finally, Udon spoke. 'Captain, I still don't know what the anomaly is, but the ancestor vision I had, proves to me that it is extremely dangerous. The other strange thing is we can find no reference to a ship called Frederickson... the ancestor vision was most insistent on the name.'

Joseph had not actually seen Altarian ancestor visions before, but had seen the results of them. In every case the vision had been accurate, if sometimes cryptic.

'But did the vision actually name the ship?' Bruce McGill asked.

Udon thought before answering. 'Not exactly... I got the name as I **saw** the ship, so I believed that it must be the name. Why?'

Bruce moved to the console and began interrogating the data base; when he was satisfied he turned back to the group. 'I don't think it was the name of the ship,' he put his findings up on the view screen.

'Ernst Stanislaus Frederickson, Professor Frederickson to give him his professional title. He is the Galaxy's leading authority in a number of areas. Quantum Physics and Astro Physics are two of his specialities, but he is the leader in the little known field of Temporal Mechanics. Frederickson was heading up a research team into sub space and Temporal Mechanics. But what that has to do with your vision, is beyond me.'

While Bruce had been speaking, Joseph had been busy at another terminal. He beckoned Udon over to the screen. 'Is this the ship you saw?'

Udon looked at the image, shaking his head. 'Yes Sir, the exact one.'

'Coalition Space Corps prototype, Horowitz class frigate; it's very fast, heavily armed and potentially a game changer for the war... here's something else about Frederickson. A couple of years ago, I attended a prospectus meeting for a start-up company, Frederickson was one of the directors seeking funding. The company was involved in developing a new weapon system, something about delivering a displacement-torpedo.

'The theory was to be able to fire a torpedo equipped with a displacement drive, and use the worm hole to bypass detection. But the major idea was for it to materialise inside an enemy stronghold... then it would detonate and destroy everything. As I recall, nobody wanted to take the risk of something going wrong, no-one was willing to fund the project, and the company folded.'

'Why?' Udon inquired.

Bruce McGill had the answer. 'Simple... with the technology, in theory anyway, you could send a torpedo directly into the core of an enemy's planet, detonate it and destroy their home totally.'

Molly Renwick's face lost its colour. 'You must be wrong, nobody is that stupid! What happens if one of these missiles detonates in its worm hole?'

Joseph looked up from the console. 'I think that question has been answered. Udon, the tear you encountered in the Rift, is it small compared to what your vision displayed?'

'Yes... I am bemused by that as well. The vision also showed planets that I know are still there as being destroyed... most perplexing.'

'Not really,' McGill interjected. 'Consider the anomaly in the Rift may be part of the research... a small yield weapon that accidentally detonated in hyperspace. Your vision showed what will happen if a full yield weapon does the same... it just hasn't happened, yet.'

'But it's not rational to do this,' Molly exclaimed.

'Molly, when has man ever been rational about weapons of mass destruction, remember your history from the Academy? The old nuclear weapons of the past... did man ever stop to consider how many times he could destroy Earth? No, we just kept on building more of them. This is no different, the bigger the bang, the better the weapon. Don, is your crew ready?'

'Almost Sir.'

'Ok, Udon, you need to get going ASAP. I'll send some messages and check if I can find out any more. When you arrive on Earth, I'll try to have a meeting with the Coalition Council arranged. We need to stop this before it happens.' Joseph closed the meeting.

Chapter 8: First Visitor

'This is taking too fucking long!'

Boris Adler swore as he sat in his shuttle, counting the freight containers left to load.

He was frustrated; loading the 1200 containers on Kidman was way behind schedule, and Mahmoud Dashiki, Kidman's Loadmaster, wasn't helping. Mahmoud was a stickler for regulations and wouldn't change his methods no matter how much Boris complained. He swore again, for good measure.

Drake calling Betty B; are you receiving? Danielle St Clare's voice interrupted his stream of profanities.

'Drake, Betty B receiving,' Boris growled. On the other end of the communication Dannie held back a chuckle. She knew her deputy well and understood his frustrations, maybe her news would cheer him up.

Boris, Captain Jones wants you to return to Argos, he has a new assignment for you. She quickly cut the comm. She could picture Boris's reaction, and she couldn't hold back the mirth any longer.

'Come on, I'm trying to light a fire under this bureaucrat's bloody arse! Talk about a pencil pusher.'

*Sorry, Boris. The boss wants you back here **now**. I suggest you get moving.*

'Yes, Ma'am,' Boris begrudgingly initiated the drive and turned the shuttle for Argos. 'By the way, Kidman wants us to take some redundant freight, they're sending the manifest; you should have it by the time I arrive.'

*I'll find it, but I need you to calm down. You're the only one stressing over the load out... take your time getting back and **relax**.* Dannie emphasised the last word.

'Yes Ma'am, I'll relax.' Boris cut the link.

***

Gail Mossberg sat in her office on Earth; she read the message from Jones a fourth time. Initially the contents were innocuous, a series of instructions regarding purchase of equipment, sourcing contractors and supplies as per an attached document. It was the last paragraph, in fact the last few lines that rattled her.

Need to discuss many issues re Argos. Commander Hopmann will be returning with new ship, could you join him. Come to Argos and discuss options. These words hung in her mind. 'What are you thinking, Joe?' She buzzed her father and told him she was coming to his office, she also sent him the message.

'About bloody time,' HG Mossberg called as she walked into his office. 'Maybe I'll get those grandkids yet.'

'Oh, for Pete's sake will you drop that. What is he doing? Read the list he wants us to source; what in heaven's name is he up to?' She countered.

'That's bloody obvious; Jonesy's setting up a new colony and a new colony needs rules and regulations quick, hence he needs a lawyer; and you my dear are his lawyer. Do I need to remind you how much Jonesy's operations mean to our little firm?'

'No, he's still our most valuable client, but if he starts his own colony, what will he need Earth lawyers for?'

'My dear daughter, you may be one of the smartest people I know, but you can still be so dumb. He wants you there to form all the laws of Argos...' HG paused and called

Anderson into the room. The door opened, and he continued. 'Anderson, what pressing matters do Gail and I have for the next...' he paused again, working something out in his mind. 'Say for the next nine months.'

Anderson consulted the company calendar. 'There are a couple of matters that Gail has, but nothing that couldn't be handled by her teams. Why?'

'Because my dear Anderson, we're going to Argos.' He turned to his daughter. 'Don't start... we're going, end of story. Our most valuable client has requested representation from Mossberg and Partners, and he's going to get it. Now what's this about physical conditioning? What's different on Argos?'

***

Boris took his time, as Dannie had suggested, and twenty minutes later a much more relaxed man walked out of the shuttle's airlock. He went straight to the Loadmaster's office to find out what the fuss was about. Dannie admitted she was no wiser, so they left for the Captains ready room.

Joseph was waiting for them. 'Boris, I hear that you're some sort of big game hunter?'

'Well, yes Sir, I do try to do some hunting when I'm on leave. Why?' Boris was intrigued.

Joseph's tone was serious. 'Well, as you know, our food stocks are low; we're looking at testing some of the local indigenous animals and plants. We have set up some rudimentary fish traps, we have people collecting various plants but, I believe we have a plentiful food source in those cattle-like creatures. We need to bag some to ascertain if they are compatible with our digestive system so... we need someone to do the hunting. I've had some experience, back in my youth, but I'm a tad rusty and, from what the Drake rumour mill says, you're on the top of your game.'

'I probably am but, we have a slight problem, I didn't bring my guns on this trip; there wasn't time for leave, so I left them on Earth,' Boris added.

'We have plenty of weapons, blasters, disruptors. Won't they do?' Dannie asked.

Boris shook his head. 'That's where we have a problem; a beast as big as these things won't go down easy. To drop one with a blaster, you'd vaporise it and a disruptor would probably turn its internal organs into mush... either way you end up with nothing. I assume the Doc and his crew want to vivisect the creature to check what, if any of it we can eat?'

As he finished, Joseph's communicator buzzed. He took the call before speaking.

'Ok, blasters and disruptors are out, but I may have a solution,' Joseph said. 'I have to speak with Udon; go grab yourself some lunch and I'll call for you when I'm free.' Boris and Dannie stood and left the room, passing Captain Tellyz at the door.

'Udon, your message said you had a problem, how can I help?'

'Sir, we are carrying some redundant cargo and I need to do something with it.'

'What do you mean redundant cargo?'

Udon sat and began to explain. 'We were contracted to take cargo from the Garrick factory on Kandos to New Britain. When we arrived, New Britain was embroiled in a huge industrial dispute and the planet was in lock down; evidently the cargo we were carrying was the problem. It turned out that the Government had bought the items we were carrying off world, angering the workers as the product could have been sourced locally.

'We sat in the dock for two weeks, impounded almost, until the Government relented and cancelled the deal with Garrick. We contacted our agent on Kandos only to be informed that Garrick was refusing to pay the cost of returning the goods and had cancelled the payment for delivery. I must apologise but this trip has been a financial disaster.'

'But you still have the goods?'

'Yes Sir.'

'What are we talking about?'

'I really don't know, it was all hush-hush, but I believe it to be some sort of sensor system. There was a lot of talk on New Britain that the system could be made locally, hence the unrest,' Udon responded.

Joseph paused, his mind weighing options. 'And it's all there... a complete system?'

'I believe so... there are four containers and the manifest lists them as one complete unit.'

Joseph reached for his communicator and called Dannie, telling her to liaise with Mahmoud on Kidman and bring the mystery cargo down to Argos. He looked to Udon who was showing concern. 'Offload the cargo here, I'll take responsibility for it; our company has incurred substantial costs in transporting it and the principal has reneged on payment. Interstellar law allows us to recoup this type of loss from the disposal of the goods. Give me all the details and I'll have our lawyers look at the situation.' Udon's relief was clearly etched on his face.

'Thank you Sir, I will return to Kidman and expedite our departure.'

Joseph sat back as Udon left. He checked the time and realised how hungry he was. He went into the kitchen area and hastily threw a sandwich together, then called both Boris and Simon Carpenter to his quarters. The doctor arrived first and sat opposite Joseph.

'Where are you up to with the food analysis, Simon?'

Simon took a few moments before answering. 'So far, we have only analysed three possible plant sources, everything is fine with two; the third may have some residual toxicity. I have, this morning, received six different types of marine creature, but we haven't started to test as yet. I need about four days to get a reliable picture.'

'So what about the larger, land based animal we have seen? When can you examine that?'

'In truth, any time. We have a team now testing the fish and I can start an autopsy whenever we need... just say the word.' At that moment Boris announced he was at the door.

'Boris, the Doc and I have been discussing the food situation, and he's ready to start looking at land based creatures. We need you to bring one of those creatures down, so we can analyse it. Now before you say anything,' Joseph keyed a code into the console. 'Have a look in here.'

A section of the bookcase behind Joseph's desk had sprung open. Boris took his Captain's invitation and opened the concealed door further, lights automatically came on. The room was about four metres square, with a workbench in the centre, but the walls were lined with gun racks. Boris let out a tuneless whistle.

'Thinking to start a war Skipper? If you are you've certainly got enough firepower!' Boris couldn't believe his eyes. In here he found guns he had only seen in old books, or in a museum. Slowly he moved around the room as Joseph and Simon joined him.

'No, not a war; but like you I enjoy a good hunt. Most are really museum pieces, some haven't been fired in centuries, but the ones at the back to your right are the ones I keep ready.' He reached up and picked a rifle off the rack. 'I think this one might do the job.'

Boris took the offered weapon, almost with reverence, 'An Evans twelve mill, these things were supposed to stop anything, even armoured vehicles. I certainly think it'll stop those oversized cows.'

'Excellent,' Simon broke in. 'I need the animal to die instantly, without getting spooked. All animals, that we've so far encountered, have a basic survival instinct; fight or flight and all have an adrenal system, or something similar. I don't want the carcass contaminated with adrenalin or some other stimulant, understood.'

'Loud and clear, Doc; with this baby I should be able to stay well clear of the herd, it'll never know what hit it.' Boris turned to Joseph. 'Thank you Sir, I'll take good care of her.' He set the rifle down on the workbench and began stripping it.

Joseph turned to Simon. 'Well Doc, I think you'll have your first subject soon, how long will you need before you have an answer?'

'Three to four days after we receive the first sample... within the next week we should know what our food prospects are. I'll head back now.' Simon left the room, so glad to be away from all the weapons. This was an aspect of his Captain he never knew. He wondered how many knew about the arsenal – the thought troubled him.

Joseph turned back into the gun room, surprised that Boris had the rifle stripped and was checking and measuring the firing pin.

'I'm impressed, the first time I stripped that rifle it took me ten minutes, with the manual open,' Joseph moved past the bench to another locked cabinet. 'What ammo do you want?'

'Depends on the cow's skull... I reckon something around four hundred grain, penetrator design would be best,' Boris responded.

Joseph selected a box from the cabinet and handed it over. 'Will these do?'

Boris inspected the cartridges, consulting the ballistic chart on the box. 'Perfect, now unless this creature has armour plate in its skull, I should be able to take one down from about a thousand metres.' He loaded ten into the magazine, reassembled the rifle and cycled a few rounds through the breach. 'She's in perfect condition, Skipper. But what's all this about?' Boris said as he gestured round the room.

'Another day... bag the creature for the Doc and then I'll tell you the story.'

Thirty seven hours later, Boris had successfully bagged the first bovine for the vivisection team; now there would be an anxious wait until the Doc gave his verdict. Kidman was loading the last three containers and Joseph was sitting in the ready room, preparing for the onslaught he had skilfully avoided, until now. The annunciator buzzed and a gruff Bruce McGill growled that he was waiting. Joseph took a deep breath and opened the door.

Bruce stormed in, his face red with anger. 'What the fuck is going on Joe! Why are you sidelining me?'

'And good afternoon to you too **Commander**,' Joseph reacted, emphasising Bruce's rank.

'Don't pull that bloody rank thing; we've been through too much for that shit. What's going on?' McGill shouted in reply.

'Ok, first sit down and shut the fuck up,' Joseph shouted back. Years of working with the engineer had taught him that, sometimes, the only way to get through to him was a direct attack. Bruce took his seat.

'Now, you aren't being sidelined, I need you here, not babysitting a new ship on her first trip. Hell, Don's going, three of the other senior Bridge team are going so who does that leave, from senior ranks?' Joseph raised the question, forcefully. 'Only you... now... think about it for a moment, what message would it send the crew if I sent you back?'

Bruce sat back, he knew Joseph was right, but he didn't want to admit it. 'But what happens when she returns, who's going to man her then?'

Joseph shook his head. 'Bruce, we've worked together for over twenty years, so I won't bullshit you. Neither of us will be in Freedom's crew, not permanently anyway; we have too much to do here. Do you think I like the idea of giving my newest ship, the one that was to replace Drake, to someone else? No, old friend, our days of space hopping are slowing down, so we better get used to it.'

Bruce sat still, his face showing his disappointment but also his realisation that Joseph was right. 'Yeah, you're probably right, but that doesn't mean I have to bloody well like it.'

Joseph laughed quietly. 'No mate it doesn't!'

***

It was three days since Kidman had departed. Everyone, including Joseph felt a little more alone than before. The turn around and return trip was expected to take fourteen weeks at least, and the isolation of Argos was now on everyone's mind. To add to the situation, there was a crew delegation that had requested a meeting. He glanced at the time; they would be here in ten minutes and still Joseph didn't know what they were going to ask.

On a positive note, he re-read a message from Phillipe Alvaris confirming he had the equipment Joseph needed available. Phillipe also said he was on his way to Argos and, according to the time stamps on the message, should arrive sometime tomorrow. All Joseph needed was a site for the permanent settlement.

His thoughts were interrupted by the buzz of the door annunciator, the door opened on Joseph's command and Molly Renwick walked in. 'Molly, what can I do for you?'

'We may have a problem, Sir. May I?' She was pointing to his console. Joseph turned it toward her.

'Be my guest.'

'Thank you, but you may not like this.' Molly set about pulling up some sensor logs. 'Are you expecting anyone?'

'I have a meeting with a crew delegation in a few minutes, but they can wait.'

'No, are you expecting another ship?' she turned the screen back toward Joseph. 'One that appears to be cloaked?'

The word cloaked piqued Joseph's interest, cloaks took huge amounts of energy to run and only Krell warships routinely used them. 'Ok, you've got my attention… now details please.'

Molly ran him through the logs, commenting on her findings. The evidence was convincing, there was something orbiting the planet. Something that appeared to have entered the system at the same time Kidman had left. So far, all it had done was enter a stable orbit and with the cloak active, confirming its location was almost impossible.

'How have you done this? I thought the cloak would prevent discovery?'

'It does, but all drives leave a residual trace, we picked this up by accident. It intrigued me, so I analysed the trail, it led here, and now it's dead. Once the orbit was established, the drive was powered down, so the trace has gone. All this,' she pointed to the orbit track, 'is supposition. The only thing I can say for certain is it hasn't left orbit yet.'

Joseph leaned back in his chair. 'There's more, isn't there?'

Molly sat down. 'Yes Sir. Our problem is we don't have any orbital sensors; all we have is what's on the Drake and the shuttles. That means that for most of a day we are blind, or partially so. We can only scan a very small part of space from here and, unless the bogie enters a geosynchronous orbit above us, we have no real idea where it is.'

'But these readings, you got them from our sensors? That's what you based your orbital simulation on?'

'Yes Sir, I used what data we had in the sensor logs, why?'

'If they're accurate, can you extrapolate the orbit, in real time? Can you predict when they will be over this site again?'

'I could do that, but I don't know how accurate it would be.' Molly sounded bemused at the question.

'Ok, for now Molly keep this between us and start working on that orbit. Call me the instant you think you've got it.' Joseph said. Molly stood and began to head for the door. 'Remember, Molly, between us **only**.'

'Yes, Sir, I understand.' The door slid open and she left. Waiting outside were four grim faced crew men led by Bosun's Mate, Clive Barber.

'Gentlemen, come in, please make yourselves comfortable.' Joseph greeted them as he moved from behind the desk. He indicated they all take a seat in the lounge area and when they were all settled, he asked. 'Now, what can I do for you?'

'Well first you can tell us how you're going to get us off this bloody rock.' One of them blurted out.

Barber cut him off. 'Enough of that! Captain, there are a number of crew members who are concerned about how we're going to get home, considering it's common knowledge that you intend to start a new colony here.' He stopped to allow Joseph to answer.

'Continue, Mr Barber, I'll answer your concerns when I have them all.'

Barber gave Joseph a long, hard look, sizing the Captain up. 'Sir, some of the crew is interested in the possibility of a new colony but, we need to know what's in it for us. Most of us have homes on Earth or other planets so, to join this colony we'd need to divest ourselves of these properties and build new homes here.'

Another of the group spoke up, 'and what of our families and possessions? It'll cost a pretty penny to transport everything here.'

Now Joseph had the picture, he considered his answer and began to speak. 'Gentlemen, if anyone wants to leave and return to Earth, they can. When Kidman and Freedom return, their first priority will be to take any who want to leave back to Earth. Any who elect to stay will be accommodated as best we can, until we build permanent accommodation. Those accommodations will have facilities for you to bring your families and as time goes on we will assist any who want to build their own dwelling. You will be granted land for this, and other assistance that we agree on. Please understand we've only been here about a week, so details and specifics of the colony are few, but Freedom will return with our lawyers, and then we will negotiate. Is that acceptable?'

'Considering the circumstances, I suppose so,' Barber agreed, 'but there is one other issue... food. How are we going to sustain ourselves for the next four months?'

'Mr Barber, we have already identified a number of plants that can be eaten, three different types of fish and, hopefully by the end of today, we'll have a decision on the land animals we're testing.' Joseph answered, honestly.

The discussion continued, a number of other subjects and concerns were raised and a program of meetings was scheduled to work through them all. Finally, Barber and the others stood, said their goodbyes and left, their mood was a little better than when they arrived.

Joseph looked to the console; the meeting had taken slightly over an hour. He wondered how Molly's project was progressing; the thought of a cloaked Krell warship overhead was worrying. Then he remembered, Phillipe Alvaris was due to arrive tomorrow morning. Another coalition registered vessel may be problematic; he activated his comm unit and called Molly. She had a result, of sorts, and sent it to Joseph. He called the engineer and began to view the data from Molly the seed of an idea growing in his mind.

***

'Are you absolutely mad?' Bruce McGill cried. 'You're telling me we have a cloaked Krell warship, in orbit and you want to contact it? For fuck's sake why poke the dragon?'

'Well for one thing, it's the only way we'll know for sure if anything's there; second we have another ship arriving in a few hours, the last thing we want is for our Krell friend up there to get trigger-happy. In case you forgot, the Coalition and the Empire are still, technically at bloody war. This system is now not part of the Empire **or** the Coalition, so I can understand their curiosity.' Joseph countered.

'Curiosity... where in the bloody universe did that come from? The Krell are **never** curious.'

'Well, in that case, why haven't they blasted us to hell and back? They've certainly got the firepower to do it.' Joseph mused.

'Alright, you may have a point, but why prod a sleeping monster; let them get bored and leave.'

'No, I think we have an opportunity here, we'll proceed as I outlined. Now, Molly how long do we have?'

Molly had shrunk back into the far corner of the room, while Joseph and Bruce had been shouting at each other; she stepped forward. 'Well... if my simulation is correct, half an hour.'

'Did you hear that... if her simulation is correct? Jesus Joseph... of all the half arsed, crazy notions you've had, this may take the cake,' McGill grumbled again.

Joseph turned to the engineer. 'Bruce, will you please shut up and get with the program. Like it or not I believe this is our best shot, and we're doing it... understood?'

'Yes Sir, understood, but I don't like it! Ok.'

'Noted... now Molly, have you programmed the sensors as I asked?'

'Yes Captain, but I don't know what good it'll do.'

'If it works, you'll see, if not...' Joseph didn't finish; a groan from McGill was the only answer. 'Now, give me the countdown.'

Molly busied herself timing the operation and, at the precise second she had calculated, she initiated the sensor program. Thirty seconds later, she had her result, and she nodded to Joseph.

'Argos control to cloaked Krell warship in orbit; please deactivate your cloak and state your intentions,' Joseph was transmitting via a specific narrow band system, favoured by Krell battleships. He nodded to Molly again; she initiated the sensor program again; then nodded to Joseph who repeated his message; still no reply.

'Once more, Molly,' they repeated the transmissions. This time it worked, their sensors showed a large vessel starting to appear in orbit, exactly where Molly had predicted.

'Now what?' McGill gasped.

'Krell warship, this is Captain Joseph Jones at Argos control, please respond.'

The response was almost instant.

Argos control, this is Krell battle cruiser Zotrik, Captain Nadroc speaking; can you transmit visually?

'Yes, Captain, visual transmission commencing.' The view screen in his ready room now showed the Cruiser's Bridge and Captain Nadroc sitting in his command chair. 'Captain, I must ask what your intentions are?'

Nadroc appeared to be considering his answer, for quite a while. *Captain Jones, we weren't aware of any colony on this planet. Out of security concerns we are investigating but somehow you've been able to negate our cloak. This is puzzling.*

'Captain Nadroc, I assure you our intentions are peaceful. To demonstrate, I invite you, and a small delegation, to come to the surface; I always prefer to carry out any negotiations in person. Or, if you prefer, I can come to your ship.' Joseph stopped and waited for an answer.

Perhaps in this instance, we will trust you. I will come to your site and I will bring three of my officers with me, is this acceptable? Nadroc asked.

'Perfectly acceptable, I look forward to meeting you in person.' Joseph cut the link.

'Now I know you're completely fucking mad.' McGill shook his head.

Joseph issued his instructions. McGill raced to alert the crew and organise a greeting party. Molly kept a sensor lock on the Krell ship and waited for a shuttle to leave. Twenty minutes later she called Joseph, a shuttle had just left the Krell ship. Joseph assembled his greeting party and spoke to them.

'As Commander McGill has told you, we are about to receive a visit from the Commander of a Krell battle cruiser in orbit above us. Now this is unusual, to say the least. If they wanted to harm us, they have had plenty of time to do so and, remembering this is now a neutral sector of space, we will treat them as guests, understood?'

A chorus of *Sir, yes Sir*, greeted his words. Molly called with the news that the shuttle was on final approach. Joseph dismissed the party who took their positions at each side of the entry ramp.

The Krell shuttle turned toward the shuttle bay ramp, and slowly followed the signal lights into Drake's belly. The pilot carried out a perfect landing and began to power down. It was roughly the same size as Drake's units, although it did have a rather menacing plasma cannon attached to the tail. The wings were short and swept back, the flight deck protruded above the fuselage. In all, Joseph thought the design was practical and utilitarian. An airlock opened and four Krell officers descended the short ramp that extended from the craft.

Captain Nadroc led the group. He was tall, like most Krell, and walked with confidence. His hair was jet black and long, tied back behind his head; his eyes, a steely grey and his features angular. He stepped forward, Joseph responded. They stopped, a couple of metres separating them.

Nadroc snapped the traditional Krell greeting; his left arm flashed across his body and came to rest above his primary heart, located in the right half of his chest. This showed he had no weapon in his fighting hand and came in peace. Unsure of how a human should respond, Joseph simply snapped a formal salute and then offered his hand, a smile crossed Nadroc's lips as he took the offered hand and shook it.

'Welcome, Captain. Welcome to Argos.' Joseph greeted the newcomers sincerely.

Chapter 9: New Friends

The first meeting with the Krell went well.

It started with a formal greeting complete with honour guard; then a quick tour of Drake which ended at the wardroom where a casual buffet had been laid out.

'So as I understand, you crashed on the planet?' Nadroc asked.

Joseph smiled as he guided his guest through the buffet. 'In essence you're correct. I'm afraid this old girl will never go back into space. We intend to move her to a permanent site and use her as the base for our colony.'

Nadroc nodded slightly. 'And you say you have been able to gain absolute title to the system, from the Coalition Council?'

'Correct. One of my companies, Argos Limited, now holds the title.'

'So this will be a Coalition colony?' Nadroc's question revealed his true concern.

Joseph recognised where this could lead. 'Emphatically no... I represent the Independent Traders Guild. We are a group of merchants and traders who want freedom from the impost of Coalition rules and laws. This outpost will be the first Free Trade colony, and we reserve the right to trade with anyone, or no-one.

'Captain, I have seen how destructive this war has been, to both sides and personally, I want no part of it. I'd bet that even the Emperor wouldn't know what caused it. Hell, the Coalition has had four Presidents since it started, and a new one is soon to take over. Neither side knows what the war is about.' Joseph watched his guest's face, trying to read his emotions, something exceedingly difficult with a Krell.

Nadroc sighed. 'I agree, the effort has become exceedingly taxing, for both sides. But you must understand that when we became aware of a potential Coalition outpost so close to our space, we had to investigate.'

'I expected no less in fact, I was hoping the Empire would come to investigate. Let me reiterate our philosophy. The Guild is dedicated to free trade, we have a charter that calls for each member to actively seek out new opportunities and let's face it, it's in our interests to do so. Our biggest problem has been the Coalition Corporations, and their strangle hold on the best trade routes. This causes us an immense amount of trouble. For years, I have looked for ways to engage with non-aligned cultures, and I've had some success but, if we can end this stupid war, I believe that the opportunities for everyone will far outweigh any downside.'

'So, Captain Jones, I take it you would like to start a dialogue with the Empire?' Nadroc took a bite from a small cake. 'By the way, these food items are excellent.'

'I'll tell our cook you approve, and yes I'd be very pleased to start a dialogue. One thing you must understand, we will not trade any contraband or sensitive technology, from either side. I believe in ethical trade agreements, and any member of our Guild who breaks this code is automatically banned and their membership is cancelled.'

Nadroc stood back, examining his counterpart. It was some time before he spoke. 'Captain, I like your philosophy and I detect no threat to the Empire from your colony.

What I ask is that you allow our ships to enter your space, from time to time, to keep an eye on things?'

'Nadroc, again I would expect no less, in fact we will welcome them with a couple of conditions... only one ship at a time and no cloaks. We were lucky in detecting your vessel; I don't think we can do it again. Also, I ask that the Empire respects our neutrality and takes no hostile actions in this system; we will have Coalition ships calling as well.

'In fact, I'll make that the first colony declaration. From this day forward, Argos and the entire Zedak system is not aligned to any Government except Argos. As such, all vessels and species are welcome, as long as they also respect our neutrality. What I'll do is have our legal team on Earth draft the declaration. Once complete, I'll send a copy to both the Coalition Council and the Emperor.'

Nadroc was impressed by Joseph's sincerity and made a commitment to petition the Emperor on behalf of Argos, he agreed with the neutrality declaration. 'Now the politics have been sorted, I believe you are trying to harvest the local beasts? We may be able to help.

'As a young boy, I was fortunate to have a father who embraced traditional Krell ideals. He believed his children should be self-sufficient and brought us here on a number of occasions to hunt. One thing with the Dab Korac, the things you call cattle, they must be bled well and the meat aged. If you like we can show you the best way of doing this?'

Before Joseph could answer, Molly interrupted. 'My apologies, Captain. We have a message from Omnicron; Mister Alvaris's ship will arrive soon.'

Joseph nodded. 'Thank you, Molly. Captain we will soon have another ship in orbit, it is not hostile, it's a private vessel. Could you inform your ship?'

Nadroc called one of his Officers, they conferred and the other moved away. 'It is done; he will contact our ship and tell them. Would you prefer if we cloaked?'

'No, I want this to be transparent. Molly, contact Alvaris's ship, inform them that we are being assisted by an Imperial Krell vessel and that Argos is now neutral ground.' Molly nodded and left quickly. 'Now Captain, about hunting these Dab Korac?'

Joseph called Boris to the meeting, introduced him to Nadroc and left them to work through the hunting and preparation of the animals. The Krell were intrigued with the Evans rifle and Boris was only too pleased to offer a demonstration. Joseph agreed and the group left Drake and went down to the shoreline where Boris had set up a firing range.

He used a drone to drop targets at various distances and the demonstration began. From inside the ship Joseph could hear the reports of the rifle and smiled; this bonding exercise appeared to be working.

An hour later, the group returned and Joseph met them as they entered the shuttle bay. 'Captain Nadroc, I believe you're going to inform me that a very large vessel has just reinserted into our system?'

Nadroc nodded. 'You are correct. I received a communication from my ship, but from their description, this new visitor is massive.'

'Walk with me.' Joseph moved to the closest console. 'The vessel you have detected is the one we are expecting; they're called Terra-Trucks.' Joseph activated the console and brought up an image of the vessel. He spent the next half hour explaining the design and purpose of the ship to Nadroc.

It consisted of three sections; the forward section of the ship was over one hundred metres in diameter and cone shaped; this housed command, control and accommodation areas. The rear was similarly dimensioned except it was squared and not cone shaped; engineering, power generation and the drive systems were all located here. Connecting both sections was a fifty-metre square tube – one thousand metres in length – giving the vessel a total length of fifteen hundred metres. The design allowed Omnicron to transport eighty standard equipment pods which meant they could use one vessel to set up a complete terra-forming operation.

Nadroc studied the images closely. 'In reality I would call this an elegant design – elegant in the way of supreme functionality. I will call my ship, and tell them not to be concerned.'

***

Placing a Terra-Truck into a stable orbit is a delicate operation, and takes time as well as expertise. Phillipe Alvaris left this to the Captain and crew and took a shuttle to the surface. He parked beside the Krell shuttle, powered down and opened the air lock.

Joseph met him as he left his ship. 'Phillipe, welcome to Argos.'

'Joseph, good to see you again; I would say you are now truly Laird of all you see,' Phillipe responded.

'I suppose so, but there's more... much more.'

'Like a Krell battle cruiser in orbit? Joseph are you sure of this? Last I heard, the Coalition and the Empire are still at war.'

'Phillipe, I've got so much to tell, follow me.' Joseph turned and led him to the transport pod. They arrived at Joseph's quarters and went inside, tea and biscuits were waiting.

'You remembered,' Phillipe chortled. Tea, accompanied by sweet biscuits was a favourite for him, but something his wife blamed for his generous proportions. They sat and Joseph explained the situation starting with the accident; Phillipe listened intently. After it had been explained he spoke. 'So this system has always been designated as neutral ground, which explains why no-one wanted it. But what now... how does this help you? Without any alignment, how secure is this planet?'

Once again, Joseph explained the philosophy which was the basis of the Independent Traders Guild and his belief that these principles would be the best security.

'I understand the theory, but the practicality... who's paying for everything?'

Joseph poured another cup of tea, before answering. 'I am, in fact, I believe in this so strongly I'm willing to sink everything I have into it. And before you ask, yes, I do have a plan to recoup at least some of the expenditure.' Joseph took a sip from his cup, before continuing.

'For a limited period, any who wishes to join will do so without cost, land will be made available for bases and operations. After this period there will be charges, including the sale of land which Argos Ltd is sole owner. I know the costs. I expect at least half of my wealth to be sunk into Argos in the next year. I've even instructed my agents to dispose of some superfluous assets, but I firmly believe I'll recoup the lot.'

Phillipe picked up his cup and drained it, he poured another and picked up his fifth biscuit before he spoke. 'I always knew you were slightly nuts, but in a good way. Tell you what, Omnicron will throw in with you, we need a base in this vicinity in any case. We'll contribute in kind. Any terra-forming needed in the initial stages will be free of charge and I'll accept the offer of free land.'

Joseph's smile split his face; he offered his hand which Phillipe took. 'It's a deal! I was hoping you would want in. Now would you like to meet our Krell guests?'

Phillipe had to wait until the evening to meet the Krell. Nadroc and Boris had taken another hunting party out and returned late with another two beasts. This time, they had been field prepared as per Nadroc's instruction. The Doctor, having already studied the Krell data on the animals, declared they would be fit for consumption, so a butchery team set about preparing the meat for ageing.

At twenty hundred hours the senior team met in Joseph's quarters. The senior officers' mess staff provided a banquet to mark the occasion. The first time in two hundred years Krell and human sat down to take a meal together.

The auspiciousness of the occasion was not lost on Joseph who marked it with a toast and a gift. He presented Nadroc with an inlaid box, with an inscription that read, *For Peace and Friendship*. Nadroc opened the box, inside was an ancient Glock pistol, complete with magazines and one hundred rounds of ammunition.

'This weapon was carried by one of my ancestors, into battle in the late twenty-first century. He kept it as a memento of the futility of war. I hope his vision of peace lingers on it, and we can start down a path of reconciliation.' Joseph raised his glass. 'To peace and friendship.'

Nadroc replaced his glass and replied by thanking Joseph and pledging himself to doing whatever he could to hasten peace. He sat down and turned to Joseph. 'Do you think there will be repercussions over all this?'

'Definitely! I was surprised when we found out that the whole system had to be transferred... I originally only wanted this planet. But why the Council transferred the lot is beyond me... but you are correct... when the Conglomerates find out, I am expecting some sort of backlash.'

Phillipe joined the conversation. 'The reason it all had to be transferred is the way our friends originally ceded it to the Coalition. They relinquished title and all claims on the provision that this system was never militarised, it must always remain neutral. That's why they didn't do anything with it, to accept it into the Coalition meant the Council must ratify the neutrality. Then you come along and seem like a godsend, at least at first. I'll bet there are some on Earth who are screaming for blood even now. Believe me my friends, the next few years will be interesting, very interesting indeed.'

Everyone saw the smile on Nadroc's face. 'An excellent observation. We did make the move in good faith but, to have a potential enemy on our doorstep was unacceptable, so our Emperor decided to add the neutrality provision. History will tell us if it works... or not.'

He reached for his own data pad. 'I sent your message of intent to the Emperor, and he has responded. It is decreed that no Krell vessel will enter your system cloaked, unless they have your permission to do so. Also, no Krell ship will enter with any offensive weapons active, only defensive systems. If there is to be progress toward peace, then the Krell will walk the path with honour.'

Nadroc transmitted the document to Drake's data core. 'Unfortunately we will have to leave... in the next day... we still have a patrol to complete. But with your permission, we will return in six Argos months and check on your progress.'

The rest of the evening and all the next morning was spent downloading all information the Zotrik data base had on Argos. There were a number of possible sources of animal protein, as well as some rather disturbing revelations. The Zartol, the fire bird that Joseph had seen, was one of the more benign creatures, even though its hunting was spectacular.

There were a number of large and dangerous predators, at least ten extremely deadly reptiles and many plants that had proved deadly, at least to Krell physiology. The Doctor decided that if these things could kill a humanoid as robust as the Krell, humans were even more susceptible. Finally, with all available information downloaded, Nadroc and his team left. Minutes later Zotrik broke orbit and headed out of the Zedak system and back into Krell space.

Phillipe turned to Joseph. 'Well you've certainly advanced Human/Krell diplomacy hugely. From what I've just seen, Argos may be the best chance we have of ending this stupid war. Believe me, old friend I'm impressed. In a few short days you've done more than any Coalition politician or diplomat has in a couple of centuries. Maybe you should consider standing for President?'

'Not a chance in hell. When we write the constitution for Argos, politics will be outlawed. The petty bickering in the Council got us into this war initially, and all they do now is hide; hundreds of light years from the fight, back on Earth. No, Phillipe, if I have any say in the future of this planet, politics will be curtailed.'

Phillipe chuckled and clapped his friend on the back. 'It's always good to feel your passion, and to get a bite.'

Chapter 10: Anomaly

She was old, older than any working lady should be, but still she kept going.

The freighter, Lady Philomena, was tired; tired and falling apart. Her owners, Galactic Freight, were renowned for penny-pinching, and her maintenance was basic, at best. She had recently loaded 13.5 million tonnes of highly refined Barainium at Aegis six and, considering her current safe mass certificate was for 11.5 million tonnes her systems were straining under the load. On the outward journey, two of her five old hyzene reactors had shutdown, and no amount of effort or cursing from her engineering staff could coax them back online.

Her drive system only just passed her last space worthiness examination – something her engineer considered a miracle. Chief engineer Collingwood was amazed that she hadn't been converted to a Coalition Space Corps range target by now.

Her hull showed signs of multiple patches and repairs, and to make things even worse, her primary sensor suite had shut down. All she had now was close range sensors, giving her no more than one hundred thousand kilometres range and, at her current velocity of 0.3 light, she would have a little over a second warning of any obstruction in her path.

According to the chief engineer, anything larger than a baseball would tear her apart. Safe navigation regulations stated that under these circumstances, the ship must slow to a speed that would allow them to manoeuvre out of any difficulty.

Unfortunately the Captain, Alistair Naismith, was on a mission to prove himself to the board. Galactic Freight had just released the short list for command of their newest ship and his name was at the top.

This was the third time in the last five years he had been top of the selection list. He wasn't going to let anything damage his chances of promotion this time. Lady Phil - as most of the crew called the old ship - was bound for Greenbach Technologies on Earth, and to deliver late would certainly spell the end of this opportunity.

With the reduced generating capacity, Lady Phil couldn't generate a worm hole that would hold her colossal mass; the only alternative was to utilise the displacement gate at Aegis One, which was now their next destination.

Cordoba Corporation, Aegis Mining's parent company, had purchased many of the old Exodus gates, refurbished them, and set them up at their major mining sites. This allowed heavily laden freighters to traverse the distance back to Earth, and other destinations, without needing to update their drive systems. This suited the financial guys back at Galactic very well.

With all the problems the old ship now had, her crew were a little edgy. Navigating along the asteroid belt could hold some nasty surprises and, even at their reduced speed, disaster was a real threat.

The First Officer, Adelle Simpson, was standing in front of her Captain. 'But Captain Naismith, we are essentially blind. If we encounter anything in our path, we won't have the time to manoeuvre.'

'Lieutenant Simpson, I am the Captain and I make the decisions. I will not allow us to delay delivery... it won't look good.' Naismith was a prickly customer whose career had been helped by his family, one of the larger shareholders in Galactic.

He was a company man and held to company policy and delivery timetables above all else; bending space regulations was second nature to him. 'As you are aware; this old ship has an enviable record for *on time delivery* and I am not about to sacrifice that for petty fear. We know this area of space, we know what to expect, so I have decided the risk is acceptable; that is all.' His dismissal of her was as arrogant as she expected.

'Understood, Sir; but I would like my protest to be placed on the record.'

'You have that right, but it will be accompanied by an adverse note on your record... do you really want that?'

'Captain, I really don't care what sarcastic remark you make, I am justified by the regulations, and if anything happens I want the record to show what transpired here!' Simpson demanded.

'Your decision, the record shall show both your protest and your insubordination; dismissed.'

Simpson left the room. 'Stupid, arrogant fucking arsehole,' she swore as she headed back to her station.

'I take it our illustrious leader didn't listen?' Chief engineer Collingwood asked, a wry smile creasing his face.

'Oh, he listened and then told me to get out; nothing is going to damage his bloody delivery record. Navigator, what's our position?'

'Coming up on Aegis Five, we're approximately seven hundred and fifty hundred million kliks from the gate.'

'So we're what... three and a half hours from the gate?' Simpson verbalised her thoughts.

'Close enough... depends on our deceleration and any queuing.'

'So, three and a half hours flying blind. Comms, keep a constant scan on all frequencies just in case.' She turned back to the engineer. 'Chief, are you sure we can't do anything?'

'Sorry, but unless someone can somehow materialise a new signal converter, we're screwed.'

'Chief, what about the shuttles... can we use their converters?' the comm operator voiced an idea.

'No, they're far more advanced than this old girl, the systems are totally incompatible.'

Simpson added a new idea to the mix. 'Hang on, what if we put two of the shuttles on the outer hull, one forward and one aft; could we use their long range sensors and relay the signal in here?

'It might work. We would need to send the data by comm link and it'll be slow, but better than what we have now.' Collingwood shook his head. 'But his highness would never agree to it.'

'He doesn't have to. He's off duty for the next six hours. Technically, I'm in command, so hop to it.' Simpson held to the theory that it is sometimes better to ask for forgiveness, than permission. This rough patch might, at least, give them some eyes. The comms operator started to work on a conversion algorithm, so they could display any data on the main viewer.

Fifteen minutes later the Collingwood returned. 'Both shuttles are in place, we should be seeing their data now.'

Simpson turned to the comms operator. 'Anything?'

The comms operator worked her console, finally declaring 'main viewer now.' The screen flickered and settled; now split in two with the left side showing the sensor data aft and the right forward. 'There's a point five second delay... sorry ma'am, it's the best I can do.'

'Who cares, slow sight is way better than none.' They all watched the screen. Forward was their real concern, so they minimised the aft feed, giving it ten percent of the screen. The view forward showed their path as being clear, at least for the next thirty minutes; the range only allowed them to detect one hundred and fifty million kliks ahead. 'Looks like we're clear to Aegis Four,' Simpson said, relief evident in her voice.

The entire Bridge relaxed and the normal hubbub of operation returned and the tension dissipated.

Ten minutes later the comm operator spoke. 'Ma'am, I'm getting some weird messages from four. It appears they've lost contact with five.' She was referring to the Aegis mining operations. 'Also, the transponder on five has gone dark.'

'Dark? What do you mean?'

'It's like it... vanished. Usually if there's a problem with the transponder, it transmits a shut-down signal and the back-up takes over... standard redundancy. This just stopped, like it vanished.' The comm operator's voice trailed off.

'Ok, enhance the rear sensor feed, and contact four, maybe... they can give us more information.' Simpson ordered. While she knew that five would now be at extreme sensor range, she had a bad feeling in her gut. The screen changed – now they were getting data mainly from the aft shuttle – but it told her nothing.

'Ma'am, I have four on the line. They're getting some strange readings from where five should be.'

'Should be? What's going on? Patch me through to four,' Simpson directed.

'Aegis Four this is Lady Philomena, we've lost five's transponder. Can you confirm status?'

It's gone... gone, a terrified voice replied, *there appears to be something carving a path through the belt, it's heading toward us eating everything in its path.* The transmission from Aegis Four boomed out of the comm system, fear verging on panic evident in the voices. Then it went quiet, until another voice returned.

This is Melissa Stokes, chief operating officer on Aegis Four. Who am I speaking with?

'Adelle Simpson, First Officer on Lady Philomena. What's your status?'

Ok, please record this transmission. Stokes waited for confirmation of the recording. *Fifteen minutes ago we lost all contact with Aegis Five; no warning,   it just vanished. Our sensors have detected some sort of spatial anomaly heading in our direction. As this anomaly passes a point in space, that point... vanishes. The anomaly has no signature and no energy expenditure; it's like a void, a hole in space. We have projected the path it is taking and believe it will reach Aegis Four in the next ten minutes. We advise all ships to take evasive action and move at least fifty million kilometres away from normal shipping routes. Evacuation of Aegis Four is underway, and we have advised all other Aegis outposts to monitor the situation and take whatever action they deem appropriate. End of transmission.* There was a pause before the voice returned, *all ships receiving this message please re-transmit on a continual loop until the situation is resolved; Aegis Four out.* The transmission ended and the link was cut.

'Comms please comply, set up a continuous loop on all hailing frequencies,' Simpson stood from the command chair and examined the image on the screen. 'Navigator, plot a course away from the normal lane.' She was concentrating on a section of the screen. 'Can we enhance this area?'

The comm operator worked quickly and soon had the sector filling the screen; all she could see was blackness. As she watched, a group of asteroids accelerated into the blackness, and vanished. There was no reading from the anomaly, no light, no radiation; nothing.

'And what the hell are you?' Simpson looked at the image. 'Chief, what do you make of this?'

Before the engineer could speak, the Navigator announced 'escape course laid in, ma'am.'

'Execute,' Simpson replied; the old ship started to turn slowly.

'Number One, this is weird,' the engineer was studying the sensor feed as he spoke. 'That anomaly appears to be eating everything in its path; there's nothing coming back from it. If I didn't know better, I'd say it was a black hole, but black holes don't move, and this thing is coming fast! From the data the Navigator has, about point eight light... we're never going to avoid it.'

'Not unless we can use the displacement drive.'

'With all this cargo, we'll never get a stable field established. The old girl would tear herself apart.' The engineer was right, and Simpson knew it. A few seconds later he added, 'but without the cargo?' Collingwood didn't need to expand his comment; Simpson was already thinking the same.

'Navigator, what's our optimum course for a displacement insertion?'

'095 by 122... it'll allow us to insert in seven minutes. We'll be on a course for Altar, the closest planet.'

'Chief, how fast can you dump the cargo?' As Simpson spoke, the ready room door opened.

'Nobody is dumping my cargo. Why are we off course?' Naismith was back on the Bridge.

'We don't have time to explain. We've got to act now!' Simpson argued.

'Lieutenant Simpson, you are relieved from duty. Chief, arrest her for mutiny.'

'No Sir, she's doing the right thing, there's some sort of black hole heading our way; look at the god-damned screen. If we don't get out of here, we'll all die!'

Naismith glared at the engineer. 'Absolute rubbish... she's hysterical... a stupid hysterical woman. She's not fit for her job; now the rest of you do as I have ordered.' His bluster didn't work. The engineer took the two steps necessary and opened all the cargo holds; concentrated Barainium ore began pouring out of them.

'**Stop! No!** I will not have my cargo lost by a pack of gutless fools.'

Simpson had heard enough, she moved closer to Naismith. 'Captain Naismith, under article seventeen of Coalition space transport regulations, I am relieving you of duty. You are now to be considered under arrest for recklessly endangering your ship and crew.'

'You can't, you need at least three senior officers to make that charge... you're finished Simpson.'

The engineer spoke next. 'I, chief engineer Collingwood, concur with the First Officer's assessment.'

Next the Navigator spoke. 'Let the record show that I, Ensign Holloway also concur. I believe that makes the three senior Bridge officers, currently on duty.'

'Cargo is gone; we can initiate a worm hole.' The engineer's voice broke the stand-off.

'You'll all hang for this, I guarantee it!' That was the last thing Naismith screamed. The engineer's right fist cut any further tantrums short.

'Feel better now?'

'Shit yeah, I've wanted to do that for ages.' Collingwood turned back to the console, 'Displacement probes deploying, we should be able to initiate a field in about three minutes.'

Simpson continued to study the screen; the anomaly was getting very close; as it moved, everything in its path vanished. There was no show, no explosions; asteroids, debris, equipment, everything just vanished. 'Navigator how long until it hits us?'

'Five minutes. Look how the cargo is being sucked in,' she was correct, the Barainium was being pulled towards the blackness, its velocity increasing exponentially each second. Time ticked by.

'Initiating displacement field,' the engineer's voice rang out. Still, the blackness kept coming.

'Come on, we've only got seconds left,' Holloway's voice was filled with fear. 'Four's gone dark!' Then everything slipped out of phase for an instant. They had entered the worm hole with only a few seconds to spare. The last thing they saw as they transitioned was a brilliant flare from the anomaly, it flashed almost as bright as the sun, and then it was gone, lost behind their worm hole.

***

On Argos, Phillipe Alvaris received a call from his ship. He asked that they relay it to Drake and set off to find Joseph. He located Joseph in the shuttle bay, about to head out to the hyzene plant. After a brief discussion, they both left for the Bridge at double time.

'What's it all about?' Joseph asked.

'Don't know; they think that the Aegis mining operation is under attack. If it is, then we need to ascertain where Nadroc went.' Phillipe was running down the last corridor before the Bridge.

The implication that the Krell could somehow be involved weighed heavily on Joseph; he had entertained them for over a week. Quickly he did some mental calculations, which made him feel better. Unless the Krell had some new type of drive that instantly transported them through space, there simply wasn't enough time for them to reach the belt.

'Comms, open a channel to the Omnicron vessel.' The channel was opened, and soon they were listening to the emergency transmission. The word anomaly stopped Joseph in his tracks. 'Replay it.'

'No need Sir, it repeats every fifteen seconds.' On cue, the message began again, fifteen seconds after it finished.

'Phillipe, can your ship's sensors reach out that far?'

'Not a hope, way too far for us, but we can receive their comm traffic. There'll be a bit of delay, but it might help. Why, what do you know?'

'Come to the ready room.' Joseph said and cut the link.

As the door closed behind Phillipe, Joseph turned his console on, accessed his private files and brought up the Udon experience. 'Watch this, and then we'll talk.'

Phillipe watched in awe and horror as he followed the path Udon had recorded.

'And you think this is the same anomaly?'

'Has to be, the chance of two is remote. Even one like this must be man-made.' Joseph recounted his ideas on Frederickson.

'Come on, I know Ernst is a bit loopy, but even he isn't mad enough to create this,' Phillipe responded. A call from the Bridge cut their conversation and had them racing back.

This is Aegis One, the emergency has subsided. The anomaly reported has dissipated. Aegis Five and four are uncontactable and there has been significant disruption to the asteroid field. We advise all but essential vessels stay well clear of the Daldaro Belt; Aegis One out. Phillipe and Joseph looked at each other, bemusement written on their faces.

'Comms, did you pick up any transmissions earlier?' Joseph called.

'No, Sir, we weren't listening.' Phillipe's comm unit buzzed. He indicated the ready room, and Joseph agreed. Several minutes later, he came back out.

'That was Silvio Cordoba; he wants us back at the Belt to help out. Don't worry, I've told him we're on a new contract and I've arranged for another unit to head there, it has three weeks before it's required at the next job. But things must be bad for Silvio to call in person.' Phillipe turned back to the screen, the message from Aegis One still being displayed. 'I'd love to see what has happened.'

Joseph called Bruce McGill and asked him to meet them in his quarters. Ten minutes later the three were sitting comfortably as Joseph began.

'Bruce, can you run things here for a few days?'

'Sure, are you planning a holiday?' Bruce replied, sharply.

'Something like that.' They both began to bring Bruce up to date with the Aegis situation, including Udon's Rift Run. 'So now you know why we want to have a look, first hand.'

'Yeah, before the spin doctors turn it into a picnic. Ok but what about the survey. We've got three sites already and the teams want to go further afield. How many sites do you want to evaluate?' Bruce asked.

'Have the survey crews prepare a briefing for oh eight hundred tomorrow,' Joseph replied. 'We'll examine the current sites and make a decision. If they check out, we'll use one of them. If not, we'll keep looking.' He turned back to Phillipe, a conspiratorial wink from his left eye. 'Come on. I'll show you a secret.' Bruce and Phillipe followed.

'You're gonna love this.' McGill was grinning from ear to ear as they entered a small alcove in the far wall of the room. The alcove housed an elevator pad. Joseph activated it, and they ascended toward the ceiling. At the last moment, the ceiling opened and the pad came to a stop inside a hangar. 'Very few of us even know this is here, it's the Captain's secret.' Lights came on and there before them stood a beautiful, sleek space ship.

'It's an Askari, built on New Nippon. Isn't she beautiful?' Joseph announced – his pride in the ship evident.

The ship was sleek; her forward section tapered into a delicate point, the fuselage was oval on the upper surface but flattened out below. Two wings started slightly aft of the obvious Bridge area and swept back to form an old delta wing shape. Incorporated into the underside of these were two nacelles, housing two MAM reactors and twin Gravitron drives.

'She's fast. In space, she can hold point nine five, and can run at a displacement factor of fifteen, all day,' Joseph spoke factually.

'Impressive, but what's her duration?' Phillipe ran a hand on the smooth underside of the nose.

'We haven't actually tested it, but the designers believe at fifteen, something like two hundred hours. Should get us to the Daldaro Belt in about thirty-six hours... fast enough?' Joseph was beaming with pride. Apart from Bruce McGill and a couple of others, Phillipe was the first person to see his newest acquisition. 'Come aboard.'

As he spoke, a boarding ramp lowered to give them access. Bruce took his leave, saying he needed to arrange the briefing for tomorrow.

Phillipe was fascinated, the ship was more than he expected. 'She's far more advanced than anything I've ever seen, what's the story?'

Joseph went back to the Bridge, took the command chair and offered the seat next to him to Phillipe. 'She's the first ship built away from Earth, but utilising all the newest technology available there.

'Askari is a joint venture, the company name is actually Askari AG; the partners are Askari Industries, on new Nippon, Abracorp and Greenbach Technologies. It appears that two of Earth's largest companies are moving away from the home planet.'

'That's inevitable; Earth's no longer the centre of our civilisation; in fact, it's really at the far end of human colonisation. Operations moving out to the colonies was always only a matter of time.' Phillipe observed. They spent the next hour discussing the ship and the journey they needed to take. Joseph's chief concern was that his crew would be anxious if their Captain was seen deserting the ship but a suggestion from Phillipe had the potential to save the day. They left the ship and returned to Joseph's quarters.

At 18:30 hours, Joseph Jones instigated a ship wide broadcast to inform his crew of the events in the Daldaro Belt. He told the truth and kept nothing back, even describing Kidman's journey through the Rift. When he finished, he introduced Phillipe.

'Crew of the Drake,' Phillipe began. 'My company, Omnicron, built the installations for the Aegis mining venture and I find it difficult to understand how these could just vanish. Each station, both four and five, were usually staffed by one thousand people. If they have been destroyed, two thousand people are gone. I have been in contact with the Cordoba group, and we are sending one of our vessels to the sites as we speak.

'Captain Jones and I have decided to go to the belt and try to assist if we can. Now to do this, we will be taking the Captain's personal shuttle, but we need three additional crew members to come with us, so we're asking for volunteers.' He stopped and let Joseph continue.

Joseph opened. 'This may be a waste of time, also it may be dangerous but here's what we are asking. We need some particular skills, mainly medical and engineering. Our sensor specialist, Ensign Renwick, has already volunteered, and I am grateful to her... her expertise will be fantastic. So I ask you to think about this and if you wish to volunteer, contact me by twenty-one hundred hours tonight. Thank you, that is all.'

At 21:00, Joseph checked his console; there were twenty offers to join the group. He called Phillipe and together they sorted the list. They settled on the new crew. Lieutenant Cobal Latric was selected for his ability as both a pilot and an astrophysicist. Next was medical and med-tech Jennifer Turbut was the standout, her experience in trauma medicine making her the ideal candidate. The final spot was given to Petty Officer Rajiv Singh, an accomplished and thorough engineer. Joseph responded to all that had put their names forward and thanked them. To the ones chosen, he requested they meet in his quarters at 07:00 the next day.

'Well, we have a crew.' Joseph looked at the time; 24:50 was showing on the console. 'Time for some dinner and then I think I'll turn in.'

***

At exactly 07:00 the next morning, the door annunciator to Joseph's quarters buzzed. 'Right on time,' he observed, impressed with his crew's punctuality.

He opened the door and let everyone in. The meeting was short, with Phillipe doing most of the talking. He had arranged for supplies from his ship to be used for the mission, so he called and asked for a shuttle to collect the crew. Then they all followed Joseph to the hangar, here things changed.

Cobal Latric let out a low whistle. 'Sir, is that what I think it is?' His eyes not leaving the gleaming silver hull before him.

'Yes, Lieutenant, it is.'

'An Askari, I've only read about them, and you have one!'

Joseph wanted to diffuse this now. 'It's not such a big deal. We do a lot of business with the three joint venture partners. So, when I said I was looking for a personal boat, they made me an offer I couldn't refuse, at least not with any degree of sanity. She's the second production unit, and part of the deal is regular updates on her performance. So now Lieutenant those updates can be part of your job.'

'Does that mean I get to fly her, regularly?' Latric's voice was almost reverent.

'Well, you can hardly give them updates if you don't. Now, we will have only a limited amount of space, so here's what is available for each of your specialities. Make your selections carefully and collect the gear from the Terra-Truck, in orbit.'

Jennifer Turbut joined the conversation. 'What facilities are available where we're going?'

Phillipe had the answer. 'They have full medical facilities, but most was located on Aegis Four. Aegis One and Six, have good trauma suites but most of their medical staff was also on Four, and we don't know if they survived. If I may make a suggestion, take one of our twenty man trauma kits; from experience, that should be enough to treat any victims close to the zero point; all others will be sent to one of the Aegis trauma units.'

The discussion lasted for another ten minutes, until the shuttle arrived and Phillipe took them back to his ship. Joseph had just enough time to return to his desk before the survey teams arrived. This meeting took much longer; their briefing was thorough and well documented. After two hours, Joseph called a halt.

'So which site would you recommend?'

Without any delay, Bruce McGill answered. 'Site one, the plateau we can see from here. It is close to a source of water, we already have the hyzene plant up and running and transport to that site would be easy. Additionally, it only appears as a plateau from where we are, in reality, it's relatively flat land that continues to the mountains behind.'

Joseph looked to the four Omnicron people who were part of the team. 'What do you guys think?'

The senior Omnicron member, Goran Illych, responded. 'Sir, what your engineer said is correct. We have sampled all three sites and that is by far the best. For an initial colony you need certain things and this site has them all, in abundance. Plus, the ground is solid and there is little evidence of seismic activity. That's the site we recommend.'

'Well that settles it. Goran, we need to move this ship to that spot, so we need your people to prepare the final site. Bruce, can you handle this while we're gone?' Joseph asked.

'Definitely, with these Omnicron guys here, it'll be a breeze,' McGill said confidently.

'One thing, Captain,' Illych cut in, 'how big do you want this site to be, how many people are you intending to house there, for say... the next three years?'

'Around, ten thousand in the next year, and one hundred thousand in three years... aim big!' Joseph replied, grinning.

'Easy, one hundred thousand it is. We should have the site prepped and ready in about a week.'

'A week!' Bruce exclaimed. 'Shit we better get our arses into gear, it'll take at least two to get the ship ready.'

Illych smiled. 'Listen, we have gear and people on the Terra Truck that can help; I'll have them talk to you.'

Joseph let the conversation take its own path; the crews from both ships appeared to be working well together. At length, everything was talked out and everyone left. It had taken three hours to get things sorted, but he felt it was three hours well invested.

Chapter 11: Daldaro Belt

Joseph had only taken delivery of the Askari three weeks prior to their accident.

They had arrived on New Nippon to collect their final trade cargo, and he was notified that his new ship was ready. Wasting no time, he had arranged for the final transaction to be made and had it delivered to Drake.

So far, he hadn't done more than the two-hour test flight required for his familiarisation, and he was eager to spend more time in her. Before he could do that, there were formalities to action. First he had to complete the registration. Being an independent trader, this was relatively simple, initially. Joseph called up the ITG ship register and completed the data input for his vessel. His only stumbling block was a name.

All through the six-month build he had considered, and discarded, numerous names. Now eight weeks after taking delivery, he still had no clear idea of what to call her. Joseph sat back. He turned up the volume of the ancient recording he was playing. The Marriage of Figaro by Mozart filled the room. Joseph had a love of ancient opera and this was his favourite and, in one of those rare light bulb moments, it came to him.

He completed the registration, giving the home port of the ship as Argos; he locked the entry and smiled. ITS Amadeus, registry number 225-1 was now officially in existence; the first independent trade ship to be registered on Argos. While he was in the registry, he entered the details for Freedom, and her home port as Argos. Her registry number ITS225-2 was now locked into the data base, the last number in her registry sequence indicating she was the second vessel registered on Argos.

The registry details complete, Joseph headed for the hangar; there he had the ground crew affix the name and registry number to the hull, forward of the Bridge. The number would also be displayed on both wings. He went aboard and downloaded the information into the ship's data core and activated the transponder. The newest vessel in the Jones Trading fleet was now ready for space.

Amadeus's construction was new, utilising a composite/metal hybrid called Acrilan. The details of this new material were a closely guarded secret, but it was said to be 5 times stronger than previous materials and less than a third of the weight. It also allowed for more complex shapes to be formed and still hold their strength.

In all, Amadeus had eight cabins and two staterooms, three small holds and room for 2 small shuttles. Each of the holds was now filled with the equipment needed for this trip and all crew members already on board. Joseph entered the Bridge, finding the others at their respective stations, Lieutenant Latric occupying the Pilot's chair.

'Well Mister Latric, think you can fly her?'

'Damn straight... I'm ready!'

'Excellent,' Joseph said as he took the command chair, 'well then, let's get underway.' At his Captain's word, Latric initiated the exit procedure; the hangar roof opened, all umbilicals retracted and both airlocks sealed.

The hangar exit was tight, with less than a metre clearance to any extremity of the ship, but Latric and the ship's AI systems were more than up to the task. Gently, Latric guided Amadeus out of Drake and to freedom in the atmosphere of Argos.

Joseph turned to the nav station. 'Ensign Renwick, do you have a course for the Belt?'

Molly Renwick was acting Navigator, on this trip. 'Yes Sir, I've programmed the orbital parameters and the initial course into the nav system. Pilot, you should be able to see it now.'

'Thanks, Molly.' Latric entered the course change. Although the ship's AI systems were capable of totally autonomous operation, the history of the human race precluded this from being a standard mode of operation.

Latric reflected on his role and this history. Hundreds of years in the past, Earth had embraced autonomous technology. Over time many modes of transport had been automated and eventually human presence was removed. Everyone thought this was a great leap in safety and comfort, until the inevitable happened - a fringe anarchist group found a way to break the security walls on these autonomous systems. They waited until the best opportunity to cause maximum disruption before actioning their new power.

One Monday morning the group pounced; they took control of most forms of transport, in every part of the planet. Trains, planes, ships, private vehicles were hacked. The ensuing melee resulted in total disruption across the world; trains were derailed, vac tubes ruptured, road transport was devastated, but the worst was in the sky; hundreds of planes crashed.

Over four million lives were lost in that one attack and the fantasy of autonomous transport was dashed forever. Now people like Latric were always in command, no matter what the assurances; machine control didn't have the allure after that incident.

The chime of the nav system brought him back to the present. 'Coming up on the first insertion point,' he checked the system, confirmed the insertion was correct and initialised the displacement drive. Moments later, they all felt the fraction of a second disorientation that signalled the transition to sub space, and then they were safe inside their worm hole.

Latric checked the system and reported the status. 'Displacement field stable, currently holding at twelve point five, our time to reinsertion is twelve hours and eight minutes.'

'Well done Mister Latric,' Joseph commented. 'We'll now split into shifts, six hours each. Mister Latric and Ensign Renwick will take the first shift, Phillipe and Mister Singh the second and Miss Turbut and I will take the third.'

Two hours later, Joseph and Phillipe each received a call to the Bridge; arriving quickly they found Latric and Renwick huddled over the nav console.

'What's the problem?' Joseph asked.

Latric explained his concerns. 'Sir, our current course will have us reinserting approximately fifty thousand kliks from Aegis One. The problem is we have no real information as to any destabilisation the Belt has suffered. If both Aegis Four and five have been destroyed, it stands to reason that some; if not all the surrounding asteroids suffered the same fate.'

'So?' Joseph wasn't following their logic.

Phillipe butted in. 'Shit, why didn't I see this? Joseph, an asteroid belt is a mass of broken bits of other heavenly bodies; planets, moons or comets. The reason it forms a belt is attraction; each chunk of rock exerts a form of gravitational force, either repelling or attracting the other pieces around it. This is something we work with very carefully when we set up any mining operation like the Aegis field. What do you suggest, Mister Latric?'

'We change our last reinsertion point to at least fifty million or even one hundred million kliks from Aegis One. We do a long range analysis and then proceed as the situation dictates.'

Joseph studied his two crew members, quietly proud of them. 'Do it,' was all he said, then as he stood to leave. 'Well done... well done indeed.' He and Phillipe left and as they passed through the door, Latric and Renwick shared a high five, knowing their call had been correct.

'Impressive... how many other trade crews would even think of that?' Phillipe said.

'Exactly why I always try to secure the best; it costs a bit more, to attract the right people, but I believe it's a smart investment.' Joseph sounded more like a proud father than their boss.

Thirty two hours later, Amadeus reinserted into normal space, 97,000,000 kilometres from Aegis One. Molly Renwick was glued to the sensor console and Latric was in command. Joseph and the others held back, allowing the two who had formulated the plan to work it. A few minutes later, Renwick let out a slow whistle.

'Oh my god,' her words were almost a whisper.

'Come on Molly, share it around.' Joseph coaxed and Molly directed the feed to the main viewer, the image coalesced.

'All stop, shields to maximum!' Latric spoke quietly as he carried out the functions. He stood and offered the seat to Joseph, before taking the Pilot's chair. Joseph sat, still mesmerised by the image on the screen.

'Singh, on comms please,' Joseph called, 'try to raise anyone in that mess.'

Rajiv moved to the console and began transmitting on all hailing frequencies. 'All stations, this is ITS Amadeus calling any station in the Daldaro Belt.' His call was met with silence. He tried again, no reply.

None of the Aegis plants were registering on sensors, and this concerned Joseph. The Aegis stations were built either on the extremities of the field, like Aegis Six and One, or on larger, more stable asteroids. Amadeus's sensors didn't register any of them; all that could be seen was the gate, 2,000,000 kilometres off their starboard quarter. But even it refused to respond to hails.

'Molly, can you find a way through this, to Aegis One?' Joseph was clutching at straws. Normally the Daldaro Belt was an organised flow of asteroids and smaller rocks, 750,000,000 kilometres long, 300,000 wide and 12,000 deep. It had been, according to the boffins, in that arrangement for many millions of years; now it was a massive jumble of constantly moving debris. They watched in awe as asteroid after asteroid collided, some disintegrating, others fusing to form a larger body. Singh set the hails on auto-transmit and joined the others.

Phillipe sat in the spare chair next to Joseph and activated its console. He worked at it for a few minutes before speaking. 'Petty Officer Singh, can you contact my ship back at Argos?'

'Of course Sir,' the comm dwell from Argos to the Belt was only a couple of minutes; Phillipe took a headset and waited.

'Lieutenant, are we still moving?' Joseph asked.

Latric checked his console. 'Yes Sir, slightly... must be the gravitational effect of what we're watching.' As he spoke he set the ship to station keeping. 'That should correct it, sorry Sir.'

'Don't worry, it was only an observation, but if we can feel the effect out here, what's it like in there?' Joseph indicated the melee now unfolding on the screen.

Latric was spellbound by the sight they all saw; as an astrophysicist this sight was something like the Holy Grail. 'Skipper, I may be a bit premature, but I think we are watching the forming of a new planetoid. As more pieces fuse together, the gravitational effect increases and more are pulled in. It's fascinating.'

The scene was becoming more violent by the second, more debris was being sucked into the central mass, more explosions and fusing of material but, more worrying were the gravitational waves being generated. Amadeus was constantly being pulled and pushed by conflicting waves, much like the chaos of a violent atmospheric storm. Holding position was becoming difficult.

'I think we should move, and soon,' Phillipe said as he replaced the headset he had been talking on. 'My guys agree with your assessment, Mister Latric, but there could be two outcomes.' He consulted his console. 'May I?'

He minimised the view from the Belt and replaced it with a simulation. 'These are two possible scenarios for situations like this.' The screen changed and showed what they were now watching, except it was a simulation. As it progressed, it showed a new planet forming and, when the asteroids feeding the growth were depleted, activity stopped and the gravity anomalies subsided. 'This second one is, historically, more accurate. If this is what we're looking at, we need to clear out soon.' He ran the second scenario.

In this scenario, the same initial activity was shown, asteroids colliding and fusing together. Where it differed was obvious; at some stage, the mass became so hot and unstable it exploded, debris was thrown far out into space, well past their current distance. 'If this is the end result, we're sitting ducks here.'

***

On board Lady Philomena things were going from bad to terrible. Now the displacement drive was failing.

'Our field has destabilised, we're now only able to hold one point six, and I don't know how long it's going to last.' The engineer's voice was despondent.

Simpson watched the readout on the screen; it showed how bad the field was. There appeared to be holes forming in it.' 'How long mister Collingwood... until it collapses entirely?'

Collingwood was about to answer when alarms started screaming from the engineering station. 'I'd say about now.' A failure of the displacement field was the greatest fear any space traveller had. An uncontrolled reinsertion was extremely dangerous as there was no way of knowing where the ship would rematerialize. It might be in clear space, or in the centre of a star, or in the gravitational pull of a planet; it was never something that any sane spacer would want to try. Lady Phil had no choice, her field collapsed, and she reinserted back into normal space.

'Deflectors, shields?' Simpson cried.

'Deflectors and shields not responding,' Collingwood called back. 'Shit, we've lost another reactor; it's what dumped the drive!'

'Comms, what do our sensors show?' Simpson asked.

'We're clear, for now.'

'Well, that's one decent piece of luck.' Simpson beckoned the engineer. When they were out of earshot of the rest of the Bridge team she wanted answers. 'Ok chief, what's the situation?'

'Awful, we're down to two reactors, and one of them is suspect. We can manage to run life support and either the Ion drive or the deflectors and shields, not all three. We either run the risk of being pulverised as we move or we sit here, dead in the water so to speak.' His tone was grim and matter of fact.

'What about the shuttles? could we put them all outside and use their shields?'

'What do you mean **all**... we only have four,' Collingwood said angrily.

'Four? We normally carry twenty; where are the others?'

'Maybe we should ask the Captain, he was the one who authorised them to be removed prior to leaving Earth; I checked the shuttle logs. Naismith authorised for sixteen shuttles to be offloaded for repairs, or so the log shows.'

Simpson searched her mind. No Skipper could be that stupid; to run without enough escape vehicles broke at least a dozen rules. 'Make a copy of all the logs, I have a feeling that if we get out of this, Naismith will have them erased, try to make us the villains.' She turned back to the rest of the Bridge team. 'Comms, what's showing from the Belt?'

The screen flickered and then displayed what it could. 'Holy shit, look at that!'

Their feed was showing the direct feed from the Aegis outpost. 'Looks like a new planetoid forming... what's our distance?' Simpson mused.

The Navigator looked confused. 'I'm sorry Ma'am, but the instruments seem to be failing. It says we're only ninety thousand kliks from the zero point, but it can't be right. The displacement run should have us at least four million kliks by now.'

Simpson's heart sank. 'The anomaly... it must have interfered with the field, held us back; Nav what's our velocity now?'

'We're not moving, no forward motion at all.' A deathly hush fell over the Bridge, everyone knowing what it meant.

Simpson felt their eyes boring into her, they all looked to her for a solution, and there wasn't one. 'Chief, what's our Ion drive's status?'

Collingwood shook his head. 'It's at max now, Skipper; and it can't hold that for long.'

Simpson was frantically considering options but each second depleted the pool. She was running out of ideas when the comm operator spoke. 'Ma'am, we're getting a signal from six!' She relayed the signal, a new voice sounded in the room. *This is Aegis six, calling any ships in our sector of the Daldaro Belt?*

Simpson opened the channel. 'Aegis six, this is Lady Philomena, what's your status?'

Lady Philomena, we only loaded you a few hours ago. Six is operational, but only just. We sustained some damage, but we're still able to function. How did you fare?

'Not well, we have damage to our reactors, and we're short on shuttles. At this time we are being pulled towards the zero point, are you able to assist?' Simpson felt a pang of hope.

Sorry, all our shuttles were lost, but our bays are clear, if you can get here.

'Six, wait one.' She ran her finger across her throat, signalling for the comm to be muted. 'Chief, could we use the shuttles we have to transfer our people to six?'

'Skipper, we could, but we don't have time. We have one hundred and fifty aboard; the four shuttles we have can only take ten at a time, including the Pilot.' He turned to the nav console. 'The time it would take for a return trip to Six, hell ... we'd be lucky if we got two trips in, that's eighty at most, before the drive fails completely.'

The Navigator interrupted. 'Hang on, what if we turned Lady Phil and headed toward Six, ourselves. Instead of trying to defy the gravity well, we use it... like a whirlpool. Run across but with the current, the least it would do is give us more time; each trip would be slightly shorter. Who knows, Lady Phil may even build up enough velocity to break free.' He worked his console and displayed his idea on the screen. All eyes now fell to the engineer.

'Damned if I know if it'll work, but it's way better than doing nothing.'

'Ok, Navigator get things started. Chief, bring those two shuttles back inside, fuel them up and start an evacuation. Comms start a mayday; inform any and all ships of our predicament. Right people, we have a purpose, now let's move!' Those words spurred everyone to action. Simpson sat at the command chair and activated a ship wide broadcast, this would be the most difficult part, getting the entire crew ready to evacuate, while stopping any panic.

***

'Captain, we're getting some transmissions from Aegis Six and what sounds like a freighter,' Renwick stated. Joseph signalled for it to be put on speaker and the conversations boomed across the Bridge. They all listened, a sense of dread creeping into the group.

'Can we see them yet?'

Renwick worked the sensor console. 'Not clearly, too much interference from the Belt, but I have the ship's location.'

Joseph studied his console as the relative location of both ships was displayed. 'Pilot, can we get there, in time?'

'We can't use the displacement drive; the mess in the belt would distort it too much, but, if this ship is as fast as you say,' he paused while he did some calculations. 'Allowing for acceleration and deceleration, we could be there in under an hour.'

'Right, make it happen. Molly, keep scanning the mess in there, look for anything left of the other Aegis operations and,' he looked at the others. 'Phil, you and Jennifer start on prepping a rescue scenario; we need to know what we can do before we arrive. Rajiv, on the comms; try to contact any ships that are out there, we're going to need all the help we can muster.' As he finished issuing instructions, Amadeus began to accelerate, hard. Latric had opened the throttles to the twin Gravitron drives all the way, feeding raw antimatter into the reactor to create drive plasma which powered the oversized engines. Amadeus was having her first real test.

Molly kept a sharp eye on the sensors and, even though they would automatically alert the Bridge to any obstruction, she had the shields fully powered.

Latric was in awe of the small ship. The acceleration was incredible, almost each minute it ticked off another decimal of light speed. 'Sir we're at point five light and climbing.' He had set the ultimate speed limiter at .9 light or 240,300 kilometres per second, his estimate of their travel time was proving accurate.

Damn, I love this ship he thought as they passed through .7 light. At the speeds they were now operating, even the smallest speck of dust could cause damage to the hull. Latric said a silent prayer, for help and safety to any deity that may be listening. He checked the speed, .75... and then less than a minute later .8. Finally, he spoke again. 'Point nine light and holding.'

Suddenly the screen flared brilliant white; a tiny vibration was felt by all. 'Nothing to worry about, some of the junk from the Belt, shields and deflectors took care of it.' Molly said relief, evident in her voice.

'No need for alarm. One of the things with this ship, it has the same shield and deflector system that we will have on Freedom, and she's about one hundred times bigger. We'll have some of the debris hitting us while we travel, but it isn't a problem. But Molly, try to find any big bits... I'd rather avoid them,' Joseph joked. His words were greeted with a nervous chuckle from the others, but it did help to lower the tension.

Thirty minutes later Molly spoke again. 'Sir, we have a visual on the freighter.' She put it up on the screen. The image showed Lady Phil desperately trying to run across the gravity field, and making hard work of it.

'Molly, hail them!' Joseph turned to the Pilot. 'Cobal, how long?'

'We're still eighteen minutes out, with minimum decel time.' To arrive at that time they would need to wait until the last moment and then perform a crash stop. 'We'd better make sure everything is tied down.'

'Captain,' Rajiv moved to his Captain's side. 'That old ship can't take the stress much longer, bits are breaking off now.' As he spoke, one of the ancient antennas crumpled and flew toward the Belt.

Joseph nodded. 'I know.'

'Sir, we have an answer to our hail.' Molly fed the comm to the speakers.

ITS Amadeus, this is Lady Philomena... we're in trouble, can you help?

'Lady Philomena, this is Joseph Jones on board Amadeus, how many do you have still on board?'

Captain Jones, our shuttles have just returned, they will take another eighty, we're double loading; but we will still have fifteen on board. The shuttle transit time is over thirty minutes, and this old girl will break up long before they get back.

'Don't worry, we're only about fifteen minutes out, have all your crew suited and ready to leave.' While he was talking Singh, was trying to find the engineering specs for the freighter, 'who am I talking to?'

First Officer, Adelle Simpson.

'Where's your Captain?'

Long story Sir, he's in the brig. Captain, I have a request... can I transmit our logs to your ship?

Joseph sensed that something drastic must have happened. 'Of course... begin transmission. We'll record and store them for you, but we'll be there in thirteen minutes now. You better prepare your people.' He saw Singh signalling him. 'Wait one.'

'Sir, I can't find any specs on that ship, it must be older than anything.'

Joseph looked at the old ship again. 'If ships were living creatures, that old girl would be Drake's great grandmother.' He shook his head and called for the comm to be reinstated. 'Simpson, what docking system do you have?' Joseph knew he wasn't going to like the answer.

Teradyne Systems mark two.

Singh gasped. 'Sir those systems are ancient, almost older than the Coalition. We'll never mate up to it.'

Joseph looked grave. 'I know... looks like we're going to have to be creative.' He unmuted the comm and continued. 'Simpson, we have a problem. We won't be able to mate with your docking system... wait while we reconfigure an alternative.' He ran his finger across his throat and Molly cut the comm. 'Ok what are our alternatives? One way or another we're getting these people off that derelict.' Silence greeted his words; nobody seemed to have an answer, until Singh spoke.

'Sir, does this vessel have a tractor beam?'

'Yes, all our vessels do... why?'

'Mister Alvaris are you familiar with the rescue of miners from the Caperstan disaster?' Singh asked.

Phillipe nodded. 'Yes I am, come on, let's set it up. Joseph, where's the tractor control?'

'Here,' Singh replied. The two of them worked desperately, they only had five minutes until Amadeus arrived.

'Joseph, ask her where their nearest docking port is,' Alvaris called. Joseph contacted Simpson and got the answer.

'Now, highlight it on the image on our screen.' Joseph transferred the data, as Phillipe looked up from the console. 'Nearly ready, Pilot, you have your target, get us a close as you can, as fast as you can.'

'No worries, three minutes.'

Phillipe turned to Joseph. 'Here's what we're going to do. When we stop, Latric will match us to that docking port; we close in, deactivate part of the shields and activate the tractor beam.

'Before then, Simpson needs to have her people as close to the port as possible, inside the airlock, if she can. They will need to hold on to something substantial. When they open the hatch, the tractor beam will pull them into the lower hold airlock. I'd also suggest she have them tie each other off, just to be safe.'

Joseph grinned. 'You're going to use the tractor beam as an elevator, brilliant!' He signalled for Molly to call Lady Philomena again; Simpson answered, and he explained what was going to happen. He finished the conversation with 'don't worry, this is a standard rescue technique in the mining industry, and we have Phillipe Alvaris here organising it.'

Before anyone could say more, Latric called. 'Hang on, decelerating now.' There was no need to hang on, the inertial dampeners, like the shields, were massively over specified. Amadeus slowed immediately and within minutes was in position.

'Amadeus calling Lady Philomena... Simpson, are your people ready?'

Yes, Captain, and we've got our Captain as well.

Joseph turned to the engineering station; Singh gave him the thumbs up.

Joseph opened the comm link. 'Simpson, we've established the rescue elevator, open the hatch.'

Nothing happened.

'Simpson, what's the delay?'

It won't budge, looks like the mechanism has been welded closed.

'Fuck,' Joseph swore, 'Ok can you blow it?'

I think so, unless some arsehole has removed the emergency bolts. Joseph could only imagine what everyone on the old ship was going through; fear, desperation - it was all up to his crew now.

'Here's what we're going to do. We'll deactivate the elevator, you blow the hatch when we say, and make sure everyone is holding on when you do. Then, when the hatch has blown, we'll reinstate the elevator and you can all come aboard, only take a few seconds.'

Understood, Sir; waiting on your command.

Turbut was standing at the sensor console. 'Better hurry Sir.' She was indicating a huge piece of debris heading their way.

'I know... Phillipe, are you ready?'

'De-energising the tractor beam now,' he waited until the control indicated zero tractor power. 'Now, Joseph.'

'Simpson, blow the hatch!' Immediately Joseph gave the order, the docking hatch flew off its mount toward Amadeus. It hit the deflector field and was flung safely away. As soon as it was gone, the tractor beam was re-established, and Phillipe gave the go signal.

'Simpson, send your people out, now' he turned to Turbut. 'Jennifer, you better take your kit down there.' He turned back to the screen and watched as fifteen people, all tied together, were pulled into Amadeus's airlock.

Joseph turned to the Pilot. 'Cobal, as soon as engineering gives you the sign, get us the hell out of here.' They both saw the huge lump of rock tearing toward them.

'You don't have to tell me twice, Skipper,' his hands were already on the controls. The thumbs up signal from Alvaris, and he pushed the engine controls to full power. Amadeus leapt away from the freighter, but the rock was still a threat. Latric threw the ship into a hard climbing left turn, to clear Lady Phil, and then pushed it completely over and dived under the approaching rock.

The rogue piece of rock was huge and it took all Latric's skill to keep Amadeus from being smashed on its surface.

On the Bridge it felt like hours of extreme manoeuvring, zigging and zagging, the small ship was thrown about in a desperate attempt to avoid a fiery death.

One last desperate rolling turn, and they broke free of it; ten seconds later the rogue collided with Lady Philomena, vaporising them both. There was no cheering, just a collective sigh of relief from those on the Bridge.

'Molly, please contact Aegis Six and inform them we have the last of the crew from the freighter on board,' Joseph requested.

'Yes Sir, but what about the debris from the collision?' As she spoke, Molly changed the screen, now it was focused aft of the ship. It centred on a rapidly expanding cloud of rock and wreckage, hurtling away from the collision epicentre.

'Shit, never just rains, does it?' Joseph mused, 'Mister Latric I think a hasty retreat would be in order.'

'My thoughts exactly,' Cobal said as he turned to a new heading and opened the engines up to maximum. 'Heading towards Aegis One, it's the quietest place around here.' Amadeus responded like the thoroughbred she was and the distance between her and the ever expanding debris field grew quickly.

Once he knew they were out of danger, Joseph stood. 'Well done Mister Latric, you have the con. I'll be in the dining room, greeting our guests. Molly, please get an update on Six's disposition.' He left the Bridge as Cobal Latric assumed command.

Chapter 12: Diplomacy

Joseph was greeted with pandemonium as he entered the dining room. Everyone was trying to speak at once and the volume was building.

'**Silence!** He yelled above the din. '**Everyone... be quiet**!' Joseph stood quietly waiting for the noise to subside. 'Thank you. I'm Joseph Jones, Captain of this vessel; which one of you is Simpson?'

Before Simpson could answer, a figure leapt forward, 'I'm Captain Naismith I demand you free me and arrest these mutineers.' He held his arms in front of him to emphasise the restraints on them.

'Ah, Captain Naismith... I'm sorry but I can't do that. Your crew has filed a serious set of charges against you and, according to interstellar law; you remain confined until the charges are resolved.'

'Captain Jones, do you have any idea who I am?' Naismith shot back.

Joseph looked hard at the man before him. Average was the way he would have described Naismith, average in every way. 'Yes, I do; Alistair Naismith, the youngest child of Graham and Zena Naismith, employee of Galactic Freight and former Commander of the freighter Lady Philomena.'

'Then, Captain, you know the trouble I can bring to you.' Before he could make any more threats, Joseph cut Naismith off.

'Mister Naismith, I've known your father since long before you were born and if you think that by invoking his name I'll cave in, you better think again. You're not at

Galactic now. In fact, Galactic has no jurisdiction out here; the relevant authority is the Cordoba group and the operators of Aegis.

'So here's what has to happen... we'll contact Cordoba and have them decide what course of action they wish to take. Until then you will remain as you are, understood?' As he finished, a call from the Bridge came through.

Sir, we've established a link to Aegis One... their comm antenna was damaged in the initial blast. Their COO (Chief Operations Officer) would like to speak with you.

'Ok, I'm on my way,' Joseph turned back to the group. 'Our Med Tech, Jennifer Turbut will check you all out and I'll return as soon as I take this call. Now, again, which one is Simpson?'

'I am, Sir.' Adelle Simpson stood forward. 'Thank you for rescuing us.'

'Lieutenant, when all this is sorted, you may wish to revise that statement. As for now, I will leave things as they are. In fact, I have no jurisdiction to do anything else. All I ask is you keep your people in line; we'll try to sort this out as soon as we can.' He turned and left the room.

Back on the Bridge he took the call from Aegis One; the situation on the station was better than envisaged. The only real damage was the loss of the comm tower, but this had now been replaced and, apart from a few scratches and dents, the station was fully operational. The COO on Aegis One was also the senior officer for the whole installation and when Joseph started to discuss the Lady Phil saga, she stopped the conversation.

Look, Captain, this is something I'm not equipped to deal with. I'll need to speak with our head office and, as you are aware, I have rather more pressing issues to deal with. My suggestion would be for you to either dump them at the nearest Galactic base or hand them all over to the Coalition.

'That won't be necessary.' Phillipe interrupted. 'I have spoken to Silvio... he's on his way and should be here in a few days... we'll let him sort it out then.'

The Aegis COO broke in. *I don't think there'll be much left here in a few days. Our brains trust believes the whole field will be totally destabilised in less than twenty hours. After that, they won't speculate except to say they want to be a long way from here by then.*

Joseph and Phillipe looked at each other. 'Then we have some bad news. The Terra truck that Omnicron is sending is the closest vessel and it won't be here for sixty-eight hours, the Coalition has nothing and no others have responded.' Phillipe's reply sounded flat.

Then we're in deep shit. Responded Melissa Stokes, chief operation officer for the Aegis Mining group, her voice edged with defeat. Joseph couldn't think of anything to say.

Molly was absorbed with the nav console. 'Sir, how many shuttles do they have?'

Phillipe shook his head. 'Running in shuttles won't save them... just delay the inevitable. Most don't have a displacement drive and those that do, well, it's only a token unit, only capable of short range hops.'

'Sir, I understand that; but what about the gate? Couldn't they use it to escape?'

Her idea stunned Joseph; he hadn't considered the possibility. 'Melissa, how many shuttles do you have, enough to get everyone off the station?'

Yes, but what good will that do, we can't survive long in shuttles.

"No... but what about your gate? Why not use it to escape? Anywhere will be better than here in a few hours.' Joseph suggested.

The Bridge was now quiet. Singh and Phillipe were working with Molly on something, Latric was busy at the controls, the effects of the gravitational waves were increasing and a steady hand on the controls was required.

Captain, the comm activated again, *our guys here confirm what you suggest may be an option; I am sending a team to activate the gate. We're evacuating Two, it's in deep trouble, and their reactors are already running at one hundred and twenty percent. They can't hold position much longer; but what about Six? We still can't raise them and there's no way they can get here in shuttles. Are you sure there are no other ships close by?*

Singh went back to the comm console and began hailing again, on all frequencies. His efforts were in vain. The closest ship to respond was a Coalition frigate and that was thirty-two hours away. Frustration began to build, there was a way to save these people, but they couldn't get them to the gate in time. Joseph, while not being a religious man, found himself asking for a miracle.

Then it happened.

ITS Amadeus, this is Krell Battle cruiser Zotrik, can we be of assistance?

Joseph answered. 'Captain Nadroc, any assistance will be greatly appreciated, how far away are you?' Neither Nadroc nor Joseph mentioned the obvious issues with a Krell battle cruiser entering Coalition space.

Three hours, at our maximum velocity.

'Fantastic, I'll transmit the coordinates and meet you there. I also suggest a broadcast announcing your intentions of assisting in the rescue.'

It will be done, my friend. Moments later, the announcement began.

This is Captain Nadroc commanding the Krell Battle cruiser Zotrik. We are entering Coalition Space to assist in the rescue of people stranded on Aegis Six. We will remain uncloaked and with our offensive weapons offline for the duration of this rescue. I repeat we will have our weapons offline and are only entering this sector to rescue the miners on Aegis Six.

Five minutes later there was a Coalition response.

Cruiser Zotrik, this is Coalition frigate Eureka, you have no authority to enter Coalition space. Do not breach or we will consider this an act of war and respond accordingly.

Silence followed the transmission; Joseph was first to answer. 'Coalition frigate Eureka, do you understand the seriousness of this situation? If we don't evacuate Aegis Six in the next few hours, over one thousand people will die. Do you understand this?'

The dwell time was still a few minutes, indicating Eureka was a long way off.

That is of no concern to me. My orders are to patrol and stop any Krell incursions into Coalition space. I am only following orders.

'Then whoever issued those orders is a murdering arsehole, just like you.' Joseph couldn't help the outburst. Before any reply could come through, another voice entered the conversation.

This is Silvio Cordoba, President and CEO of Cordoba Corporation and legal entity for the Daldaro region of space. I am formally requesting the Cruiser Zotrik assist in the rescue and, as of this time, I am rescinding all rite of passage to any and all Coalition vessels. Eureka, be warned, if you enter this sector, we will consider it an act of piracy and you will be dealt with accordingly.

Molly summoned Joseph to the nav station. 'Sir, I've pinpointed Eureka's position. The only way she can reach the Belt is by traversing through our system.' The grin on her face told Joseph exactly what he needed to know.

'Activate the comm.' He waited until she signalled him, 'Coalition frigate Eureka, this is Joseph Jones, President and CEO of Argos Limited. We are now the sole authority in the Zedak system; please record this directive.

'All right to navigation of Coalition registered vessels is hereby rescinded. Any Coalition registered vessel, military or commercial entering this system, will be classified as a pirate and dealt with accordingly. I will not repeat this warning. **Do not** enter the Zedak system.' He ran his finger across his throat and Molly cut the comm.

Amadeus, this is Aegis One may I join you on your vessel? Joseph approved and had Latric move closer to the station. A small shuttle approached and docked, one person boarded Amadeus and then the shuttle left. Joseph opened the airlock and greeted his guest.

'Joseph Jones,' he said as he held out his hand.

'Melissa Stokes... pleased to finally meet you. We have something of a problem... the shuttles are now leaving for the gate, but we can't find anywhere to send them.' The woman standing before Joseph was of average height, she had blonde hair and striking blue eyes. Her face showed the signs of extreme stress, something this situation would do to anyone.

'Come with me, I'll have our Navigator look at it for you. Do you need to go back to the station?'

'No, my deputy will handle things now.'

They entered the Bridge and Joseph told Latric to head back to Six; Molly took the newcomer to the nav station. They were deep in discussion for about eight minutes until Molly straightened and beckoned Joseph over.

'Sir there's only one system that they can reach in the shuttles... Zedak.'

Phillipe was standing behind Joseph when Molly spoke, and he couldn't hide his amusement. 'Well done, Joseph. You have just shown your true talent for diplomacy. Believe me this day will be forever marked in our history; talk about David and Goliath!' Phillipe's chuckle developed into a full belly laugh. Joseph grasped the irony of the situation. He smiled, shook his head and turned to the Aegis official.

'We have settled on Argos, formally AG48-5. If you wish, your gate can send the shuttles there, but be warned we have only just arrived on the planet; conditions are basic at best.'

Stokes nodded. 'Still, better than freezing to death in a shuttle with no power. May I call the gate?' She gave the operator the coordinates and then called all the shuttles. After a brief announcement she advised that this was the only viable alternative, and that they would all now survive.

Ten minutes later Latric announced they were coming up on Aegis Six. Stokes called the station and explained what was happening. 'I emphasise that all weapons be deactivated and no-one is to carry any weapons of any type, please confirm.' She finished her call.

Are you sure a Krell cruiser is rescuing us? Almost on cue Zotrik de-cloaked above Amadeus, *I guess that confirms it, ma'am. We will comply, but we've gotta evac quick, the reactors are burning Barainium off the lining; they can't last much longer.*

While Stokes was talking to her people, Joseph had called Nadroc and arranged for Amadeus to be brought aboard his ship. The massive cruiser re-positioned slightly forward and now below Amadeus; a hangar door opened and the path into Zotrik was illuminated.

'Now Mister Latric, I would appreciate it if you could take us inside,' Joseph suggested and Cobal gently edged Amadeus forward. For the first time in two centuries, a human ship berthed inside a Krell warship, Latric performed a perfect landing and gently edged Amadeus into the docking bay allocated to it. He powered the ship down and did the usual atmospheric checks before declaring that they could disembark.

Before they did, Joseph broadcast to the ship, telling them what had happened and asking for all to respect the danger that the Krell crew had placed themselves in to help. Finally, he opened the airlock and extended the boarding ramp; Nadroc waited at the foot of the ramp. Joseph and Stokes led the Bridge team to the waiting welcome.

'Jones, my friend, I didn't think we would meet again, so soon,' Nadroc boomed.

'Neither did I, but I am very glad we can. Thank you, and your crew; you have taken a huge risk to help. We will always be in your debt,' Joseph replied; then introduced Stokes. 'How are you going to collect the crew on Six?'

'We have started to dispatch our troop carrier transports. They will easily accommodate all the crew, and return them to us in safety.' Nadroc took Joseph aside. 'You have risked much to save these people, my friend, more than you needed to. Believe me, it has been noted on Gaddok Prime... the Emperor is interested in meeting you.'

Joseph shook his head, realising just what was at stake, now. 'All I have done is make threats to the Coalition, and alienate us from them. I hope they don't take up the gauntlet... we've got nothing to back up what I threatened.'

'Not true! We have seven ships this size, at your disposal, should anything unwanted happen. As I said, you have impressed the Emperor.'

At that moment, the first shuttle from Six arrived. It was directed to a vacant bay where the fifty aboard were quickly disembarked. Stokes left Amadeus and met her people; she directed them to an assembly area as more shuttles began arriving.

Phillipe joined Joseph and Nadroc. 'Well Joseph, I just spoke to Silvio. He asked if you would head up the inquiry into this event, and also that it be held on Argos. Your style of diplomacy must have struck a chord with him.'

'Why me? Why Argos?'

'Simple,' Phillipe explained. 'Argos is now classed as a sovereign world. Its neutrality gives weight to an impartial investigation and, as for you... he believes you are an honourable man who will only work towards the truth. I took the liberty of directing him there... he'll be waiting when we arrive. Perhaps we should speak to the crew of the freighter... they're at the centre of this.'

They returned to Amadeus and explained the situation to the crew of Lady Philomena.

'Argos? I've never heard of it!' Naismith's blustered. 'I demand this issue be handled by Galactic Freight, not some nobody from an outer world.'

Rajiv Singh couldn't help himself, he grinned and spoke. 'Actually, Mister Naismith, Captain Jones is Prime Citizen on Argos and therefore, under interstellar law Cordoba can request him to be the adjudicating authority. If you care to check the Coalition data base, you'll find what I say is true.'

Singh's comments quietened the situation; Naismith was dumbfounded.

***

'What do you mean, prepare to receive shuttles?' Bruce McGill asked.

Danielle shook her head. 'That's all I know. It was a garbled transmission from Amadeus... and something that sounded like twenty hours.'

McGill stood and started pacing round the room, deep in thought. Finally, he stopped and spoke, 'Dannie, get me all the info we have on the Aegis operation. If I'm correct this is going to be interesting.'

Dannie called up the data he requested, together they scrutinised it. 'Yes!' McGill exclaimed.

'Yes what?' Dannie asked.

'They have a gate, that's how they're sending the shuttles.' He looked at the time on the transmission and now, eight hours had passed. 'Did they send any coordinates?'

'Sort of, but they were a bit confused. We have no idea what the base reference is, that part of the message was lost.'

'Right, let's get to astrogation.' Bruce said as he headed for the door.

One part of all Jones Trading ships was a full astrogation suite, something many traders refused to install because of the cost and space it required. The suite was a holographic generator that could call up any section of space and display it inside a special room, the astrogation chamber.

They both went to the console in the centre of the room. 'Bring up both systems.' Dannie worked the console. 'Now, let's locate that gate.' Even after enhancing the region around Aegis One, nothing showed.

Bruce started pacing again. 'What's your range from the station?'

'A million kliks.'

'Expand it to five. Hang on; check if the system can recognise a gate.' Together they interrogated the system, 'nothing; we'll never find it if the system can't recognise it. Fuck, what do we do now?' Bruce swore.

Dannie was a little confused. 'Why are you looking for an old gate?'

'Because it's the only way these shuttles can get here. Each gate can direct worm holes to a limited number of sectors. Cordoba use them to transport bulk freight, saves them money. But we need a precise location, so we can decipher the actual meaning of the coordinates. We need to know where the shuttles are going to enter sub space. Can we pull the info off the main data base?' Bruce asked as Dannie started to interrogate the system.

Ten minutes of frantic work and she had the data they needed. She fed it into the astrogation program and repeated the search. Instantly, the gate showed up as a red ball, hanging in space 2.5 million kilometres from Aegis One.

'There it is.' Dannie's voice was a whisper as she reduced the magnification of the Daldaro Belt. The Zedak system and the Belt were displayed in their true relationships.

'Using Argos as a base reference, plot a course to that gate.' Dannie's fingers flew across the keyboard and a thin blue line snaked from the Zedak system toward the Daldaro Belt. 'Now, factor in orbital movements for twenty hours from your estimated time the transmission originated.'

'But Sir we could be horribly wrong.' Dannie protested. 'The transmission was badly degraded.'

'Damn it, Dannie. It's all we've got... just do it.' She shrugged, entered the parameters and the celestial ballet was performed. Every planet, asteroid and other body moved as it would in reality, until the twenty hours had transpired. Now the simulation displayed what McGill wanted.

He slowly walked round the room, trying to view the image from different perspectives. 'Hang on a minute, reconfigure using Drake's landing as the reference.'

Dannie complied, the blue line moved slightly. 'Why did you want that?'

'Simple... if I was Joseph I'd use the ship's data base as reference, and Amadeus would have Drake's hangar as its point of origin! Look... how much has the line moved.' He pointed to both tracks now displayed.

The course trace had moved only slightly in the simulation, but in space this small movement equated to 3 million kilometres. 'Now, we use standard navigation rules and put in an outer limit marker.' A few moments passed as the information was loaded. 'There... we need to be right **there** to receive these shuttles.' The simulation now showed a point twenty eight million kilometres from Argos. 'Log that location. We're going to need some help, call the Truck, and see if they have anything that can assist. We only have,' he checked the time, 'nine and a half hours until they arrive... if they arrive at all.'

Chapter 13: Escape

Kidman was ready to depart Earth.

She had loaded all the supplies that Joseph had ordered as well as the two passengers, now settling into their berths. Initially, Gail and HG were to travel on Freedom, but at the last minute they had transferred to Kidman. While she wasn't a cruise liner, Kidman did have a few guest cabins and did quite a fair trade in interplanetary passengers. Gail finished unpacking when the door annunciator buzzed; it was her father.

'What shit has Jonesy got into this time?' HG asked as he entered the cabin.

'So you've read the last comm from him?'

'Not just that... Anderson's contacts have come back to him. Here read this.' He handed his data pad to his daughter. Gail read the report, her face showing increasing fear and stress as she did.

'This can't be true. The Coalition is mobilising against him?'

'Certainly looks like it... he really knows how to keep us entertained.' HG had a quiet laugh.

'Don't be so bloody silly, this is serious! They could send in the military.'

'And what good would that do? It was only a few weeks ago they agreed to his ownership of the system. Hell, even the President ratified the deal and accepted his declaration of neutrality. If they move against them, there'll be hell to pay in the Council Chamber. Besides, how can the military justify attacking a colony for effecting the rescue of three and a half thousand people? If they do, it'll spell the end of the Coalition; even a President as inept as the idiot we have now isn't that stupid.' HG let his opinion of politicians be widely known. Further discussion was cut short by the buzzing from the door. Gail opened it. Standing before her was Captain Tellyz; she stood aside to allow him to enter.

'I trust you are finding our accommodation acceptable?'

'Yes, Captain, most acceptable.' Gail's answer was sincere.

'I have had a communique from Captain Jones; he has asked that we get to Argos with a degree of urgency. To do this we have secured a new departure window; we are currently disengaging from the dock and will leave within the next few minutes. If you wish, I invite you both to the Bridge; some find a departure highly informative.' Tellyz paused for an answer.

'We accept,' HG responded.

'Excellent, if you are ready, we can proceed,' he stood aside to allow Gail to leave first. 'Something interesting... Captain Jones has changed the registration of this vessel, and all his others I believe. Our new home port is Argos.' He said this in his usual matter of fact way but to Gail, there was an undertone of concern.

'Yes, it appears that Argos is now the base for the Independent Traders Guild. I think Captain Jones will encourage all to follow his lead.' Gail knew Joseph's passion for the Guild.

'An astute move... it should remove many of the unfair conditions imposed by Coalition registration,' Tellyz replied. The Bridge door opened and HG and Gail were ushered to the vacant guest seats. Set behind, and slightly elevated from the command position, the guests were given a complete view of the Bridge and, more interestingly, the view screen. As they watched, the huge ship turned away from the dock, appearing to clear the berth by scant millimetres.

'This is Captain Udon Tellyz, commanding ITS Kidman. We have cleared the dock and are proceeding to the outer mark. Thank you for your assistance Dock Commander, we will see you next trip.' Udon then cut the comm and moved to his pilot's side. A short, covert conversation ensued with the pilot nodding in agreement.

Phillip Barton, the First Officer sat beside HG. 'Normally, we keep our speed to approximately point three of light in this sector. But the upper limit is point five; on this trip we will be pushing that.'

'Not breaking any laws, I hope,' HG said, a huge smile splitting his face.

'Just bending them a little,' a conspiratorial wink flashed from Phil's right eye as he returned to his post beside the Captain.

The outer mark was pinpointed on the view screen; Kidman seemed to take forever to reduce the distance to it.

'Outer mark in twenty minutes, Sir; speed now point five-five light.' The Pilot confirmed.

'Sir!' the sensor operator called. 'We have a Coalition patrol ship approaching, port rear quarter.'

'On screen,' Udon ordered.

'They're hailing us.'

'Acknowledge the hail.'

ITS Kidman, this is Coalition patrol ship Scaramouch, you will heave to and allow us to board you.

'And what justification do you have for this action?' Udon challenged as he indicated to the Pilot to keep going.

We believe two prominent citizens of Earth are on board, against their will. You will stop, so we can remove them.

HG stood and approached Udon. 'Captain, allow me to handle this?' Udon nodded.

'Scaramouch, this is HG Mossberg. My daughter and I are the only passengers on this vessel and I assure you we are under no duress.'

Sorry Sir, but my orders are to remove both you and your daughter and take you back to Earth.

'And what idiot issued those orders?'

Sir they come directly from Admiral Cartwright.

'Well listen to me, young man! If you wish to end your career in a blaze of politics, proceed as you are. I am telling **you**, that Bill Cartwright has no jurisdiction over either my daughter or me. Add to that, this vessel is registered to a gazetted neutral planet. If you continue with your present course of action, it will be classified as an act of piracy and you will be branded forever as such.

'Now if Cartwright wishes to end his career that way, it's his choice. But understand this... I will personally have you charged as a pirate and prosecuted to the fullest of the law. You do know the penalty for piracy, don't you?'

But Sir I have my orders. They state that both you and your daughter are to be rescued at all costs.

'Listen, young man, I don't give a flying fuck what that idiot Cartwright has said! I am telling you we are under no threat. We are heading to Argos to purchase property, and for a well-earned holiday. Now, fuck off and tell Bill Cartwright that I said he can do the same!' HG winked at Udon.

'Sir the outer mark...' the Pilot whispered. Kidman had reached the control limit.

'Engage displacement drive.' Moments later Kidman entered the worm hole and disappeared from the solar system.

HG looked at Udon as they entered sub space. 'What was that all about?' He shook his head. 'Talk about a load of crap. Neither of us is worth a kidnap attempt like he suggested.'

Udon nodded in agreement, 'I don't believe you were the issue, just a desperate attempt to board this ship.' He considered his next few words. 'Mister Mossberg, would you please join me in my ready room?' He indicated for Gail to join them as well. As the door closed Udon started the console on his desk. 'Have you heard of the troubles in the Daldaro Belt?'

'Only that there's been some sort of mining accident and that Jones and his crew are involved.'

'I thought as much, a much sanitised version of the truth.' Udon sent the data on his console to the screen. 'This is a log recording from our last Rift Run and following, a copy of an ancestor vision I had afterwards.'

For twenty minutes HG and Gail watched the recordings, the effect becoming more evident from the look of fear and horror their faces wore. As the recording finished HG spoke, 'Frederickson... do you mean... Ernst Frederickson?'

'I believe so. I believe he has been experimenting with some sort of weapon delivered via sub space. I also believe that what we encountered is the result of it detonating prematurely, inside a worm hole. This has led me to the conclusion that the incident in the Belt was caused by this event. If I am correct, then the Coalition is complicit in this, and the attempt to board this ship was a ruse to suppress the information.'

'Does Jonesy know all this?'

'Yes, he has a complete copy.'

'Then, he's in deeper shit than he knows. Stranded on a virgin planet, no real weapons and no one to call for help.' HG turned to Gail. 'Can you get a message to him, using his codes?'

'Yes, I think so.'

'Do it. And I'll try to find out what Ernst is up to.' He saw the concern on Udon's face. 'Don't worry, we have our own sources, and security'

Udon nodded and answered the door annunciator, the Navigator and First Officer entered. 'Navigator, did you file our flight plan as ordered?'

'Yes Sir, exactly as you suggested, but we're not taking that course.'

'I know, thank you. Number One, please initialise all weapons and shields... also raise the alert status to yellow. This may all be a small paranoia, on my part, but I would rather be prepared for any further incidents.' He dismissed the officers and the Mossbergs went to their quarters to work on their part of the puzzle.

***

Freedom had no such troubles; although Joseph had already registered her and her home port as Argos, she was still, technically, owned by Abracorp. The logs indicated she would be undergoing trials for the next two weeks so the bureaucrats ignored her.

Secretly, all her cargo had been delivered to the Abracorp facility in orbit above Earth. After an initial two days in a simulator, the crew were allowed to make a couple of runs in the ship. With these successfully completed, the ship was returned to the dock to undergo some further fine-tuning. In reality, it was a ruse to hide loading the cargo. Two days later, Freedom slipped out of the dock and headed out for her final trials. As she quietly initiated a worm hole, Abracorp filed the final release documentation and Freedom was away, free from any official entanglement.

Don Hopmann sat in the command chair; Allison Thompson taking the Navigator and comms duties, Doug Harris was piloting Freedom and the engineering duties were handled by Gabrielle Simona. This made up the entire crew of this huge ship.

Don had decided against hiring any new crew after his last message from Argos. The interest shown by Coalition officials in when Freedom was to be officially launched reinforced his decision. If all went well, they could handle her from the Bridge. Most functions could be performed by the ship's systems; not his ideal solution, but considering what he read into current events, acceptable.

'Displacement holding firm at fifteen... we should reach Argos in four weeks,' Doug announced.

Don had decided to run hard and deep, cutting two weeks off the normal *Earth to Argos* transit. The designers at Abracorp had been insistent on Freedom's ability to do just what she was doing now; Don now felt that this ship and its attendant capabilities would be needed sooner rather than later.

Freedom's design differed from the usual trader. First she had a moderate cargo capacity of five million tonnes, carried in five holds. Her accommodation could only be described as luxurious – when compared to other trade vessels – and her systems were state of the art. While most trading companies sought to cut costs at every opportunity, the Jones group did the opposite.

The shape of Freedom was different. From the side she looked like an egg – with one end cut square. From above, she appeared to be a flat oval shape, with the end squared. There were no protuberances, no antenna arrays, no displacement spears or towers – her surface looked smooth and moulded. The narrowest part of the bow housed the deflector array; this had emitters running the length of the ship giving the deflector one single control point. The displacement drive emitters were housed in the skin of the ship, allowing for deeper and more accurate worm-hole control. And weapons, where most traders paid this lip service, again, Jones' ships were different.

Every Jones' Group ship had the best and latest defensive and offensive systems available. Freedom may be designed to travel to places not before seen by man, but she was also designed to take care of herself and her crew. Everything was over-specified. She would carry more food and water than most other trade ships even those twice her size; there were no bunk rooms – and the hydroponic garden was extensive.

Joseph had designed her for long trading missions and creature comforts were high on his must have list. And the engines – they were the same as used in the latest Space Corps battle cruisers, giving Freedom massive displacement capability and unequalled in-space performance.

Don smiled to himself. *This ship really is a wolf in sheep's clothing,* he mused.

***

Back on Argos, things had proceeded far quicker than Bruce McGill had expected. Site preparation that he thought would take weeks, only took a few days and the time to move Drake was at hand.

Four huge tugs from Omnicron's ship had arrived at 06:00 and were now attached and ready to start. Bruce sat in the command chair on Drake, while Goran Illych was high above in a small shuttle, orchestrating the entire operation. It had been agreed that only Drake's antigrav system would be used, the real lifting and moving being left up to the tugs.

Drake, this is Illych... prepare for initial lift.

'Roger.' McGill replied. As he did, he felt the powerful tractor systems of the tugs begin to take the strain; this was the most dangerous part of the exercise. With Drake's compromised structural integrity, balance was critical.

Increase antigrav to sixty percent, Illych's voice commanded. Bruce complied. He believed he could feel the old ship protesting and suddenly realised he was holding his breath.

'Come on old girl, just one tiny trip,' he spoke aloud. Everyone on the Bridge was silently asking the same thing. The screen showed a structural diagram of Drake, and the attendant stress points. His primary concern was a section of the upper spine where they had discovered the worst cracking. A series of temporary struts had been installed to hold the structure, but it was showing signs of excessive stress.

'Hold on Goran, we've got a small problem with the struts.' Bruce's hands flew over the console as he balanced the antigrav system to improve the load distribution. It worked and the stress levels in the critical area dropped back into the safe zone. 'Ok we're right to proceed.'

Almost at a snail's pace, the tugs increased their efforts on Drake. Reluctantly the old ship lifted, finally breaking contact with the ground altogether, Bruce increased the power to the antigrav, compensating for the lifting effect of the tugs. Now the system was running at eighty-five percent.

Drake, how's your stress levels?

'All in the green... Drake's ready to move.'

Gradually the tugs began to drag Drake forward, keeping her fifty metres above the ground. The old ship protested – groaning and creaking constantly. Bruce kept a close eye on the stress levels, compensating for any peaks he detected.

While the distance from the landing site to Drake's new permanent home was only a few kilometres, it took nearly an hour to lift and move her; the tension on the Bridge of Drake growing every minute.

Dannie was manning the comm suite. 'Sir, we're getting a message from Amadeus.'

'Dannie, I don't care. We've got our hands full at the moment Record it, and we'll listen later.' McGill replied, curtly.

The final half hour of the operation was the worst. Bruce knew what Joseph's long term plan for Drake was and correct orientation of the ship was critical. Slowly and deliberately the tugs reduced height, holding Drake ten metres off the ground. Next, they had to turn her one hundred and eighty degrees so the forward observation lounge had an uninterrupted view of the original landing site.

Another twenty minutes passed and now, with orientation correct, Drake had to be gently lowered to the prepared foundations. Not someone easily impressed, even Bruce McGill was amazed by the skill of the tug operators as they effortlessly lowered Drake to her final resting place.

The foundations were a complex structure designed to hold and spread the mass of Drake over the site. Antigrav would be needed only until Freedom arrived with the materials needed to make a permanent repair to the backbone of the old ship. Bruce kept one eye on the stress readouts as he incrementally decreased the power to the antigrav system.

Two of the four tugs had detached and the final duo had reduced their tractor systems so that the vast majority of the bulk of Drake was now supported by the foundations and her systems. Finally, the last two tugs shut down and Drake was on her own.

Gradually, Bruce reduced antigrav power further, achieving an acceptable balance between stress and power consumption. Finally, with just fifteen percent of the system operating the outcome was much better than anyone imagined; Drake was finally home.

'Drake to Omnicron Tug control... Drake is secure. Thank you for an excellent job.' Bruce slumped back into the command chair, clearly tired and relieved.

Our pleasure, the old girl looks like she belongs there.

'Well, she's never going anywhere again. How about you and your guys join me later for a drink?' Bruce asked. Goran replied, *I thought you'd never ask... how about seventeen hundred?*

'Done,' Bruce cut the comm link. 'OK Dannie, let's hear what the Captain has to say?'

'Sorry Sir, I can't... it's addressed to you and encrypted.'

'Ok, send it to the ready room console.' He stood and walked to the door. *This can't be good,* he thought as he entered the ready room.

Bruce was extremely tired; slowly he sat in the chair and activated the console. He called up the message, the screen held a jumble of letters, numbers and symbols, unintelligible. He activated the decryption program and the screen morphed into a clear message; he read it, swore out loud, and read it again.

'What the fuck are you playing at Joe?' he groaned. 'We're too old for all this shit.' He was about to swear again when the buzz from the door stopped him. 'Come in,' he growled.

Goran Illych walked in; one look at Bruce told him everything. 'Had a message from your Captain I see?' Bruce nodded. 'Don't worry, I got one from my boss too; looks like we're going to be in the middle of some rather heavy shit.'

'Yeah, that doesn't really worry me that much; it's the three and a half thousand extra bodies he's bringing back that concern me. Where are we going to put them and how will we feed them?' Bruce commented.

'Accommodation's, no problem... we have a number of prefab mining accommodation blocks on the ship, easily house them. We can have them down here and constructed, fully, in two days. The civil works here have already been done to take them; Alvaris thought they'd be a good start for Argos. They may not be luxury, but they are comfortable and dry.

'Food is another issue. We have sufficient on our ship for our people for the next three months, so we could spare some, but I think indigenous sources will need to be more heavily exploited. It's the Coalition inference that worries me. What's your take?'

Bruce agreed and activated the comm. 'Dannie, get in here!' He barked.

'Bit snarly,' Goran chipped back.

Dannie opened the door and cautiously entered. 'Yes Sir?'

'Sorry, Dannie, just a tired, cranky old man,' Bruce turned the console toward her.

From the moment Amadeus had left, Dannie had assumed a lot of responsibility. While she was Loadmaster she was also a qualified and first-rate engineer, a licensed pilot and navigator. Bruce had been impressed with her performance and had already placed a message on Joseph's message board recommending a promotion.

Dannie shook her head. 'This must be a mistake, surely?'

'No mistake, Alvaris has confirmed it. Where are we up to with that sensor system Udon dumped here?'

'Well, all we needed was to move Drake. Now, we need to tune the receivers and test the system; all the sensor drones are in place.' Dannie spoke with confidence.

'And what is the range?'

'Not sure until we test, but we should have long-range capacity of around three to five light years from the system; and I believe we can have it up and running in a couple of hours. We can fine tune as we go.'

'Good, then get your team on it, we may need it soon.' Bruce dismissed her.

The next hour was spent analysing the logistics of suddenly having all the extra people to house and feed. Boris and the Doctor were called in to discuss food supply and how to augment it. Meat supply would be Ok for a short while. As the meat from the Dab Korac needed an extended time to age, Boris had stocked up rather well, but even that wasn't going to be enough. He was tasked with increasing the supply dramatically, and he left to arrange a harvesting team.

The Doctor had approved several of the fish and plants as being suitable for consumption; the only problem was catching enough marine creatures. Shore based fishing was ok for a small group but now it wouldn't do much. The solution was in orbit above them. The Terra Truck was equipped with a number of aquatic craft that could be used as fishing boats. Goran left to make the arrangements for both the boats and the accommodation.

Finally alone, Bruce went to the cupboard on the side of the room, poured a stiff scotch and sat back in the chair. He sipped the amber liquid, relishing in the fact that Joseph really knew a good scotch. He reclined the chair and within a few minutes was fast asleep; his first downtime in over two days.

Chapter 14: Settlement

Joseph felt some trepidation as he accompanied Nadroc to the Bridge; it had been two centuries since any human had been on a Krell ship, let alone on the Bridge.

How the war started was lost in time, but Joseph believed it had to be because of human greed; all he knew for certain was that four Presidents and five Emperors had continued the fight. Now there was a chance of some reconciliation. Steven Chang, the incoming President, was a moderate who favoured talking instead of shooting. The current Krell Emperor was an unknown, but Joseph believed that if the current situation was any indication, Gorth Todarij may also be ready to talk.

The Bridge was similar to any ship of the Coalition; there was a command chair, various operational stations and the view screen. The command chair on a Krell ship was normally placed above and behind all other stations, set against the rear wall of the Bridge for security. It was well-known that one of the ways for an officer to be promoted was to kill his Captain and take command.

Humans called this mutiny, to a Krell it was just business as usual. Here on the Zotrik it was in the more conventional human setting, behind the pilot and navigator, but in line with the other stations. It seemed that the rumours of a softening in Krell philosophy were accurate.

Nadroc stood beside the command chair. 'Today is an auspicious one,' he began. 'For the first time in over two hundred years, this crew, and those of Captain Jones have proved that Krell and human can work together for the common good. Our actions have been endorsed and approved by the Emperor himself, so each one of you should feel proud of what has been achieved.'

The announcement was met with cheers and, what looked like fighting – punches and slaps – simply Krell congratulating Krell. 'While we have the opportunity, we will record as much of the phenomena as we can, but once all the shuttles have left, we will follow them to Argos.' He turned to Joseph. 'Now, Captain, allow me to introduce my Bridge crew.'

The introductions and discussions that followed were open and sincere, not at all what Joseph expected.

'Captain, we have arrived,' the pilot advised. The view screen was filled with the gate, hovering in space. 'Sir, the last shuttle is entering the event horizon.' As these words reached Joseph's ears, the shuttle was surrounded by a brilliant blue flash then it vanished. The gate was programmed to hold the worm hole event horizon open for ten minutes. At that time it would shut down and the worm hole would start to collapse from this end – the source. All eyes on the Bridge now returned to the chaos that was the Daldaro Belt.

Nadroc stood in awe. 'This is what the birth of the universe must have looked like.' The mad jumble of asteroids hurtled towards the central core, their speed increasing exponentially until they slammed into the huge ball of rubble adding their mass to the already unstable pile. 'Science station, what are the readings?'

The officer manning the station looked up, disbelief etched on his face. 'Unbelievable Sir, we've never seen anything like it. The temperatures are as hot as our sun and the gravity fluctuations are incredible.' As he spoke, alarms started screaming, the huge ship lurched and the view screen changed again.

'What was that?' Nadroc called.

The science officer worked his station frantically. 'Huge gravity spike, look at the gate... it's starting to break up!' His words were true. Before their eyes the massive gate began to deform; bits flew off directly towards the centre of the Belt.

'Pilot, time for us to leave,' Nadroc commanded and the pilot fed more power to the huge drive system. Zotrik began to sluggishly pull away from the melee. 'Faster please pilot.'

The pilot called for full emergency power, the massive MAM reactors fed raw energy into the converters and the drive screamed in protest. 'Main drive at full power sir,' the ship's acceleration began climbing, almost imperceptibly at first, but, as each second passed, everyone knew they were increasing the distance from the Belt.

'Pilot, is the hyper drive powered?'

'Yes Captain, powered and on standby, but the gravity fluctuations make it impossible to transfer to hyperspace.' The look on the pilot's face was the closest to fear that Joseph had ever seen, on a Krell.

Nadroc moved to the navigation console. 'Agreed, but we're not going to initiate a full insertion.' He worked quickly and effortlessly at the console, plotted a course and entered it into the navigation system. 'Pilot, on my mark, initiate a jump into hyperspace for exactly twelve seconds. When we re-emerge, perform an emergency stop. Do you understand?'

'Not really Sir, but I will comply.'

'Excellent. Now everyone; brace yourself, this may be rough. Five seconds, four, three, two, one, mark.'

As Nadroc called the word mark, the pilot obeyed and Zotrik was thrown into hyperspace. Twelve seconds later she re-entered normal space and the Pilot reversed the engines. A ship the size and mass of Zotrik doesn't stop instantly – it took nearly two hundred thousand kilometres for her to come to a complete stop.

'Science officer... readings please.'

'All normal Captain no influence from the Belt.'

'Thank you. Navigator... plot our course to Argos and get us there as quickly as you can.'

The reply came immediately. 'Course is in the system, we can enter hyperspace in six minutes on heading one-five-five by zero-two-four. Our speed needs to be thirty-five percent of light.'

Very good; Pilot, please begin.'

Joseph felt the huge ship begin to accelerate again, turning to the new course.

***

In the Daldaro Belt, events were accelerating. The huge displacement gate began to break up; pieces started flying off the structure and were drawn into the vortex that was now at the centre of the event. Predictably the structure failed completely and the remaining sections of the gate crashed into the vortex.

Two of these were the huge MAM reactors and their anti-matter plasma tanks. What happened next would be debated for centuries. When that much anti-matter collides with a matter ball of the concentration in the vortex, there should be a massive explosion, as both particles annihilate each other. This didn't happen; the energy released was absorbed by the growing matter ball, increasing the gravity well and dragging much more into it. This fed the reaction and was the tipping point, no explosion, but the formation of a new star.

***

Zotrik reinserted back in the Zedak system, one million kilometres from Argos. All the crew from Lady Philomena, Aegis Six and Amadeus were on board. Joseph stood at the foot of the boarding ramp, Nadroc beside him. 'I agree it's better this way. Still, I am saddened that after all you have done, we still have this problem.'

'My friend, let's look on the bright side. Maybe what we have achieved will be the start of a true reconciliation. Unfortunately for now, we must observe the conventions. But remember, we will be close if you need us.' Nadroc smiled as he drew his fist over his heart. 'Farewell Captain.'

Joseph acknowledged the salute and walked up the ramp. Minutes later Amadeus was outside the Krell ship and heading for Argos, Joseph switched the view screen to port in time to watch Zotrik engage her cloak and disappear.

Amadeus took up position in the vanguard of the shuttle convoy. Forty two Krell shuttles and Amadeus holding fifteen hundred and thirty-five survivors began their final journey to Argos. The plan was simple, rendezvous with the Omnicron ship, and then down to the surface.

Unlike the other survivors, this group was able to descend to the surface. The Krell transport shuttles were capable of both space and atmospheric operation. All the others were not so lucky; the mining shuttles were designed as tough work boats, able to operate in the hostile environment of the Belt. Trying to land one on

Argos would be the same as trying to float a lead brick in water.

What greeted them was nothing like what they left, just six short days ago. Drake was permanently fixed in her new location and a small city had begun to grow. Accommodation blocks were being constructed to the north of Drake and other constructions needed for human habitation were in process. Cobal gently orientated Amadeus for a landing in her hangar on Drake and without any fanfare, she was home. Bruce McGill was waiting as the access ramp was lowered.

'Welcome back, Skipper. You had some fun I hear?'

'Thanks, Bruce. You could say we had an interesting journey. We have fifteen guests with us. Can you have accommodation on Drake arranged?' Joseph asked.

The request was not expected but Bruce knew that Joseph must have his reasons. 'I'll get someone on it straight away.'

'Thanks.' Joseph clapped his friend on the shoulder. 'Give me half an hour then come to my quarters; we've got heaps to discuss.'

Bruce nodded and turned to the crew from Lady Phil. 'If you would all follow me, we'll see what accommodation we can sort out for you.' He turned and started for the exit, the others following. Joseph turned back to his small crew.

'I want to thank you for the past few days. I know it's been tense and tiring but every one of you excelled, and we managed to save three and a half thousand people; people who would have died if we weren't there. So, thank you and now get lost, I don't want any of you on duty for at least three days.'

Broad smiles greeted his order, and they all headed for the exit. Joseph smiled. He had watched the relationship between Cobal and Molly progress over the last six days.

Things are happening, looks like the first Argosan romance. His smile broadened at this thought as he left the hangar and took the lift to his quarters.

His first task was a shower. He stood under the water for ten minutes, letting the flow wash away the tension of the last few days. Feeling better, Joseph dressed and ordered a coffee from the dispenser, sat at his desk and started to scan his messages. He had only started when the door annunciator sounded. Bruce had arranged for them to tour the construction site, and they left for the ground transport.

Goran Illych was driving and gave his companions a running commentary, his pride in the efforts of his crew obvious. 'The accommodation is pretty basic. This building beside us now is one of the dormitories... at each end are the amenities So far, we have completed enough for twenty-six hundred. By the end of next week we should have enough for everyone.'

'I can't believe you've done this is such a short time.' Joseph was amazed at the progress they had made.

'We should have had them all up, but we ran into some issues on the site that slowed us down; still not a bad result.' Goran grinned from ear to ear.

The buildings weren't the most beautiful Joseph had ever seen, looking more like freight containers with windows.

'They won't win any prizes for beauty, but they're strong, dry and comfortable. We use them for initial or short term mining operations and if miners don't complain, no one will... believe me!' Goran chuckled. 'Each block houses five hundred in rooms of no more than four, and each room is a suite with separate sleeping area and lounge.'

He stopped the vehicle so they could physically inspect a building. It was as Goran described, functional but comfortable. The rooms were light and appeared spacious. All the bed systems were comfortable anti grav units.

'What about services. All this must use heaps of power?' Bruce asked.

'Easy, we have two sources on this construction. Each block has its own battery and solar system that assists a small MAM unit... power is never an issue, believe me if a miner's bed fails, we would know in short order,' Goran explained. 'As for the other services, we will run a water supply from the river, through a filtration system, so water won't be an issue. That should all be finished at the same time as the construction.

'These units were last used on Daldius four, now that place is hell. Dry, shit soil... nothing really grows. Our solution was simple. These blocks have a recycling system. Waste is channelled into a composting plant and in approximately twenty-four hours we can produce ten litres of nutrient rich liquid from every one hundred litres of waste. Organic waste from the kitchens is handled by a separate system. Back on Daldius four we ended up with a very productive vegetable garden, actually grew far more than the miners could use, they started packaging the excess and selling it to other marginal outposts.'

'Impressive. It appears you have everything under control.' Joseph finished his tour and they headed back to Drake. Goran left them and went back to his crew.

Finishing the construction was now more important than ever, over one thousand people had nowhere to sleep until the work was done.

As Goran left, Joseph looked to the north; the Krell shuttles had deposited their passengers and were leaving to rendezvous with Zotrik before she left the system. A fleeting feeling of apprehension washed over him. He was saddened that because of the stupidity of politics they had to leave. Even after Zotrik had been instrumental in saving so many, war was still more important. He wished this would change, and soon.

Joseph and Bruce continued with the inspection, the preparations were well advanced for the influx of people. Food was now in reasonable supply. The work boats from the Terra Truck had proved to be excellent fishing platforms, and the stasis larders were now well stocked.

In conjunction with the seafaring food supply, Boris and his hunting parties had the ageing lockers well supplied with meats from a number of sources now. The local plants had proved to be an abundant supply of nutritious vegetables, pleasing the Doctor and his medical staff. Joseph was now fully informed with all Argosan progress, so he and Bruce returned to his quarters.

'I think this calls for a small celebration,' Joseph grinned as he opened a small cupboard. He removed an old bottle of Scotch. 'I've been saving this for the right occasion. My father gave it to me, over a hundred years ago and I think he would agree that this is the right time.'

He poured two generous measures and handed one to Bruce. 'Now you see why we, you and I, will be spending much less time in space,' he raised his glass. 'To a job well done, thank you Bruce, you've worked a miracle.'

'Thank you, but it was really Goran and his crew; I've never seen anything like it. Each day they seemed to move mountains,' Bruce's words showed how much respect he had for the Omnicron crew. 'But yes, I know what you are getting at. We'll have so much to do from now on, now that we actually have a settlement.'

As Bruce finished speaking, Joseph noticed a small icon flashing on his console; it was a message from Mossberg and Partners. He motioned for Bruce to sit and opened the message. It was a video recording from HG himself, detailing what had happened as Kidman tried to leave Earth. He also said that he had contacted Anderson to do some snooping and said he would contact again if he had any information.

HG finished with his usual dig by asking Joseph if he was going to make an honourable woman of his daughter; he never stopped trying. Joseph looked over to Bruce. His face told the story.

'Now things get serious! I'd better check how that sensor system you appropriated is getting on... I have a feeling we're going to need it.' Bruce drained his glass and left.

Joseph returned to his message board, the remainder were a mixed bag. A number of independent traders expressed interest in his proposal to base their operations on Argos, some were still hesitant. There was also a demand from Galactic that he return their crew for an internal investigation into the deliberate sabotage of the freighter Lady Philomena.

His reply was short, indicating that he had been asked by the ruling authority of the Aegis outpost, the Cordoba Corporation, to hold the crew and conduct an initial investigation. Only after consulting with representatives of Cordoba could he release any of the crew. Joseph did suggest that they send a representative to Argos to assist in the investigation.

He read his reply, smiling to himself. *Now we'll see what you bastards are really up to,* he thought as he transmitted it.

Sitting back, he poured another scotch and checked the time, 24:04 was displayed. Joseph drained his whisky and the exhaustion of the last week suddenly hit him. *You're too old for this crap*, he chided himself as he stood and went to his bedroom. *Still, tomorrow is another day.* Within minutes, he was sleeping soundly.

Chapter 15: The Die is Cast

His stride was measured; a perfect parade ground .75 metre.

Admiral William Cartwright, Commander of the Coalition of Earth Planets Space Corps was on the way to his office. He had just arrived from an inspection of Mars base, the new training facility and home to the solar system defence net. As he entered his office, his communicator chimed.

'Cartwright here,' he listened to the caller, his face slowly draining of colour. 'He said what?'

Sir, he said that I should fuck off, and he said you should do the same. Ferdor Zhirov, Commander of the frigate Scaramouch, waited, believing his career was now finished. Instead, he was greeted with a chuckle.

'Don't worry about it... that's definitely HG Mossberg; seems our information was flawed. Good work Commander, resume your normal patrol.' The Admiral's words were music to the young officer's ears.

Yes Admiral, thank you Sir. Relief was etched into Zhirov's voice.

Cartwright was angry. He had a real problem now. He switched on the security suppressor making the room absolutely secure. He opened the middle left-hand drawer of his desk, removed a false panel and took out another communicator. This one was different to the standard issue for the military. He tapped an icon, selected the recipient and made the call.

There was no voice answer, just the call being connected. 'Interception failed, rendezvous coordinates to follow.' Cartwright tapped another icon and the data package was sent. Confirmation of receipt ended the call. He sat back in his chair and initiated one more call. 'Professor, we would like another demonstration, if your modifications are complete?' The person on the other end of the call affirmed that the mods were complete and that the system would work perfectly.

'Excellent, I'm sending the data package now. You will have a window of six hours.' Cartwright didn't wait for any response. He ended the call, replaced the communicator and began to scroll through his schedule for the day.

***

'Sir, there is a problem with the insertion of one of the trade ships.' The junior flight controller handed her data pad to her chief. Lieutenant Commander Jeffery Norwich took the unit and examined the data. He was tired, having just completed a double shift. His relief had called in sick so Jeffery had no option but to stay on duty. He took the pad and scrolled through the data. If this was correct, it would mean hours of examination and reports, something he didn't want.

'Ensign, these traders are all loose cannons... a few seconds to them could mean the loss of a deal. They do this constantly.' Norwich looked at the young officer; the earnest look on her face told him she wouldn't be easily placated. 'Leave it with me, I'll analyse the data and if it appears that there is a real problem, I'll action the report. Go back to your station; I'll call you if I find anything.'

The young officer saluted and returned to her console. *Was I ever as young and dedicated as her?* Norwich grinned. He took the data pad to the control desk, called up the ship flight data and plan and began his analysis; fifteen minutes later, he made his decision.

'Ensign,' he motioned for the young woman to return. 'I have analysed the data and looked at who was in command of the ship. Captain Udon Tellyz is a dedicated officer, one of Jones Trading's best earners but somewhat prone to cutting things fine. If you analyse the flight plan, they'll end up slightly out of position on their exit from the worm hole, in dead space. All this does is force them to correct course, nothing else. I don't see any reason to log this issue, the only one disadvantaged is Tellyz.'

He paused noting the expression on the Ensign's face. 'Excellent work, to notice a deviation that small shows real dedication. Well done!' Norwich handed her data pad back, she smiled and saluted.

'Thank you Sir, I try to be efficient.'

Norwich dismissed her and turned just as the next shift entered. He approached the shift Captain and gave his report, making no mention of Kidman's departure.

***

'Captain Tellyz, we're coming up on our registered insertion point,' Phil Barton, Kidman's First Officer announced.

'Is everything ready?'

'Yes, all ready.' Barton smiled as he spoke.

'Then proceed; Number One,' Tellyz ordered.

Barton and the chief engineer stood by their consoles, monitoring what looked like a countdown. When the numbers reached zero, something was jettisoned from the ship.

'Drone away... its displacement is holding. Thirty seconds to insertion,' the engineer called. The drone was her idea. The engineering team had modified it to emit a higher sensor response than normal; they had also reprogrammed the transponder on it to mimic Kidman's. When the drone re-entered normal space it would mimic Kidman, only a close visual inspection would tell the difference. The seconds crawled by.

'Normal space reinsertion now... Drone data recording holding.' The Bridge was silent, waiting to see if the suspicions of their guests were justified. Twenty seconds, forty; every additional second that passed could be a good sign, or an indication that their ruse had failed. Kidman had only two minutes left before she also would reappear in normal space.

Barton stared at his console intently. 'Sir, the drone's picking up something at extreme range.'

'What?'

'Can't tell exactly, it has no transponder, and the sensor system can't identify it.' Then his console went dead. 'Drone has been destroyed.'

Udon turned to his guest, his face a grim mask. 'Looks like you were right Mister Mossberg.'

'Wish I wasn't... this doesn't bode well for Jonesy. Still, if that worked, we're all now dead, so we could be the ace in the hole.'

***

On board Freedom, Gabby Simona took the command chair; for the next ten hours she was running the ship. Since they left Earth, the new ship had been running perfectly, and she was impressed. The way the new AI systems were integrated, but still subservient to human command, was brilliant. It meant that one person could operate the ship for extended periods if necessary.

While her watch meant she was responsible for their safe passage, it gave her time alone; time to study the engineering of the ship. They had transitioned back into displacement mode two hours ago, just before she took over. She sipped her coffee and called up the final schematic of the drive system, quickly becoming engrossed in the simple harmony of the design. Gabby's thoughts were rudely interrupted by the computer.

Duty officer Simona, please check aft sensor readings, I am detecting an anomaly in our displacement field.

Gabby moved to the sensor console, brought up the aft array and began her analysis. A few minutes later she spoke. 'Well done computer. It appears that something is caught in our displacement wake.' She switched the console, deciding that the main viewer would give better resolution. 'Computer can you enhance the object.' The computer obeyed and the object now filled the screen, Gabby's blood ran cold. 'Computer, analyse image? What is it?' The question was unnecessary; she knew full well what was behind them.

It appears to be a modified mark nine torpedo, and it is generating its own displacement field.

While the computer was talking, Gabby was busy at the nav console. 'Computer, please confirm my findings.'

Your calculations are correct, the torpedo is advancing... it will impact with Freedom in twelve minutes.

Again, Gabby worked the nav console. 'Computer, please analyse and confirm the navigation data I have just input.' Simultaneously, she hailed the Captain.

Your navigation data is sound, but not advised.

'I know, just keep monitoring the torpedo and run the navigation scenario.' Again Gabby hailed the Captain, this time she was rewarded by a very groggy voice.

'What's the problem, Gabby?' Don Hopmann asked.

'Don, I need you on the Bridge **now**! We've got company.'

'Two minutes.'

Right on time Don Hopmann entered the Bridge. 'Ok Gabby, what's the flap?'

'We have a mark nine torpedo, equipped with a displacement drive, closing in on us... impact in less than ten minutes.'

Don studied the data, and swore. 'Damn! It appears they don't want us getting away.'

'Don, there's something else... remember Udon's ancestor vision? Take a look at this.' Gabby worked the screen controls. 'I had the computer analyse the sensor logs from our last insertion.'

The screen changed, now it showed their insertion into hyperspace, but then another image coalesced. A second ship and this ship fired something directly into the displacement wake of Freedom. 'Remind you of something?'

'The ship Udon saw in his vision,' Don gasped, 'unbelievable.' A warning from the computer spurred him into action. 'Computer, wake everyone up, sound red alert.' He turned back to Gabby. 'How long until impact?'

Gabby started to answer as the red alert alarm screamed throughout the ship. Everyone was awake now. 'Eight and a half minutes.'

'And how long until we have no alternative?'

'Less, we need to leave the wormhole no later than eight minutes from now,' Gabby answered.

Don picked up the ship comm. 'This is the Captain, we have an emergency situation; all crew prepare to abandon ship. Don emergency evac suits and enter rescue pods. Gabby and I are trying to resolve the situation, but we now have less than eight minutes to prepare.' Don waited for any response, none came. The crew were professionals and would obey. Questions would be answered later, if they survived. He turned to Gabby. 'That goes for us too, get into the suit.'

Together they opened the evac pods and pulled out a suit. The suit was designed to sustain life for a maximum of five days, even outside of a ship; the pod it was attached to could triple this time. They stripped and pulled on the suits.

'Computer, disengage displacement drive as programmed, confirm.'

Confirmed, displacement drive will be deactivated in four minutes and six seconds. Captain, the crew members are in their pods, I suggest you do the same. Don knew it was pointless to argue, the computer was right. He and Gabby entered their respective pods and locked the hatch. If the worst happened, the system would drop them out of the ship; then the real fun would start. Being ejected from a ship while still in a worm hole wasn't something any of them had ever done and none wanted to be the first.

The calm, measured voice of the computer echoed in his ears. *Time to impact two minutes thirty-eight seconds... time to drive shut down; two minutes.*

It continued every thirty seconds, *time to drive shutdown ninety seconds.* Reference to the impact had been removed.

Time to drive shut down sixty seconds.

Time seemed to stretch, every second felt like an hour, Don felt his heart rate increase and his breathing quicken. He'd been in space most of his life and couldn't remember being this afraid before.

Gabby was in the same shape, her heart pounding, she felt it was going to burst out of her chest.

Time to drive shutdown, thirty seconds.

Don said a silent prayer to whatever godhead may be listening; then the voice returned.

Drive shutdown in ten-nine-eight-seven-six-five-four-three-two-one; displacement drive now offline. Don waited for ten more seconds before opening the pod, Gabby exited a few seconds later.

Anomaly still in displacement mode, impact probability, zero.

They removed the evac suits and stood facing each other, not quite believing what had just happened. Then, realising they were naked, reached for their clothes.

'Computer, cancel red alert, and have the crew report to the Bridge,' Don directed as he dressed.

'I still can't believe this,' Gabby started to speak, only to be cut off by Don.

'We're not out of the woods yet. That thing is still out there, remember what it did in the Rift?' Don resumed command and Gabby began to interrogate the sensors. 'Find it, Gabby for the sake of the galaxy, find the bloody thing.'

The Bridge access door opened and the rest of the crew rushed in, questions as to why the drill had been called on their lips. When the explanation was given, everyone assumed their posts. Finding the torpedo was no longer a matter of just their survival – another tear like the Rift could do untold damage.

Seconds passed. Every eye strained trying to find the torpedo, every sensor at maximum, every console scanning a different sector.

'Keep watch for the ship that launched the bloody thing... it may still be close!'

Gabby was desperately scanning the projected path the torpedo was taking, nothing showed. 'I don't understand, unless it's still in displacement mode, I should be getting something.'

Nobody made a sound – their survival was in Gabby's hands. Another minute passed, and then she cried out.

'Got it; co-ordinates zero-two-five by zero-one-zero.' She placed the icon on the screen.

'Computer, full power to shields and deflectors... bring the weapons systems on line.' Don ordered. Weapons, the one system they hadn't had time to test. Now they needed them.

Freedom was equipped with the normal blaster and disruptor systems, four forward torpedo tubes and two aft. She also had been fitted with a new type of energy weapon - a Plasma cannon. No one had actually fired it; they had all only seen simulations.

'Computer, run an intercept scenario. What weapons will be most effective?' Don knew that a target as small as a torpedo would be hard to destroy, if it was fitted with AI. Most torpedoes were basically dumb, with only targeting and tracking systems. They were designed to ram a target, not fight one. But this unit had a displacement drive and that required far more intelligence to operate than a standard torpedo carried, the logical conclusion was AI.

The scenario ran and the result was predictable — the blasters took it out comfortably.

'Computer, modify the scenario... equip the torpedo with AI, simulate it being able to defend itself.' This time the result was different — blaster and disruptors were problematic — the torpedo seemed to be able to easily avoid the weapons.

Next the computer added the plasma cannon. This time the result was what they wanted. While the simulation took a number of attempts, the torpedo was eventually destroyed. 'Right, there's our solution, Gabby what's it up to?'

The screen showed the torpedo moving slowly toward Freedom. 'In search mode, it hasn't found us as yet.'

'Comms, is there any signal being transmitted or received by it?'

The comms operator shook his head. 'Nothing, or nothing we can detect.'

'Good, I think it's running autonomously, but that won't last. Whoever fired that thing will soon take control; we need to terminate it now. Helm, head toward the bloody thing, maximum acceleration.'

The pilot obeyed Don's command and Freedom began to accelerate.

'Computer, I just set up three firing solutions. As soon as it detects us, start firing using those solutions **only**.' Don moved back to the command chair. 'Transfer plasma cannon control to this station.'

Gabby moved close to Don. 'Skipper, are you sure? Won't the AI learn the patterns?'

'I bloody well hope so. One of the selling points of any AI system is that it learns, right?'

Gabby nodded in agreement.

'That means it can be taught,' Don winked. 'Believe me I'm counting on it being a good student.'

A voice from behind called out. 'Torpedo turning, I think it found us.' As the words rang through the Bridge, the screen showed the torpedo turning and accelerating towards them. Even though the range was extreme, the computer obeyed Don's command and started firing the weapons in the set patterns. The torpedo easily evaded them at that range, but the gap was closing rapidly and the manoeuvres became more violent each time.

'Computer, I just entered another two firing patterns, incorporate them in the sequence.' Simultaneously, Don's fingers flew over the icon pad on his console. 'Pilot, I have a course correction coming to you. Execute on my mark, understood?'

The plasma cannon could hold four charges; Don powered it up and loaded four into the storage chamber. As they developed he programmed in a final firing solution for the cannon.

'Computer, on my mark initiate the plasma solution I programmed. Pilot, execute the course change the instant the last plasma charge is away.' The pilot again acknowledged the order, but he was secretly worried as to the outcome.

'Distance to target, one hundred thousand kilometres.' Gabby called out.

Don watched the firing sequence. When the first program began to repeat, he issued new commands, 'computer fire plasma on my command;' he watched the blaster firing sequence. As the final bolt from the port blaster erupted from the ship he called, **'Fire!'**

Two things had to happen for Don's plan to work; first the target had to respond as he predicted second, the plasma cannon had to be fired at exactly the right moment. A fraction of a second too soon or late, and it was all over for Freedom.

The torpedo responded as predicted. As the last blaster bolt fired, and a second before the first disruptor fired, it violently changed course to port and dived, as it had learned from the previous attacks. The computer worked correctly and sent the four balls of highly charged anti-matter plasma towards the target.

As Don predicted it reacted to the first two and avoided them completely. The third slammed into its meagre shields, overloading them and the final shot impacted directly mid ship. The target exploded into a huge ball of charged energy.

Freedom was accelerating away at full throttle, but the shock wave still slammed into her. Inertial dampeners and external shields compensated for the energy rush and, except for minor turbulence, she weathered the blast well.

'Navigator, time to our next insertion point?' Don asked, his voice evidence of the relief he felt.

'Sixty two seconds,' a puzzled voice answered from the nav console.

'Excellent... helm, complete insertion as programmed. Now, I think we should check the holds, make sure nothing has broken loose. Lieutenant Simona, I believe you have the watch.'

'Aye Sir, I do. I'll keep the sensors at maximum for another thirty minutes.' She replied as the others left the Bridge and Freedom transitioned back to sub space.

***

Admiral Cartwright glanced at his console, 18:30 blinked in the top left corner. It had been a long day, and he had just finished his report to the Council on the Mars training project. He was stiff, having been cooped up in the office all day working on it. He stood and stretched.

Bill Cartwright was a fairly tall man with regulation cut brown hair. His face betrayed his age and, even with hair regularly coloured, he looked like a man approaching his 250th birthday.

He stood in front of the mirror, observing his reflection, the steel blue eyes were cold and hard, something that his ex-wife had told him was his worst feature. He smiled. *Fuck her, she'll soon be laughing on the other side of her face.* Their separation and divorce had taken a huge toll on him; both his children had sided with their mother and deserted him. Now alone, he had thrown himself into his job and had little outside the Corps.

Then he noticed the small red light on the desk drawer flash three times – he had a message. He returned to the desk, opened the drawer and took the communicator out of its hiding place. He switched the security system on before he activated the unit. Two messages were indicated.

Prototype test success confirmed. Target eliminated. No adverse results indicated.

The second was similar. *Target eliminated as planned.*

These told him everything was now back on track. He replaced the covert unit, deactivated the security field, and placed a call on his official communicator. He was answered by a familiar voice.

'Graham just thought you would like to know... the system trials were successful. You can proceed to proposal status now.' The voice from the communicator thanked him and advised that his people would start work immediately, and that he could expect further documentation in two weeks. The call ended. Cartwright closed his console and left the office, a contented feeling of achievement filling his being.

Chapter 16: Escape and Arrival

Michael Anderson entered the restaurant.

The Maître de welcomed him, escorted him to his table and asked if he wanted a drink. He returned shortly with a glass of bourbon and left two menus and a wine list. A tall elegant woman entered and scanned the room. Locating her target she walked confidently to the table.

'Michael hello, you look well.'

Michael stood and held her chair. 'Solara, you look wonderful as usual.' She sat and Michael resumed his seat. 'Care for something?' A few minutes later they both had drinks and were engaged in small talk. 'How are things at the directorate?'

'All the worse for your absence... have you ever thought of coming back? Surely private law must be rather boring,' she challenged.

'Boring? Not really... it can be predictable sometimes, but never boring.' He didn't finish, the waiter had returned for their orders. Michael took out a pair of glasses and put them on.

'Glasses... seriously? I never picked you as the glasses type. Why not just have your eyes fixed?' Solara queried.

'Oh, I don't know. Usually when I put these on, clients seem to listen to what I say more intently, I guess they have become part of the theatre of law.' He took them off and looked at them.

'Well, if you must use props, at least make sure they're clean.' She reached over and took the glasses from him, picked up her napkin and began cleaning the lenses. She held them up to the light, used her fingernail to scratch at something she obviously thought was stuck to it and handed them back. 'There, you should be able to see things much clearer now.'

Michael thanked her, took the glasses and finished studying the menu. They both selected the same meal; Lobster Thermidor, a speciality of the house accompanied by a bottle of Marlborough Semillon. The meal was wonderful and at the end they agreed to repeat the exercise in a month. Michael walked back to his office, acutely aware of the rather clumsy tail he had picked up at the restaurant. The two men he had noticed sitting at the bar had left at the same time he did. They were following him and trying to look inconspicuous, and failing badly.

Back in his office, he activated the security system and took out the glasses. Placing them in a special recess on the side of his console, he started the scan. While it was compiling he thought back to his time in the Coalition Intelligence Directorate and about the day he had met Solara Zander.

Michael was section chief, and she had started as a rookie analyst. As a rookie, she had years of training still to complete, but Michael recognised something else. She was stunning, and intelligent. Her mind was extremely sharp, and she continuously shone over all the other rookies.

Then an opening in his section came up, and he pounced on it, offering it to her. Solara accepted immediately and from that day on they had been close, nothing romantic but a very good team. They knew how each other thought, how the other would react almost as though they had a telepathic link. Over the years, they pulled off some of the Directorate's most ambitious and dangerous missions.

Then Michael had decided to retire from active duty and, in deference to his outstanding service, several senior posts were offered, but he opted for retirement. Even though he had left the service, he had a number of friends still active; Solara was one.

The file opened, and he began to read. 'Fuck me' he whispered as he continued to read. Several times he repeated the words as he progressed through the information.

Mister Anderson, there are two men here who wish to see you, the intercom announced. Michael switched to the security screen, noting the two who had been following him. He erased all the data on the screen, placed his glasses on his head and opened an innocuous looking file.

'Send them in,' the door opened and the two men entered, Michael stayed seated behind his desk. 'Gentlemen, what can I do for you?'

The shorter of the two answered. 'We actually wanted to see Mister Mossberg... it seems he's unavailable. Do you know where he is and when he'll be back?'

Michael looked at the pair. *All bluff and bluster*, he thought. 'Mister Mossberg is on holiday with his daughter. As for when they'll return, it's open-ended. Could be in a few weeks or a few months?'

'Do you know where he went?' The other demanded.

'Gentlemen... and I obviously use that word generously... where HG is and what he's doing is his business, I'm not his nanny. Now, if you don't mind I have work to do.' Michael spoke dismissively as he began to study the document on his screen.

'Stop, I don't think you know what trouble you're in,' the short one said as he moved to the left of the desk.

Michael smiled coldly, and repeated. 'Trouble? Let me tell **you** who's in trouble. First, you two amateurs tail me from a very pleasant lunch, and then you burst into my office and threaten me. So far, I have about six charges I can have you brought up on. How many more violations do you want?'

The short one moved slightly closer and was about to speak when Michael tapped a small icon on his console pad. A piece of the desk about knee height flew out and slammed into Shorty's knee. He screamed and collapsed on the floor, his knee broken.

The other one hesitated for a second. Michael leapt from behind his desk and slammed his left foot into the other's nose. He fell to the floor, unconscious. Next Michael returned to his desk, activated his communicator and called the police.

'Yes, Sargent, this is Michael Anderson of Mossberg and Partners. We have had an incident here... two thugs have entered our offices and tried to shake us down. They have been subdued so could you please send some officers over, we would like to press charges.' Then he switched to the office intercom. 'Security this is Anderson, please come to my office.' As he spoke he removed the security field, now his office could be accessed. He moved to the short guy who was still groaning in pain.

'You can't have us arrested, we're CID,' he moaned.

'Just watch me. I have recorded it all... you never identified yourselves so, for my money, you are a couple of cheap thugs, trying to shake us down. Anyway it doesn't matter... when all this blows over you two will be lucky to get jobs as janitors.' Michael felt a pang of regret. These two were obviously just out of training and a failure as spectacular as this would end their careers, but whoever sent them was the real problem.

He reached inside of the guy's jacket and pulled an item from the inside pocket. 'Good boy... at least you managed to activate your emergency beacon. Sorry, but this whole building is screened, nothing gets out unless we want it to. So, by the time your boss gets the message, you two will be guests of the local constabulary.'

Although Michael was trying to sound flippant, his mind was racing. First the information Solara had given him and now these two fools confirmed his worst fears. He had to send the information to HG immediately.

Michael quickly checked the security footage; it would support his story, so he refrained from any enhancements. As he finished, the door opened. Two security guards and three police officers walked in. He showed the police the security footage, prepared his statement, and ten minutes later they all left his office.

His first call was to Solara, a quick cryptic call that warned her to be careful. His next move was to Gail's office; her console had the Jones' encryption software. He began typing, an innocuous message telling HG and Gail of the events since their departure. To any prying eye, it would appear he was simply reporting a problem in the office.

HG and Gail could decrypt the message and unlock the file he concealed in it. Finally, satisfied that it looked banal enough, he tapped transmit. *Now things become interesting*, Anderson thought to himself.

***

Joseph stepped on the elevator pad and it started to ascend, depositing him on the hull just above his quarters.

Having decided to retain Drake as his home, he'd had a small but comfortable sitting area installed. He carried a tray with his coffee and two choc chip muffins over to a small table, turned his chair and gazed towards the east.

This was the best part of the day… sunrise. In the weeks since Kidman had left, many things had changed. The Daldaro incident was now past and the results were being keenly monitored. Argos had gone from a place of shipwreck to home, housing for the survivors was complete and daily work routines had been established. Today, both Kidman and Freedom were due to arrive with supplies and equipment they sorely needed.

In all Joseph was happy with the progress. There was still the constant harassment from the Coalition and the trade conglomerates, but Silvio Cordoba was adamant that he would only allow this independent examination of fact to be conducted by Joseph. Silvio himself would arrive in two days and then the inquiry could proceed. Joseph's ruminations were interrupted by the first fingers of colour signalling sunrise.

Clear day sunrises on Argos were spectacular, reminding Joseph of some of the impressionist art he had seen back on Earth. Colours exploded across the sky – red, violet, orange and blue all thrown together in an almost insane mix, but it was all too short. Within minutes, the colours retreated from the battlefield as the bright orange disk of Zedak conquered all.

Joseph smiled, satisfaction filling him. For the next half an hour Joseph sat and watched as Zedak rose leisurely up the horizon, and Argos started to awaken from its nocturnal slumber. Finally he rose and retreated back into the ship.

It was 06:00, Joseph checked the time again and decided to give the new pool a try. One of the issues that had flared up was the lack of recreational facilities, so a new aquatic centre had been installed. If Joseph was completely honest it was a bit rudimentary, being cobbled together from part of the wreckage of the old hyzene tank, but it worked. Swimming was a favoured way to relax but, with the limited knowledge of the creatures that inhabited the waterways, it seemed prudent to have an indoor facility, at least in the short term. Part of the redesign of Drake had included removing the two pools she had. This was something Joseph had regretted for many years.

The centre was located in number three hold and, even at this early hour, was well patronised. For the next hour, Joseph swam, working any tension out of his muscles. He returned to his quarters, showered and dressed, leaving for the wardroom at seven thirty-five. He knew that Bruce would be there early, as he always was.

'Morning Skipper,' Bruce McGill greeted Joseph as he entered the room. 'Tried the new pool I hear. How was it?'

'Morning Bruce... considering that a few days ago it was the wreckage of our damaged hyzene tank, I think it's great and being well-used. Good job!' Joseph headed to the counter where the orderly took his breakfast order. He joined Bruce and was soon in discussion about the day's upcoming arrivals.

'One thing Bruce, how many are requesting to return to Earth?'

McGill's face split into a grin. 'Three.'

'Three... is that all?'

McGill's grin broadened. 'Only three confirmed. I still have five pending a decision and twenty-five have been withdrawn. I believe that the crew committee will want to discuss their options soon, probably as soon as they find out that the Mossbergs are here.' Their breakfasts arrived and further discussion was postponed until they had finished. A call from the Bridge forced them to rush their meal.

They entered the Bridge to a welcome sight. The view screen showed two ships now in the system. Kidman and Freedom had arrived.

'They're early Sir. We weren't expecting them for another four hours.' A jubilant sensor operator announced. 'They should achieve orbit in two hours.'

Joseph turned to Bruce. 'We better check with Phillipe. We may need their space port sooner than expected.' He sat in his old command chair and initiated the comm link.

Thought you might call. The landing pads are complete, but we need another eight hours minimum, for the hard stands and roadways to cure. After that, everything will be normal. Phillipe's voice boomed through the Bridge.

When the second Omnicron ship had arrived, it was tasked with building a space port. A site seventy-five kilometres south-west of the city was chosen. The land was relatively flat and it ran into the plateau they had seen from the original landing site.

It also had one huge advantage; the plateau walls here were sheer and contained a vast cave system. This was modified and turned into storage and maintenance areas before the final work of building a landing field was tackled. The field was levelled and landing pads constructed for six ships. Access ways and roadways were then installed and these were almost complete.

The control tower was placed on the top of the plateau, giving unrestricted views of three hundred and sixty degrees. It had its own atmospheric sensor system and was also tied into the old system, still on Drake. Now the port controllers could plot and control all comings and goings in the Zedak system.

'Thanks Phillipe, Bruce and I will head over now; I'd like to see it firsthand.' Joseph cut the comm and led Bruce out the door. They headed for the shuttle bay where he selected a shuttle. 'I think this will do, might want to head into orbit, you know hang out the welcome mat.'

Bruce smiled and nodded. 'Not a bad idea.'

The inspection took two hours. The result was impressive. The planet based area was first class and, although eventually an orbiting space port would need to be established, this would serve very well for many years.

'Well done, Phil.' Bruce beamed. 'I never thought you could get it done in time, very impressive.'

'Wait till you see the control tower,' Phillipe led the way to the elevator. This had been installed on the outside of the cliff face as a temporary measure, while a permanent system was being bored through the rock inside.

The control tower was much bigger than it first looked, with room for eight operators and a Commander. At the moment it was manned by three under the command of newly promoted Lieutenant, Molly Renwick.

She greeted them proudly. 'Welcome Captain, Chief; welcome to our new Argos Control centre.' It was different to how Joseph had imagined. The eight controller consoles were arranged as on the Bridge of a ship, except they were in line with the command chair. Directly in front was a huge view screen and a strange looking raised section in the floor? Joseph was about to ask when Molly spoke.

'Sir, this is the coolest bit of kit we have. It came with the sensor system you impounded.' She sat at the command chair and activated the system. 'Computer, initiate the hologram.' As she spoke, the air above the strange pad began to change, a translucent blue glowing sphere formed above the pad. It took a few seconds before it started to show any form.

'Computer, transfer feed from sensor grid.'

The translucent blue mist seemed to waver, shimmer and change, forming a holographic representation of the entire Zedak system. All the planets and satellites – but more importantly the ships in orbit and on approach to Argos – were displayed in real time.

'This is the best part. We can look at the entire system and plot movements in real time and with accuracy down to a metre.' She tagged the two newcomers, gave them designations and spoke. 'Computer… track and monitor bogies one and two. Make their separation one thousand kilometres… keep them separate to all stationary vessels and project the most economical course for landing.' Now the display showed four ships, the two real vessels and two theoretical vessels on a changed heading, the most economical for landing.

'Sir all we can do now is monitor… Drake is still in control.' Joseph knew what she really wanted, so he initiated a comm link to the ship and spoke.

'Drake, this is Captain Jones. Please transfer all approach and departure control for Argos to the new control centre.'

Yes Sir, transferring control now. Was the reply

'There, Molly, you now have control.' Joseph smiled. 'Please have both ships fix in orbit, we still need a few hours for everything to be ready below, and plot a course for us to intercept them.'

'Aye Sir... Kidman and Freedom this is Argos control, new course data being transmitted now. You will establish a stable orbit and wait for further instruction, please confirm.'

Both ships replied and confirmed their new course and orbital parameters. Molly turned to Joseph, 'Sir, your flight plan has been cleared and sent to your shuttle.'

Joseph was proud of the accomplishments here. 'Well done Molly! Please keep Drake on standby just in case. We'll review the system in a few days, to see if there are any issues.' He congratulated her again and left the control room.

Back in the shuttle, Bruce worked through the pre-flight checks. Joseph called Kidman and Freedom and arranged for a meeting in thirty minutes.

'Bruce, just one question... where did all this hardware come from?'

Bruce initiated the take-off cycle as he spoke. 'From Drake, of course... the old girl will never move again so all the hardware aboard is now redundant. The control tower came from a secondary engineering station, but eventually we'll cannibalise her for more facilities.' He returned to piloting the shuttle and to give Joseph time to digest the ultimate end for most of Drake's systems. Twenty minutes later they were on approach to Freedom.

Shuttle Orion from Freedom control, you are cleared to enter the shuttle bay. Do you want manual control or would you prefer an automated entry.

Joseph answered. 'Freedom control, this is Captain Jones requesting permission for a visual inspection of your ship.' Although he owned Freedom, Don Hopmann was in command and only he could authorise this operation. Minutes passed until he received his answer.

Shuttle Orion, you are cleared for circumnavigation of Freedom, enjoy the view.

This was the first time Joseph had actually seen Freedom. He had been quite involved in the design and specification process but, when that finished, he let the experts at Abracorp and Greenbach get on with the job. He had only been present on two occasions during construction; first for the symbolic laying of the keel and later for an update half-way through the project. Orion slowly traversed round the ship. Kidman and Freedom shared a similar shape which differed from the majority of trade ships.

Freedom was vaguely ovoid with a flat underside and squared aft section. There were no protrusions from the hull giving her a very sleek appearance. The forward section housed the Bridge and living quarters. Immediately aft were the holds, these were modular and could be easily reconfigured to a number of roles. Aft of these were the engineering spaces and the drive systems. Displacement emitters were placed around the hull and weapons ports were concealed, until needed. Joseph smiled; he was pleased with the final result. Two years and a huge investment totally justified.

'Freedom control, Orion has finished the inspection, please take control and guide us in.'

Shuttle Orion, Freedom is taking control. Sit back and enjoy the ride. Joseph leaned back in his chair as the shuttle changed course toward the bay entry.

'Well, are you happy with your new toy?' Bruce asked, with a slightly sarcastic tone in his voice.

'Yes, but she's not my toy. She'll be under the command of Captain Hopmann,' Joseph replied, holding a small valise in his right hand.

'So, you weren't joking when you said our time in space was coming to an end.'

'Not coming to an end, just not our main duty from now on. Bruce, believe me... you and I will have our heads down and arses up for the foreseeable future, just getting Argos running smoothly. Besides, as I said, trading is a young man's game. It's time for me to settle down. Wouldn't do you any harm to take things a bit easier, either.'

Chapter 17: High Stakes

*A*nd *you are certain both ships were destroyed?*

The voice of Michael Husan, CEO of Galactic Freight boomed from the comm system.

'Yes, Michael. Both Frederickson and Holt have confirmed the results. Jones won't be getting any backup from them.' Admiral William (Bill) Cartwright was getting tired of the constant doubting from these civilians. He was also rethinking his decision to get involved in their petty politics, but, so far, the rewards had been worth it.

What about that Anderson character? What's he up to?' this time the question came from Naismith himself.

'As I told you, Graham, we have one of CID's best watching him. Don't worry, she is totally clueless and thinks Anderson is trying to infiltrate his old section for some info he needs for a case. She'll string him along as long as she needs to. If he becomes a problem, I'm sure our Section Five boys can sort something out.'

Correct Admiral... just say the word and Mister Anderson will cease to be an issue. Jefferson Holt, Commander of the Coalition's non-existent Black Ops group, Section Five replied, his voice cold and hard. He too was getting sick of listening to these overstuffed civilians issuing orders.

***

Unaware of his popularity with the hierarchy of the Coalition Military and the heads of one of the largest trade conglomerates, Michael Anderson entered the dining room of the Savoy Hotel. He located his dinner partner and navigated his way through the busy crowd.

'Evening Solara,' he extended his hand in greeting. Solara smiled and took his hand, palming a small round devise as she did. Michael nodded and sat, surreptitiously slipping the disk under his watch.

'Good evening Michael, glad you could join me. That device is a disruption field generator; nobody will be able to hear us speak. Did you get the file?'

'Yes, and it took a while for it all to sink in. Are you sure of it?'

'Absolutely, that's why we're here. I'm supposed to pump you for information.' Solara winked, a look of intrigue flashed across her face.

'Well, I couldn't ask for a better pumper.' Michael couldn't help himself, the opening was too good. Solara laughed and deactivated the field as the waiter arrived to take their order. Michael identified four agents entering the dining room. Two men headed for the bar and took up positions at different ends; the others were a couple who took a table several metres from him and Solara. 'We have company.'

'Yes, seems my loyalty is being questioned... time for a performance.'

Michael nodded, almost imperceptibly as the field was deactivated again. 'I hate to ask, Solara, but I'm very worried about HG and Gail. They were supposed to contact me weeks ago, and still nothing. I know it would be an abuse of your position but can you find anything out? I have a bad feeling. It's not like HG to stay out of touch this long.'

'But you did say they were going on a vacation. Couldn't it just be that he wants to be left alone?'

'HG, no way! In all the years I've known him, he's never been out of touch for more than a few days... and that was when Margaret passed. No, Solara I think something has happened to him. All I ask is; see what you can find out. Don't put yourself in danger, but I need to know. If something has happened to them, I've got a business to sort out.'

Solara gave her best impression of a sympathetic smile, 'Ok, for old times' sake I could snoop around. How about I come to your office Thursday? If I have nothing by then... there's nothing to find.' They finished their meal and Solara returned to her office, knowing that she was being followed.

Waiting for her was CID Director, Brian Bosworth, a man who had risen through the ranks in stellar form. Tall and handsome, he had the right background for the new, more politically savvy intelligence operation.

'Enjoy your dinner, Zander?' Bosworth never used first names, preferring to show his dominance by referring to subordinates in this manner.

'Yes Sir, very nice except for the fumbling of the two operatives who followed me. I take it this was part of their training... if so, they need to go back to class.' She deliberately left the other two out of the conversation.

'Yes, that is obvious; tell me what did Anderson want?' Bosworth never wanted to spend too much time with underlings; he had far more important things to attend to.

'He's concerned about his partner, HG Mossberg. He, and his daughter, left for a vacation and haven't been heard from since. He asked if I knew anything.'

'And what did you tell him?' Bosworth's supercilious attitude was beginning to annoy Solara.

'Just that I'd see if I could find anything out, I'm meeting him again on Thursday.' Sometimes the best lie is the truth. She waited for Bosworth to make the next move.

'And what's Anderson's interest?' Either Bosworth was fishing or he was too lazy to do his own research.

'Mossberg and Partners has three senior partners; HG, his daughter Gail, and Anderson. If they have met with an accident he's got a lot to do. After all, Mossberg and Partners is probably the premier law firm in the Coalition.' The truth again was the best option, but not too much of it.

'Right, well, he has reason to be concerned. It appears that there may have been an incident, maybe two. We know that Kidman inserted into sub space in an unusual fashion and, when they were supposed to reinsert into normal space something happened. The current theory is an asteroid collision. But whatever happened, Kidman's transponder went dark and so far, we can find no trace of her.

'Jones Trading's newest ship, Freedom, I believe he called it, had a catastrophic reactor failure... utterly destroyed it... nothing left. I believe the Space Safety Bureau has started an investigation into it. Greenbach Tech may be in a lot of trouble... if it was a faulty reactor. Anyway, I'm having dinner with Admiral Cartwright tonight; I should have an official report tomorrow. Tell you what, I'll send you a copy, that way you can inform Anderson of the facts.' His smile was satisfied and smug, Bosworth stood and walked to the door. 'By the way, there were four agents watching you.'

'What? The two gorillas at the bar were agents? We're in deep shit if they were out of training!' Solara fired back.

'They better go back into diapers. If it was a real op, the four of them would be in the morgue by now.'

Bosworth's smile vanished. Now his face showed his usual contemptuous sneer. He didn't say anything, just closed the door, rather forcefully.

Solara smiled. *Stuck up prick*, she thought. She turned her attention back to her desk. Data drives sat there waiting for her attention. She decided to follow the process she had set up and began the administrative tasks that took up so much of her time.

***

Joseph and Bruce were met by Don Hopmann as they exited the shuttle. 'Welcome Sir, your new ship awaits your inspection.' Don smiled, knowing that Joseph would want a tour.

'I'm afraid the inspection will need to wait. Where are we meeting the others?'

'In the conference room... you certainly made sure this ship would impress any prospective customers.' Don headed to the pod.

The conference room was all that Joseph had envisaged – large and impressive. Oversized view ports covered the far wall, with plush leather lounges positioned to allow good external views as well as encouraging conversation. In the centre of the room was a round mahogany table that would comfortably seat twenty. Two food and beverage dispensers were to either side of the entrance and more chairs and lounges were scattered in a seemingly random pattern.

The walls were most interesting, they could change colour as required. Something Joseph had learnt over the years was that colours can affect negotiations and this room could be used as a subliminal influencer. It wasn't cheap, but Joseph believed it was a prudent investment.

'Better than I expected. Abracorp certainly did a great job. Now Don, let's get down to business.' Joseph placed the small valise on the table and opened it. 'Freedom is now the flagship of Jones Trading and as such needs the best crew. Captain Hopmann, I'm offering command of this ship to you.' He took a small leather bound box from the valise and handed it to Don.

Don took the box and looked at the insignia inside. 'I don't know what to say, I thought you would be in command?'

'No, my days of tearing all over the galaxy are coming to an end. If my dream of an Independent Traders Guild is to come true, I have to work on that. Besides you've proven many times that you're every bit as good as anyone in the trading community. You deserve this Don.'

'Thank you, but what about a crew?'

'You can choose that yourself. Drake will never get off the ground again so everyone, except for Bruce and I, are available.' Joseph was interrupted by the comm unit paging them; the others had arrived. 'Well, Captain, change those pips and go greet your guests.'

As Don left Joseph, turned to Bruce. 'Let's see if everything was done to my liking.' He moved to the sideboard and opened a door.

'A-ha, they did very well!' he said gleefully. He retrieved a case from inside, opened it and produced a large bottle. 'One litre of the finest single malt Scotch available... this bottle can stay on the ship. The rest I'm commandeering; after all I did pay for it.' Joseph cracked the seal and opened the bottle, gently sniffed the contents and smiled.

'Fifty years of maturation in seasoned oak casks, an old family recipe as well. This is something the Jones Clan has made for centuries.

'My cousin Amos still makes this on Callanish and the Abraham's are one of his best customers. Silly isn't it, It's easier for me to get it from a shipbuilder than from my own cousin. Maybe one of the first industries for Argos should be a distillery!' Joseph laughed. He placed the bottle and a tray of glasses on the table and sat back to wait.

A few minutes later the door opened and in walked Don and his guests. Captain Tellyz greeted Joseph, followed by HG. Finally Gail came forward; Joseph offered her his hand in greeting.

'For pity's sake, greet the man properly! How am I ever going to have grandkids if all you two do is shake hands.' HG was in full voice. Gail threw her father a withering glance but turned to Joseph, reached up and kissed him. Not a gentle, friendly 'hello' kiss, but one full of promise and affection.

Gail broke the embrace. 'Maybe he's right, but I swear, sometimes I could cheerfully strangle him,' Gail said as she moved to Joseph's side.

The rest of the meeting was informal and happy Both Captains told of their encounter and subsequent escape – sensor data would be analysed later. HG opened the data pad he held and started to show the information Anderson had sent. The mood suddenly changed, things were gravely serious, now.

'OK, there's little we can do here. We should move on with this inquiry. To make it formal, I suggest that Gail and I act for the parties. Gail can have the crew, I'll take Naismith,' HG suggested. 'That way, if anyone takes issue with the findings, both parties will have had professional representation.' The idea was swiftly agreed to and any further discussion of the issue halted. It was now a matter for the court of inquiry.

'Good, that's sorted.' Joseph was relieved. 'I have some news! Captain Hopmann will take command of Freedom... my days of active trading are now behind me. I have also issued an invitation to all independent traders to meet us here. So far, fifteen have agreed and I suspect others will follow.

'In the next week this system will be very busy... there'll be more ships entering than at any time since we discovered it. Also, Silvio Cordoba will arrive tomorrow, and he wants to start the inquiry as soon as we can, so I suggest our advocates get to the surface and meet with their new clients.' Joseph stood and picked up the case of Scotch.

'Captain, I believe that belongs on Freedom,' Don said, half-jokingly.

Joseph held tightly to his prize. 'Well here's a deal Captain Hopmann. If you can set up a trade deal with my cousin Amos on Callanish, I'll let you have a case for every shipment.'

Don thought for a moment, and then offered his hand. 'Deal!' They shook on it and left the conference room.

The Mossberg's belongings had been transferred to the shuttle; Joseph would take Gail and HG down to the surface. Bruce elected to stay on board to have a better look at the new ship, his curiosity finally winning out. HG found a seat and settled in for the next thirty minutes while Gail took the second seat beside Joseph.

'So, Captain, your space faring days are coming to an end? I suppose that means that if I want to see more of you, I'll need to migrate to Argos... permanently?'

'Well, it's where I'll be, and I was hoping we could entice at least one good legal mind. As you know we have no actual laws and no constitutional documentation... up for the job?' Joseph asked.

'Just try to hire anyone else!' Her decision had been made.

'There's just one thing,' HG said from his seat. 'Until this inquiry is over, we need to keep a formal relationship. As you're heading it, you need to keep your distance... for appearances' sake. The last thing we need is for there to be any hint of collusion or favouritism.'

'Agreed,' Joseph nodded, his face sporting a frown.

One of the benefits of having a converted cruise liner as a base, the accommodation is first class. Joseph had arranged for two suites close to his quarters to be made ready, but Gail and HG were unprepared for what greeted them. He saw the look on both of his guests faces, and decided an explanation was called for.

'Drake started life as a luxury liner, the company went bust and I bought her for a song. I kept some of the furnishings and cabins for the crew and myself, the rest I sold off. It actually paid for the conversion and most of the purchase. Five of Jones Trading's other ships have similar pedigrees.'

'So how many trade ships do you have?' Gail asked.

'Not including Drake... twelve.'

'Does that include Amadeus?'

'Yes, I suppose it does.' Joseph didn't know where she was heading with this conversation.

'So in fact you have eleven active trade ships?'

'Ok why the interrogation?'

'Just something we discussed a couple of years ago... an idea I have. I'll explain later, now I need to see my clients.' Joseph nodded and the others followed him back to the entrance where HG was waiting there for them.

'Jonesy, we'll take it from here,' he inclined his head toward a Petty Officer standing at the base of the ramp. 'Better if we do this alone.' Joseph watched as they boarded the ground car and sped off to the accommodation blocks. He turned back into Drake. *Time to prepare for our next guest,* he thought as he took the pod to the old Bridge. He stood before the door and read the sign.

BRIDGE
Authorised Personnel ONLY

Joseph smiled as the door opened. *Nothing much left,* he mused as he entered. His thoughts were correct – most hardware not essential for the operation of what was left of Drake had been pilfered for other tasks.

The sensors had been cannibalised to augment the space control system and were now being reconfigured to operate as a ground based warning and flight control system. He sighed. So sad to see the old ship being gutted, but he knew it was essential for the survival of the small group, and his dream. His musings were terminated when his communicator chimed.

He pulled it off his belt and answered. 'Jones.'

Captain, this is Argos Control. Silvio Cordoba's ship has entered our system. We have cleared him to orbit, but he has asked that you meet him on his ship, alone.' Joseph smiled, Silvio had a reputation for making theatrical entrances; the best way forward was to entertain him.

'Control, contact him and agree to the meeting.' Joseph considered his answer and, deciding that meeting Silvio's demands should be done in style, he added. 'Also, file a flight plan and send it to Amadeus, I'll take her to the meeting.'

He contacted the ship and advised that he would be bringing Phillipe Alvaris with him and, when this was accepted, he called Phillipe and arranged to meet him in the hangar. His next call was to the newly constructed space port to arrange for a suitable greeting for Silvio.

An hour later, Amadeus was parked in orbit waiting for Minerva, Cordoba's ship, to appear. When it did, the effect was immediate. Minerva was huge, by yacht standards, almost as large as Freedom. She was bright red with black accents. On the bow was the Cordoba crest; a bright yellow diamond supported by crossed swords and a stylised letter C emblazoned in black and silver in the diamond.

'I've heard about her but have never seen this ship in the flesh. A bit ostentatious for me,' Joseph said.

'If you think of her as a yacht I agree but... she is also headquarters for Cordoba Mining and Silvio's residence. She has an operational crew of sixty but a total complement of over three hundred. He runs his entire mining operation from this ship. All negotiations and contract agreements are made on board, usually in free space. It gives Silvio a degree of... protection from some of the local laws and regulations, if you get my drift.'

Joseph nodded. 'I certainly do; a clever solution... yes very clever!'

I.T.S Amadeus this is Minerva control. You are cleared to enter hangar 2 on our port side. The glide path has been illuminated, just follow the yellow beam.

Joseph responded. 'Minerva control, this is Amadeus, thank you... proceeding on illuminated flight path.' He set the guide parameters into the nav system and Amadeus began to turn toward the target. At their distance of one thousand kilometres Joseph and Phillipe got a good view of the ship.

The sleek lines coupled with the colour scheme impressed them. 'The colour is Ferrari Red, from what Silvio has told me, it was a corporate colour from old Earth, back in the twentieth and early twenty-first century. Evidently they made what were called super-cars. Even the shape of it is based on the designs of those vehicles. Silvio is something of an expert so if you want to kill a few hours; just mention the word Ferrari,' Phillipe chuckled.

Docking was smooth and easy, with plenty of room in the hangar for a number of ships the size of Amadeus. Joseph extended the boarding ramp to the walkway to port of Amadeus, opened the airlock and followed Phillipe out of the ship.

Waiting at the end of the walkway was a tall, elegant woman. 'Welcome to Minerva, please gentlemen follow me. Mister Cordoba is waiting for you.' Her voice was clipped and efficient and the rest of her was very pleasing. With shoulder-length jet black hair, she cut an impressive sight. She seemed to sense the interest. 'My name is Martina; I'm Director of Corporate Relations. If there is anything you require, please don't hesitate to ask.' Her voice conveyed efficiency and purpose as she stood aside for them to enter a pod.

The meeting room they entered was designed for relaxing – with comfortable lounges and arm chairs, subdued tones in the decor and an intimate size – good for no more than ten people.

'I trust this room is acceptable?' We have several others all designed for specific purposes, if you prefer something else?'

'No, thank you this's fine.' Joseph answered as the door opened.

The man who entered wasn't at all what Joseph expected. His imagination had built an entirely different figure for Silvio Cordoba. The man before him was short, but large framed. Some described him as *the brick* because of his body shape. His face was round with blue eyes and a mass of dark hair. He moved forward with confidence.

'Captain Jones, my pleasure to finally meet you, I'm Silvio Cordoba.' He offered his hand.

Joseph took it, impressed with the strength of Silvio's grip. 'Joseph, please. This is some ship you have.'

'Thank you. She serves me well as home and company headquarters. But I believe you've just had some bad luck with two of yours?'

Joseph looked Silvio directly in the eyes. 'Don't believe all the rumours you hear.'

Silvio was stunned by these words. 'But I heard that your two newest ships were destroyed in separate accidents?'

'A rumour that for the moment, we would rather keep alive.'

Silvio gave Joseph a long look. 'I think I'll enjoy dealing with you Joseph. But to business, I asked you to meet here as there is something we need to discuss. Do you know anything about the political machinations developing on Earth?'

'Some... it appears that there is some sort of coup being plotted,' Joseph was deliberately being vague.

'Yes, but far more than that. My sources tell me that certain corporate interests are funding the action and that a move is imminent. There's even a rumour that President Elect Chang is to be eliminated.'

'Silvio, this is interesting but it doesn't concern me or Argos. All I want to do is set up our community and consolidate the Guild.'

'You're wrong about that... you are very much at the centre of it. Your intervention in the Daldaro incident has the main players in a spin, so much so that they destroyed two of your ships... or, so they think. Their next target is Argos... they seem to think they can destroy it. Why you're so much of a threat is beyond me, but that's what we hear.'

Joseph shook his head. 'Naismith, Graham Naismith is behind all this, isn't he?'

Joseph's words caused Silvio to pause. 'Yes, but how did you know that?'

'His son... I have his son in custody. He was the Captain of the Lady Philomena and so far the evidence is enough to put him away for a long time, maybe even call for the death penalty. He's the only reason anybody would be interested in this inquiry, and Argos. Naismith will do anything to save his family name. I've had a number of messages from Graham, first asking what he could do to assist, but now he's getting a bit more aggressive, demanding we release his son or else. He hasn't specified the *or else*, yet.'

'I think you'll find it goes a lot deeper than that. Naismith is ambitious, but he's never shown any interest in politics. No, Joseph, I fear that there's more to this than we know, so we'd better make sure we all watch our backs,' Silvio warned.

'I understand. We're working with someone back on Earth to try to find out what's behind all this. Our only issue is the comm dwell, six hours each way. Every time we send a message it's at least half a day until we receive an answer... so bloody frustrating.'

'Well Captain Jones, I can fix that. How's half an hour sound?' Silvio grinned. 'Let's get the ship on the ground and I'll show you how.'

With permission from Argos control, Minerva began its entry into the atmosphere. In space she was an impressive sight but, descending to a planet's surface was a different matter.

Silvio Cordoba was renowned for his flamboyance, and his ship was the epitome of this. In space, she was a brilliant red but the outer coating was such that in an atmosphere, where the light was filtered, she was entirely different. The ship appeared to change colours when viewed from different angles. One second red, then as the light angle changed, all the colours of the rainbow appeared to erupt from the hull.

The Captain and Pilot revelled in their charge and, with a final flourish, brought Minerva to a perfect landing on pad four, beside Freedom.

Silvio led his guests off the Bridge to the pod then hesitated. 'There's just one small detail I have left out,' he said as he accessed the pod control. 'I neglected to tell you I have another guest, Steven Chang.'

His timing was perfect. As he spoke the pod door opened and Steven Chang, President Elect for the Coalition of Earth Planets, stood before them.

While not a large man, Steven Chang's presence was always felt. He had an athletic physique that he worked hard to keep, but his intellect was his key factor. His keen mind had forged his career, both in interstellar law and politics. Even HG Mossberg believed him to be one of the best political and legal minds in the galaxy. Twelve months ago Steven had been convinced to stand for the Presidency and had won the contest in a landslide. In three months he would take control of the Coalition administration.

'Gentlemen, I must apologise for all this intrigue and ask your forgiveness, Captain Jones, for arriving unannounced.' Chang's voice was deep and well-modulated, a tool he had used to full advantage during his career.

'No apology necessary, but I am a bit mystified as to why you're here.' Joseph replied.

'All will be explained in time.' Silvio suggested. 'For now, we must ensure that the President's visit is kept covert for a few more days. In the meantime I believe you could use better communications?'

'Yes, you mentioned something about that, earlier.'

Silvio motioned for them to enter the pod. 'Shall we?'

The pod conveyed them to the administration section of the ship. 'Part of my business philosophy is to take my operation with me, but even then we need to be able to contact our outposts quickly. The Daldaro incident is one example. I stumbled across a young engineer a couple of years ago and was impressed by his ideas on how to speed up communication, I tipped in some capital and here is the result.' The pod door opened and they all exited. The room was fairly small, but filled with equipment.

'This system gives us an advantage in time. Our comm dwell time is usually less than a third of conventional systems, so we can respond faster or take advantage of situations more easily. Don't ask me how it works, that's what I pay the boffins for... all I know is that it does.' Silvio was interrupted by his comm unit; he took the call and turned to Joseph, 'It seems HG Mossberg is waiting for you?'

'Yes, he and his daughter are counsel for the inquiry. I asked them to join us here.'

Silvio spoke into the comm unit and arranged for HG and Gail to be taken to his office. The group once again boarded the pod for the same destination.

The office was in keeping with Silvio's flamboyance. Some would call the decor garish with bold colours, ultra-modern furniture and some good examples of what currently was called impressionist art. For all the extravagance the room had a warm feel, a welcoming ambience that wasn't lost on the guests.

They had just arrived when HG and Gail were announced by Silvio's assistant. As they entered he greeted them, shaking hands with HG and taking Gail's hand, bowing and delicately kissing it. Joseph experienced a slight feeling of panic at this, but dismissed it immediately. As they all settled into their seats, an assistant entered and poured everyone a drink.

'HG, I believe you have a contact on Earth who has been digging around for you?' Silvio asked.

HG nodded. 'Yes, one of the partners, Michael Anderson... he has contacts in places nobody can reach, and we're waiting on some new information he has.'

'I have a new communication system that will shorten that dwell to around half an hour, but the only system on Earth is in our offices. Can you convince him to go there?'

HG nodded and smiled. 'I think I can do that.'

Steven Chang entered the conversation at this point. 'I think we should stop skirting the issue. We all believe there is some political intrigue going on in the Coalition... something that could, if successful, change the course of human history. Everything we do from this point on comes with extreme risk, so please be clear... do you all want to proceed?' Everyone in the room agreed. 'Then we are all now in the highest stake poker game in history.'

Chapter 18: First Draw

Michael Anderson answered the knock on his office door and in walked his PA.

'Your morning communication, Sir... and there's a representative from Cordoba Corporation asking to see you.'

Michael smiled. 'Good morning Nyah, how are you?'

An embarrassed grin flashed across her dark face. 'Sorry Sir. Good morning, I feel well thank you.' Michael had brought Nyah Diallo up from the secretarial pool on the floor below. He had worked with her on a couple of cases and found her to be efficient and very effective. When HG had left for Argos, he had to step up and take on some extra workload. He needed his own PA and Nyah was his first thought. So far he had been right.

'Is something bothering you?' Michael asked.

'Nothing, it's really nothing.'

'Come on Nyah, we're a team... if you have a problem, so do I.'

'Well... just a feeling... I don't have any proof but I think someone has been following me. The last couple of days I think I have seen the same man on the pod each morning and afternoon and I think the house is being watched.' Clearly she was concerned. Since HG left, Michael had been lead on a couple of important cases and knew that it was possible that at least one of those involved may look for any advantage.

'Leave it with me; I'll see what I can do. If you like, I'll have security tail you so don't worry, ' Michael offered. 'Give me five minutes and then send in the Cordoba rep.'

Nyah nodded and left. Michael called the head of company security, gave him the information and arranged for twenty-four-hour security on Nyah and her family.

He had just finished when the door opened and Nyah ushered in Jasmine Cordoba, one of Silvio's nieces and operations manager for Earth and the solar system. While most of the company's operations were based in the colonies, Cordoba Corp still had several that were administered from Earth and, as Silvio really only trusted family, it was run by a family member.

'Good morning, Mister Anderson, thank you for seeing me.' Her voice was clipped and efficient. Her clothing, a smart suit, also spoke of her business motivation.

'Not at all, I'm intrigued as to why a senior member of your company needed to see me so urgently.'

She didn't reply, simply handed him a data drive. Michael plugged it into his console, carried out the usual security checks and activated it. There was only one file, a message from HG. Michael read it three times before he looked up.

'You have read this?' he asked.

'No, but I had a communication from my uncle informing me to assist you in every way. It appears we are now joined at the hip,' she chuckled, dispersing some of the tension currently in the room.

Michael read the message again and activated his comm, 'Nyah, what's my schedule for today?'

Fairly clear this morning... there is a three o'clock with David Buckman and a team meeting at four thirty.

'Ok, the Buckman thing, have Adrian briefed to fill in, and make sure you're there too, I should be back by then but just to be sure. And open a new file for the Cordoba Corporation, mark it as general counsel.'

Yes Sir... oh almost missed this... Ms Zander is coming by at ten, do you want to cancel?

Michael looked at the time on the console; 09:42 was displayed. 'No, I'll see her first.' He looked back to Jasmine. 'Does 10:45 work for you?' They agreed that the time would work, and she left the office.

At exactly 10:00 Solara Zander exited the elevator and walked into Mossberg and Partner's reception area. She announced herself to the young man behind the desk and waited for a response. Two minutes later, Nyah came through the large frosted glass doors and greeted her. Together they walked the short distance to Michael's office.

Nyah opened the door and Solara entered, when the door closed Michael triggered the security screen. Although the entire building was screened and isolated, each office and meeting room was also individually secured. Mossberg handled some of the most sensitive legal cases in the Coalition; information discussed was, at times, delicate and extremely valuable. In the entire life of the company, there had never been a breach of security but today, Michael was taking no chances.

Solara was relieved he felt this way considering what they were doing could be construed as treason, and that was still punishable by death. She handed him a small data drive and he repeated the process of checking it, once satisfied it was clean, he opened it. The file was damning, and he had to read it a number of times before he spoke.

'Are you serious?' he asked.

'Most definitely... the sources are impeccable. There is a coup underway and your friend Jones is a huge fly in the ointment. They are planning an all-out attack on Argos; some excuse like collusion with the Krell will be used as justification. The only thing stopping it is Naismith, but I don't think he can stall much longer. The reference to Section Five suggests they will try a covert rescue of his son soon. Once they have him, Argos and everything on it is to be obliterated.'

'I don't get it! Naismith is ambitious and wealthy, but even he doesn't have the grunt to pull this off. What, or better still, who, is really behind it?' Michael asked.

'I agree, but we have no evidence or even a suspicion of who that may be. At this stage all roads lead to Naismith. Oh, and another interesting development, there seems to be a panic over where the President Elect is... his security detail appear to have lost him.'

Michael shook his head. 'Still as efficient as ever, I see. I now have access to a new comm system, one that will cut the dwell time down to less than thirty minutes. I'm due to send a message in about twenty minutes, so I'll call you later if I have any more info. And, by the way, are any of your guys following my assistant?'

'No, none that I know of, but as we've learned things here are not always clear.'

'Well, she's convinced she's being followed and her house is being watched. I've assigned her a security detail, and we will be watching. If anyone is tailing her, we'll take care of it, just so you're warned.'

'Point taken, I'll look into it,' Solara said as she stood to leave. As soon as she had, Michael started compiling the message he was going to send HG.

At 10:28 he called the shuttle pilot. The company always had a shuttle standing by for last minute meetings. He assured Michael that the craft would be ready for immediate lift off when he arrived.

At 10:34, Michael left the elevator in the rooftop hangar; the shuttle was powered and ready to go. As soon as he had entered, the door closed and the Pilot's voice asked him to take his seat and prepare for take-off.

At 10:42, Michael disembarked the shuttle and was met by Jasmine Cordoba. They took the elevator down three floors to her office. At 10:45, Michael's first message was transmitted.

'Now we wait,' Jasmine commented.

***

On Argos a secure comm link between Minerva and Drake had been established, Joseph sat in his office with HG and the others, waiting for the message from Earth to arrive. He had twin clocks showing on the console, one for Argos time and the other displayed Eastern Standard Time for Sydney, Australia on Earth.

According to Argos time it was 19:42 but for Earth 11:16 was displayed. The message should arrive any second. It seemed like no one was breathing and the tension and expectation in the room was almost physical. 11:17 now showed on the console, then 11:18. The message notification was a single chime, everyone in the room jumped. There it was, in his *in box*. HG opened it and verified it was from Michael. He decoded it and put the text up on the screen for everyone to read.

The disbelief in the room was palpable, the plot and proposed actions were laid bare. 'I don't believe they are this stupid. How do they think they'll get away with it?' Chang asked.

HG replied, sadly. 'Quite simple... fear. I have a bit more to add. Naismith has been forming various alliances, mainly with the defence industry. He has taken positions in a number of those companies, some of which are just surviving and their share price is very low. Consider what would happen if suddenly, the Coalition faced a new threat... a renewed war with the Krell.

'Those companies would suddenly find their order books full and massive profits would start flowing. But a new and non-aligned Argos is a real threat. If you, Jonesy, started to work independently with the Krell, maybe other colonies would follow suit and pretty soon Naismith's profits would vanish.

'That's why they must destroy you, and this planet... to keep the rest in line. It's also where Frederickson and his new displacement torpedo will come in. He'll simply fire one, have it materialise in the centre of Argos and boom all their troubles are over. It would even look like a natural disaster.'

It was Phillipe who spoke next. 'No, that's not what would happen. The Daldaro incident was caused by an accidental detonation... I'm sure of that. An accident in hyperspace that resulted in a massive tear in the very fabric of space/time... imagine what one detonated inside a planet would do. If they do it, then this will be a disaster of biblical proportions. Joseph, I need that astrophysicist of yours and young Molly. This madness has to be stopped.' He stood and hurried from the room.

'HG, see if Anderson can dig up more definitive information,' Joseph said as he and Silvio followed Phillipe.

'Also inform your people that I am here,' Chang added.

Joseph stopped at those words, 'Mister President, can you still contact your security detail?'

'Joseph, please, I'm not the President yet so Steven will do nicely, and yes, I have a communicator on Minerva.'

'Excellent, here's what I think we should do.' Joseph took the next few minutes outlining his idea, Steven agreed, and they went separate ways to put the plan into action.

***

Back on Earth, Michael Anderson had returned to his office and checked his messages. As discussed, any communication from Argos would now come from the Cordoba system; each would be heavily encrypted and buried in seemingly harmless legal and business documents. Part of this deception would entail Mossberg and Partners taking over as chief legal counsel for Cordoba Corporation. If nothing else came from this exercise, Mossberg would benefit. 'Win, win.' Michael smiled, very pleased with developments so far.

While he had been waiting for Cordoba's techs to set up the encryption system, Michael was asked to investigate a purchase Cordoba was trying to make: an asteroid belt similar to Daldaro, but negotiations had stalled. He read through the documents with Jasmine, noted a couple of issues that he believed he could assist with and the deal was sealed. Michael decided to up the ante. He accessed his communicator and made a call. While waiting, he opened a file and began completing some of the details it required, a self-satisfied smile creasing his face.

When the call was answered he introduced himself, deliberately sounding official. 'Solara, Michael Anderson, 'there's something I'd like to discuss with you. How about dinner tonight, say eight at Raphael's?' He spoke as he worked on the document. He waited for an answer. 'Excellent, I'll see you then.' And he cut the link. When he was satisfied with the document in front of him he registered it on the company system, and downloaded a copy to a data drive.

***

Solara looked vacantly at her comm unit, not quite understanding what Michael was up to. Contacting her openly and without any covert cover, just an invitation to dinner could be problematic. The door opened and in walked her boss, Bosworth.

'What was that about?' He asked.

Solara looked indignantly at him. 'Are you tapping my comms?'

'Only those from Anderson... so what does he want?' Bosworth blustered.

'I have no idea; just that he invited me to dinner at one of the best restaurants in the city. You obviously heard the conversation... make your own bloody conclusions!' She fired back.

'Well, we'll have to bug you for it.'

'Not bloody likely. You know Raphael's... no surveillance is permitted. If you get caught, well you know what happened to the last person who tried. You'll just have to trust me.' Solara was right, and Bosworth knew it.

Raphael's was neutral ground; members of the Council, even the President, and most of the Diplomatic core of the Coalition frequented the place. The last time CID tried to eavesdrop, it ended badly for the then assistant director, Bosworth's predecessor; he ended up as Warden on Gulag, the Coalition's maximum security prison planet. Bosworth grunted something and stormed out of the office.

***

Michael leaned back in his chair and checked the time: 16:45, *time for a drink*. He went to the cabinet and removed a bottle of bourbon. He hesitated and took out two glasses, went back to his desk, accessed his intercom and called his assistant. Moments later, his door opened and Nyah walked in.

'Yes Mister Anderson, what can I do?' She asked.

'Please, Nyah sit down. Would you like a drink?' Michael asked as he poured the liquid.

Nyah noted the bottle and agreed. 'Thank you Sir. It's not often I get to enjoy this.'

Michael flashed a knowing smile. 'Well, that may be about to change. I noted from your file that you've been working on your law degree, part-time, and that you've almost finished.'

'Yes Sir, I thought it might be appropriate, seeing as I am working for a law firm. And I don't want to stay in the secretarial pool forever.'

'Ambitious... I like that. I need a full time PA and I need someone who is sharp. The last few weeks have shown that you are a perfect fit, so here's what I am offering. You will become my PA and move into the office next door. You need to select someone from the pool to fill the job you've been doing. Now, before you say anything, a couple of other things.

'The company will pay your tuition fees and give you the time you need to complete your degree.' Michael stopped, thought for a moment and wrote something on a piece of paper. He folded it and handed it to Nyah. 'This will be your new salary, along with the normal benefits and conditions that come with the position. Now the downside: lots of work, long hours and, as you are no doubt aware, there are some strange things going on at the moment. Be warned... they will get stranger. Now how do you feel about it all?'

Nyah hadn't unfolded the piece of paper; she held it tightly in her left hand. She took a deep breath and a sip of her drink. 'I don't know what to say... yes... yes, I accept. Thank you, Sir.'

'Nyah, you haven't even looked at the salary, maybe it's not enough?' Michael grinned. Nyah opened the folded paper, her eyes growing wide as she read it.

'Thank you Sir, this is wonderful!'

'Excellent! A couple of other things... drop the Sir, you are my assistant and as such we will be working closely so less formality will be required. Michael will suffice most of the time. The other thing, I think you should finish your drink, go home, and celebrate with your family. I'll send the memo to HR, and they will complete the formalities tomorrow. I'll also backdate the salary to when you moved up here.'

'Thank you Sir, err Michael,' Nyah stuttered.

'Wait a few weeks before you thank me'

Nyah savoured the last of her drink and left. As she closed the door, Michael noticed a message icon on the bottom of his screen; it was from Cordoba. He opened it, scanned the business documents and forwarded them to Nyah. All that was left was the highly encrypted message from HG. Michael opened it and ran it through the decryption system. What came back, he read and read again.

'Fuck!' He said quietly as he read the message a third time. 'Fuck me… now things will get bloody hot.' The final paragraph actually caused him to laugh; HG reminded him that, as he and Gail were considered to be dead, Michael should arrange a memorial service for them. He poured another drink and gathered his thoughts.

Ok HG, if you want it that way, Michael thought as he began to enter a memo to all staff. The subject line was titled *Memorial for the Mossbergs*. When he finished, he smiled again before sending it to all employees. Checking the time again he decided not to go home.

Like most executives, Michael kept several changes of clothing in his office. He selected a suitable combination and called the garage to book a car for the evening. Next he showered, and changed. At seven thirty he was ready.

Michael arrived at the restaurant ten minutes early, his now customary tail following ineptly behind. He decided to wait at the bar and asked the Maître de to escort Solara to him, when she arrived. He ordered a drink and sat at a small corner table that gave him a good view of the entrance and the dining area.

As he expected, two agents followed him in. Both young, they tried to give the impression of a couple just out for an enjoyable evening. Sadly their trade-craft was poor and their actions gave them away in seconds. Michael smiled to himself. Remembering the old days when he was a field agent, if he was that obvious back then, he knew he wouldn't be here now.

Raphael's was the most discrete venue in the city and Michael was a regular customer. He was seated at his usual table, and he watched, with some amusement, as the new couple unsuccessfully tried to change their table to be closer to his. He was smiling as the waiter brought Solara to him.

'Michael, you seem to be in high spirits, care to share your thoughts?' She asked.

Michael waited until the waiter left with her drink order before he spoke. 'Yes, I've been watching the two who are tailing me. Were we ever that young and hopeless?'

'Speak for yourself, Mister Anderson. I remember a time when you removed me from an operation for the same indiscretions... give them a break.'

'I suppose you're correct but in my day, they'd be dead by now.' His voice was grave. 'But here's to a good night.' He raised his glass and Solara responded.

'Thank you but why are we here? Bosworth was very intrigued when you rang; in fact, I thought he was going to have a seizure when I told him it was just dinner. So I suppose that, if for no other reason tonight is already a screaming success.'

'Well it's not only dinner, so here's the pitch. It appears that my partners are now officially dead and that leaves me, and the firm, in a bit of a quandary. We're short two senior counsels and a work load that I won't be able to manage. Ever thought of ditching the cloak and dagger routine and joining the private sector?'

Solara appeared stunned by his words. 'Are you offering me a job?'

'Yes I am! You have a Masters with honours in Corporate Law and you minored in forensic economics, so you would be a great fit. I need someone to run our interstellar corporate division.' Michael reached into his pocket, withdrew the data drive and held it out.

He made a great show of handing it to Solara, mainly for the benefit of the two agents watching from the dining area. 'It's all on this: the offer, benefits, title and responsibilities. I'm serious... we could use someone with your credentials and I think you'll find this offer and package a huge step up from what you have now.'

Solara was silent. She held his hand, trying to decide whether to take the drive, or not. 'Michael, I'm flattered but you understand I haven't actually practised law for years.'

'I know, but your mind is sharp and your instincts well honed. The legal mumbo jumbo is the easy part; the real talent is what you have. Anyway, no need to answer now. Think it over and let me know your decision. But, this is a real offer; I need to fill this gap in the firm quickly.' Michael emphasised the last word.

Solara nodded and with a deliberate and obvious move, took the drive. Simultaneously, and secretly, she palmed a similar unit back into Michael's hand. 'I'll think it over and let you have an answer by three tomorrow.'

With business concluded, they went to their table to enjoy dinner. Conversation was general and mainly small talk, the only serious subject was the memorial for the Mossbergs. Solara agreed that an invitation should be sent to the Directorate. HG had tried several cases both for and against CID and had been successful in most. They finished dinner just after eleven and decided to call it a night.

Michael couldn't contain himself. He approached the couple who had been tailing him and spoke quietly to them.

'Now, listen to me. You two have lousy trade-craft and, take it from an old spy, in my day you'd both be in the morgue by now. So to help, I'm going home where I will spend the night. At seven in the morning I will rise and have breakfast. At eight, I'll take the car you have been following and return to the office by nine. Now you two can continue to follow me or take the night off and tell Bosworth that I'm insulted he sends students to keep tabs on me. Or, I will see you tomorrow.' He stood and left, before they could say anything.

'That was a bit brutal,' Solara chided.

'Not really, it was more for the benefit of the two clowns at the bar who followed you; they now think they went unnoticed,' Michael whispered as they left the restaurant. Solara's car was waiting, and she said goodnight just as Michael's Bentley arrived.

***

Nine am the next morning, Solara had just logged onto her console when Bosworth stormed into the room.

'Well, what happened? What did he want?' He demanded.

'And good morning to you Sir,' Solara replied, naked sarcasm in her words.

'Yes, good morning, now what is fucking Anderson up to?'

'Well, he offered me a job. That's what last night was about and believe me it's a very good offer.'

'Bullshit! He made two of our agents... he's up to something.'

Solara smiled. 'Wrong, again. He only spoke to two of them, the others he ignored, and while we're at it, why wasn't I informed of the operation? I thought CID was a team. Why were agents from a separate group watching me?' Solara took the initiative.

'Need to know and you didn't need to fucking know. Now how the hell did he make our guys?' Bosworth looked as if he was about to explode.

'Do you have any idea who you're dealing with?'

'Who... Anderson? He's just some bloody old lawyer, a lawyer who is starting to annoy me.'

Solara smiled. Bosworth had always been like a bull in a china shop. 'I suggest you look up his file, find out who you are really pissing off.'

'Don't be stupid, I've already read his file. We started it, remember!'

'Not that file... his employment file here with CID.' Her smile grew as she watched Bosworth stop. Her words hit him like a hammer.

'He worked here? There's no record of it on the system.' He blustered.

'Maybe that should tell you something.' Solara sat back at her desk. 'Now if you've finished, I've got work to do.'
***

While Solara was engaging with Bosworth, Michael entered his own office. He took the data drive she had given him and ran it through a full security scan before connecting it to his console. Most was data on the various coup players she had been able to identify, but the last file was probably the most important.

He scanned it, not really understanding all the engineering stuff, but quickly realised the advantage it might give Argos. He decided that the best course would be to send everything to HG, let them sort it out. Michael activated his DND status and began to draft the message. Once done he sat back, satisfied with what he had written.

He had included an update on the firm, what decisions he had made and finally a draft and timetable for the memorial. Michael took a little perverse pleasure as he imagined what HG would say about that. Finally, he ran it through the compression and encryption programs and embedded it into an innocuous business proposal to Cordoba, pressed transmit and deactivated his DND status.

A knock on his door brought him back to reality. Nyah entered, and they began discussing the list of applicants for their assistants. The work of running the firm was now his focus, with conspiracies relegated to the background.

Chapter 19: Ducks in a Row

Bosworth spent several hours scouring through the computer system.

Try as he might to find any reference to the employment of Michael Anderson in CID, he came up blank – not a single reference could be found in any of his searches. He was starting to think Zander had lost her mind when his final search responded – a single word *Vault*. He queried this and was immediately locked out. Seconds later a call came from the Director's office. He was wanted there immediately!

A summons from the Director was almost as important as a call from god, Bosworth hurriedly left his office. Five minutes later he was ushered into the Director's office by two guards.

Ivan Pankov, Director of CID motioned for the guards to leave. 'Bosworth, what's your interest in the vault?' Pankov never made small talk; he was always direct and blunt.

'Anderson... Michael Anderson. He's a person of interest and I've been told he used to work here but there's no record. One of the searches came back with that word, Sir.' Bosworth stammered.

'Why is he of interest?' Pankov's piercing black eyes bored into Bosworth like twin lasers.

'It's part of the investigation into the Daldaro incident, we believe that the law firm he works for may be involved.' Bosworth was regaining his composure.

'Daldaro, wasn't that was some sort of temporal accident? How can a law firm be involved?' Pankov asked quietly.

'That's exactly what we're trying to find out.' Bosworth answered confidently, but his thoughts were different *pompous ass; I'll enjoy watching you die.*

'Well, if there is anything to find... and I doubt there is; the Vault is located on sub-basement level twelve. I'll set it up. Take the express elevator to the lowest level, someone will meet you there.' Pankov dismissed Bosworth.

The door of the elevator opened at a discrete level, officially basement level five; a tall, young woman met him. 'Deputy Director Bosworth, if you would follow me.' She turned and started down the corridor. She stopped in front of another elevator, placed her hand on the scanner and the door opened. 'Please place your hand on the scanner.'

'What happens if someone tries to access and they're not in the system?' Bosworth tried to sound calm.

The woman gave Bosworth a steely, threatening gaze. 'They're never seen again.'

They entered the elevator and the doors closed. It dropped like a stone, down twelve floors in a couple of seconds. The door opened and she stood to one side. Another young woman approached.

'Follow me, Mister Bosworth.' Just ahead was a massive door, there were no locks and the door looked like it was part of the wall. Again this woman repeated the DNA access system. The door swung open. Inside were rows of what looked like individual safes. 'Now Sir, who were you interested in?'

'Anderson... Michael Anderson.' She entered the name into a console and pointed to a side room.

'Please wait in there, the files will be delivered shortly. When you're finished place the files back in the tray they are delivered on, and remember nothing can be copied or removed. Our security is total,' she said threateningly.

As the door closed behind her, a tray materialised from a slit in the wall. It came to rest on the table, Bosworth took his seat. On the tray was an old legal file, tied with tape. He broke the seal and opened it. Inside was a single folder, again sealed.

He broke this seal and dumped the contents. All that was there was a single sheet of paper with the words "Anderson, Michael: Retired." Bosworth picked it up, turned it over, held it up to the light but found nothing.

'Is that all?' he asked no-one, 'just a bloody name and the word retired?' He replaced the file in disgust, furious at the time wasted. 'Who the fuck is this guy?' He left the room and returned to his own office, seething at his failure.

***

Several thousand kilometres away a sleek black and silver shuttle touched down on the landing pad of Kynetis Limited's headquarters in what used to be Malawi, Africa. Nothing remained of the old city, Blantyre - everything had been devastated in the ancient Jihad wars. But, out of the ashes, Kynetis had built a gleaming new complex.

The location was chosen as it was far enough away from anywhere, that prying eyes rarely ever looked their way, something that Kynetis was grateful for. The door to the shuttle opened and the boarding ramp extended. A single occupant stood at the door. He turned to his left and thanked someone for the flight before exiting.

The landing pad was attached to the executive office floor, giving senior company officials discrete access. The occupant from the shuttle walked briskly to the office entrance. He was feeling particularly enervated this morning. Yesterday had seen the culmination of years of work with the takeover of Integrated Defence Technology, the major supplier of shield and ship defence systems to the Coalition. With this one move, Kynetis had become the major weapon system supplier to the entire Coalition. He smiled a huge beaming smile, something that was rarely, if ever seen on his face.

He approached the reception desk. 'Good morning Adam.' He greeted the young man at the desk.

'Good morning, Mister Naismith.' Clearly young Adam was startled by the cordial greeting from the company CEO. He quickly regained his composure. 'There are a number of communication drives on your desk Sir, and President Abercrombie's office rang... he would like to see you at your earliest convenience.'

'Thank you, Adam I'll deal with the communication, and then we'll arrange a time.' Naismith smiled again, and walked to his office. The room was huge, with windows covering the entire southern wall. He moved to the desk that faced the windows and sat down, activated his console and brought up a display on the centre screen. This detailed all the company's operations, something Naismith was extremely proud of.

Every type of weapon, space ships, even drive systems could be supplied by Kynetis and all transported by his family company, Galactic Freight. Now all he needed was to extract his stupid son from the farce on Argos, and all would be back on track. This thought returned his face to its normal scowl.

Graham Naismith had two children but only one son, Alistair - Captain of the former Galactic Freight ship Lady Philomena. The thought of his son's actions raised his blood pressure, h*ow could he have been so bloody stupid,* he thought but the anger was short-lived. With the plans now in place, Alistair's dilemma would soon be over.

He returned to his communications. Most were routine but the fifth one piqued his interest, it was from Joseph Jones. Naismith connected the drive and opened the file. It was a video file and the face of Joseph Jones filled the screen A*t last, Jones has seen sense* he gloated prematurely as he pressed the execute icon. The message was short but it caused the colour to drain from Naismith's face, disbelief replaced the confidence he displayed earlier.

'How?' the single word escaped his lips, then his comm unit buzzed. 'Naismith.'

*Graham, we need to talk. I've just had a strange discussion with the leader of the Council; it appears that our errant President Elect has turned up… **on fucking Argos**! How do you explain that?* The caller was President Abercrombie, and he sounded even more panicked than normal.

'Luthor, what do you mean, the leader of the Council told you? How'd he find out?'

*A message from Chang's security detail! Evidently he called them, told them where he was and also that he had deliberately slipped them so he could try to help in the Daldaro inquiry. The detail chief contacted his boss to fill her in and the entire team left for Argos. It appears that Chang dumped the team three weeks ago, supposedly to check on some **humanitarian** issue. According to the time frame, they should be there by now. What do we do next?* The mild panic was still in Abercrombie's voice.

'Do? You do nothing. Just keep cool and go about business as usual. I'll make some calls and see you around four, agreed?' Naismith's patience with whining politicians was very thin and Abercrombie was shaving it even closer. Naismith cut the comm before Abercrombie could say anything else. He retrieved another unit from a locked drawer in his desk and made a call.

Frederickson, was the one word reply.

'Ernst, we may have a problem. I'll come to you, say in an hour and a half?' Naismith asked.

Ninety minutes... agreed, Frederickson replied, and cut the link.

Ernst Frederickson reclined his chair, placed his booted feet on the desk and processed what he had just heard. Frederickson thought he knew all Naismith's machinations; but the current situation caused him to doubt his perceptive abilities. Development of the new weapon was one thing, but this rumoured coup – he still didn't believe it was the goal.

He knew Graham Naismith to be a very astute businessman, an entrepreneur who had, to date, made no mistakes. But with all that, Frederickson didn't believe Naismith was the one behind this move. To Ernst, he didn't have the brains, balls or, most importantly, the free capital to orchestrate and fund such an operation. *No, there's someone else behind all this... someone with incredible resources and technology.* For Naismith to risk coming to his base, Frederickson knew something dire must be in play. He settled back to wait.

***

Joseph sat on his new balcony, watching the sunrise. Gail had decided to go to the gym; she was starting to really feel the changed gravity and atmosphere of Argos and was trying to acclimatise as fast as possible. He was grateful that the inquiry was now out of his hands; his only involvement now was that of a witness, giving him and Gail the freedom to spend more time together and explore the possibilities of their relationship.

Finally, Zedak peeked above the horizon. There were none of its usual colour shows, the sky was too full of dark belligerent clouds; rain was finally a real possibility.

It had been twenty weeks since they had landed on Argos and in all that time there had only been three days when any rain fell, even the level of the river had fallen quite dramatically. While he was contemplating what this meant for the colony, the first drops of rain hit him. It was only seconds later that it came down in earnest. Huge drops of water crashed on the balcony and, as it had no cover, Joseph was drenched very quickly.

He smiled and went to the elevator platform, feeling refreshed and alive after his soaking. As he squelched his way through his quarters, a small robot cleaner darted out of its alcove and began to follow him, cleaning up his wet footprints and puddles from his clothing.

He removed his clothes and dumped them into the sanitiser, turned the shower on and entered the cubicle. He stood under the deluge, enjoying the hot water massaging his back, but he sensed something else. Joseph turned, opened his eyes and saw Gail standing beside him.

'Mind if I join you?' She asked as she moved closer. Joseph smiled and reached for her, she melted willingly into his embrace. They held each other for ages, Gail finally breaking the spell. 'See what surprises you get when you stay in one place long enough?' She stifled any answer with her lips, crushing them to his. The sound of his comm unit buzzing interrupted the moment; sheepishly he broke the embrace, his interest evident as he reached for a towel.

'Keep that thought,' Gail suggested as she smiled at his reaction. Joseph nodded and reached for a robe, clearly the towel wasn't going to work.

He went to his office and activated the console; there was a message from Earth. He read it and laughed. The message was from Naismith, accepting President Elect Chang as adjudicator but with a veiled warning that he considered nothing short of total exoneration of his son as an acceptable result.

'Arrogant arsehole;' Joseph said under his breath.

'Who's an arrogant arsehole?' Gail's voice came from the doorway. She stood provocatively, wearing nothing but a towel wrapping her hair.

Joseph groaned. 'I'll never get anything done if you keep dressing like that.'

'Oh, so you'd prefer me in head to toe garments? Believe me, I have some but I don't think they'd make you feel any different.' She giggled as she turned and left for the bedroom. Joseph was about to follow when the comm buzzed again; this time it was HG.

Jonesy, just getting out of bed… sorry, but we've just finished decrypting the message from Anderson. I think you need to see this, we're in engineering.

'Ok, I'll meet you in engineering in half an hour,' he said as he cut the link.

He found Gail, now dressed, in the kitchen making breakfast – Dab Korac sausages and eggs. One of the items he had insisted Freedom or Kidman bring to Argos were chickens, now they had fresh eggs every day. They took their time with the meal, savouring the tenderness and flavour of the sausages. 'That was great, thanks,' Joseph said gratefully, as he took his plate to the kitchen sanitiser.

'My pleasure,' Gail quipped, and then she looked seriously at him. 'I'm a bit overawed with all this. The incident seems so cut and dried but now to have the President Elect of the Coalition as adjudicator, well... I'm a bit nervous.'

'Interesting I've never seen you as the nervous type... you're always so calm and focused.'

'I suppose all the veiled threats and demands from Naismith senior are getting under my skin. You're right he is an arrogant bastard.' Gail's confidence reappeared as she left the table. 'Well I've got to present my initial argument in an hour, see you tonight.' She kissed Joseph lightly as she picked up her briefcase and data pad and headed for the door.

Joseph dressed and left for engineering. He was greeted by a delegation: HG, Bruce McGill, Don Hopmann and Rajiv Singh.

'This looks serious,' Joseph said as he entered.

'See for yourself.' Don activated the screen to the left of the desk. The display showed the schematics of a ship, but one Joseph didn't recognise.

'Ok, what am I looking at?'

'Ernst Frederickson's ship... somehow we've got everything, including...' he changed to another image, 'the special transponder system and code it uses.'

'And what's special about it?' Joseph asked, quietly.

'Well it doesn't register on normal transponder systems. To most, the ship just isn't there; it's invisible to transponder interrogation. But the signal is still there, just in the background noise. I asked Udon to bring all the transponder system logs from his Rift trip here.'

Udon entered the room and handed a data drive to Don who set it up on the console. Rajiv started working on it and minutes later, there was the signal. He quickly superimposed it over the flight log from Kidman and the result was startling. Frederickson was in the vicinity when the torpedo attack on Kidman took place. Then Rajiv isolated a second signal; he traced it from the source to its conclusion.

'Captain that was the torpedo they fired at you. Your transponder system recorded it even in hyperspace.' Singh's revelation astounded everyone; the secret transponder system used was now damning evidence of the attack.

'Make a recording of all this... I have an idea how we can use it,' Joseph ordered. 'Great work, everyone... really great work.' He left and raced back to his quarters, the call he had to make could be one of the most decisive he ever made.

***

The court of inquiry took the full five days Chang had allocated but finally, all evidence was exhausted, and he asked both legal representatives to sum up. This in itself was unusual. A court of inquiry was only about the evidence and facts, not legal argument, but he had decided to allow each side to summarise their position, allocating just fifteen minutes each. The court was adjourned for two hours to allow each to organise their thoughts.

Two hours later, HG was standing ready to deliver his summary; Chang took his seat just as Joseph entered the room. HG began his summation of the facts, and fifteen minutes later, he offered his final words.

'And; in closing I offer the following points for clarity. First, Captain Naismith acted in the best interest of his employer, Galactic Freight. He and his crew had made this trip no less than eighty-two times without incident. In fact, they had never needed to launch more than two of their shuttles at any time during these trips.

'Yes the ship was old... this was to be her last trip before she was decommissioned, and this in itself is a testament to the good maintenance record previously shown. In hindsight, it may have been more prudent to wait to transfer the shuttles, but we must remember this transfer was authorised by Galactic Head Office.

'And as for the strange anomaly, nobody knows where it came from or what caused it. Nothing like this has ever been recorded before. The testimony from Captain Tellyz shows that in all his crossings of the Rift he has never encountered anything like it.

'Now, I'm certain that the crew of the Lady Philomena were rightly concerned for their safety, but to mutiny? Well that is something they must all justify to themselves... but the real cause of this disaster is not Captain Naismith but the spatial anomaly that destroyed so much before it extinguished.' HG concluded and took his seat.

Damn, he's good Joseph thought, his mind now wondering what Gail could pull out of this for her clients.

Gail stood, her face a mask of concentration. She let her gaze roam the room. Finally seeing Joseph she smiled and gave him a conspiratorial wink.

'Adjudicator Chang, this case before you rests on one thing, and one thing only, a Captain's duty. It has nothing to do with corporations, profit or reputation; it is about a Captain's duty and responsibility.' She reached for a folder on the desk.

'I have here the standard contract a Captain signs when he qualifies to command a ship. It is a lengthy document, so I'm not going to read it entirely, just one paragraph. This paragraph is to be found on page three of the document, and it lists the critical responsibilities the rank and command position encompasses. Again there are a lot of words, so I'll only read these few, the first few lines of the paragraph, titled as critical responsibilities.

Any person assuming the command of a starship of any designation shall have as their first and foremost duty and responsibility, the safety and well-being of the crew under this command. In all aspects of said command this is the overriding responsibility of any person in the command position.

Gail looked up from the document. 'I see no mention of any employer or corporation as a responsibility, no mention of profit, no mention of any *on time* reputation, simply the responsibility of a Captain to his, or her, crew.

'Adjudicator Chang, it matters not at all whom, or what created the anomaly. It is inconsequential where it came from. The evidence is clear; Captain Naismith put his reputation, his corporation's profits before the safety of his crew.

'His actions were in direct violation of his sworn duties as a starship Captain, and these actions forced his crew into a position where the only way to ensure their safety was to remove him from command. Had they not done this, the evidence shows that all would have perished.'

Again Gail paused to allow her words to sink in. 'Captain Naismith has, by his own actions, demonstrated he is unfit to ever command a starship again. Thank you.' Gail finished and resumed her seat.

Chang rose. 'The court thanks all who have assisted in this matter. I will now adjourn to consider my findings... any such findings will be made available two days hence.' He turned and left the room.

Joseph left his seat and approached Gail and HG just as HG spoke to his daughter. 'Damn well done, I'm glad I never had to oppose you before.' His voice was filled with pride. 'Jonesy how about we go and have a drink, Gail's buying.' She shook her head and led them out of the room.

Now outside, they headed towards a new construction. Some of the crew were amateur brewers and, with Joseph's blessing, had set up a small brewery in what was becoming a commercial precinct of the accommodation area. A couple of small enterprises had started; a butcher, a bakery and now a brewery and pub. The name said it all *"Four Horns"*. Hanging over the entrance was a carved representation of the head and horns of the indigenous cattle.

They entered and took a table near one of the windows, ordered three beers and sat back to enjoy. Joseph smiled a very satisfied and contented smile.

'A penny for them?' HG asked, bringing Joseph back to reality.

'Just thinking, we've only been here for a few weeks, in reality, and already a colony is starting. We have a pub and a small retail sector, soon there'll be more and I reckon within a year this area will be thriving.' His voice was filled with enthusiasm.

HG nodded. 'In that case you'll need some laws and that means lawyers as well. Tell you what Jonesy, how about Mossberg and Partners sets up an office here.'

'Are you for real? I asked Gail to help with the basics... you know a constitution and such. I never thought you'd want to move here.'

'Listen Jonesy, every year less and less of our business is from Earth. Hell, our offices on Coltara now generate more income than Earth. In fact, most of the work on Earth is done in support of off world operations. The reality is that while Earth is still the headquarters of the Coalition, and I believe will always be, it is becoming a distant destination for the majority of the human race. Shit Argos is actually closer to most, than Earth.

'That being said, if we set up now we can start a process of transferring our operation closer to most of our clients... got to be good for business. So what do you say

'Hang on a minute dad. Have you thought this through or is it one of your knee-jerk reactions?' Gail interjected.

'Believe me, this is something Anderson and I talk about constantly... how to take the firm from a backwater Earth centric operation to a truly galactic one. Argos is the answer we've been looking for. Location is perfect, the neutrality Jonesy keeps rabbiting on about is ideal, and this way I'll be able to be closer to my grandkids.' HG was grinning broadly, as he spoke.

Gail threw her hands up, 'I give up... you're incorrigible! So what happens to Earth?'

'Anderson... he's better connected there anyway. He can take over running Earth and gradually we'll transfer operations here. Once word gets out that Mossberg and Partners are here, business that used to be sent to Earth will flow here instead. We've been looking for a base like this for a couple of years now.' HG's logic was sound and Gail had to admit he really had thought it through.

Joseph entered the conversation. 'Well that's settled. We'd be very glad to have Mossberg and Partners set up as our first law firm.' He was cut short by the buzzing of his communicator. 'I'm needed back on Drake, see you tonight.' He bent down and kissed Gail tenderly.

Chapter 20: Inclement Weather

Joseph walked onto the Bridge on Drake.

Molly Renwick and Goran Illych were concentrating on a console. 'Captain… sorry I didn't hear you come in,' Molly apologised. 'This is why we called you here.' She moved aside so Joseph had a better view.

'What am I looking at?' He asked.

'A huge low pressure system headed our way,' Goran answered. 'Since we got here, we've been building a global weather monitoring system… this is the first result.'

'How big, how bad…and how long, before it hits us?' Joseph asked, studying the screen.

'We sent a shuttle into orbit, to survey it. This storm is two thousand kliks across.' Molly changed the image to the shuttle feed. It looked like a massive cloud, swirling in a clockwise direction. Solid white, the cloud obscured everything below it while at the centre a small opening showed a clear view down to the sea below.

'We have a climatologist on the truck, she's monitoring it, but she says it's going to be bad. Probes we sent into the storm registered wind speeds of two hundred and fifty kph… our buildings will handle that, it's the ships I'm concerned about,' Illych said. 'I would advise to get any we can into orbit… safer there, but Drake is my real worry.'

'Why? We've anchored her solidly haven't we?' Joseph stood back, waiting for an answer.

'Yes, I think so, but we didn't factor these conditions into the footings, and she's awfully exposed here.'

Joseph gazed round the Bridge, now largely devoid of equipment. 'She's withstood so much… I think the old girl will survive this, but in any case, there's not much we can do.' He paused. 'Molly, have all senior officers join us, we're going to need to get things happening. How long Goran?'

'At present speed, eight hours.'

'Ok! We've got eight hours to well and truly batten down the hatches, so we better get started. 'Molly, when you call the senior officers here contact Phillipe and Silvio, they may want to ride this out in orbit.' As he finished Phillipe and Silvio entered the Bridge.

'Bit of a storm brewing?' Phillipe asked.

'Yes, a rather nasty hurricane by the looks of it.' Joseph confirmed. Minutes later, the senior officers joined and a hasty plan was thrashed out. The doors to the hangar were now installed so some of the ships could be accommodated in there. Freedom was too large so Don left to gather his crew and return to orbit. Kidman, being slightly narrower, was already in the hangar and would be left there while Silvio's ship was to be moved inside as well.

The buildings Omnicron had installed were more than capable of withstanding the coming onslaught but Drake and the Hyzene plant were the main concerns for everyone. Two engineering teams were dispatched, one to secure the Hyzene plant and pipeline, the other to install additional tethers to Drake. The latter proved to be complex, any failure of the primary structure would cause cascade of problems for the team.

Six and a half hours later Bruce McGill called a halt. 'There's nothing more we can do; the old girl is on her own now.' He stood back, letting his gaze roam over the work they had completed.

A spider's web of high tensile cables secured into deep holes drilled into the ground, and filled with a special composite compound, now gave Drake additional anchor points.

Bruce checked the time. 'Well done everyone, now let's get back inside and make sure she's locked up tight.' He had to shout over the increasing sound of howling wind. A quick check around the ship showed that, except for the main access ramp they were heading for, Drake was locked up.

The team double timed back to the ramp, the wind increasing in intensity with each step. Again, Bruce checked that each member of his team was aboard before he activated the ramp mechanism.

Slowly, the huge structure began to rise. The massive magneto-hydraulic rams straining against the constant pressure of the howling wind outside. It took a full ten minutes to close and seal and by that time the floor of the hold was awash.

This was something that the ship wasn't designed to handle and Bruce called for pumps to be found. The problem he now faced was where to pump the water. With Drake sealed against the storm, it couldn't be dumped outside.

One of the engineering ratings found a solution. He took three colleagues and returned shortly after with three Hyzene storage tanks, the ones used to extend the range of the tugs. They set these up and soon had all the water off the floor, Bruce smiled at the solution... another testament to the spirit of the crew.

'Good job! Now I suggest we all change into some dry clothes and get some rest... nothing else to do at the moment.' He dismissed them and headed for his cabin.

Dry, and dressed in fresh clothes, Bruce walked onto the Bridge. Joseph was sitting in his command chair watching the storm on the main screen. The readout in the left corner indicated the wind speed, currently showing two hundred and sixty kph, Silvio, Phillipe and Goran were also watching the screen, all so intent on the view they didn't notice his entrance.

He went to the engineering station — luckily it hadn't been cannibalised yet. He initialised it and started to interrogate the stress data — the old ship was holding up well. He let out a sigh of relief. So far his lock down system was working. It was then he noticed the shield system was operating. Bruce called Molly over, she explained that she had suggested this to Captain Jones, and they had modified the system to operate as a ground based shield wall.

'Impressive, Lieutenant, very impressive.' Bruce congratulated her for her foresight. Modifying the system to this new function wasn't easy and Molly Renwick wasn't an engineer, making her actions even more impressive.

'Bruce... didn't hear you come in.' Joseph turned his chair, to face the engineer. 'Are you happy with Molly's idea?'

'Extremely! She'd make an excellent engineer,' he fired back as he left the station and moved to Joseph's side. 'Any idea how long this will last?'

Phillipe answered. 'No, this is just the tip, and it's slowed. Current estimate is for around forty hours of this, if the system stays on course.'

The answer concerned Bruce. 'If this is just the tip, as you said, how much worse can it get?'

Phillipe paused; his face told Bruce what he really wanted to know. 'The last probe we sent in recorded three hundred kph wind speed, before it stopped transmitting.'

The screen changed and now focused on the accommodation blocks. Torrential rain was falling, so heavy that the drainage system wasn't coping. Flooding was evident; nothing to worry about, at the present stage, but enough to cause concern later, if things didn't change.

'What about the Hyzene plant?' Bruce asked. Joseph changed the feed again and now the plant was visible.

'We have five feeds from here... so far it seems to be holding,' Joseph offered. The plant was, indeed, holding. All structures were intact and very little appeared to be reason for alarm. 'I suggest we set up a monitoring team, one for each sector... four hour shifts should keep attention levels where we need them.'

McGill nodded and called Molly over; together they began setting up the teams for the job. Once completed Bruce handed the data pad to Joseph, who read the lists and gave his approval.

'Fifteen minutes to the hour... we can begin at four, agreed?'

Bruce agreed and sent the notifications out to each team member as Joseph changed the feed to the control station atop the bluff. Here things were worse; the bluff was actually giving Drake and the settlement some protection, but clearly not helping the new structure. Already one of the smaller buildings had suffered damage with cladding panels missing. So far, thankfully, the sensor domes were intact as was the control tower.

Next he checked the landing pads, but with only two feeds, he couldn't see much. Joseph cycled through all the feeds again, noting that little had changed, only the flooding in the accommodation area seemed to be worse, but still well below any point of real concern. The door opened and ten crew members walked in.

'Good afternoon,' Joseph welcomed them. 'Your tasks will be to monitor the feeds coming in. Any changes will need to be noted and given to one of the senior officers for action. Lieutenant Commander Thompson is duty officer for this watch; she will be here in the command chair.'

Right on cue, Allison entered the Bridge and went to the chair as Joseph vacated it. 'Now the rest of us will leave. Commander you have the con.'

'Aye Sir, I have the con.' Allison settled into the seat.

***

For the next twenty hours the storm raged over the settlement, wind gusts exceeded predictions and more than five hundred millimetres of rain fell; finally it changed direction and moved down the coast. Orbiting above, the Terra Truck kept a watch as the hurricane weakened, and eventually dissipated.

Now with clear skies overhead, the new settlement began the task of cleaning up. Surprisingly, damage was relatively light and, except for a couple of flooded areas, repairs would be easy. It did show, however, that weather patterns on Argos were unpredictable. Given the limited knowledge of the planet, a new data system was set up to record any weather fluctuations. To help this, Omnicron made the global monitoring system, incorporating both land based and orbital elements, its top priority. This was a standard system they used in planning any terra-forming operation, Joseph agreed and the team in orbit began assembling the necessary hardware.

Three days after the storm, Steven Chang called Joseph to arrange for the handing down of his findings. To allow for all involved to be present, the time was set for 11:00 hours the next day, Friday as per Earth calendar.

At 18:00 Joseph entered his quarters, the smell of roasting meat greeting him. Deciding to be flippant he called out, 'Honey, I'm home,' chuckling to himself as he did.

Gail came round the divide between the kitchen and the living area. She was dressed as he had never seen her before, sporting a new floral apron. 'About time... much later and my dinner would have been ruined. Now get cleaned up while I serve.'

Joseph grinned from ear to ear and couldn't resist the temptation. 'What a wonderful thing. The lord and master returns home to find a hearty cooked meal is waiting,' he ducked and ran for the bedroom, as the spoon she was holding sailed towards him.

'Another crack like that and all you'll ever eat again is dry bread... two days old at least!'

Dinner was wonderful, roast haunch of Dab Korac with local roasted root vegetables. A very pleasing aged red accompanied the meal. As he finished, Joseph smiled and leaned back in his chair.

'I must say, you really are a surprise package. I never saw you as the domestic type and that meal was definitely fit for any royalty.'

Gail fidgeted a bit and then replied. 'I have a confession... I rarely ever cook, except when I'm nervous, and I'm very nervous about tomorrow.'

'Why? You did a great job!'

'I did the best I could, but I'm concerned about what the outcome will do to Argos and your dream, about how Naismith and Galactic will respond, if it goes against them.' Gail was serious and very worried, Joseph could see that.

'Look, the outcome will be what it is. Any fallout, we'll face together, so stop worrying.' He stood and moved to her side, took her hand and continued. 'Gail, from a space farer's view point, Captain Alistair Naismith should be blown out an airlock for placing his crew in that situation and I don't give a damn what his father says. I'll meet Graham Naismith head on, as I have in the past, so forget about the finding. You did your job and so did HG. Remember, we have the President elect of the Coalition acting as adjudicator so the outcome is owned by the Coalition, not us.

Now, let's finish dinner and see what mischief we can get up to after that.' His smile seemed to calm her, and she returned to her meal.

Chapter 21: Counter Coup

Michael Anderson sat quietly at his desk, contemplating the evening's mission.

He looked at the time readout on his screen for the tenth time, 21:48 was displayed. *Twelve minutes* he thought to himself. He reviewed all the information, again coming to the same conclusion, now must be the time to act.

His past was a great advantage in this situation, and he had been able to put together most of his old team. Every one of them ready to put their lives on the line for a cause they believed in. These brothers in arms had been together for years, in the service; now they were lawyers, bankers one was even a restaurateur, but they never forgot their past.

When Michael had made initial contact it was like he had woken a dragon, and to a man, and woman, they agreed to the mission. A mission which, if unsuccessful would see them end up in an unmarked grave somewhere.

The time readout changed again, 21:53, time to go.

Timing on this job was critical, the smallest delay or deviation could jeopardise everything. He stood, adjusted the shoulder harness, took the old Evans pistol from the hidden drawer in his desk, attached the silencer and checked the load. Satisfied, he holstered the weapon, donned his coat and placed five spare magazines in the special pockets in the lining. He carefully checked his reflection in the now opaque, office window. Satisfied, he checked the time for the last time, 21:56.

Michael smiled. *'Show time'* he said to himself.

Michael exited the elevator and approached the building entrance, 22:00 showing on the digital clock behind the security desk. He nodded to the guard and walked through the door, right on time.

As he stepped out to the footpath he casually glanced down the street, like anyone looking for a taxi. What he did note was the grey ground car half a block to his right on the opposite side of the street. Michael smiled; *these guys are nothing if not consistent.* His mind cleared as he prepared for his first involvement in the operation.

He turned to his left and started to walk down the street, noting the window on the fourth floor of the building opposite was slightly open, and the room in darkness. In itself, this could be meaningless, but with the rest of the building ablaze with light it was a clue that a seasoned operative would twig to.

He counted his steps. At thirty-five he pressed a button on his belt sending the go signal to his team. Instantly he ducked into the alley now on his left.

Things happened quickly and invisibly. The two operatives in the grey car tried to start the vehicle, but the system refused to initialise. They next tried to open the doors – again the system refused their command. Then they noticed the old woman standing in the doorway of the building they were parked near. She was holding a data pad. She smiled, blew them a kiss and tapped the pad. Both men felt a sharp sting in their buttocks; then everything went black.

The old woman tapped her pad again, sending a confirmation signal to the rest of the team. The soft chime, in Michael's ear told him that phase one was complete.

Phase two was just as quick. The open window that Michael noticed was actually a hide for a sniper, as he suspected – just far enough inside to be totally concealed. She brought her weapon to bear, the scope trained on Michael's head. She moved her finger to the trigger and took the first pressure, just as her target disappeared into the alley.

'Fuck,' her last word of frustration left her mouth just as the door flew open. She didn't hear or see anything. The only sound that was made was the cycling of the Evans 10 mm pistol as it fired and cycled twice. The sniper was dead before she could hear the first pop. The tall man in the doorway tapped an icon on his communicator, telling Michael he had completed his task.

Michael felt a twinge of remorse; three dead and the two now entering the alley behind him not for this world much longer.

'Anderson, CID... **stop**!' One of the men following him called.

Michael already had his pistol in his right hand. As he turned, he pressed a button on his belt and activated a personal dispersion field. His rationale was that these two wanted him alive and would be using sonic disruptors.

Both of the CID agents saw his weapon.

'**Drop the gun!**' The lead agent called.

Michael just smiled.

'I said drop it, I won't tell you again.'

Michael felt the recoil of the Evans a fraction of a second before he saw the neat 10 mm hole appear in the first guy's forehead. The next two hit the second agent squarely in the chest, both died before they even knew they had been shot.

Michael didn't give them a second glance. He simply turned and continued down the alley, exiting at the far end just as a black ground car pulled to the kerb. The door opened and Michael Anderson climbed in. The first mission of the evening was complete, now it was up to Solara to complete hers.

***

Brian Bosworth, Deputy Director of CID, entered the restaurant feeling a little apprehensive about the evening. For several weeks he had been watching one of his subordinates, Solara Zander, unsure as to where her loyalty lay. He had made overtures that he could help her career, but she seemed to be impervious to his words. The fact she had agreed to dinner tonight, puzzled him. Still, he was here, and she would be joining him shortly. He went straight to the bar, ordered a gin and tonic and sat at one of the corner tables.

Solara entered the restaurant a few minutes later, recognised Bosworth and walked to his table. He stood as she approached.

'Good evening, Sir.'

'Please Solara... tonight we're just two people out for dinner, so please call me Brian.' His usual snide voice was gone; he was trying to be charming. 'Now, what would you like to drink?'

Solara gave a seductive smile. 'A Vodka Martini... dirty please.' He moved to the bar to order her drink. Solara checked the time − 10:15, *seven minutes more*, she thought.

Bosworth returned and took her coat, his eyes roaming over her body, the elegant dress accentuating every curve. 'You look ravishing tonight,' he complimented her.

Solara smiled and thanked him. Her drink arrived and Bosworth's attention was diverted, just for a moment. Solara surveyed the room, a casual glance to any observer.

'I'm glad you chose this place, I've heard a lot about it but have never come here. The decor is wonderful.' Her gaze flowed round the room, taking in everything. What she did notice, there were no other agents. Bosworth's arrogance was working to her advantage.

'Yes, very intimate, and the food is wonderful.' Bosworth was doing his best to impress.

Solara glanced at the time readout behind the bar – 20:22, – time was up. She moved closer to Bosworth, placed her right hand on his left and smiled, inviting him to move closer. He did, just as she activated the small injector in the ring on the right hand. Bosworth felt the sting, but the pressure from Solara's hand held him in place.

'Brian, you're about to pass out. To everyone here it'll look like you're having a seizure of some kind. Don't worry; an ambulance will be here in minutes to collect you.' Her voice was calm and icy, Bosworth wanted to cry out, but he couldn't make a sound. His arms and legs felt like lead and his head started to spin.

Solara pushed her chair back, just as Bosworth started to foam at the mouth. 'Help me! Please someone, help me! He's having a fit. Call an ambulance!' As she cried out, she lowered Bosworth to the floor, loosened his tie and started searching his pockets. In the left side coat pocket she found what she was looking for, his emergency transmitter. Deftly, she palmed it and replaced it with an emergency syringe.

'I found it!' She cried, trying to sound concerned, as she removed the protective cover and exposed the instrument.

She pushed the needle through his trouser leg and into his thigh, administering a lifesaving drug, or so it would appear. As she withdrew the unit, two paramedics raced through the door. They worked on Bosworth for the next five minutes, stabilising him before a gurney was brought in, and he was transferred to the waiting ambulance outside.

'You probably saved his life, ma'am,' the paramedic said to Solara. 'Do you want to accompany him to the hospital?'

'Yes, please.' She stood but stumbled.

'A good idea, you've had quite a shock.' With that the paramedic took her arm, and supported her to the waiting ambulance. Once the door closed it left the curb and raced away, siren blaring. Solara noted the time – 20:32 – the schedule was intact.

The ambulance raced through the city, Solara and the paramedic constantly watching for any sign of pursuit. Finally, satisfied they were not being followed Solara called, 'Kill the noise... time to be stealthy.' With the siren and lights off, the ambulance slowed to normal traffic speed until it entered a warehouse precinct.

Now they took a number of turns to reach their ultimate destination. The building ahead was dark, no streetlights showed the way. The driver killed the headlights. To any possible spying eyes, this was just a dark street.

Slowly, they crawled up to the building. As they did a door opened in front of them. They drove inside and the door closed. The driver pulled up beside an elevator and Solara and the paramedic got out, pulled Bosworth out behind them and replaced the gurney with one standing adjacent to the elevator door.

Once the door was closed, the ambulance moved off – the plan was to have it back at the hospital before 23:00. Solara pushed the gurney into the elevator, closed the doors and inserted a key into the control pad. She pressed the down button, noting that there were no floors indicated, and the elevator began to descend.

***

At the same time that Solara first entered the restaurant, Admiral William Cartwright was pouring himself his fourth whisky of the evening. He was sitting in his favourite chair in his study, and he was drinking more heavily than usual. His companion for the evening knew it was best to leave him to his demons; she had retired at his third glass.

The Admiral was worried. He had a long and distinguished career – first, as a frigate Captain, where he had shone in a number of battles. He was promoted quickly, taking command of larger vessels and displaying impressive leadership to his superiors. His first promotion to Admiral gave him command of a full battle group of twelve ships. In this role he had proved himself to be the equal of any Krell commander and gained a reputation that elicited respect, even from his enemy. He kept rising through the ranks to end up as Fleet Admiral, commanding the entire Coalition Space Corps. But, as sometimes happens, Cartwright bored quickly in his present role. He was a field Commander, and a good one. Now, as the Commander in Chief, his main role was to meet with politicians, press the flesh and generally make nice to the powers that be.

Boredom brings new challenges, but it was the risk, the adrenalin rush of battle that Cartwright craved. Sadly his boredom led him to gambling. At first, just a little flutter, but as time went on it became an obsession, an expensive one.

That was when Naismith had first approached him. The Admiral was deep in debt, too deep. After a period of befriending, Naismith had made his offer. Cartwright had no option, the alternative was exposure and the loss of everything, so he accepted Naismith's offer and became a puppet of the unfolding political drama.

The Admiral swore, threw the glass into the old fireplace and swore again. He stood, went to the cabinet and selected another glass. He had just filled it when the door opened.

'Sorry, Admiral, you don't have time for that drink. Come with me now.' The commanding voice of Jefferson Holt burned through the fog now enveloping the Admiral's brain. He nodded and put the glass down, following Holt out of the room.

'Don't worry, when your young lady wakes in the morning, she'll find the message from you telling her you were called to the office... an emergency.' They left through the front door and approached a waiting ground car. Holt stood aside and indicated for the Admiral to get into the rear seat.

The door opened just as two distinct pops were heard. Cartwright turned just as Holt dropped – two holes in his chest. He hadn't even hit the ground when three people rushed up; one pushed the Admiral into the car while the other two placed Holt into a body bag.

Cartwright looked at the man now beside him. 'Who are you? Do you know who you just killed?'

Michael removed his balaclava and smiled to Cartwright. 'Michael Anderson, lawyer, at your service Sir, and yes, I know who I just killed... a real piece of shit. Now settle back and enjoy the ride.'

He opened a small cabinet in front of them. 'I think you'll find this a particularly fine single malt, Admiral.' Michael produced two glasses and poured two fingers for each of them. 'Now Admiral, please regale me with the story of how you fucked up and joined with Naismith and co?'

It was 23:35 when Michael's car entered the warehouse. He had been correct about the whisky, it was good. Unfortunately for the Admiral his glass had been treated with an exceedingly effective drug; under its influence, Michael had found him to be a very accessible source of information. He deposited the now comatose Admiral in the elevator with one of the operatives; now the final part of the mission was under way.

The door to the car opened and Solara stepped in. 'Evening Michael, you seem to have had a productive time?'

'You have no idea.' He started to play the tape of Cartwright as the car left the building, the driver taking a circuitous route to their destination. As it finished, Solara reached for her communicator, placed a call and asked the recipient to meet her at the office in twenty minutes. Ten minutes later they arrived at CID headquarters and left the car.

'You'll need to leave the cannon,' Solara suggested.

Michael shook his head and smiled. 'No I won't. Just watch, it'll pass through your security unnoticed.' As he predicted, he walked straight through the scan. Solara had to hand in her blaster though. They reached her office before she asked. 'Ok how did you get that thing in here?'

Michael chuckled. 'I used to work here and when we changed over to energy weapons, they changed the security protocol. Some genius in a suit and tie decided that projectile weapons were no longer necessary and the new security system was set up. It only scans for energy signatures. Hell, I could probably walk in with an old rocket launcher and those idiots would think it was an umbrella stand.'

As he finished, the door burst open and a tall well-built man strode in. 'Zander, what's so important you drag me out of bed and demand a meeting?' he paused, looked hard at Michael, 'and who the hell is this?'

Solara moved between the two men. 'Michael Anderson... Michael, this is the Director of CID, Ivan Pankov.'

Pankov looked hard at Michael, his grey eyes trying to bore through Michael's soul, but not achieving much. 'Anderson, I've heard that name somewhere,'

Michael answered. 'Probably, I'm a senior litigator with Mossberg and Partners.'

Pankov shook his head. 'No, you used to work here, I'm sure of it.'

'Yes Director, a long time ago; but we can reminisce some other time, right now we have a crisis that needs to be managed.' Michael produced the recording of Cartwright and handed it to Solara; she brought it up on her console and started the playback.

Twenty minutes later, Pankov's face looked drawn and grey. 'And this is for real?'

Solara answered. 'Yes Sir. We've run an operation tonight and caught most of the players; some are already off world and will be handled by others. The thing now is, can we trust you?'

'And if you can't, what then?' Pankov asked.

Michael's hand movement appeared to be a blur; one instant it was by his side, the next he was holding the Evans to Pankov's head. 'In that case, you'll never leave this room. Now shall we dispense with the bullshit and save the Coalition?'

Pankov didn't flinch; he just stared at the gun. 'How the fuck did you get that antique in here?'

Michael smiled, holstered the gun and answered. 'I'll tell you some time, but for now we have work to do.'

Pankov moved to the desk. 'OK what do you need from CID?'

'The President, he's in on it and, we suspect, some of the Council as well. We need to keep a close eye on him and the Council, see if we can catch them out. We also have Bosworth, and he's singing very nicely. As soon as we've finished with him we hope to have more names, so are you in?'

Pankov just smiled and nodded. He opened his coat to reveal the butt of an old revolver. 'I remember where I heard of you... you warned the then Director about the security system. Still, it works for me... we'll keep it our secret. And yes I'm in.' he turned to Solara. 'Now, acting Deputy Director Zander, what's your next move?'

'What did you just call me?'

'Acting Deputy Director... Bosworth had a seizure tonight, which makes him medically unfit for duty. You're currently section chief so you can fill his role until the situation is rectified. You can have whatever resources you need. What are you going to do?' Pankov stood back to allow Solara to take charge.

She thought for a few minutes, and then spoke. 'First we need to secure the President, let's say we have a credible threat to his safety. Next, we lock down the Council; part of the threat is a possible breach of security protocol. This will give us a reason to start snooping and, under the constitution CID is the only agency who has the authority to investigate. To start with I'll need twenty agents and three rapid response teams.'

Pankov moved to the console. 'May I?' Solara agreed and he began to issue a directive. When he finished he asked her to check it. The directive announced her as acting Deputy Director of CID, and authorised her to second any and all operatives and materiel needed to counter a credible threat to Coalition security, effective immediately. Within seconds, every operative and employee of CID had the information, now it was up to Solara.

Michael moved towards the door. 'You two have heaps to do, I'll leave you to it.'

'Just a moment, I'll come with you, at least to the front door,' Pankov replied. 'I think we need to issue you a pass... I have a feeling you'll be here periodically, at least until we sort this mess out.'

***

The concierge at the Grand Hotel was enjoying the peace of the late shift. Most of the guests had returned and the hotel was quiet, now he could relax a bit. He was finalising the administrative tasks for the shift when four large black vehicles pulled up under the portico.

People clad in tactical armour spewed out of the first and last vehicle and raced to form a perimeter in front of the hotel. The rear door of the limo in the convoy opened and a tall, elegant woman got out. She walked purposefully towards the front door, her eyes dancing through every angle covering the entrance; two well-armed men fell in behind her. Solara walked through the door and over to the reception desk, the two men taking up flanking positions either side of the main entrance. She held her right arm out, so he could read her implant.

'Solara Zander, Deputy Director CID,' she announced. 'This hotel is now in lock down, nobody gets in or leaves, is that understood?'

The concierge swallowed, hard. He passed his scanner over her right forearm and read the screen. She was who she said, and there was an order to lock down the hotel.

'Now I believe President Abercrombie is here... in the Presidential Suite I believe?' She asked.

'I'm not at liberty to say, ma'am,' the concierge stammered, 'we can never confirm or deny his presence.'

'Listen, my friend, we have evidence of a credible threat to Coalition security and that includes the President. We are here to secure him and transfer him to a new location; you can either help us or be charged with obstruction... your call.' Solara's voice carried a grim threat.

'Yes ma'am, he's on the twelfth floor... elevator three is the only one programmed to stop there.'

Solara looked at his name tag. 'Thank you, Justin. Just stay here, this will be over in a few minutes.' She turned and beckoned to someone outside. Five more heavily armed men entered the foyer and followed Solara to the elevators. Solara and one of the men entered number three. The others took two separate elevators, one to the floor above and the other to the floor below. Solara waited for thirty seconds after the other elevators moved before entering hers, giving them time to get into position, just in case.

The Presidential Suite was the entire twelfth floor. It was located at this level for security reasons, not at the top or bottom of the hotel as these were too easy to breach. The twelfth floor was in the middle of the relatively low rise building, giving it a degree of anonymity and making ingress more difficult.

The elevator took thirty-eight seconds to traverse the twelve floors and, when the computer announced they had reached the destination; Solara tapped a small device in her right coat pocket. This device generated a signal that disabled the Presidential Protection Detail (PPD) comms while signalling to her team that the operation had started. Time was now of utmost importance. They had allowed five minutes to get to the President, rouse him and return to the elevator.

The door opened and Solara stepped out. The elevator was at the far end of the corridor. Three PPD operatives were stationed along its length. Three more would be in the suite and the floor above and below would also be secured.

She held up her hand, displaying her ID. 'Solara Zander Deputy Director CID,' she called out as she walked forward. The operative immediately in front of her drew his weapon and covered her. 'Stand down agent, that's an order!' Solara barked.

'No, you stop!' Solara stopped as the young woman walked up to her, the other two now rushing in support, weapons drawn.

'Look at the ID and holster your weapons... I won't tell you again!' Solara's voice was firm. The woman reached her and took the ID, examined it and holstered her weapon as the other two joined her.

'Sorry ma'am, just doing our job.'

'I understand, but I am ordering you to stand down. We have a credible threat to the President... we're here to take him to a secure location.' Solara retrieved her ID and started to walk toward the entrance of the suite.

'I'm sorry ma'am; I can't allow you to go in there,' one of the other operatives said.

Solara turned to him, her eyes boring into him like lasers. 'And just who the hell are you? I know PPD, but PPD works for me, so this is a direct order. Stand down or suffer the consequences!'

The young operative stood his ground. 'Sorry ma'am, but the President gave orders he wasn't to be disturbed.' He got no further. Solara's right hand flashed out, the blow catching him in the solar plexus, knocking the wind out of him and temporarily stopping his diaphragm. As he doubled over, Solara's companion moved out from his place of concealment on the left side of the elevator car, behind the control panel.

'I wouldn't if I were you.' his voice menacing as the other two turned to look down the barrel of his long arm blaster. 'Drop the weapons on the ground. Now, hands behind your heads.'

Solara turned to the young man on the ground, took his weapon and spoke quietly to him. 'The credible threat we have implicates PPD. Now understand this, you're under arrest.' She took the door key from him and left her companion to deal with the three as she ran toward the suite door, two other agents joining her from the stair well.

Solara drew her weapon as they reached the door, used the coded key and threw the door open.

'CID, drop your weapons!' She ordered as she burst into the room. The three PPD guards were all sitting watching a hockey match on the screen; instantly they leapt up but the sight of drawn weapons staring at them forced them to comply.

'Where's the President?' One of the guards gestured to the door to Solara's right; she went to the door and threw it open.

The scene that greeted her was a simple confirmation of many rumours. 'A bit young, even for you Mister President,' she spat as the two young girls hastily reached for their clothes.

'Who are you? I'll have your head for this!' Abercrombie blustered.

'Not likely Sir. Solara Zander Deputy Director CID, we have a credible threat to security. I'm here to take you to a more secure location. Now I suggest you get dressed, quickly.'

She pulled the two girls to one side. 'I'm not going to ask your age but listen up. I will have you taken home and neither of you will ever speak of this again. If you do, I will find you and believe me, you really don't want that.' Her eyes told the girls she was serious. 'Are we clear?'

They both quietly responded. 'Yes ma'am.' One seemed to find some courage and asked. 'Do we still get paid? He got what he wanted!'

Solara grabbed the wallet on the bedside table, opened it and saw a wad of cash withdrew all the notes and handed it to the girls. 'Now remember... tonight never happened.' Both girls nodded their agreement.

'Harrow!' One of the agents leapt through the door, Solara beckoning him to her. 'Have a car brought to the car park; the driver is to leave it there. Take the girls home and do it discretely.'

Harrow nodded, understanding what had transpired. 'Yes ma'am.' And he gathered the girls and took them to an adjoining room while he arranged transport.

Abercrombie returned to find only Solara waiting. 'Thank you, Deputy Director.'

'Don't thank me, you filthy piece of shit! I'm not doing this for you, but for the office and the Coalition. You, Abercrombie, I'd rather take my blaster and blow that pathetic excuse you call your dick off... if you weren't the President... I would.

'But unfortunately, you are still President of the Coalition and my sworn duty is to protect both, but think on this... soon, you'll just be a memory, just a citizen. If I ever even hear a rumour that you're up to this behaviour again, one morning you'll wake up with that tiny lump of flesh in your throat... now get moving.' She pushed Abercrombie out of the room.

The elevator door opened and the foyer was secured by five heavily armed agents, Solara led Abercrombie through the foyer and out the door. Three limos were waiting; they took the second one. Each car now had three occupants — the driver and two in the rear — the convoy set off. The operation had taken seven minutes and thirty-eight seconds; thirty-eight seconds too long.

'Egress plan Gamma three five,' Solara spoke into her communicator as the three cars and four armoured transports sped off. They headed for the cross city tunnel, entering at speed. Once inside, the lead vehicle activated a transmitter that blacked out all security in the tunnel.

Five minutes until emergency response arrives. The voice from the lead vehicle announced.

Two minutes later, the first car took the City East exit, thirty seconds later their car took the City South exit. Just as they exited the tunnel, the car stopped; two people were standing by the emergency access door. Solara pushed Abercrombie out of the car and the two newcomers took their place.

She wasted no time, forcing Abercrombie through the access door as the car sped off. Forty five seconds later they burst through the access door to the opposite traffic flow tunnel and their waiting transport. They climbed in and sped off in the opposite direction.

There were two people in the front – the driver and the passenger – who turned to the rear seat. 'Well done Solara.' He looked at the President. 'Mister President, allow me to introduce myself, Michael Anderson, I bring warm greetings from Admiral Cartwright, and some entertainment.' Michael switched on the view screen in the rear of his seat, just in front of Abercrombie.

Chapter 22: All In

'Fuck me!' HG cried as he read the message from Anderson.

He paused to refill his glass with bourbon. *Things better get sorted soon* he thought, remembering he only had two bottles left after this one. He shrugged and continued with the message, opening up the vid file that was included. As he watched, the colour drained from his face faster than he drained his glass.

He was watching the confession of Admiral William Cartwright, followed by Brian Bosworth, the plot to take control of the Coalition now laid bare.

'Fucking Naismith, who the hell does he think he is?' HG yelled at the screen. He reached for his communicator and called Joseph.

'Jonesy, you've got to see this, get down to my quarters **now**! This is a time bomb!' Minutes later the door announced Joseph's arrival.

'What's so important?' Joseph asked as he entered.

'Oh, I dunno, maybe a foiled coup on Earth and your mate Naismith is at the centre of it. Sit down and watch.' HG pushed Joseph into the chair, activated the vid playback and poured two stiff drinks. Joseph's face also lost colour as he watched.

'The message contains lots more,' HG explained. 'Naismith left Earth nearly six weeks ago... in company with at least three Coalition frigates... heading here to get his son. Plus, we don't know where Frederickson is but I guarantee he's skulking somewhere close enough to send one of those hyper torpedoes to Argos. Anderson will take care of things on Earth, but we're essentially on our own, with a small fleet of Coalition warships bearing down on us.'

'I'm not worried about them, I have taken steps; it's Ernst we've got to find. If he sends one of those torpedoes here, he'll destroy Argos and everything on it, but worse than that, it could release another anomaly, much larger this time. Most of this sector will be destroyed, millions of lives... who knows, it may be too big to stop!' Joseph paused before asking. 'How long until Naismith arrives?'

'I guess about four days, why?'

'Gives us four days to find Frederickson and his damn torpedoes,' Joseph replied grimly. 'The frigates won't pose too much of a threat. We'll have around fifteen armed trade ships here in the next two days and Chang will hand down his findings tomorrow, so we'll have no reason not to let Naismith take his son.

'If we can neutralise Frederickson, Graham Naismith is hanging onto a very small branch. Look, his coup on Earth has failed but he doesn't know it yet. Cartwright gave us the codes to convince Naismith that all's going to plan... with any luck, he won't know anything's wrong until it's too late.'

'Well, we better call Steven and let him in on this.' HG said, pointing to the console.

'No, not until after he's handed down his findings, then we show him. This way, there can never be any suspicion of collusion. What time tomorrow?' Joseph asked, his mind racing ahead.

'Ten am, why?'

'Can you send Anderson a message? I think it's time for Abercrombie to resign... say around thirteen hundred tomorrow, Argos time.' Joseph smiled. 'I've got to contact someone. Give me an hour then meet me in my quarters.' HG agreed as Joseph left the room.

Back in his quarters, Joseph quickly activated the comm system Nadroc had given him. It took a few minutes to make contact, and then Joseph outlined events and his plan. Nadroc agreed to present the details to his high command immediately and the comm went dead. All Joseph could do now, was wait.

***

On Earth, Michael read the message from HG twice.

'Easy... just force the President to resign and then fucking what?' He sat back in his chair, thinking. He saw Nyah enter her office, and he called her in. 'Nyah, you're currently studying constitutional law. What is the process for an emergency change of power? Let's say a President dies... there must be a process for the transfer of power?'

'There is, if a successor is known. All that's needed is for the Leader of the Council to swear the new President in. Once done, everything is in order. Why has something happened to Abercrombie?' She quizzed.

'No, not yet, it's just hypothetical. Now, let's say the President Elect is a long way from Earth, in another part of the Galaxy... what happens then?'

'Same thing; the Council Leader can still swear the new President in, via proxy even, if need be. A formal ceremony would then be held at the earliest convenient time and place. Come on, what's going on?' Nyah was sharp, Michael knew that.

'Ok, there's a huge political scandal about to break, and we're at the centre of it. I'm just looking at possible angles.'

Nyah gave her boss a hard look. He was holding back, she knew that, but maybe a tactical retreat would be best for the moment. 'I don't believe that's all, but I can see it's all I'm going to get, so I'll get back to work.' She turned and walked back to her office.

Michael immediately called Solara, filled her in and asked if she could persuade Abercrombie to resign and do it at eight that night.

The answer caused him to sit back a bit. 'Not a problem, he'll resign at eight and I'll have all the papers ready for him.'

'Excellent, now for the really hard part... the Leader of the Council will need to swear the new President in ASAP... let's say at eleven tonight. Can you also arrange that? And who is actually the current Leader?'

'Alfred Hawes... and I don't know if he'll do it, he's a stickler for protocol.' Solara sounded doubtful.

'Leave Hawes to me, just get Abercrombie organised. I'll call you later.' He cut the comm. Next he initiated a call to Jasmine Cordoba and asked her to meet him in his office; she agreed to be there in half an hour. The time raced away and before Michael could finalise preparations, Jasmine was in reception; he left his office to greet her.

Back in his office, a tray with coffee and biscuits was waiting for them. Michael poured the coffee and began his story. It took over an hour to bring his guest up to date, now was the time for the big ask. The instant he asked this question, Cordoba was technically part of what could be called an act of treason, but Michael asked anyhow.

'Jasmine, given all I've told you I need to ask something that will place you right in the firing line. Can we use your communication system to swear in the new President?'

That one question could mean so much. Michael realised he was sitting on the edge of his seat. Slowly he settled back, for the answer.

'Michael... my uncle and CEO of the company is on Argos assisting President Elect Chang with the inquiry. When he told me to work with you his instruction was clear; to give you any and all assistance required... no reservations. So, in answer to your question, yes, we'll assist in any way we can, but we cannot remove the comm system from our office... the transmission must be made from there. I'll set up one of the conference rooms in suitable fashion, make it official and ceremonious, which will please Hawes. Now, when will he arrive?'

'I'm waiting on a call from him at the moment. As soon as we make arrangements, I'll let you know.' The meeting continued, and they even discussed real business. Cordoba was in the early stages of negotiation for the takeover of a small mining operation and needed legal input and representation. Michael told her he had just the person and escorted her to Nyah's office.

***

Alfred Hawes was old, but his mind was incredibly sharp. He returned Anderson's call and was soon in deep discussion. Both men had served in the military – Special Service to be exact – and Michael knew just what to say to tweak Hawes's interest. The conversation was short and, to anyone listening, inconsequential; just two men who had served in the same branch reminiscing.

In reality, it was nothing like that. The short exchange told Hawes that a delicate political issue was unfolding and that he would be instrumental in the resolution. The dinner invitation was a cover for him entering the fray. He agreed to the time and to Michael sending a car to collect him, and the conversation ended.

Michael looked at the time. Nyah and Jasmine were still deep in conversation, out in the main office everyone was busy at their desks and three of the meeting rooms were active. He sat back, happy that normal life was still going on and people were oblivious to the grimy political machinations currently in play.

***

Joseph entered the hall where Chang was to hand down his decision at 09:57. He took his seat, again glancing at his watch. Timing was critical in this venture, a couple of minutes either way could spell disaster.

Earlier, he had spoken to Chang to emphasise the need for keeping to the timetable; Chang's response was predictable as he questioned the reasons. All Joseph could do was assure him that it was essential and that he would explain everything after the hearing was finalised.

At exactly 10:00, the door to the small ante room at the rear of the stage opened and in strode Chang accompanied by Phillipe Alvaris and Silvio Cordoba. They took the three seats behind the large desk that had served as the adjudicator's bench. Once the crowd settled, Steven Chang stood and addressed the room.

'The inquiry into the loss of the freighter Lady Philomena has concluded... all that is left is the findings. But, I have a few people to thank: first Joseph Jones and his people, for allowing this inquiry to be held on their fledgling colony. Holding it here has been of great benefit due to the neutrality of the settlement.

'Second, I wish to thank Silvio Cordoba and Phillipe Alvaris for their assistance in this matter; their expertise has been invaluable to the findings.' He looked up and surveyed the room before he continued.

'I will not go through all the evidence but I hereby inform you that, as this is a public inquiry, all data, evidence and findings will be freely available at the conclusion of this morning.

'My findings are twofold. First, in regard to the charges of mutiny against the crew, it is the finding of this inquiry that no such crime took place. If the crew hadn't assumed control of the ship all hands would have been lost. If we examine the transcripts and logs, we see that the First Officer, supported by the senior officers, advised the Captain of the problems the ship was experiencing and adequately warned him of the probable consequences. In their assumption, the ship was doomed if they kept trying to complete the freight run.

'Coalition law, space regulations and the shipping regulations of Aegis Mining and the Cordoba Corporation are clear in this matter and exonerate the crew's actions. It is the finding of this inquiry that they acted within all laws and regulations and therefore are free of any blame.

'Second, the actions of the Commander, Captain Alistair Naismith, were in error, at best. To leave port without sufficient means of evacuation violates Coalition laws and regulations.

'To put the completion of a freight delivery above the safety of crew and ship, also violates these laws and regulations.

'To refuse to act on the expert advice of senior officers as to the safety of the crew and ship, is both foolhardy and in breach of several regulations. There are a number of other charges that have been levelled at Captain Naismith and, to save time, this inquiry finds them upheld.

'It is the recommendation of this inquiry that Alistair Naismith be stripped of rank and privilege, and that his record be so endorsed as to ensure he is never in any command situation again.

'It is also the finding of this inquiry that Alistair Naismith be held, in custody until such time as he can be transferred to a Coalition facility for trial on criminal charges arising from this inquiry.

'In closing, I thank all for their candour and participation. I hereby declare this inquiry closed.' With those words, he turned and left the stage, the others close behind.

Joseph checked the time again, 10:32. *Now for the hard part*, he thought as he stood to leave the room.

As arranged, HG waited for ten minutes before he approached Chang's quarters; he announced himself and was admitted by one of the security team. After the customary scan, he was ushered through to Chang.

'Steven,' HG began. 'I'm sorry, but we have no time for pleasantries. I need you to come with me, now.'

Chang looked up from his desk, studying the face now staring at him; all he saw was concern and a degree of urgency. 'And I suppose you can't tell me why?' He was smiling as he stood. 'Don't worry, one thing I've learned about this place is that there's never a dull moment... lead on.'

They exited the pod close to Joseph's quarters and soon were at the door. HG announced them and Joseph answered. He looked at the three man security detail as he spoke. 'Steven thanks for coming so quickly but I must ask that the security detail wait out here.'

The head of the detail moved forward. 'Not going to happen. President Elect Chang is under my protection so where he goes, I go.'

Chang saw a stand-off in the making and moved between them. 'Gerald, it's ok... form a perimeter out here... I'll be fine.' While the agent was clearly not impressed, he obeyed his boss's order and the three took up positions that could defend the door now closing behind them.

Once inside, Joseph led them to his office, offered seats and started to explain. 'Steven, there's been developments on Earth. A coup was initiated, but has been foiled and most of the players have been neutralised, including President Abercrombie.' Joseph saw questions forming in Chang's mind, 'before you ask... please watch this, we don't have much time.'

He began the replay of Admiral Cartwright's confession. Joseph waited for a couple of minutes while Chang assimilated the information. 'In less than five minutes, the Leader of the Council will announce the resignation of Abercrombie... health reasons I believe. He will also begin the process of swearing you in as President... we've set up my office as the venue. The process will take just over ninety minutes to complete, but we must be ready Mister President.'

'But how did you know all this? Who foiled the plan and what was to become of me, if it succeeded?' Chang asked.

'We don't know all the details except that some people in CID stumbled on the plot. The: who, what, where and how we'll find out later, but now, we only have three minutes. Are you ready Sir?' HG asked.

'As ready as I can be! Let's get this show on the road.' Chang stood and followed HG to the office. Silvio, Phillipe and Gail were already waiting. Joseph went to the door and called the detail in. Now there were four witnesses who were classed as beyond reproach, plus the President's security detail. The requirements for the transfer of power were now complete.

Chang sat at the desk with the Coalition flag draped behind him, HG and Silvio to his left with Phillipe and Gail to his right and the three security agents directly behind. Exactly on time, the screen came to life and displayed the face of Alfred Hawes in the centre. Flanked by ten members of the Council, Jasmine's office made an impressive sight, as Hawes began to speak.

'Fellow members of the Coalition, it is with sadness that I address you. There has been an attempt to wrest control of the Coalition from our elected leaders. This coup has failed and most of the players are now in custody, or dead. The few who managed to flee are at this moment, being hunted and will be apprehended.

'Unfortunately, during the attempted coup our President, Luthor Abercrombie was critically wounded. Sadly, I must inform you that he has subsequently succumbed to his wounds. So, as leader of the Council, it is my duty to swear in our new President, Steven Chang.'

The view changed and an image of Chang was flashed on the screen.

'Currently, President Elect Chang is on one of the outer colonies, on a legal and humanitarian mission, but we have been able to secure him and the swearing process will take place in accordance with section three, paragraph five through seven of the Coalition Constitution.' He began to read out the relevant section and state the oath of office, and then he transmitted a document that held a code that must be used when Chang took the oath.

The thirty-minute delay was an irritation, but better than the usual six plus hours it took for communication between Argos and Earth.

Finally, an hour later, the screen once again showed the image of Hawes as he concluded the formalities, noting the President's oath and the identity of each witness. Steven Chang was now officially, President of the Coalition of Earth Planets.

Joseph approached to offer his congratulations. 'Congratulations Mister President.' Chang took the offered hand enthusiastically. 'I have one more favour to ask.'

'Joseph, it seems that you, and your compatriots, have somehow foiled a plot on Earth and probably saved my life... ask away.'

'There's someone I want you to meet, but it must be secret, no security.'

Chang studied Joseph's face, but could find no indication of duplicity, 'when?' he simply asked.

'Now, if you please.'

Chang agreed and the two headed to the door Gerald was there blocking the way.

Chang waved him aside. 'Please Gerald, stand down, I'm in good hands.'

The agent obeyed, reluctantly, and the two headed to the pod. They exited on the hangar level and went straight into a small meeting room, one that was used, in the past, for final trade negotiations.

Inside were three Krell who all stood and saluted the President as he entered. Joseph walked forward and greeted Nadroc. 'Welcome, my friend. I appreciate this chance we have been given.'

'As do we,' Nadroc bowed to Chang. 'Mister President, may I introduce the Leader of the Krell Empire, Emperor Gorth Todarij,' he turned and bowed lower.

The door behind them opened and in strode the Emperor, resplendent in his golden armour and brilliant red robe. He walked past the now bowed Krell and Joseph, and stood before Chang. Nadroc completed his introduction. 'Emperor Todarij, may I present President of the Coalition of Earth Planets, Steven Chang.'

Todarij flashed his best salute, his left fist covering his right heart, then he bowed, something rarely seen from a Krell ruler.

Chang responded by bowing as deep as Todarij. He extended his right arm, offering his right hand. The Emperor took it, and they shook, finalising the greeting. Everyone took their seats and the first meeting between Krell and Human leaders in two centuries began. It lasted for four hours with many issues discussed. Very early it was evident that neither side had the will to continue the war, a conflict that neither actually knew the reason for.

Finally, a decision to continue discussions with full diplomatic attendance was agreed. Unfortunately, the choice of venue was a sticking point. The only neutral ground was Argos and, with Joseph's declaration that no ship could enter with offensive weapons active, the whole Zedak system was acceptable.

HG brought up the one problem that might derail the plan. While Argos and the Zedak system were owned by

Argos Ltd, there was no active government. HG argued that it could be construed, in legal jargon, that no declaration was valid without a working Government to authorise it.

It was Gail who solved the dilemma. As Joseph wanted the Independent Traders Guild to be based and operate from Argos, and as he was CEO of the company, Argos Ltd could simply defer administration of the system to the Guild, for a nominal fee. Also Joseph was the current President of the Guild, so he could assume that role in the system administration, problem solved.

It was agreed and Gail was given two days to have the necessary documents ready. Emperor Todarij made the comment that law practitioners were the same – race or species seemed to make no difference. The meeting concluded with an agreement to meet again when the documentation was finalised.

Chapter 23: Showdown

The next two days were frantic, Joseph didn't see Gail as she was locked away with a team of people working on the correct wording for the documents they needed.

In the end she adopted the majority of the Guild constitution for Argos, including the governing hierarchy. The word President was dropped and replaced with Prime; this was the role that Joseph held and would for another five years.

As Prime, Joseph had the authority to accept the offer for the Guild to run Argos and the Zedak system, but this was the sticking point. While the Guild would be administrating the system, it was owned by Argos Ltd, one of Joseph's companies and that company alone had rights to allocate land or any exploitation rights, not the Guild.

Joseph's answer was simple; he allocated all exploration rights to Omnicron, any subsequent mining rights to Aegis and all freight and trade rights to the Guild. Argos Administration would receive a royalty from all exploitation and in turn pay Argos Ltd a percentage of this royalty. Taxation was to be simple and based on a flat rate on all transactions or income, with the rate to be reviewed each year and adjusted to reflect the management costs the Guild incurred.

Joseph's dream of a free and equitable society was also enshrined in the document which started as a two-page declaration, but was supported by thousands of words in legal mumbo jumbo.

While all this was happening, the trade Guild members started to arrive. First was Duncan McLeod – his ship

Galway Lady, taking a geosynchronous orbit above what was being called Drake city. Next to arrive were Izzy Dolando and Maris Legrand; Izzy choosing to ground his ship while Maris followed Duncan's lead and set her ship in a similar orbit.

Joseph was waiting at the landing field, now called Argos Spaceport, when the three arrived. Izzy was first and as soon as his ship Eldorado was grounded, two shuttles landed. Joseph greeted each Captain as they stepped on Argosan soil, for the first time. He guided them to the waiting ground car, and they were soon on board Drake.

Duncan was first to comment on the old ship. 'So the old girl is permanently grounded?'

'Yes, landing here was her last voyage.' Joseph's words carried a hint of sadness. 'Now, I know you all have a million questions, so let's get down to business.' He ushered them into his office. Once they were seated he began telling the story, deliberately omitting the parts relating to the Krell and human dialogue. An hour later he finished and buzzed for Gail to come in and discuss the draft constitution.

With initial introductions completed, she produced the document. 'Initially the document had sixty points. Captain Jones wanted a simpler version so here are the twenty that form the basis of the Constitution of Argos.' They all read the document in silence until Izzy spoke up.

'Joe, we've all known you for a long time and you always have had this idea of an independent Guild but this is crazy. You own Argos Limited. So far you've borne all the costs of establishment; and from what we see they've been pretty high. Now you basically hand it over to the Guild. How will you make anything on the deal?'

Joseph smiled. 'Izzy, so far the terra-forming hasn't cost Argos a cent. Both Omnicron and Cordoba are setting up bases here, so their payment for land has been in kind. Also, as the document states, Argos Limited owns the system so any land sold will be sold by that company, and the appropriate tax to Argos administration will be paid.

'In addition, as you will see in the supplemental documents, the administration of Argos will pay Argos Limited a fee equal to zero point five percent of revenue raised, so believe me, I will make a profit from the deal.' He waited for other comments; none came, so he continued.

'There are a couple of other issues we must discuss.' Joseph entered into the briefing on political developments and where he saw Argos in the mix. No-one spoke while he told the story; only when he finally finished did anyone speak.

Maris Legrand – tall and elegant with long blonde hair, sparkling blue eyes and a wide sensuous mouth – looked anything but a successful trader. She looked too innocent – too gentle – but looks can be deceiving. Maris was as ruthless as any pirate. 'I never liked Naismith, trust him to be in this. What do you need us to do?'

'Work with the others who are on their way, help me build our Guild and hence all our businesses. Help me stop the total destruction of this sector of the galaxy because if Frederickson fires his torpedo at us, that will be the eventual outcome. Now there are a couple of people you need to meet.'

The door opened and two men entered. 'Allow me to introduce Steven Chang, President of the Earth Coalition of Planets and Gorth Todarij, Emperor of the Krell.'

***

Graham Naismith was on the small Bridge of his ship, pacing nervously, and that was a problem. 'Captain how long, to our destination?'

'Thirty two hours, Mister Naismith.' The Captain replied.

'Comms, any word from Earth?'

'No Sir, nothing as yet.' The reply wasn't what Naismith wanted to hear. He moved to the comm console and began entering a message. When he was satisfied, he tapped the transmit Icon. Four hours later he was rewarded with a simple phrase. *The Sun is shining,* Naismith smiled. This simple phrase told him that events on Earth were proceeding as planned.

His smile broadened until it resembled a demonic leer. *Soon, I'll be in control of the entire Galaxy and Jones and his useless Guild will be non-existent.* He relished this thought.

He began composing a new message to the three frigates in his small armada. Next he called Frederickson to check on his progress. The conversation lasted less than a minute, but it confirmed Frederickson was on station. Naismith began to relax. Everything was going to plan; he checked the time — twenty-eight hours to go. He announced he was returning to his cabin and left the Bridge, much to the relief of the crew.

* * *

All twelve senior Guild members were now on Argos, their ships dispersed around the globe or on the ground. Discussions had been going on since they first arrived and were still raging. Some were opposed to the deal, while the majority were in favour. Joseph was at his wits end, nothing he said could placate the two opponents. Even a plea from President Chang fell on deaf ears. Now Todarij stood and called for quiet.

'This is stupid! For over two hundred of your years we have been at war. Neither of us knows why it started or why we are still fighting, but understand this, the Krell want it ended. The opportunity for your Guild is huge. To be the only truly neutral trading post in the Galaxy, will give you great opportunities, but still you two refuse to see the truth.

'Please understand this, from our perspective, the war is over, and we are prepared to enter into a peace treaty that President Chang and I have been discussing. But what will that mean for your Guild? Don't look shocked, at least two of you are thinking that and rightly so. Here's what the Krell offer the Independent Traders Guild.' Todarij looked at each person in turn before completing his statement. 'Any and all trade between Coalition and Krell societies and worlds will go through your Guild, if you all agree to the Argos proposal.'

Silence gripped the room; this was a huge concession and one that could make everyone in the room immensely wealthy.

Legrand cleared her throat and spoke. 'Allow me to repeat your offer, Emperor. All trade between our races will be handled by the Guild and no-one else?'

Todarij nodded. 'That is correct. All trade will be through the Guild, and further we would offer to work with you, through the Guild of course, to enhance all ties, cultural and commercial, if you agree.'

This final concession extinguished all opposition, and the motion was passed. With this decision, the Free Traders Guild and Argos were truly born. The formality of each Council member signing the Argos Resolution, as the document was known, took another twenty minutes, the two witnesses being Todarij and Chang. Then Joseph took the floor.

'Thank you for helping in this historic occasion... now we must prepare for the next one. Graham Naismith and his small battle fleet will be here in less than twelve hours, so we need to be ready. We know he has three Coalition frigates with him and the theoretical area he must arrive at. Our battle plan is simple. If each of you moves your ship out to the locations indicated, we will be able to cover all the main routes he can take to Argos. Plus I don't think he'll do anything until he gets his son... and that's another issue. The court of inquiry has ordered him to stand trial in a Coalition court, so Naismith will not be happy. Now I suggest we get started... time is not on our side.'

Chang stood to address the room. 'The situation we all face is one of Coalition making, so I ask you all to allow the Coalition to rectify it.'

Dolando took the floor. 'Mister President, with all due respect, you don't have any assets in the area and, as far as we know, those en route are still two days away. There's really nothing the Coalition can do.'

Chang smiled. 'You are correct Mister Dolando, our assets are a long way off, but we do have allies.' He stood aside slightly to allow Emperor Todarij to move to his side. 'The Emperor and I have worked out a rather sneaky strategy. Believe me, even Naismith isn't stupid enough to tackle what we have in mind.'

Todarij nodded. 'The Krell often refer to one of our most revered ancestors, a military genius and philosopher, General Edroc Satar. One of his teachings is, *the best way to win a battle, is not to enter battle*. I know it sounds strange. Believe me it sounds worse during our training as his teachings and strategy are the foundation of our military academies. But in this instance, it will be the truth. All I ask is you move your ships to the outer orbit of this system and allow us the honour of assisting our new allies.'

Twelve hours isn't a lot of time when repositioning large space ships is concerned. Time rushed by and finally the control tower announced the space over Argos was free of trade ships and four new re-insertions were detected, precisely where they had been predicted.

These newcomers were hailed. *Unidentified vessels in sector five alpha of the Zedak system, this is Argos control, please respond.*

The comm officer on Naismith's ship called to the Captain, 'Sir, Argos control is hailing us.'

'Do not respond!' Naismith ordered as he entered the Bridge, 'We'll let one of the frigates do that.'

Unidentified vessels in sector five alpha of the Zedak system, this is Argos control, we have detected active offensive weapons. This is a violation of transit authority, please respond immediately.

Naismith grinned. 'That sounds like they're getting worried. Comms have Scaramouch reply, here's what they are to say.' The comms officer sent the message, a feeling of dread building in his stomach.

In Argos control, Molly Renwick was OOD, and she was sick of waiting for an answer. She was about to hail again when the reply came through.

Argos control this is the Coalition warship Scaramouch, Commander Zhirov speaking. We are at normal operational readiness for any Coalition ship entering hostile or unknown territory. You will stand down any defensive systems and allow us to approach your planet.

Molly was about to answer when a hand rested on her shoulder. She looked up to see Chang standing behind her. 'Allow me to respond, please.' Molly nodded and left her post.

'Commander Zhirov, this is Steven Chang, President of the Coalition of Earth Planets. It is you who are in violation of protocol. I order you to stand down and power your weapons down. Failure to do so will be construed as an act of war against a neutral system and you will be held accountable. Do you understand?' Chang's voice showed just how angry he was.

The reply was immediate and less aggressive. *I understand the message but cannot comply, Luthor Abercrombie is still President and you are not due to take over for three months. Again, I demand you allow our approach to the planet... we have legitimate business with Joseph Jones.*

Chang chuckled; he was starting to enjoy this banter. 'Commander Zhirov, it would serve you well to check the status of the Coalition. President Abercrombie fell victim to a failed coup. I was sworn in by the Leader of the Council two days ago. As such, Commander, I am now your boss and I am ordering you, and all Coalition vessels in this sector, to power down their weapons and hold current positions.

'Failure to obey will be viewed as mutiny and you will be treated accordingly. I will not repeat the order, you need to decide whether to obey or follow the traitor Naismith to your death.'

I am no traitor, Chang and you're not President. Now surrender or we'll reduce that planet and all on it to a cinder. Naismith's voice screamed over the comm system.

Chang spoke calmly. 'Naismith, you finally come out of hiding… excellent… now listen. You have only a few seconds before we destroy your little fleet, so I suggest you come to a full stop and power down. This is a one-time offer, refuse and you will condemn all with you to death.'

On his ship, Naismith was fuming. 'Jumped up little ambulance chaser! Who does he think he's dealing with? Captain, are we close enough to send them a message?'

The Captain knew what he meant, quickly checking the relative positions of Argos and his fleet. 'Only just… we are at extreme torpedo range, but they will hit the planet.'

'Good, tell the others! We fire a full spread from each ship on my signal. I'll show these idiots who's in charge.' He watched as the Captain followed his instructions, then he opened the link to Argos again. 'Chang, I make you this one time offer… power down any defences and surrender to us, or we will begin our bombardment… you have ten seconds.' Naismith started counting down in his head as Chang replied.

You have our terms, proceed with this action and you will be condemning all with you.

'Fuck you, Chang. Now you die.' Naismith spat as he gave the signal for each frigate to fire.

A wicked evil leer slashed his face as each ship fired a full ten torpedo spread, the optical sensors taking a few milliseconds to adjust to the drive flare. Just under two minutes later, his leer changed to a grimace of pain as the view screen was blinded by a series of huge explosions. All forty torpedoes detonated less than half way to Argos.

'What happened?' Naismith was dumbfounded. 'Fire another volley!' The order was delayed, as the screen rebooted. Then they saw the reason. Four huge Krell battle cruisers materialised in the space where the torpedoes had exploded, their distinctive shape and bulk coalescing as their cloaks disengaged.

Coalition renegade vessels, this is Emperor Todarij on the Krell battleship Basog. Power your weapons down, or be destroyed.

'Fucking Chang, he's a puppet of the Krell, and he calls me a traitor! Captain, target the lower ship, fire everything!' Naismith ordered.

The Captain took his seat in the command chair and opened a channel to the other ships. 'This is Captain Bartholomew... I'm ordering each ship to comply with the Krell demand. Stop all engines and power down your weapons.' He then hailed the Krell ships. 'Emperor Todarij, we are complying with your demands we surrender.'

'What?' Naismith screamed. 'Bartholomew, you craven coward, we will not surrender!' He threw the comm officer out of his chair and activated another comm channel. 'Naismith calling Frederickson, respond,' he waited for a few seconds before repeating his hail; this time he was answered.

Frederickson responding.

'About time Ernst, fire the torpedo! We are under attack from Krell warships. You have the coordinates; fire that damn torpedo, before it's too late!' Naismith's voice was calming down, his ace was about to be delivered. He waited for confirmation, it should come in a few seconds... time ticked by. After a full minute he tried again, 'Ernst what's the delay? I need you to fire that torpedo **now**!'

A new voice responded, *I must apologise, Frederickson is unable to comply. This is Captain Nadroc of the Krell battleship Zotrik, now de-cloaking, off your stern. We have captured Ernst Frederickson and his ship... there's no torpedo to be fired. I suggest you prepare for your ship to be boarded.*

***

The mop up was anticlimactic. Each of the frigates was boarded and a Krell over-watch crew monitored the final passage to Argos. Naismith was restrained and delivered to Argos for confinement.

The situation regarding Naismith was now complex. The nature and depth of the failed coup had been minimised. Every news outlet reported it as a fringe group's attempt to gain recognition. The death of the President was announced as stress induced heart failure due to the coup. All the protagonists were removed and with Abercrombie dead from natural causes, the vast majority of the population really paid it no heed.

The fact that Naismith had attacked a sovereign neutral planet and fired on Krell ships was the major complication to the issue, and only those on Argos knew it had happened. What to do with him was something Chang wrestled with, and he didn't have much time. In less than twenty hours a Space Corps battle group would be arriving and Chang wanted a solution before then. He called for Joseph and Todarij to meet him.

Chang greeted both as they arrived and explained his dilemma. His prime concern was maintaining the secret of the coup attempt and metering a suitable punishment for the coup leader, Graham Naismith.

All this amused Todarij. 'It appears we have much more in common than we realised. This sounds like a number of Krell political problems we have faced. We need to keep news like this out of the general population and punish the wrong doers. And then the crews and Frederickson... you must do something with them.'

Joseph entered the discussion. 'I may have a solution... for Frederickson and the crews at least. I have spoken to them, and they all realise their lives as they know them are over. They can never go back to the Coalition, so I suggest they stay here.'

'Frederickson didn't know that his torpedo caused the anomaly. It seems that the reinsertion into normal space was the problem, at least for the prototype; somehow it caused the warhead to detonate. Evidently, he found a malfunction in the control circuitry that sent a false signal to the detonator. With this rectified, he believes his design would work as designed... something I don't think any of us want to risk.

He is distraught that he was the cause of the Aegis debacle, and it seems that Cartwright kept him in the dark as to what he was actually doing. Even the attacks on my ships... he believed he was demonstrating against drones. He didn't know exactly what Naismith was up to but, like many people, he doesn't have a high opinion of politicians. He thought a change would be good for the Coalition.'

Both Todarij and Chang smiled at this.

Chang interrupted. 'And you believe him?'

'Yes, I do. Plus I've had my people dig deep into his ship and data... it all supports his story.' I want to set up our own training and education system and someone with Frederickson's intellect would be a great fit.' Joseph replied.

'The crews could stay here, on Argos, and either join some of the traders, or form a small defence force... but we'd need ships for that.' Joseph's hint was recognised by Chang.

'Ok we can arrange that. The ships they came in will stay here, if you wish. Call it a gift from the Coalition for keeping the President secure,' Chang replied. 'But Naismith is the real problem. As Coalition law states, any person involved in this sort of operation is a traitor. The gazetted punishment is forfeiture of all their wealth, property and finally execution,' he explained. 'Treason is the only crime, in Coalition Law where there is zero room for leniency. But... that means lawyers, a trial and all the publicity that goes with it. The confiscation of assets will be a formality. It appears that Naismith and his cronies have invested heavily into the war effort, buying companies that deal specifically in that arena.

'With an outbreak of peace, he'd be broke anyway, he's that heavily geared. His son will be tried as normal; he had no involvement or knowledge of the coup.' Chang stopped, trying to find a solution.

Todarij stood and walked to the window. 'I may have a solution... it is different but, hear me out. Naismith fired on Krell ships. That action is either an act of war or an act of piracy. As he wasn't acting for any government but as a private citizen, I would interpret his actions as an act of piracy against the Empire.

'This crime carries either a death or life imprisonment sentence. If this is held true, then I can order his immediate transfer to Mortuk, our prison planet... and no-one ever leaves Mortuk.' This offer sealed the fate of Graham Naismith; the last loose end was now tied.

Epilogue

Six months later, Emperor Todarij and President Chang officially met, back on Argos, to sign the peace treaty. The war between the races was now legitimately over. This heralded a massive wave of interest in Argos as the opportunities brought about by peace were becoming apparent.

While he was on Argos, Chang advised Joseph that an offer to purchase Galactic would be a wise move as it was in massive difficulty with the failure of some of the Naismith investments. Joseph took the advice and an offer was made and accepted.

During the visit by both Krell and Coalition heads of state, two sod turning ceremonies were held. Both were setting up Embassies on Argos and the symbolic sod turning signalled a new upsurge in construction.

The purchase of Galactic could have been a huge issue as it had nearly one hundred ships and according to the rules of the Guild and Argos the maximum number of individually owned ships one entity could hold, was twelve. Once again Gail solved the problem, referring to a section of both constitutions which allowed a senior, one who owned twelve ships, to be a partner in any number of other operations.

She registered all the Galactic assets on Argos and dispersed their ownership through a number of companies. Now all she had to do was find partners who had the capital to buy into these operations. Eventually this was easy, with many investors looking to this new frontier hoping to cash in on the potential of trade with the Empire, plus the Galactic purchase was for the company – all assets and existing contracts.

Joseph and Gail were sitting on the patio on the roof of the old Drake. Stretched out before them was a massive construction site, one of three now on Argos. Omnicron had designed the city to incorporate the Drake site in its centre. Now called Central City, it would be the hub of Argos for centuries to come, and the seat of Government.

Part of the development was the official residence of the Prime and the seat of the Administration. The site was chosen on an elevated position less than twenty kilometres from Drake. Construction had been quick and efficient and the next day, Joseph Jones was to take up residence, as the first Prime to live there.

'How are you feeling about tomorrow?' Gail asked.

Joseph took a swig from his whisky glass. 'A bit nervous... I've called this old girl home for so long it feels strange to be deserting her.' He looked round, gazing over the lines of his old ship. 'She served me well... made me, I suppose. But at least she'll continue to be part of Argos. After we move out, the refurbishment starts. In a year she'll be opened as the Drake Museum and all this area will be a park... Freedom Park.' His face showed a satisfied, contented smile.

'Well I for one am glad we'll be living in a real house. An old grounded space ship is no place to raise a family,' Gail said, her voice full of conviction.

'A family... we never actually discussed that!'

'Discussion is now irrelevant, seeing that in about seven months you'll be a father.' She looked directly into Joseph's eyes.

'What, when, how...' he stumbled for words.

'Well, as for *what and when*, that's easy but if you don't know how, we're in deep shit.'

Joseph leapt to his feet, knocking his glass over as he did. He scooped Gail up and kissed her, then let her go. 'Sorry, I shouldn't grab you like that now.'

'I hope you bloody well keep doing that! I'm pregnant not incapacitated.' She giggled just as the comm unit announced they had a visitor. 'That'll be HG; I couldn't wait to watch you tell him the news.'

They took the elevator down to the living area, the last thing they saw as they descended was the plasma flash from a hunting Zartol as it closed in on its prey.

THE END.

Also by the same Author available from all good bookstores or online.

Chronicle of the 12th Realm
Book 1: **REUNION**
Book 2: **SEDITION RISING**
Book 3: **HUNT FOR BALEROPHON**

Coming December 2021
A new 12th Realm adventure
INCIDENT AT ZYRALIN 4

Set in a military board of inquiry, JT Abraham is fighting for his career. The incident at Zyralin 4 is examined and played out in a holographic suite. As he tries to clear his name, more political intrigue and treachery unfolds.

www.ingramcontent.com/pod-product-compliance
Lightning Source LLC
Chambersburg PA
CBHW020553120726
47903CB00001B/249